THE
SACRED BOOKS OF THE EAST

Translated by

VARIOUS ORIENTAL SCHOLARS

Edited by

F. MAX MÜLLER

Vol. 17

SACRED BOOKS OF THE EAST

(50 VOLUMES)

Series Editor : *F. Max-Müller*

ISBN: 978-81-208-0101-1 (Set) Rs. 15000 (Each Vol. Rs. 350)

These volumes of the Sacred Books of the East series include translations of all the most important works of the seven non-Christian religions that have exercised a profound influence on the civilisations of the continent of Asia. The Vedic Brahmanic system claims 21 volumes, Buddhism 10, and Jainism 2; 8 volumes comprise Sacred Books of the Parsis; 2 volumes represent Islam; and 6 the two main indigenous systems of China. Translated by twenty leading authorities in their respective fields, the volumes have been edited by the late F. Max Müller. The inception, publication and the compilation of these books cover almost 34 years.

I. BUDDHISM

Vol. 49: Buddhist Mahayana Texts (2 Parts)
Vol. 11: Buddhist Suttas
Vol. 10: The Dhammapada and Sutta Nipata
Vols. 35 & 36: The Questions of King Milinda (2 Parts)
Vol. 21: The Saddharma Pundarika or the Lotus of the True Law
Vols. 13, 17 & 20: Vinaya Texts (3 Parts)

II. CHINESE

Vol. 19: The Fo-Sho-Hing-Tsan-King
Vols. 3, 16, 27, 28, 39 & 40: The Sacred Books of China (6 Parts)

III. A GENERAL INDEX

Vol. 50: A General Index to the Names and Subject-matter of the Sacred Books of the East

IV. ISLAM

Vols. 6 & 9: The Qur'an (2 Parts)

V. JAINISM

Vols. 22 & 45: The Jaina Sutras (2 Parts)

VI. PARSIS

Vols. 5, 18, 24, 37 & 47: Pahlavi Texts (5 Parts)
Vols. 4, 23 & 31: The Zend-Avesta (3 Parts)

VII. VEDIC-BRAHMANIC SYSTEM

Vol. 8: The Bhagavadgita with the Sanatsujatiya and the Anugita
Vols. 29 & 30: The Grihya-Sutras: Rules of Vedic Domestic Ceremonies (2 Parts)
Vol. 42: Hymns of the Atharva Veda together with Extracts from the Ritual Books and the Commentaries
Vol. 7: The Institutes of Vishnu
Vol. 25: The Laws of Manu
Vol. 33: The Minor Law Books
Vols. 2 & 14: The Sacred Laws of the Aryas as Taught in the Schools of Apastamba, Gautama, Vasishtha and Baudhayana (2 Parts)
Vols. 12, 26, 41, 43 & 44: The Satapatha Brahmana According to the Text of the Madhyandina School (5 Parts)
Vols. 1 & 15: The Upanishads (2 Parts)
Vols. 34 & 38: The Vedanta Sutras (2 Parts)
Vol. 48: The Vedanta-Sutras (with the commentary by Ramanuja)
Vols. 32 & 46: Vedic Hymns (2 Parts)

VINAYA TEXTS

PART II

THE MAHĀVAGGA, V—X

THE KULLAVAGGA, I—III

Translated from Pāli

T.W. RHYS DAVIDS

HERMANN OLDENBERG

MOTILAL BANARSIDASS PUBLISHERS

PRIVATE LIMITED • DELHI

8th Reprint: Delhi, 2012
First Published by the Oxford University Press, 1882

ISBN: 978-81-208-0118-9

MOTILAL BANARSIDASS
41 U.A. Bungalow Road, Jawahar Nagar, Delhi 110 007
8 Mahalaxmi Chamber, 22 Bhulabhai Desai Road, Mumbai 400 026
203 Royapettah High Road, Mylapore, Chennai 600 004
236, 9th Main III Block, Jayanagar, Bangalore 560 011
Sanas Plaza, 1302 Baji Rao Road, Pune 411 002
8 Camac Street, Kolkata 700 017
Ashok Rajpath, Patna 800 004
Chowk, Varanasi 221 001

UNESCO COLLECTION OF REPRESENTATIVE WORKS— Indian Series
This book has been accepted in the Indian Translation Series of the UNESCO Collection of Representative Works, jointly sponsored by the United Nations Educational Scientific and Cultural Organization (UNESCO) and the Government of India

Printed in India
By Jainendra Prakash Jain at Shri Jainendra Press,
A-45 Naraina, Phase-I, New Delhi 110 028
and Published by Narendra Prakash Jain for
Motilal Banarsidass Publishers Private Limited,
Bungalow Road, Delhi 110 007

RASHTRAPATI BHAVAN,
NEW DELHI-4
June 10, 1962

I am very glad to know that the Sacred Books of the East, published years ago by the Clarendon Press, Oxford, which have been out-of-print for a number of years, will now be available to all students of religion and philosophy. The enterprise of the publishers is commendable and I hope the books will be widely read.

S. RADHAKRISHNAN

PREFATORY NOTE TO THE NEW EDITION

Since 1948 the United Nations Educational, Scientific and Cultural Organization (UNESCO), upon the recommendation of the General Assembly of the United Nations, has been concerned with facilitating the translation of the works most representative of the culture of certain of its Member States, and, in particular, those of Asia.

One of the major difficulties confronting this programme is the lack of translators having both the qualifications and the time to undertake translations of the many outstanding books meriting publication. To help overcome this difficulty in part, UNESCO's advisers in this field (a panel of experts convened every other year by the International Council for Philosophy and Humanistic Studies), have recommended that many worthwhile translations published during the 19th century, and now impossible to find except in a limited number of libraries, should be brought back into print in low-priced editions, for the use of students and of the general public. The experts also pointed out that in certain cases, even though there might be in existence more recent and more accurate translations endowed with a more modern apparatus of scholarship, a number of pioneer works of the greatest value and interest to students of Eastern religions also merited republication.

This point of view was warmly endorsed by the Indian National Academy of Letters (Sahitya Akademi), and the Indian National Commission for UNESCO.

It is in the spirit of these recommendations that this work from the famous series "Sacred Books of the East" is now once again being made available to the general public as part of the UNESCO Collection of Representative Works.

PUBLISHER'S NOTE

First, the man distinguished between eternal and perishable. Later he discovered within himself the germ of the Eternal. This discovery was an epoch in the history of the human mind and the *East was the first to discover it.*

To watch in the Sacred Books of the East the dawn of this religious consciousness of man, must always remain one of the most inspiring and hallowing sights in the whole history of the world. In order to have a solid foundation for a comparative study of the Religions of the East, we must have before all things, complete and thoroughly faithful translation of their Sacred Books in which some of the ancient sayings were preserved because they were so true and so striking that they could not be forgotten. They contained eternal truths, expressed for the first time in human language.

With profoundest reverence for Dr. S. Radhakrishnan, President of India, who inspired us for the task; our deep sense of gratitude for Dr. C. D. Deshmukh & Dr. D. S. Kothari, for encouraging assistance; esteemed appreciation of UNESCO for the warm endorsement of the cause; and finally with indebtedness to Dr. H. Rau, Director, Max Müller Bhawan, New Delhi, in procuring us the texts of the Series for reprint, we humbly conclude.

CONTENTS.

PÂTIMOKKHA.

MAHÂVAGGA.

FIFTH KHANDHAKA.

(RULES FOR FOOT-CLOTHING, SEATS, VEHICLES, ETC.)

1.

1. At that time the blessed Buddha dwelt at Râ*g*agaha at the Vulture's Peak.

Now at that time Seniya Bimbisâra, the king of Magadha, held rule and sovranty over eighty thousand townships[1]. And at that time there was at *K*ampâ a Se*tth*i's son named So*n*a Ko*l*ivisa[2], delicately nurtured, on the soles of whose feet hair had grown.

Now when Seniya Bimbisâra, the king of Magadha, was holding an assembly of the eighty thousand overseers over those townships, he sent a message to So*n*a Ko*l*ivisa on some matter of business, saying, 'Let So*n*a come hither. I desire So*n*a's presence!'

2. Then spake the parents of So*n*a Ko*l*ivisa to him thus: 'The king, dear So*n*a, wishes to see thy feet. But stretch not out thy feet, dear So*n*a, towards the

---

[1] Gâma, which should be understood in the sense of parishes, not of villages.

[2] This So*n*a is the reputed author of one of the Theragâthâs. It is interesting to notice that *K*ampâ, the capital of Aṅga, is here included under Magadha. Compare Aṅga-magadhesu in Mahâvagga I, 19, and the beginning sentences of the So*n*ada*nd*a Sutta (Dîgha Nikâya), in which it is said that the revenues of the town of *K*ampâ had been bestowed by king Bimbisâra on the Brâhma*n*a So*n*ada*nd*a.

king. Take thy seat cross-legged before the king, that the king may see thy feet as thou sittest there.' And they carried So*n*a Ko*l*ivisa in a palankeen (to Râ*g*agaha).

And So*n*a Ko*l*ivisa went to the place where Seniya Bimbisâra, the king of Magadha, was. And when he had come there, and had bowed down before Seniya Bimbisâra, the king of Magadha, he took his seat cross-legged before the king. And Seniya Bimbisâra, the king of Magadha, saw that hair had grown on the soles of the feet of So*n*a Ko*l*ivisa.

3. Now after Seniya Bimbisâra, the king of Magadha, had instructed the eighty thousand overseers over those townships in the things of this world he exhorted them, saying, 'Ye have now received from me instruction in the things of this world. Go now, and wait upon the Blessed One. The Blessed One himself shall instruct you in the things of eternity.'

Then the eighty thousand overseers over those townships went on to the Vulture's Peak.

4. Now at that time the venerable Sâgata was the attendant on the Blessed One. And the eighty thousand overseers over those townships went to the place where the venerable Sâgata was. And when they were come there they spake thus to the venerable Sâgata:

'The eighty thousand overseers over the townships are come here, Sir, to visit the Blessed One. It were well, Sir, that we should be granted an audience of the Blessed One.'

'Then do you, Sirs, stay here yet a moment, while I let the Blessed One know.'

5. Then the venerable Sâgata disappeared down the steps[1] from before the very eyes of the eighty thousand overseers over those townships, and appeared before the Blessed One, and spake to the Blessed One, and said:

'Lord, the eighty thousand overseers over the townships are come here to visit the Blessed One. Let the Blessed One do as seemeth to him fit.'

'Do thou then, Sâgata, make a seat ready in the shade of the house[2].'

6. 'Even so, Lord!' said the venerable Sâgata, in assent, to the Blessed One. And taking a chair, he disappeared from before the Blessed One, and reappeared up the steps before the very eyes of those eighty thousand overseers over those townships, and made ready a seat in the shade of the house.

And the Blessed One came out of the house and sat down on the seat made ready in the shade thereof.

7. Then those eighty thousand overseers over the townships went up to the place where the Blessed One was. And when they had come there they bowed down before the Blessed One and took their seats on one side. But those eighty thousand overseers over the townships paid more respect in their hearts to the venerable Sâgata than to the Blessed One[3].

And the Blessed One perceived by his mind the thoughts of the minds of those eighty thousand

---

[1] Pâ*n*kâya nimu*gg*itvâ 'ti sopâ*n*assa he*tth*â addha*k*andapâsâ*n*ena nimu*gg*itvâ (Comm.).

[2] Vihârapa*kkh*âyâyan ti vihârapa*kk*ante *kh*âyâyam.

[3] Samannâharantîti pasâdavasena punappuna*m* manasikaronti (Buddhaghosa).

overseers over the townships; and he addressed the venerable Sâgata, and said: 'Show them now, Sâgata, a still greater wonder, beyond the power of men.'

'Even so, Lord!' said the venerable Sâgata, in assent, to the Blessed One. And rising up into the air he walked, and stood, and sat, and lay down, and gave forth smoke and fire, and disappeared in the sky.

8. Then the venerable Sâgata, when he had shown in the open sky wonders of various kinds beyond the power of men, fell down with his head at the feet of the Blessed One, and said to the Blessed One:

'My teacher, Lord, is the Blessed One; and I am the disciple. My teacher, Lord, is the Blessed One; and I am the disciple.'

Then those eighty thousand overseers over the townships thinking, 'Wonderful is it, most marvellous! If even the pupil be so mighty and so powerful, how much more then the master!' paid more respect in their hearts to the Blessed One than to the venerable Sâgata.

9. Then the Blessed One perceived by his mind the thoughts of the minds of those eighty thousand overseers over the townships, and held to them a discourse in due order; that is to say, he spake to them of giving, of righteousness, of heaven, of the danger, the worthlessness, the depravity of lusts, and of the advantages of renunciation. And when the Blessed One perceived that they had become pliant, softened, unprejudiced, upraised and believing in heart, then he proclaimed that which is the special doctrine of the Buddhas; (that is to say), Suffering, its Origin, its Cessation, and the Path.

Just as a clean cloth, from which all stain has been washed away, would readily take the dye, just even so did those eighty thousand overseers over the townships obtain, even while sitting there, the pure and spotless Eye of the Truth; (that is to say, the knowledge that) whatsoever has a beginning, in that is inherent also the necessity of dissolution.

10. And having seen the Truth, having mastered the Truth, having understood the Truth, having penetrated the Truth, having overcome uncertainty, having dispelled all doubts, having gained full knowledge, dependent on nobody else for the knowledge of the doctrine of the Teacher, they said to the Blessed One: 'Glorious, Lord! glorious, Lord! Just as if one should set up, Lord, what had been overturned, or should reveal what had been hidden, or should point out the way to one who had lost his way, or should bring a lamp into the darkness, in order that those who had eyes might see visible things, thus has the Blessed One preached the doctrine in many ways. We take our refuge, Lord, in the Blessed One, and in the Dhamma, and in the fraternity of Bhikkhus; may the Blessed One receive us from this day forth while our life lasts as his disciples who have taken their refuge in Him.'

11. And So*n*a Ko*l*ivisa thought: 'As I understand the Dhamma proclaimed by the Blessed One, it is not easy to a person living as a layman to lead a wholly perfect and pure and altogether consummate[1] life of holiness. What if I were to cut off my hair and beard, and to put on yellow robes, and give up the world, and go forth into the houseless state.'

[1] Sankhalikhita. See Boehtlingk-Roth s. v. Likhita.

And those eighty thousand overseers over the townships, having expressed their joy and delight at the words of the Blessed One, rose from their seats, respectfully saluted the Blessed One, and passing round him with their right sides towards him, went away.

12. And So*n*a Ko*l*ivisa, soon after those eighty thousand overseers over the townships had departed, went to the place where the Blessed One was. And when he had come there he bowed down before the Blessed One and took his seat on one side. Sitting on one side So*n*a Ko*l*ivisa said to the Blessed One: 'As I understand the Dhamma proclaimed by the Blessed One (&c., as in § 11, down to:) and go forth into the houseless state. I desire, Lord, to cut off my hair and beard, and to put on yellow robes, and to give up the world, and to go forth into the houseless state. May the Blessed One, Lord, ordain me.'

Thus So*n*a Ko*l*ivisa received from the Blessed One the pabba*gg*â and upasampadâ ordinations. And the venerable So*n*a, soon after his upasampadâ, dwelt in the Sîtavana grove.

13. As he, with eager determination, was walking up and down there, his feet were injured, and the place in which he walked became covered with blood, like a slaughter-house for oxen. Then in the mind of the venerable So*n*a, who had gone apart and was plunged in meditation, there sprung up this thought: 'Though I have become one of those disciples of the Blessed One who live in the exercise of strenuous determination, yet my heart has not been set free from the Âsavas through absence of craving. And there is much wealth laid up for me at home. It is possible both to enjoy that wealth, and to do good

deeds. Let me now, then, returning to the lower state[1], enjoy my wealth and do good deeds.'

14. Now the Blessed One perceived in his mind the thought of the heart of the venerable So*n*a; and as quickly as a strong man can stretch forth his arm, or can draw it back again when it has been stretched forth, he disappeared from the hill of the Vulture's Peak, and appeared in the Sîtavana grove. And the Blessed One, as he was passing through the sleeping-places (of the Bhikkhus), came up, with a multitude of Bhikkhus, to the place where the venerable So*n*a had walked up and down.

When the Blessed One saw that the place where the venerable So*n*a had walked up and down was covered with blood, he addressed the Bhikkhus, and said: 'Whose walking-place[2] is this, O Bhikkhus, which is covered with blood, like a slaughter-house for oxen?'

'As the venerable So*n*a, Lord, was walking up and down here with eager determination, his feet were injured; and so this place has become covered with blood, like a slaughter-house for oxen.'

15. Then the Blessed One went on to the house in which the venerable So*n*a was living, and sat down there on a seat made ready for him. And the venerable So*n*a bowed down before the Blessed

[1] That is to say, the state of a layman (Hînây' âvattitvâ).

[2] *K*aṅkama, for which there is no real equivalent in English. In speaking of later periods the word 'cloister' is sometimes a correct rendering, for the places in which the recluses walked up and down, thinking, were then in some cases paved and even roofed. The Chinese pilgrim I-tsing has a description of such a stone *k*aṅkama, which he saw at the great monastery at Nâlanda (Indian Antiquary, X, 192). In this passage it only means a narrow, open, space of ground, levelled and cleared for the purpose.

One, and took his seat on one side. And when he was thus seated, the Blessed One addressed the venerable So*n*a, and said: 'Is it not true, So*n*a, that in your mind, when you had gone apart and were plunged in meditation, there sprung up this thought: "Though I have become (&c., as in § 13, down to the end)?"'

'Even so, Lord!'

'Now what think you, So*n*a,—you were skilled, were you not, when you formerly lived in the world, in the music of the lute?'

'That was so, Lord!'

'Now what think you, So*n*a,—when the strings of your lute[1] were too much stretched, had your lute then any sound, was it in a fit state to be played upon?'

'Not so, Lord!'

16. 'Now what think you, So*n*a,—when the strings of your lute were too loose, had your lute then any sound[2], was it in a fit state to be played upon?'

'Not so, Lord!'

'Now what think you, So*n*a,—when the strings of your lute were neither too much stretched nor too loose, but fixed in even proportion, had your lute sound then, was it then in a fit state to be played upon?'

'Yes, Lord!'

'And just so, So*n*a, does too eager a determination conduce to self-righteousness, and too weak a deter-

[1] Vî*n*â. On the construction of the ancient Indian lute, see Milinda Pañha (p. 53, ed. Trenckner), where all the various parts are mentioned. Compare also the Guttila *G*âtaka (No. 243, ed. Fausbøll).

[2] There is a misprint here in the text, savaratî for saravatî.

mination to sloth. [17.] Do thou, therefore, O So*n*a, be steadfast in evenness of determination, press through to harmony of your mental powers. Let that be the object of your thought[1]!'

'Even so, Lord!' said the venerable So*n*a, and hearkened to the word of the Blessed One.

And when the Blessed One had exhorted the venerable So*n*a with this exhortation, then, as quickly as a strong man can stretch forth his arm, or can draw it back again when it has been stretched forth, he vanished from the presence of the venerable So*n*a in the Sîtavana grove, and reappeared on the hill of the Vulture's Peak.

18. Thenceforward the venerable So*n*a was steadfast in evenness of determination, he pressed through to harmony of his mental powers, that did he take as the object of his thought. And the venerable So*n*a remaining alone and separate, earnest, zealous, and resolved, attained ere long to that supreme goal of the higher life for the sake of which noble youths go out from all and every household gain and comfort to become houseless wanderers—yea, that supreme goal did he, by himself, and while yet in this visible world, bring himself to the knowledge of, and continue to realise, and to see face to face! And he became conscious that rebirth was at an end, that the higher life had been fulfilled, that all that should be done had been accomplished, and that after this present life there would be no beyond!

[1] Buddhaghosa says: Tattha *k*a nimitta*m* ga*n*hâhîti: tasmi*m* samathe sati yena âdâse mukhabimben' eva nimittena uppa*gg*itabba*m*, ta*m* samatha-nimitta*m* vipassanâ-nimitta*m* magga-nimitta*m* phala-nimittañ *k*a ga*n*hâhi nipattetîti (? nipphâdehiti, nibbattehîti) attho.

So the venerable So*n*a became yet another among the Arahats.

19. Now when the venerable So*n*a had attained to Arahatship there occurred to him the thought: 'Let me now make known my Insight in the presence of the Blessed One[1]!'

Then the venerable So*n*a went to the place where the Blessed One was, and bowed down before the Blessed One, and took his seat on one side. And when he was thus seated, the venerable So*n*a said to the Blessed One:

20. 'Whatsoever Bhikkhu, Lord, is an Arahat whose Âsavas are rooted out, who has lived the life, who has accomplished the task, who has laid aside every burden, who has gained the end he had in view, who has quite broken the fetter of a craving for (future) existence, who is completely set free by insight, six things doth he reach up unto[2]—unto renunciation, unto the love of solitude, unto kindness of heart, unto the destruction of craving, unto the destruction of thirst, unto the getting free from delusions.

21. 'Now it may be, Lord, that it might occur, regarding this matter, to some brother, thus: "For the sake of faith merely[3] hath this brother attained

---

[1] It is often represented in the Pâli Pi*t*akas to have been a customary thing for any one who thought he had attained to Arahatship to deliver a discourse in the presence of Gotama, as a kind of proof, or test, of his emancipation; and to receive the decision of Gotama thereupon. Buddhaghosa says: *Aññam* vyâkareyyan ti: arahâ ahan ti *g*ânâpeyya*m*. Compare *G*âtaka I, 140; II, 333.

[2] Adhimutto hotîti: pa*t*ivi*ggh*itvâ pa*kk*akkha*m* katvâ *th*ito hoti (B.).

[3] Kevala*m* saddhâmattakan ti: pa*t*ivedha-rahita*m* kevala*m* pa*t*ivedha-paññâya asammissa*m* saddhâmattaka*m* (B.). On the lower position here assigned to faith, compare Mahâ-parinibbâna Sutta VI, 9.

unto renunciation." But not thus, Lord, should this matter be regarded. For the Bhikkhu in whom the Âsavas are rooted out, who has lived the life, who has accomplished the task, he looks not upon himself as one who has anything yet to do, or to gather up, of (the fruit of his past) labour; but he attaineth to renunciation by the destruction of lust, by the very condition of the absence of lust; he attaineth to renunciation by the destruction of ill-will, by the very condition of the absence of ill-will; he attaineth to renunciation by the destruction of delusions, by the very condition of the absence of delusions.

22. 'Now it may be, Lord, that it might occur, regarding this matter, to some brother, thus: "Seeking after gain, hospitality, and fame hath this brother attained to the love of solitude." But not thus (&c., as in § 21, down to the end, substituting "love of solitude" for "renunciation").

23. 'Now it may be, Lord, that it might occur, regarding this matter, to some brother, thus: "Returning, verily, to the dependence upon works, as if that were the true essence (of spiritual welfare), hath this brother attained to kindness of heart." But not thus (&c., as in § 21, down to the end, substituting "kindness of heart" for "renunciation").

24. 'He attaineth to the destruction of craving by the destruction of lust (&c., as in § 21, down to the end, substituting "absence of craving" for "renunciation"). He attaineth to the absence of thirst (&c., as in § 21). He attaineth to the absence of delusions (&c., as in § 21, down to the end).

25. 'When a Bhikkhu, Lord, has thus become fully emancipated in heart, even though many objects

visible to the sight should enter the path of his eye[1], yet they take not possession of his mind: undefiled is his mind, firm, immovable; and he sees into the (manner which that impression) passes away[2]—even though many objects audible to the ear, smellable to the nostrils, tastable to the tongue, feelable by the body, sensible to the intellect should enter the path of the ear, the nose, the tongue, the skin, the intellect, yet they take not possession of his mind: undefiled is his mind, firm, immovable, and he sees into the (manner in which that impression) passes away.

26. 'Just, Lord, as if there be a mountain of rock, undivided, solid, one mass, and much wind and rain should fall upon it from the direction of the East, or of the West, or of the North, or of the South, yet they would not make it shake, or tremble, or quake; just so, Lord, when a Bhikkhu has thus become fully emancipated in heart (&c., as in § 25, down to the end).

27. 'He who has attained to renunciation, to solitude of heart, who has attained to kindness, and to the rooting out of craving,—

'He who has attained to the rooting out of thirst, to the absence of delusions from the mind, he sees the source of sensations, his mind is quite set free.

'To such a Bhikkhu, so emancipated, and with calmness in his heart, there is no gathering up of what is done, nothing to be done still remains.

'As a rock, all of one mass, is not shaken by

---

[1] *K*akkhussa âpâtham âga*kkh*anti; that is, should come within reach of his vision.

[2] Vayañ *k*' assânupassatîti: tassa *k*ittassa uppâda*m* pi vaya*m* pi passati (B.).

the breezes[1], just so never can shapes and tastes, and sounds, and smells, and touch—the whole of them

'Things wished for, things unwished—make tremble such a one. Firm is his mind, set free. He sees into the end thereof.'

28. And the Blessed One addressed the Bhikkhus, and said: 'Thus, brethren, do young men of worth make their insight known. The truth is spoken, and the self is not obtruded. But herein some foolish ones, methinks, make known their insight to be a thing ridiculous, and they, thereafter, fall into defeat!'

29. Then the Blessed One said to the venerable So*n*a, 'You, So*n*a, have been delicately nurtured. I enjoin upon you, So*n*a, the use of shoes with one lining[2].'

'I have gone out from the world, Lord, into the houseless state, abandoning eighty cart-loads of gold[3], and a retinue of seven elephants[4]. It will be said against me for this matter: "So*n*a Ko*l*ivisa went out from the world into the houseless state, abandoning eighty cart-loads of gold, and a retinue of seven elephants; but the very same man now accustoms himself to the use of shoes with a lining

---

[1] This half *s*loka recurs in Dhammapada, verse 81.

[2] Ekapalâsikan ti eka-pa*t*ala*m* (B.).

[3] Asîti-saka*t*a-vâhe hira*ññ*a*m* (so correct the misprint in the text). Buddhaghosa says: ettha dve saka*t*abhârâ eko vâho 'ti veditabbo; but compare Rh. D., 'Ancient Coins and Measures,' &c., p. 18, § 32, and p. 14, § 23. Vâha occurs also in the Mahâva*m*sa, p. 22.

[4] Sattahatthika*ñ* *k*a a*n*îkan ti: ettha *kh*a hatthiniyo eko *k*a hatthîti, ida*m* eka*m* a*n*îka*m*, îdisani satta a*n*îkâni sattahatthika*m* nâma (B.).

to them." [30.] If the Blessed One will enjoin their use upon the Order of Bhikkhus, I will also use them. If the Blessed One will not enjoin their use upon the Order of Bhikkhus, neither will I use them.'

Then the Blessed One, on that occasion, having delivered a religious discourse, thus addressed the Bhikkhus:

'I enjoin upon you, O Bhikkhus, the use of shoes with one lining to them. Doubly lined shoes, Bhikkhus, are not to be worn, nor trebly lined ones, nor shoes with many linings[1]. Whosoever shall wear such, is guilty of a dukka*t*a offence.'

2.

1. Now at that time the *Kh*abbaggiya Bhikkhus were in the habit of wearing slippers all of a blue, yellow, red, brown, black, orange, or yellowish colour[2]. People were annoyed, murmured, and became angry, saying, '(These act) like those who still enjoy the pleasures of the world[3].' The brethren told this thing to the Blessed One.

'Do not wear, O Bhikkhus, shoes that are all of.

---

[1] Dvi-gu*n*â 'ti dvi-pa*t*alâ. Ti-gu*n*â 'ti ti-pa*t*alâ. Ga*n*a*m*ga*n*û-pâhanâ 'ti *k*atu-pa*t*alato pa*tth*âya vu*kk*ati (B.).

[2] Nîlikâ ummâra-puppha-va*nn*â hoti; pîtikâ kanikâra-puppha-va*nn*â; lohitikâ *g*ayasumana-puppha-va*nn*â; ma*ñ*ge*tth*ikâ ma*ñ*ge*tth*i-va*nn*â eva; ka*n*hâ a*t*âri*tth*aka-va*nn*â; mahârangarattâ satapada-pi*tth*i-va*nn*â (Mahâra*g*ana is saffron; the colour of the back of a centipede is brownish yellow), mahânâmarattâ sambhinna-va*nn*â hoti pa*nd*u-palâsa-va*nn*â, Kurundiya*m* pana paduma-puppha-va*nn*â 'ti vutta*m* (B.).

[3] Read gihikâmabhogino (as corrected at vol. ii. p. 363).

a blue, yellow, red, brown, black, orange, or yellowish colour. Whosoever does so, is guilty of a dukka*t*a offence.'

2. Now at that time the *Kh*abbaggiya Bhikkhus were in the habit of wearing shoes with edges of a blue, yellow, red, brown, black, orange, or yellowish colour.

People were annoyed, murmured, and became angry, saying, 'These act like those who still enjoy the pleasures of the world.' The brethren told this thing to the Blessed One.

'Do not wear, O Bhikkhus, shoes that have edges of a blue, yellow, red, brown, black, orange, or yellowish colour. Whosoever does so, is guilty of a dukka*t*a offence.'

3. Now at that time the *Kh*abbaggiya Bhikkhus were in the habit of wearing shoes with heel-coverings (?[1]); mocassins[2]; laced boots[3]; boots lined with cotton[4]; boots of various hues, like the wings of partridges[5]; boots pointed with rams' horns, and with goats' horns[6]; ornamented with scorpions'

---

[1] All the names of boots or shoes are of doubtful meaning; and as the use of every sort of foot-covering has long been given up among those Buddhists who have preserved the use of the Pâli language, Buddhaghosa's explanations are not very reliable. He says here: Khallaka-baddhâ 'ti pa*n*hi-pidhânattha*m* tale khallaka*m* bandhitvâ katâ.

[2] Pu*t*abaddhâ 'ti Yonaka-upâhanâ vu*kk*ati, yâva *g*aṅghato sabbapâda*m* pa*t*i*kkh*âdeti.

[3] Pâligu*nth*imâ 'ti paligu*nth*itvâ katâ upari-pâda-mattam eva pa*t*i*kkh*âdeti na *g*aṅgha*m*.

[4] Tûlapu*nn*ikâ 'ti tûlapunnâ pûretvâ katâ.

[5] Tittirapattikâ 'ti tittira-patta-sadisa-vi*k*itra-baddhâ.

[6] Me*nd*a-visâ*n*a-baddhikâ 'ti ka*nn*ika-*tth*âne me*nd*aka-siṅga-sa*nth*âne vaddhe yogetvâ katâ. A*g*a-visâ*n*a-vaddhikâdisu pi es' eva nayo.

tails [1]; sewn round with peacocks' feathers [2]; or shoes of all kinds of colours [3].

People were annoyed (&c., as in § 2, down to:) told this thing to the Blessed One.

'Do not wear, O Bhikkhus, shoes with heel-coverings (&c., as in § 3, down to:) shoes of all kinds of colours. Whosoever does so, is guilty of a dukka*t*a offence.'

4. Now at that time the *Kh*abbaggiya Bhikkhus were in the habit of wearing shoes adorned with lion-skins [4], tiger-skins, panther-skins, antelope-skins, otter-skins [5], cat-skins, squirrel-skins, and owl-skins [6].

People were annoyed (&c., as in § 3, down to the end, substituting 'shoes adorned with lion-skins, &c.,' for 'shoes with heel-coverings, &c.')

3.

1. Now the Blessed One, having dressed early in the morning, went into Râ*g*agaha, duly bowled and robed, for alms, with a certain Bhikkhu as his companion. And that Bhikkhu followed limping step by step behind the Blessed One.

---

[1] Vi*kkh*ikâlikâ 'ti tatth' eva vi*kkh*ika-nangu*tth*a-sa*nth*âne vaddhe yo*g*etvâ katâ.

[2] Morapi*ññkh*aparisibbitâ (sic) 'ti talesu vâ baddhesu vâ mora-vi*ññkh*ehi (sic) suttakasadisehi parisibbitâ.

[3] *K*itrâ 'ti vi*k*itrâ.

[4] Sîha-*k*amma-parikkhatâ nâma pariyantesu, *k*ivaresu anu*v*â*t*a*m* viya sîha*k*amma*m* yo*g*etvâ katâ.

[5] Udda, an animal, feeding on fish; but Childers thinks it is not an amphibious creature, and therefore not 'otter.'

[6] Lûka-*k*amma-parikkhatâ (sic) 'ti pakkha-bi*l*âla-*k*amma-parikkhatâ. The latter is the flying fox, a large kind of bat.

Now a certain lay-disciple who had put on a pair of shoes with many linings, saw the Blessed One approaching from afar. And when he saw him, he took off that pair of shoes and went up to the Blessed One, and saluted him; and went on to that Bhikkhu, and saluted him, and said:

2. 'Why does your reverence limp?'

'My feet, friend, are blistered.'

'But here, Sir, are shoes.'

'Enough, good friend! shoes with linings have been forbidden by the Blessed One.'

'Take the shoes, O Bhikkhu[1]!'

Then the Blessed One, on that occasion, having delivered a religious discourse, addressed the Bhikkhus, and said:

'I allow you, O Bhikkhus, the use of shoes with linings, when they have been cast off by others[2]. But new shoes with linings are not to be worn. Whosoever does so, is guilty of a dukka*t*a offence.'

4.

1. Now at that time the Blessed One walked up and down in the open air[3] unshod. Noticing that, 'The Master walks unshod,' the Elders (the Thera Bhikkhus) also went unshod when they were walking up and down[3]. But though the Master and the Thera Bhikkhus went unshod, the *Kh*abbaggiya Bhikkhus walked up and down with coverings on their feet.

[1] This must be understood as spoken by the Buddha.

[2] Omukkan ti pa*t*imu*ññ*itvâ apanîta*m* (B.).

[3] This walking up and down thinking is represented as a constant habit of the early Buddhist Sama*n*as.

The temperate Bhikkhus were annoyed, murmured, and became angry, saying, 'How can these *Kh*abbaggiya Bhikkhus walk shod, when the Master and the Thera Bhikkhus walk unshod?'

2. Then those Bhikkhus told this thing to the Blessed One.

'Is it true, what they say, O Bhikkhus, that the *Kh*abbaggiya Bhikkhus walk shod, though the Master and the Elders walk unshod?'

'It is true, Lord.'

The Blessed Buddha rebuked them, saying,

'How, O Bhikkhus, can these foolish persons walk shod, though (&c., as in §§ 1, 2). For even the laymen, O Bhikkhus, who are clad in white, for the sake of some handicraft that may procure them a living, will be respectful, affectionate, hospitable to their teachers. [3.] Do you, therefore, O Bhikkhus, so let (your light) shine forth, that you having left the world (to enter into) so well taught a doctrine and discipline may be respectful, affectionate, hospitable to your teachers (â*k*ariyas), or those who rank as teachers [1], and to your superiors (upa*ggh*âyas), or those who rank as superiors [2]. This will not conduce, O Bhikkhus, to the conversion of the unconverted, and to the augmentation of the number of the con-

[1] Avassikassa *kh*abbasso â*k*ariyamatto. So hi *k*atuvassakâle ta*m* nissâya va*kkh*ati (Mahâvagga I, 35). Eva*m* ekavassassa sattavasso, duvassassa a*tth*avasso, tivassassa dasavasso (B.).

[2] Upa*ggh*âyassa sa*m*di*tth*a-sa*m*bhattâ pana sahâyâ bhikkhû, ye vâ pana ke*k*i dasahi vassehi mahantatarâ, te sabbe pi upa*ggh*âyamattâ nâma. This confirms the view expressed in a note to the first Book (chap. 32. 1), that the Upa*ggh*âya is a more important person than the Â*k*ariya. The former must have ten years, the latter need only have six years, seniority.

verted: but it will result, O Bhikkhus, in the unconverted being repulsed (from the faith), and in many of the converted becoming estranged.' Having thus rebuked them, and having delivered a religious discourse, he thus addressed the Bhikkhus:

'None of you, O Bhikkhus, is to walk shod, when your teachers or those who rank as teachers, or your superiors, or those who rank as superiors, are walking unshod. Whosoever does so, is guilty of a dukka*t*a offence.

'And no one of you, O Bhikkhus, is to wear shoes in the open Ârâma. Whosoever does so, is guilty of a dukka*t*a offence.'

5.

1. Now at that time a certain Bhikkhu had an eruption[1] on his feet. They used to carry that Bhikkhu out when he wanted to ease himself. The Blessed One as he was passing through the sleeping places (of the Bhikkhus) saw them (doing so), and going up to them, he said:

2: 'What is the disease, O Bhikkhus, from which this Bhikkhu suffers?'

'This venerable brother has an eruption on his feet, Lord, and we are carrying him out to ease himself.'

Then, on that occasion, the Blessed One, having delivered a religious discourse, addressed the Bhikkhus, and said:

'I enjoin, O Bhikkhus, the use of foot coverings

[1] Pâdakhîlâbâdho nâma pâdato khîla-sadisa*m* ma*m*sa*m* nikkhanta*m* hoti (B.).

by one whose feet hurt him, or are blistered, or who has an eruption on his feet.'

6.

1. Now at that time the Bhikkhus used to get up on to couches or chairs with unwashen feet; and the robes and seats became soiled.

They told this thing to the Blessed One.

'I enjoin, O Bhikkhus, the use of foot coverings when one of you wishes to get up on to couches or chairs.'

2. Now at that time when the Bhikkhus were going to the Uposatha Hall or to the assembly in the dark, they trod upon stakes or thorns, and their feet were hurt.

They told this thing to the Blessed One.

'I enjoin, O Bhikkhus, the use of foot coverings in the open Ârâma, and of a torch, or lamp, and a walking stick[1].'

3. Now at that time the *Kh*abbaggiya Bhikkhus used to rise up in the night towards dawn; and, putting on wooden shoes, walked up and down in the open air talking, in tones high, loud, and harsh, of all kinds of worldly things—such as tales of kings, of robbers, of ministers of state; tales of armies, of terror, of war; conversation respecting meats, drinks, clothes, couches, garlands, perfumes, relationships, equipages, villages, towns, cities, provinces, women, warriors, and streets; tales about buried treasures, ghost stories; various tales; discussions

[1] Kattara-da*nd*a. Compare *K*ullavagga VIII, 6, 3, and Childers under Kattara-ya*tth*i. Our word occurs at *G*âtaka I, 9.

on the world; disasters by sea; things which are, and things which are not[1]. And so doing they both trod upon and slew all kinds of insects, and disturbed the Bhikkhus in their meditations.

4. The moderate Bhikkhus were annoyed, murmured, and became angry, saying, 'How can the *Kh*abbaggiya Bhikkhus [do so]?'

And those Bhikkhus told this thing to the Blessed One.

'Is it true' (&c., comp. chap. 4. 2)?

'It is true, Lord.'

He rebuked them, and having delivered a religious discourse, he addressed the Bhikkhus, and said: 'Wooden shoes, O Bhikkhus, are not to be worn. Whosoever wears them, is guilty of a dukka*t*a offence.'

7.

1. Now when the Blessed One had remained at Râ*g*agaha as long as he thought fit, he set out on his journey towards Benares. And wandering from place to place, he came to Benares, and there at Benares the Blessed One stayed in the deer-park Isipatana.

Now at that time the *Kh*abbaggiya Bhikkhus, since the Blessed One had forbidden wooden shoes, used to break off young palmyra palms, and wear shoes made of the talipat leaves[2]. The young palmyra plants withered. People were annoyed, murmured, and became angry, saying, 'How can

[1] This list recurs in the Ma*gg*hima Sîla, § 7 (Rh. D.'s 'Buddhist Suttas from the Pâli,' p. 194).

[2] These are the leaves on which the MSS. are written.

the Sakyaputtiya Sama*n*as break off young palmyra palms, and wear shoes made of the talipat leaves? The young palmyra plants wither. (By so doing), the Sakyaputtiya Sama*n*as destroy vegetable life.'

2. The Bhikkhus heard those people murmuring in annoyance and indignation; and they told this matter to the Blessed One.

'Is it true' (&c., as in chap. 4. 2)?

'It is true, Lord.'

The Blessed Buddha rebuked them, saying, 'How can those foolish persons, O Bhikkhus, [act thus]? For people believe, O Bhikkhus, that life dwells in a tree. Such conduct will not conduce (&c., as in chap. 4. 2, down to:) becoming estranged.

'Foot coverings made of talipat leaves, O Bhikkhus, are not to be worn. Whosoever wears them, is guilty of a dukka*t*a offence.'

3. Now at that time the *Kh*abbaggiya Bhikkhus, since the Blessed One had forbidden talipat shoes, used to break off young bambus, and wear shoes made of the bambu leaves (&c., as in last section down to the end, substituting bambu for palmyra).

8.

1. Now when the Blessed One had remained at Benares as long as he thought fit, he set out on his journey towards Bhaddiya. And wandering from place to place he came to Bhaddiya: and there, at Bhaddiya, he stayed in the *G*âtiyâ Grove.

Now at that time the Bhikkhus at Bhaddiya were accustomed to the use of various kinds of foot coverings for the sake of ornament. They made, or had made for themselves foot coverings of tina-grass, of muñga-grass, of babbaga-grass, of the leaves of the date-palm[1], of kamala-grass[2], and of wool[3]. And they neglected[4] instruction, enquiry, morality, self-concentration, and wisdom[5].

2. The moderate Bhikkhus were annoyed, murmured, and became angry, thinking, 'How can they [do so]?' And those Bhikkhus told this thing to the Blessed One.

'Is it true' (&c., as in chap. 4. 2)?

'It is true, Lord.'

The Blessed Buddha rebuked them, saying, 'How can they [do so]?' This will not conduce (&c., as in chap. 4. 2, down to:) becoming estranged.

3. Having thus rebuked them, and having delivered a religious discourse, he thus addressed the Bhikkhus: 'Shoes, O Bhikkhus, made of tina-grass are not to be worn, or made of muñga-grass, or of babbaga-grass, or of leaves of the date-palm, or of kamala-grass, or of wool, nor [ornamented with] gold, or silver, or pearls, or beryls, or crystal, or copper, or glass, or tin, or lead, or bronze. Whosoever does so, is guilty of a dukkata offence.

[1] Hintâla-pâdukâ 'ti khaggûra- (MS. khaggari) pattehi kata-pâdukâ: hintâla-pattehi pi na vattati yeva (B.).

[2] Kamala-pâdukâ 'ti kamala-tinam nâma atthi, tena kata-pâdukâ. Ussîra-pâdukâ 'ti pi vadanti. Childers only gives lotus as the meaning of kamala. At Gâtaka I, 119, 149, 178; IV, 42, it must be kamala, and not kambala as printed by Fausböll, that is meant.

[3] Kambala-pâdukâ 'ti unnâhi kata-pâdukâ.

[4] On riñkanti (Sanskrit rik, rinakti), compare the verses in Milinda Pañha, p. 419 (ed. Trenckner).

[5] The adhisilâdi-sikkhâ-ttayam mentioned at Dhp. p. 358 is explained in the Samgîti Sutta as training in adhisila, adhikitta, and adhipaññâ. On the first, compare the note on Mahâvagga I, 36, 8.

'And clogs, O Bhikkhus, that are taken away[1], are not to be worn. Whosoever does so, is guilty of a dukka*t*a offence.

'I allow you, O Bhikkhus, the use of three kinds of clogs, that are fixed to the ground, and are not taken away[2], privy-clogs, urinal-clogs, and rinsing-clogs[3].'

9.

1. Now when the Blessed One had remained at Bhaddiya as long as he thought fit, he set out on a journey towards Sâvatthi. And walking from place to place he arrived at Sâvatthi. There the Blessed One dwelt at Sâvatthi at the *G*etavana, Anâtha-pi*nd*ika's Grove.

2. Now at that time the *Kh*abbaggiya Bhikkhus used to catch hold of the heifers crossing on the A*k*iravatî River by their horns, or ears, or dewlaps, or tails[4], or spring up upon their backs, or touch with lustful

[1] See next clause.

[2] Asa*m*kamaniyâyo 'ti bhûmiya*m* supati*tth*â ni*kk*alâ asa*m*hariyâ (sic), (B. here). Compare Pâtimokkha, pp. 106, 113 (ed. Minayeff), and Childers's interpretation of those passages under sa*m*kamati.

[3] On va*kk*a-pâdukâ, see *K*ullavagga V, 35, 2, at the end; and VIII, 10, 3, at the beginning. On the other two, *K*ullavagga V, 35; 1, 4, and VIII, 10, 3; and see also VIII, 9. The use of them was part of the sanitary arrangements enjoined upon the Order. A very ancient pair of stone va*kk*a-pâdukâ, forming part of a slab of stone, was discovered at Anurâdhapura by Rhys Davids, and is now in the Colombo Museum. As they were dug up in one of the palaces there, they were probably for the use of the king, or some high official. These ruins are among the most ancient in Ceylon, and are certainly pre-Christian in date.

[4] On *kh*eppâ, compare Sutta-vibhaṅga I, 6; and Böhtlingk-Roth under *s*epa and paru*kkh*epa.

thoughts their privy parts: and they used to duck the young calves and so kill them. People were annoyed, murmured, and became angry, saying, 'How can the Sakyaputtiya Samaṇas [act thus]? it is like men still enjoying the pleasures of the world.'

And Bhikkhus heard them murmuring in annoyance and indignation: and those Bhikkhus told this thing to the Blessed One.

'Is it true' (&c., see chap. 4. 2)?

'It is true, Lord.'

He rebuked them, and having delivered a religious discourse, he addressed the Bhikkhus, and said:

'Heifers are not to be caught hold of, O Bhikkhus, by their horns, or their ears, or their dewlaps, or their tails. You are not to get up on their backs. Whosoever gets up on their backs, is guilty of a dukkaṭa offence. And their privy parts, O Bhikkhus, are not to be touched with lustful thoughts. Whosoever does so, is guilty of a thullakkaya offence. And calves ought not to be killed. Whosoever kills them, let him be dealt with according to law[1].'

3. Now at that time the Khabbaggiya Bhikkhus used to have themselves carried in vehicles to which cows were yoked with a bull between them, or bulls were yoked with a cow between them[2]. People were annoyed, murmured, and became angry, saying, 'That is as is done at the Feast of the Gaṅgâ and the Mahî[3].'

---

[1] See the 61st Pâkittiya Rule.

[2] Buddhaghosa explains this passage in a different way: Itthiyuttenâ 'ti dhenu-yuttena. Purisantarenâ 'ti purisa-sârathinâ. Purisa-yuttenâ 'ti goṇa-yuttena. Itthantarenâ 'ti itthi-sârathinâ.

[3] Gaṅgâ-mahiyâyâ 'ti Gaṅgâ-mahî-kîḷikâya (B.). It is possible that Mahî may here mean the Earth; but it is probably the

They told this thing to the Blessed One.

'Do not have yourselves carried in vehicles, O Bhikkhus. Whosoever does so, is guilty of a dukka*t*a offence.'

10[1].

1. Now at that time a certain Bhikkhu, as he was passing through the Kosala country to Sâvatthi, to visit the Blessed One, was taken ill on the way. And that Bhikkhu went aside out of the road, and sat down at the foot of a certain tree.

When people saw him sitting there, they said: 'Whither is your reverence going?'

'I am going, friends, to Sâvatthi to visit the Blessed One.'

2. 'Come along, Sir; let us go together.'

'I cannot, friends. I am sick.'

'Well then, Sir, get up into the cart.'

'Enough, friends! The Blessed One has forbidden the use of vehicles.' And fearing to offend, he refused to get up into the cart.

And when that Bhikkhu had come to Sâvatthi, he told this thing to the Bhikkhus, and they told it to the Blessed One.

'I allow you, O Bhikkhus, if you are sick, to use a cart.'

Now the Bhikkhus thought: 'Should the carts be yoked with cows or bulls?'

---

well-known affluent of the Ganges, which is one of the Mahânadîs. Compare *K*ullavagga IX, 1, 3, Spence Hardy's 'Manual,' p. 17, and the Dhaniya Sutta in the Sutta Nipâta.

[1] *K*ullavagga X, 21 gives the rules for sisters of the Order, corresponding to the first two sections of this chapter.

They told this thing to the Blessed One.

'I allow you, O Bhikkhus, to use a cart drawn by bullocks, or by hand[1].'

Now at that time a certain Bhikkhu was exceedingly distressed by the jolting of a cart.

'I allow you, O Bhikkhus, the use of a litter or a sedan-chair.'

3. Now at that time the *Kh*abbaggiya Bhikkhus were in the habit of using lofty and large things to recline upon, that is to say: large cushions[2]; divans; coverlets with long fleece; counterpanes of many colours, woollen coverlets[3], white or marked with thick flowers; mattresses; cotton coverlets, dyed with figures of animals; rugs with long hair on one or both sides; carpets inwrought with gold, or with silk; large woollen carpets such as the nautch girls dance upon[4]; rich elephant housings, horse-rugs, or carriage rugs; panther or antelope skins; couches covered with canopies, or with crimson cushions at both ends[5].

---

[1] On hatthava*tt*aka*m* here Buddhaghosa merely says, 'itthiyo vâ va*tt*antu purisâ vâ va*tt*antu (MS. va*tt*ati) yeva.' The word recurs in *K*ullavagga X, 21.

[2] That Âsandi is a cushion, and not a chair as Childers gives, is clear from *G*âtaka I, 108.

[3] Pa*t*ikâ 'ti u*nn*âmayo setattharako (Sum. Vil. on Brahma*g*âla Sutta 9).

[4] Kuttakan ti so*l*asanna*m* nâ*t*akitthîna*m* *th*atvâ na*kk*ana-yogga*m* u*nn*âmayattharana*m* (Sum. Vil. on Brahma*g*âla Sutta 9).

[5] This list recurs in the Ma*ggh*ima Sîla, § 5 (Rh D., 'Buddhist Suttas from the Pâli,' p. 193). Childers has given the commentary on most of these terms from the Sumaṅgala Vilâsinî. Several of the items are also mentioned among the possessions of the Great King of Glory (Rh. D., loc. cit., p. 274, &c.). In several cases the exact meaning is at present quite uncertain. The comment on the last two words runs as follows: Sauttara*kkh*adan ti saha uttara-

When people, who went to visit the Vihâras, saw these things, they were annoyed, murmured, and became angry, thinking, 'This is as if they were still enjoying the pleasures of the world.'

They told this thing to the Blessed One.

4. 'Lofty and large things to recline upon, such as large cushions (&c., as in § 3, down to:) cushions crimson at both ends, are not, O Bhikkhus, to be used. Whosoever uses them, is guilty of a dukka*t*a offence.'

5. Now at that time the *Kh*abbaggiya Bhikkhus, since the use of lofty and large things to recline upon had been forbidden by the Blessed One, used to use fine skins, such as lion, tiger, and panther skins. These skins were cut to fit the couches, and to fit the chairs; and were spread inside or outside the couches or the chairs.

When people, who went to visit the Vihâras, saw these things, they were annoyed, murmured, and became angry, thinking, 'This is as if they were still enjoying the pleasures of the world.'

They told this thing to the Blessed One.

6. 'Fine skins, such as lion, tiger, and panther skins, are not, O Bhikkhus, to be used. Whosoever does so, is guilty of a dukka*t*a offence.'

7. Now at that time the *Kh*abbaggiya Bhikkhus, since fine skins had been forbidden by the Blessed

---

*kkh*adena upari-bandhena ratta-vitânena saddhin ti attho. Seta-vitânam pi he*tth*â akappiya-pa*kk*attharan*e* sati na va*tt*ati, asati pana va*tt*ati. Ubhatolohitakûpadhâna*m* sisûpadhâna*ñ* *k*a pâdûpadhâna*ñ* *k*a mañ*k*assa ubhatolohitakûpadhâna*m* eva*m* (read eva?) na kappati. Ya*m* pana ekam eva upadhâna*m* ubhosu passesu ratta*m* vâ hoti paduma-va*nn*a*m* vâ *k*itra*m* vâ sa*k*e pamâ*n*a-yutta*m* va*tt*ati, mahâ-upadhâna*m* pana pa*t*ikkhitta*m*.

One, began to use the skins of oxen. These skins were cut to fit the couches, or the chairs; and were spread inside or outside the couches, or the chairs.

Now a certain Bhikkhu of bad character was a friend of the family of a certain lay-disciple of a bad character. And that bad Bhikkhu, early one morning, dressed himself, and with his robe on and his bowl in his hand, went to the dwelling-place of that bad disciple, and sat down on a seat made ready for him. And the bad disciple went up to the place where the bad Bhikkhu was, and saluted him, and took his seat beside him.

8. Now at that time that bad disciple had a young bull beautiful to behold, quiet, and varied in colour like a panther's cub. And the bad Bhikkhu gazed with longing at the bull. And that bad disciple said to that bad Bhikkhu: 'Why does your reverence gaze so with longing at that bull?'

'My friend,' said he, 'I want that bull's skin.'

Then that bad disciple slew that bull, and skinned it, and gave it to that bad Bhikkhu. And that bad Bhikkhu, hiding that skin under his robe, went away.

9. Now the cow, greedy for her calf, followed that bad Bhikkhu, keeping behind him. The Bhikkhus said:

'How is it, friend, that this cow keeps following so behind you?'

'I don't know, friends, why it should keep following me.'

But that bad Bhikkhu's robe was soiled with blood; and the Bhikkhus asked him,

'How has this robe of yours got marked with blood?'

Then he told them the whole matter.

'How is that, Sir? You have been causing another to deprive a living thing of life!'

'That is so, friends.'

The modest among the Bhikkhus were annoyed, murmured, and became angry, saying, 'How can this Bhikkhu induce a man to deprive a living thing of life? Has not the taking of life been censured, and the abstinence therefrom been praised in many a discourse by the Blessed One?'

And the Bhikkhus told this thing to the Blessed One.

Then the Blessed One held because of this, and on that occasion, an assembly of the community of Bhikkhus, and asked that wicked Bhikkhu,

'Is it true, as they say, that you, O Bhikkhu, have been inducing another to deprive a living thing of life?'

'It is true, Lord.'

'But how can you be so foolish as to do so? Have I not censured in many a discourse the taking of life, O foolish one, and praised the abstinence therefrom? Such conduct, thou foolish one, will not conduce to the conversion of the unconverted!'

And having thus rebuked him, and delivered a religious discourse, he addressed the Bhikkhus, and said:

'Bhikkhus! No one shall cause a living thing to be deprived of life. Whosoever does so shall be dealt with according to the Laws[1]. Ox-skins are not to be worn, O Bhikkhus. Whosoever does so, is guilty of a dukka*t*a offence. And neither, O Bhikkhus, is any skin to be made use of at all. Whosoever does so, is guilty of a dukka*t*a offence.'

[1] The Laws (Dhammas) referred to are the first Pârâgika, the 11th Pâ*k*ittiya, and the 61st and 62nd Pâ*k*ittiyas.

11.

Now at that time men had couches and chairs covered or bound with skins. The Bhikkhus, fearing to offend, would not sit down upon them.

They told this thing to the Blessed One.

'I allow you, O Bhikkhus, to sit down on seats arranged by laymen, but not to lie down upon them.'

Now at that time the Vihâras were bound together by thongs made of skin[1]. The Bhikkhus fearing to offend, would not sit down upon them.

They told this thing to the Blessed One.

'I allow you, O Bhikkhus, to sit down upon (skins when they are) only used for binding things together.'

12.

Now at that time the *Kh*abbaggiya Bhikkhus used to go into the villages with their shoes on. The people were annoyed, murmured, and became angry, saying, 'That is how those behave who are still enjoying the pleasures of the world!'

They told this thing to the Blessed One.

'You are not to go into the villages, O Bhikkhus, with your shoes on. Whosoever does so, is guilty of a dukka*t*a offence.'

Now at that time a certain Bhikkhu was sick, and unable to go into the village without shoes on.

They told this thing to the Blessed One.

'I allow a sick Bhikkhu, O Bhikkhus, to go into the village with his shoes on.'

[1] Ogumphiyantîti bhitti-da*nd*akâdisu ve*th*etvâ bandhanti (B.).

13[1].

1. Now at that time the venerable Mahâ Ka*kk*âyana was staying in Avanti on the hill called the Precipice, near Kuraraghara[2]. And at that time the lay-disciple named So*n*a Ku*t*ika*nn*a[3] was the personal attendant upon the venerable Mahâ Ka*kk*âyana.

And the disciple So*n*a Ku*t*ika*nn*a went to the place where the venerable Mahâ Ka*kk*âyana was, and saluted him, and took his seat beside him. And when he was thus seated, he said to the venerable Mahâ Ka*kk*âyana:

'As I understand the doctrine laid down by the venerable Mahâ Ka*kk*âyana, it is difficult for the man who dwells at home to live the higher life in all its fulness, in all its purity, in all its bright perfection. I wish therefore to cut off my hair and beard, to clothe myself in the orange-coloured robes, and to go forth from the household life into the houseless state[4]. May the venerable Mahâ Ka*kk*âyana receive me into the Order of those who have renounced the world!'

2. 'Hard is it, So*n*a, your life long to live the

[1] Sections 1–6 of this chapter were published and translated by Alwis in his 'Ka*kk*âyana's Pali Grammar,' pp. 92 and following.

[2] Buddhaghosa spells this name Kuduraghara, and says it was there that Ka*kk*âyana had been accustomed to go for alms, and that he dwelt on the precipice itself.

[3] Buddhaghosa has a curious explanation of this name, Ko*t*i-agghanaka*m* pana ka*nn*a-pilandhanaka*m* dhâreti, tasmâ Ku*t*ika*nn*o 'ti vu*kk*ati. This is evidently merely drawn from the word itself, which may just as well have meant 'with pointed ears.'

[4] This is a common phrase. Compare Tevi*gg*a Sutta (Rh. D., 'Buddhist Suttas from the Pâli,' pp. 187, 188).

higher life using only one bed, and with but one meal a day. Do you, therefore, So*n*a, remain in the state of a householder, and practise only for a time the higher life, the precepts of the Buddhas, using only one bed, and with but one meal a day.'

Then the desire for renunciation[1] which had arisen in the disciple So*n*a Ku*t*ika*nn*a abated in him.

A second time the disciple So*n*a Ku*t*ika*nn*a [made the same request, and received the same reply with the same result].

And a third time So*n*a Ku*t*ika*nn*a made the same request. Then the venerable Mahâ Ka*kk*âyana conferred the pabba*gg*â (ordination) on the disciple So*n*a Ku*t*ika*nn*a.

Now at that time in the Southern country and in Avanti there were but few Bhikkhus. And it was only after the lapse of three years that the venerable Mahâ Ka*kk*âyana was able, with difficulty, and with trouble, to get together a meeting of the Order in which ten Bhikkhus were present[2]. And then he admitted the venerable So*n*a into the higher rank of the Order.

3. Now when the venerable So*n*a had passed the rainy season there sprang up in his mind, when he was meditating alone, this thought:

'I have heard indeed that the Blessed One is such and such a one. But I have not as yet seen him face to face. I should like to go and visit the Blessed One, the Arahat Buddha, if my superior would allow me.'

And in the evening the venerable So*n*a, leaving his solitude, went to the place where the venerable

[1] Compare gamikâbhisa*m*khâra, Mahâvagga VI, 31, 2.
[2] On the necessity of this, see Mahâvagga IX, 4, 1.

Mahâ Ka*kk*âyana was, and saluted him, and took his seat beside him. And when he was thus seated, he said to the venerable Mahâ Ka*kk*âyana:

4. 'When I was meditating alone, venerable Sir, the following thought occurred to my mind, "I have heard (&c., as above)." Now I would go and visit the Blessed One, the Arahat Buddha, if you, as my superior, allow it.'

'That is good, that is good, So*n*a! Go then, So*n*a, to visit the Blessed One, the Arahat Buddha. [5.] You shall see, So*n*a, how the Blessed One arouses faith, is worthy of faith, calm in his senses, calm in his mind, gifted with the highest self-control and quietude, an elephant among men, subdued, guarded, with his senses in subjection to himself. Do you therefore, So*n*a, bow down in my name at the feet of the Blessed One, and say, "Lord! my superior, the venerable Mahâ Ka*kk*âyana, bows down in salutation at the feet of the Blessed One!" and add, "In the Southern country and in Avanti there are, Lord, but few Bhikkhus. And it was only after the lapse of three years that with difficulty and with trouble an assembly of the Order was got together, in which ten members were present, and I could be received into the higher rank of the Order. May the Blessed One be pleased, therefore, to allow the higher ordination in the Southern country and in Avanti before a meeting of a lesser number. [6.] In the Southern country and in Avanti, Lord, the soil is black on the surface [1], rough, and trampled by the feet of cattle [2].

[1] Ka*n*huttarâ 'ti ka*n*ha-mattik-uttarâ upari-vaddhitâ ka*n*ha-mattikâ (B.). Alwis translates, 'overrun with thorns.'

[2] Goka*nt*aka-hatâ 'ti gunna*m* khurehi akkanta-bhumito samu*tth*ehi go-ka*nt*akehi upahatâ. Te kira goka*nt*ake ekapa*t*alikâ upâhanâ

May the Blessed One be pleased, therefore, to allow the use, in the Southern country and in Avanti, of shoes with thick linings. In the Southern country and in Avanti, Lord, men attach great importance to bathing, and are pure by use of water. May the Blessed One be pleased to allow, in the Southern country and in Avanti, the constant use of the bath[1]. In the Southern country and in Avanti, Lord, skins, such as sheep-skins, goat-skins, and deer-skins, are used as coverlets. Just as in the Middle country[2] the eragu, moragu, ma*ggh*âru, and *g*antu grasses[3] are used for coverlets, so are sheep-skins, goat-skins, and deer-skins in the Southern country and in Avanti. May the Blessed One be pleased to allow the use of such coverlets there. [7.] At present, Lord, people are in the habit of giving a set of robes to Bhikkhus, who have left the district, saying, 'We give this set of robes to (a Bhikkhu) of such and such a name.' When they return, the Bhikkhus tell them, 'A set of robes has been given to you by a person of such and such a name.' But they, fearing to offend, do not accept it, saying, 'Let us not be guilty of a Nissaggiya.' May the Blessed One be pleased to make a detailed statement in the matter of robes."'

rakkhitu*m* na sakkonti, eva*m* kharâ honti (B.). Alwis takes goka*n*-*t*aka as a plant (Ruellia Longifolia).

[1] Compare the 57th Pâ*k*ittiya.

[2] See below, § 12; and compare Rh. D., 'Buddhist Birth Stories,' p. 61.

[3] Imâ *k*atasso pi ti*n*a-*g*âtiyo. Etehi kata-sâ*t*ake *k*a ta*tt*ikâyo *k*a karonti. Ettha eragû 'ti ekaraka-ti*n*a*m*, ta*m* o*l*ârika*m*. Moragu-ti*n*a*m* tamba-sîsa*m* sukhuma*m* muduka*m* sukha-samphassa*m*; tena katâ ta*tt*ikâ nipa*gg*itvâ vu*tth*itamatte pana uddhumâtâ hutvâ ti*tth*ati. Ma*gg*ârunâ (sic, and so Alwis) kata-sâ*t*ake pi karonti. *G*antussa ma*n*i-sadiso va*nn*o hoti. Ta*tt*ikâ is a mat; see *G*âtaka I, 141. Compare Sanskrit Eraka, and Mayûraka.

'Even so, Lord,' said the venerable So*n*a in assent to the venerable Mahâ Ka*kk*âyana, and, rising from his seat, he departed thence, keeping his right side towards him. And taking up his bed, he went on with his robe on, and his bowl in his hand to Sâvatthi.

8. And wandering from place to place he arrived at the place where the Blessed One was, at Sâvatthi in the *G*etavana, Anâtha-pi*nd*ika's park. And when he had come there he saluted the Blessed One, and took his seat beside him.

Then the Blessed One said to the venerable Ânanda: 'Make ready a sleeping-place, Ânanda, for this Bhikkhu who has just arrived.' And the venerable Ânanda thought:

'Inasmuch as the Blessed One commands me to make ready a sleeping-place for the Bhikkhu who has just arrived, the Blessed One evidently desires to dwell in the same Vihâra with that Bhikkhu, he desires to dwell in the same Vihâra with the venerable So*n*a.' And he made ready a sleeping-place for the venerable So*n*a at the place where the Blessed One was staying.

9. Then the Blessed One, after spending the greater part of the night in the open air, entered the Vihâra. And also the venerable So*n*a, having spent the greater part of the night in the open air, entered the Vihâra. And the Blessed One rose up, early in the morning, towards dawn, and requested the venerable So*n*a, saying,

'May the Dhamma so become clear to you that you may speak [1].'

---

[1] Pa*t*ibhâtu ta*m* bhikkhu dhammo bhâsitu*m*. Compare Buddhaghosa's commentary on the similar idiom used in the Mahâ-

'Even so, Lord!' said the venerable So*n*a in assent to the Blessed One; and he intoned all the verses in the Book of the Eights (A*tth*aka-vaggikâni[1]).

And the Blessed One, at the conclusion of the venerable So*n*a's recitation, expressed his pleasure, saying,

'Excellent, most excellent, O Bhikkhu! Well have the Eights been grasped by thee, well thought over, well learnt by heart: and with a fine voice art thou gifted, distinct, pleasant[2], able to make things understood. How many years is it since thou hast been ordained?'

'One year, my Lord!'

10. 'But why have you postponed it so long?'

''Tis long, Lord, since I saw into the danger of the passions, but life in a household is crowded with business and with cares.'

And the Blessed One, when he heard that matter, gave utterance at that time to the expression of emotion:

'When he has seen the danger of the world, when he has understood the Truth, when he has become free from Upadhi[3],

---

parinibbâna Sutta II, 31 as given by Rh. D. ('Buddhist Suttas from the Pâli,' p. 36).

[1] A*tth*aka-vagga is the name of the fourth book in the Sutta Nipâta. See Professor Fausböll's translation, p. viii. It may also be the name of divisions of other books, but probably that portion of the Sutta Nipâta is here referred to.

[2] On Ane*l*agalâya compare ne*l*â vâ*k*â in § 6 of the *K*ûla-sila.

[3] Ariyo is the man who has entered the Path, Su*k*i is locative. Nirûpadhi, he in whom there remains no longer the cause of the renewal of existence as a separate individual (the cause referred to being thirst or excitement and craving, Ta*n*hâ, Upâdâna).

'The pilgrim finds in sin no pleasure, his delight is in the word, the pure.'

11. Then thought the venerable Sona: 'The Blessed One is pleased with me. This then is the time which my superior spoke of.' And rising from his seat, and arranging his robe on one shoulder, he bowed down with his head at the feet of the Blessed One, and said:

'Lord! my superior Mahâ Kakkâyana bows down in salutation at the feet of the Blessed One. In the Southern country and in Avanti there are (&c., as in §§ 4–7, down to the end of the message).'

Then the Blessed One on that occasion and in that connection, having delivered a religious discourse, addressed the Bhikkhus and said:

'The Southern country and Avanti has but few Bhikkhus. I allow the upasampadâ (ordination) in border countries to be held in a meeting of only four Bhikkhus, beside the chairman, who must be a Vinaya-dhara.'

12. 'In this passage the following are the border countries referred to[1]. To the East is the town Kagangala, and beyond it Mahâsâlâ. Beyond that is border country; this side of it is the Middle country. To the South-east is the river Salalavatî. Beyond that is border country; this side of it is the Middle country. To the South is the town Setakannika. Beyond that is border country; this side of it is the Middle country. To the West is the Brâhman district of Thûna. Beyond that is

[1] Compare Cunningham, 'Ancient Geography of India,' I, 440; Childers, Khuddaka Pâtha, p. 20; Alwis, 'Introduction to Pali Grammar,' XXIX; Lassen, Indische Alterthumskunde, I, 119 (2nd ed.); Rhys Davids, 'Buddhist Birth Stories,' p. 61.

border country; this side of it is the Middle country. To the North is the mountain range called Usîradhaga. Beyond that is border country; this side of it is the Middle country. In such border countries, I allow, O Bhikkhus, the upasampadâ (ordination) to be held in a meeting of only four Bhikkhus, beside the chairman, who must be a Vinayadhara.

13. 'In the Southern country and in Avanti, O Bhikkhus, the soil is black on the surface and rough, and trampled by the feet of cattle. I allow the use, in all the border countries, O Bhikkhus, of shoes with thick linings.

'In the Southern country and in Avanti, O Bhikkhus, men attach great importance to bathing, and are pure by use of water. I allow the constant use of the bath, O Bhikkhus, in all the border countries.

'In the Southern country and in Avanti, O Bhikkhus, skins, such as sheep-skins, goat-skins, and deer-skins, are used as coverlets. Just as in the Middle country, Bhikkhus, the eragu, moragu, mag*gh*âru, and *g*antu grasses are used for coverlets, so in the Southern country and in Avanti are used skins, such as sheep-skins, goat-skins, and deer-skins. I allow, O Bhikkhus, the use of skins, such as sheep-skins, goat-skins, and deer-skins, as coverlets, in all the border countries.

'There also, O Bhikkhus, people are in the habit of giving a set of robes to Bhikkhus who have left the district, saying, "We give this set of robes to (a Bhikkhu) with such and such a name." I allow you, O Bhikkhus, to accept such robes. The set of robes does not become subject to the ten-days' rule, before it reaches the hand (of the person for whom it was intended)[1].'

---

[1] On this last clause compare the first Nissaggiya, and our note there. The clause here means that the ten days of the rule in the Pâtimokkha are not to begin to run, under the circumstances specified, till the set of robes has actually reached the hand of the Bhikkhu for whom they were intended.

Buddhaghosa says here: Yâva âharitvâ vâ na dinna*m* tumhâka*m* bhante *k*ivara*m* uppannan ti pahinitvâ vâ nâro*k*ita*m*, tâva ga*n*ana*m* na upeti, anadhi*tth*ita*m* na va*tt*ati. Yadâ pana ânetvâ vâ dinna*m* hoti, uppannan ti vâ suta*m*, tato pa*tth*âya dasâham eva parihâra*m* labhati.

SIXTH KHANDHAKA.

(ON MEDICAMENTS.)

1.

1. At that time the Blessed One dwelt at Sâvatthi, in the *G*etavana, the park of Anâtha-pi*nd*ika. And at that time Bhikkhus, attacked by the sickness of the hot season[1], threw up the rice-milk they had drunk, and the food they had eaten. And thereby they became lean, rough, ill-favoured, yellow and ever yellower, and the veins stood out on their limbs[2].

And the Blessed One saw those Bhikkhus thus lean, rough, ill-favoured, yellow and ever yellower, and with the veins standing out on their limbs. And on seeing it, he asked the venerable Ânanda: 'How is it, Ânanda, that the Bhikkhus are become now so lean, rough, &c.?'

'At this time, Lord, the Bhikkhus are attacked with the disease of the hot season; and they throw up the rice-milk they have drunk, and the food they have eaten. Thence is it that they are become lean, rough, ill-favoured, yellow and ever yellower, and that the veins stand out on their limbs.'

2. Then there occurred to the mind of the

[1] Sâradikena âbâdhenâ 'ti sarada-kâle uppannena pittâbâdhena. Tasmi*m* hi kâle vassodakena pi tementi, kaddama*m* pi maddanti, antarantarâ âtapo pi kharo hoti. Tena tesa*m* pitta*m* ko*tth*abbhantara-gata*m* hoti (B.).

[2] Read in the text Dhamani-santata-gattâ; and compare Lalita Vistara, p. 226, and Professor Weber's 'Bhagavatî,' II, 289.

Blessed One, when meditating alone, this consideration: 'At this time the Bhikkhus (&c., down to:) on their limbs. What medicaments shall I now prescribe for the Bhikkhus, as may be authorised as common medicine, and may be diffused through the body, though it be not regarded as ordinary (material) food?' And the Blessed One thought: 'These five medicaments—that is to say, ghee, butter, oil, honey, molasses—are such medicaments. Let me then prescribe them as medicines which the Bhikkhus may accept at the right time, and use at the right time.'

3. And in the evening, when the Blessed One had arisen from his meditation, having delivered a religious discourse, he addressed the Bhikkhus in that connection, saying,

'When I was meditating alone, O Bhikkhus, then occurred to my mind this consideration: "At this time (&c., as in § 2, down to:) material food." Then I thought: "These five (&c., as in § 2, down to:) at the right time." I prescribe, O Bhikkhus, these five things as medicine to be accepted at the right time, and to be used at the right time.'

4. Now at that time the Bhikkhus accepted those five things at the right time, and used them at the right time. And foods which though rough, were ordinary foods, they could not digest[1], much less greasy foods[2]. Then they—attacked both by the hot-season disease, and by this want of appetite[3]—became by both at once still more lean, rough,

---

[1] Na *kkh*âdenti na *g*îranti, na vâtaroga*m* pa*t*ipassambhetu*m* sakkonti (B.).

[2] Senesikâni siniddhâni (B.). Compare Sanskrit snaihika.

[3] Bhattâ*kkh*andakenâ 'ti bhattam aro*k*akena (B.).

ill-favoured, yellow and ever yellower, and with the veins standing out on their limbs.

And the Blessed One saw the Bhikkhus thus still more lean, &c. And when he saw it, he asked the venerable Ânanda: 'How is it, Ânanda, that the Bhikkhus are become now still more lean, &c.?'

5. 'At present, Lord, these Bhikkhus, who use the five medicaments only at the right time, cannot digest foods which, though ordinary, are rough, much less greasy foods. Then they, attacked (&c., as in § 4, down to:) standing out on their limbs.'

Then the Blessed One on that occasion, having delivered a religious discourse, addressed the Bhikkhus, and said: 'I permit you, O Bhikkhus, not only to receive those five medicaments, but to use them both at the right time, and at other times.'

2.

1. Now at that time the Bhikkhus who were sick had need of fatty substances as medicine.

They told this thing to the Blessed One.

'I allow you, O Bhikkhus, the use of the fat of bears, of fish, of alligators, of swine, and of asses, if received at the right time, cooked at the right time, mixed at the right time, to be partaken of with oil.'

2. 'If the fat be received, O Bhikkhus, at the wrong time, cooked at the wrong time, and mixed at the wrong time, and then taken, the Bhikkhu is guilty of three dukka*t*a offences.'

'If it be received, O Bhikkhus, at the right time, cooked at the wrong time, and mixed at the wrong time, and then taken, the Bhikkhu is guilty of two dukka*t*a offences.'

'If it be received, O Bhikkhus, at the right time, cooked at the right time, and mixed at the wrong time, and then taken, the Bhikkhu is guilty of a dukka*t*a offence.'

'If it be received, O Bhikkhus, at the right time, cooked at the right time, and mixed at the right time, and then taken, the Bhikkhu is not guilty.'

3.

1. Now at that time the Bhikkhus who were sick had need of roots for medicine.

They told this thing to the Blessed One.

'I allow you, O Bhikkhus, the use of roots as medicine—turmeric, ginger, orris root, white orris root, ativisa, black hellebore, usîra root, bhaddamuttaka, and whatsoever other roots are used for medicine, and impart an appetising flavour to foods, either hard or soft, which the sick Bhikkhus could not otherwise eat[1]. They may be received, and stored up your life long; and, if there be necessity, they may be eaten. If eaten without necessity, (the Bhikkhu who uses them) is guilty of a dukka*t*a offence.'

2. Now at that time the Bhikkhus who were sick had need for medicine of different sorts of flour made from roots.

They told this thing to the Blessed One.

---

[1] Literally, 'which impart the quality of eatableness to not eatable food, either hard or soft.'

'I allow you, O Bhikkhus, the use of a grindstone, and of another stone to grind upon[1].'

4.

1. Now at that time the Bhikkhus who were sick had need of astringent decoctions as medicine.

They told this thing to the Blessed One.

'I allow you, O Bhikkhus, the use of astringent decoctions as medicine—the nimba[2], the ku*t*a*g*a[3], the pakkava[4], the nattamâla[5], and whatsoever other astringent roots are used for medicine, which impart an appetising flavour to foods, either hard or soft, which the sick Bhikkhus could not otherwise eat. They may be received, and stored up your life long; and, if there be necessity, they may be eaten. If eaten without necessity, (the Bhikkhu who uses them) is guilty of a dukka*t*a offence.'

5.

1. Now at that time the Bhikkhus who were sick had need of leaves as medicine.

They told this thing to the Blessed One.

'I allow you, O Bhikkhus, the use of leaves as

[1] Compare the Sanskrit root puth. Buddhaghosa says: Pisanasilâ *k*a pisana-poto *k*a. Pestle and mortar is in Pâli udukkhala*m* musalañ *k*a: see below, VI, 9, 2.

[2] Azadirachta Indica. Compare Mahâvagga III, 12, 5.

[3] Wrightia anti-dysenterica. Wise, p. 142, gives the botanical name as Echites anti-dysenterica, and says it is an emetic.

[4] A kind of creeper, says Buddhaghosa.

[5] Pongania Glabra (the same as Karañ*g*a, says Buddhaghosa).

medicine—the leaves of the nimba[1], of the ku*t*a*g*a[1], of the pa*t*ola[2], of the tulasi[3], of the kappâsika[4], and whatsoever other leaves are used for medicine, and impart an appetising flavour to foods, either hard or soft, which the sick Bhikkhus could not otherwise eat. They may be received, and stored up (&c., as in last chapter, down to:) guilty of a dukka*t*a offence.'

6.

1. Now at that time the Bhikkhus who were sick had need of fruits as medicine.

They told this thing to the Blessed One.

'I allow you, O Bhikkhus, the use of fruits as medicine—the vi*l*añga[5], the pippala[6], and mari*k*a peppers; the harîtaka[7], and vibhîtaka[8], and âmalaka[9] myrobalans; the go*th*a fruit[10]; and whatsoever other fruits are used for medicine, and impart an appetising flavour to foods, either hard or soft, which the

[1] See the last chapter for these plants.

[2] A species of cucumber, Trichosanthes Dioeca.

[3] That is, basil; but the reading is conjectural only. The text has sulasi.

[4] This is ordinary cotton.

[5] Erycibe Paniculata.

[6] This is not the Ficus Religiosa, but simply pepper. Childers, following Subhûti's edition of the Abhidhânappadîpikâ, spells both this word and the allied form Pippalî with pph instead of pp. So also Fausböll at *G*âtaka, vol. i, p. 29, verse 218. We prefer the spelling with pp in accordance with the Sanskrit.

[7] Yellow myrobalan.

[8] Beleric myrobalan.

[9] Emblic myrobalan.

[10] We cannot suggest any explanation of this word. Buddhaghosa has no comment on any of these medicinal fruits or seeds.

sick Bhikkhus could not otherwise eat. They may be received and stored up (&c., as in chap. 4, down to:) guilty of a dukka*t*a offence.'

7.

1. Now at that time the Bhikkhus who were sick had need of various kinds of gum as medicine.

They told this thing to the Blessed One.

'I allow you, O Bhikkhus, the use of gums as medicine—hiṅgu[1], hiṅgu lac, sipâ*t*ikâ[2], taka[3], taka-patti[3], taka-pa*nn*i[3], sa*gg*ulasa[4], and whatsoever other gums are used for medicine, and impart (&c., as in chap. 4, down to:) is guilty of a dukka*t*a offence.'

8.

1. Now at that time the Bhikkhus who were sick had need of various kinds of salt[5] as medicine.

They told this thing to the Blessed One.

'I allow you, O Bhikkhus, the use of salts as

[1] Ferula assa foetida. Böhtlingk-Roth (sub voce) say it comes from Persia. It is much used in Hindu medicine. See Wise, 'Hindu System of Medicine,' pp. 152–154.

[2] The correct spelling is probably sivâ*t*ikâ. Böhtlingk-Roth under *S*ivâ*t*ikâ and Hiṅgu-*s*ivâ*t*ikâ say it is the same as Va*m*sa-pattrî.

[3] Buddhaghosa merely says these are kinds of lac. According to Wise, p. 152, lâkshâ is used as errhine.

[4] Resin.

[5] On these salts compare Abhidhânappadîpikâ, verse 461; Su*s*ruta, vol. i, pp. 226, 227, of the edition by Madhusûdana Gupta; Wise, 'Hindu Medicine,' p. 117.

medicine—sea-salt[1], black salt[2], rock salt[3], kitchen salt[4], red salt[5], and whatsoever other salts are used in medicine (&c., as in chap. 4, down to:) is guilty of a dukka*t*a offence.'

9[6].

1. Now at that time the venerable Bela*tth*asîsa, the superior of the venerable Ânanda, had a disease of thick scabs; and by reason of the discharge thereof his robes stuck to his body. The Bhikkhus moistened those robes with water, and loosened them (from his body).

The Blessed One as he was wandering in search of a lodging-place for the night saw them [doing so], and going up to the place where they were, he asked them:

'What is the matter, O Bhikkhus, with this Bhikkhu?'

'The venerable one has the disease of thick scabs; and by reason of the discharge thereof his robes stick to his body. So we moisten those robes with water, and loosen them (from his body).'

---

[1] Sâmuddikâ 'ti samudda-tîre vâlukâ viya ti*tth*ati (B.).

[2] Kâ*l*a-lo*n*an ti pakati-lo*n*a*m* (B.).

[3] Sindhavan ti seta-va*nn*a*m*: pabbate u*tth*ahati (B.). It was probably called Sindh salt because it was found there, though, like Sindhava horses, it is always supposed to be white.

[4] Ubbhidâ 'ti bhummito aṅkuya*m* (sic) u*tth*ahati (B.).

[5] Bilan ti dabba-sambhârehi saddhi*m* pa*k*ita*m*: ta*m* ratta-va*nn*am (B.). It is Sanskrit vi*d*a, Hindustâni bi*l* laban, and the same as bilâla in the Abhidhânappadîpikâ.

[6] This introductory story recurs as the introduction to the rule laid down in VIII, 17.

2. Then the Blessed One on that occasion, having delivered a religious discourse, addressed the Bhikkhus, and said:

'I allow, O Bhikkhus, the use of chunam as a medicine by whomsoever has the itch, or boils, or a discharge, or scabs, or whose body is ill-smelling, and to those in health the use of dry dung[1], and of clay, and of colouring matter[2]. I allow the use, O Bhikkhus, of a pestle and mortar[3].'

10.

1. Now at that time the Bhikkhus who were sick had need of sifted[4] chunam as medicine.

They told this thing to the Blessed One.

'I allow, O Bhikkhus, the use of a chunam sieve.'

They had need of the chunam very fine.

'I allow, O Bhikkhus, the use of a cloth sieve.'

2. Now at that time a certain Bhikkhu had a disease not human. Though his teacher and his superior nursed him, they were not able to make him well. He went to a place where swine were slaughtered, and ate the raw flesh, and drank the blood. Thereby his sickness abated.

They told this thing to the Blessed One.

'I allow, O Bhikkhus, in the case of a disease not human, the use of raw flesh and of blood.'

---

[1] *Kh*akanan ti gomaya*m* (B.).

[2] Ra*g*ana-pakkan (sic) ti ra*g*anakasa*t*a*m*. Pâka*t*ika-*k*u*nn*am pi ko*t*etvâ udakena temetvâ nhâyitu*m* va*tt*ati, etam pi ra*g*ana-nipakka-sa*m*khepam (sic, read sa*m*kham) eva ga*kkh*ati (B.). Sa*t*a*m* in this passage must be equal to *sr*i*t*a*m*. On sa*m*kha*m* compare below, Mahâvagga VI, 16, 1.

[3] Compare above, VI, 3, 2.

[4] *K*âleti has often a more definite meaning than 'shake.' Compare *G*âtaka I, 71.

11.

1. Now at that time a certain Bhikkhu had disease of the eyes. They used to carry that Bhikkhu out to ease himself. The Blessed One as he was passing through the Bhikkhus' sleeping quarters saw them [doing so]. When he saw them, he went up to the place where they were, and asked those Bhikkhus:

'What is the disease, O Bhikkhus, from which this Bhikkhu suffers?'

2. 'This venerable one, Lord, has disease of the eyes. Therefore do we carry him out to ease himself.'

Then the Blessed One, on that account, having delivered a religious discourse, addressed the Bhikkhus, and said:

'I allow, O Bhikkhus, the use of eye ointments[1]; to wit, black collyrium[2], rasa ointment[3], sota ointment[4], geruka[5], and kapalla[6].'

They had need of perfumes to grind up into ointments.

---

[1] Añgana, which is here a generic term, inclusive of all the following; sabba-samgâhika-vakanam, says Buddhaghosa.

[2] Kâlañganan ti ekâ añgana-gâti (B.).

[3] Rasañganan ti nânâ-sambhârehi katam (B.). Böhtlingk-Roth say it is made with vitriol.

[4] Sotañganan ti nadisotâdisu uppaggamakam añganam (B.). It is called in Sanskrit srotoñgana, and was made with antimony.

[5] Geruka is the Sanskrit gairika, ochre; and the kind meant is yellow ochre. Geruko nâma suvanna-geruko, says Buddhaghosa. Compare the Sanskrit Kâñkana-gairika and svarna-gairika.

[6] Kapallan ti dîpa-sikhâto gahita-masi, 'soot taken from the flame of a lamp' (B.).

'I allow, O Bhikkhus, the use of sandal wood, tagara[1], black anusâri[2], kâlîya[3], and bhaddamuttaka[4].'

12.

1. Now at that time the Bhikkhus used to put pulverised ointments into pots and saucers. They became sprinkled over with herb-powders and dust.

They told this thing to the Blessed One.

'I allow, O Bhikkhus, the use of a box for ointment.'

Now at that time the *Kh*abbaggiya Bhikkhus used to carry about various kinds of boxes for ointments—gold ones, and silver ones. People were annoyed, murmured, and became angry, saying, 'Like those who still live in the world.'

They told this thing to the Blessed One.

'Various kinds of boxes for ointments, gold ones, and silver ones, are not, O Bhikkhus, to be used. Whosoever does so, is guilty of a dukka*t*a offence. I allow, O Bhikkhus, the use of such boxes made of bone, or ivory, or horn, or of the na*l*a reed, or of bambu, or of wood, or of lac, or of the shells of fruit, or of bronze, or of the centre of the chank-shell[5].'

---

[1] Tagara as a fragrant flower is mentioned in verse 54 of the Dhammapada quoted in Milinda Pañha, p. 333.

[2] A kind of dark fragrant sandal wood.

[3] Read so in the text as corrected on p. 381. It is a kind of sandal wood.

[4] A perfume made from the grass of the same name (mentioned above, VI, 3).

[5] Saṅkha-nâbhi, the meaning of the latter part of which compound is not quite clear.

2. Now at that time the boxes of ointment had no lid. (The ointment) was sprinkled over with herb-powders and dust.

They told this thing to the Blessed One.

'I allow, O Bhikkhus, the use of a lid.'

The lids used to fall off.

'I allow you, O Bhikkhus, to fasten the lid with thread, and to tie it on to the box.'

The boxes used to fall.

'I allow you, O Bhikkhus, to sew the boxes on with thread[1].'

3. Now at that time the Bhikkhus used to rub the ointment on with their fingers: and the eyes were hurt.

They told this thing to the Blessed One.

'I allow, O Bhikkhus, the use of a stick or holder to put the ointment on with.'

Now at that time the *Kh*abbaggiya Bhikkhus used to keep various kinds of ointment-sticks—gold ones, and silver ones. People were annoyed, murmured, and became angry, saying, 'Like those who still live in the world.'

They told this thing to the Blessed One.

'Various kinds of ointment-holders, O Bhikkhus, are not to be used. Whosoever does so, is guilty of a dukka*t*a offence. I allow, O Bhikkhus, the use of ointment-holders of bone, or of ivory, or of horn, or of the na*l*a reed, or of bambu, or of wood, or of lac, or of fruit, or of bronze, or of the chank-shell.'

[1] Buddhaghosa has no comment on this. It may mean that the ointment boxes might be sewn either on to some place in the Vihâra, or on to some part of the Bhikkhu's dress. The latter is more in accordance with § 4 below.

4. Now at that time the ointment-sticks used to fall on the ground and become rough.

They told this thing to the Blessed One.

'I allow, O Bhikkhus, the use of a case for the ointment-sticks[1].'

Now at that time the Bhikkhus used to carry the ointment-boxes and ointment-sticks about in their hands.

They told this thing to the Blessed One.

'I allow, O Bhikkhus, the use of a bag to put the ointment-box in.'

They had no shoulder strap.

'I allow, O Bhikkhus, the use of a shoulder strap (by which to carry the ointment-box), or of a thread (by which to sew or tie it on).'

13.

1. Now at that time the venerable Pilindava*kkh*a had head-ache[2].

'I allow, O Bhikkhus, the use of a little oil on the head.'

(The disease) became no better[3].

'I allow, O Bhikkhus, the practice of taking up (medicine) through the nose[4].'

---

[1] Salâkodhâniyan ti yattha salâka*m* odahanti susiradantaka*m* vâ thâlika*m* vâ anuganâmî 'ti attho (B.).

[2] Sîsâbhitâpo, literally 'heat in the head.'

[3] Compare Mahâ-parinibbâna Sutta II, 31, and below, 13. 2; 14. 3.

[4] Natthu-kamma. In the commentary on the Dhammapada, pp. 83 and foll., there is an example of the way in which a physician administers medicinal oil in this manner to a sick Bhikkhu.

The nose ran.

'I allow, O Bhikkhus, the use of a nose-spoon[1].'

Now at that time the *Kh*abbaggiya Bhikkhus had various kinds of nose-spoons—made of gold, and of silver. People were annoyed, murmured, and became angry, saying, 'Like those who still live in the world.'

They told this thing to the Blessed One.

'Various kinds of nose-spoons, O Bhikkhus, are not to be used. Whosoever does so, is guilty of a dukka*t*a offence. I allow, O Bhikkhus, the use of such nose-spoons made of bone (&c., as in chap. 12. 1, down to:) or of the chank-shell.'

2. The nose took up the medicament in unequal proportions.

'I allow, O Bhikkhus, the use of a double nose-spoon[2].'

(The disease) became no better.

'I allow you, O Bhikkhus, to sniff up the aroma.'

They used to spread the drugs on a wick before they sniffed up the aroma[3]: and their throats got burnt.

'I allow, O Bhikkhus, the use of a pipe to conduct the aroma.'

Now at that time the *Kh*abbaggiya Bhikkhus had various kinds of pipes (&c., as in the last clauses of § 1, down to the end).

---

[1] Natthu-kara*n*î, that is, an instrument to hold up the nose, so that the medicinal oil does not run out.

[2] Yamaka-natthu-kara*n*î, that is, one that would go up both nostrils. The last sentence of § 1 would come in better after this clause.

[3] They used to burn the drugs by smearing them on wicks, and then inhale the smoke through their nostrils.

Now at that time the aroma-pipes came open: and worms got in.

'I allow, O Bhikkhus, the use of a lid to the pipes.'

Now at that time the Bhikkhus carried the pipes about in their hands.

'I allow, O Bhikkhus, the use of a bag to carry the aroma-pipes in.'

The aroma-pipes rubbed against one another.

'I allow, O Bhikkhus, the use of a double bag.'

They had no shoulder strap.

'I allow, O Bhikkhus, the use of a shoulder strap (by which to carry the double bag), or of a thread (by which to sew it on).'

14.

1. Now at that time the venerable Pilindava*kkh*a was troubled with wind in the stomach[1]. The physicians said he must drink oil.

'I allow you, O Bhikkhus, a decoction of oil.'

It was necessary to put strong drink into the decoction.

'I allow you, O Bhikkhus, to put strong drink in decoctions of oil.'

Now at that time the *Kh*abbaggiya Bhikkhus used to put too much strong drink into their decoctions of medicinal oils: and they got drunk.

'Oil should not be drunk, O Bhikkhus, when too much strong drink has been put into it. Whosoever does so, shall be dealt with according to law[2].'

'I allow you, O Bhikkhus, to drink such decoctions

[1] Compare chapter 17. [2] See the 51st Pâ*k*ittiya.

of oil with strong drink in them, as wherein neither the colour, nor the smell, nor the taste of the strong drink shall be sensible.'

2. Now at that time the Bhikkhus had a quantity of decoction in which too much strong drink had been put. Then those Bhikkhus thought: 'What shall we do with this oil, which has too much strong drink in it?'

'I allow, O Bhikkhus, to use it as an ointment.'

Now at that time the venerable Pilindava*kkh*a had a quantity of oil-decoction; but he had no vessel for it.

'I allow you, O Bhikkhus, the use of three kinds of pots, bronze pots, wooden pots, pots made of the shells of fruits [1].'

3. Now at that time the venerable Pilindava*kkh*a had rheumatism.

'I allow you, O Bhikkhus, to bring on sweating [2].'

(The disease) became no better.

'I allow you, O Bhikkhus, to bring on sweating by the use of herbs which have that effect [3].'

(The disease) became no better.

'I allow you, O Bhikkhus, the use of a great steam bath [4].'

(The disease) became no better.

---

[1] Compare VI, 12, 1.

[2] Perhaps fumigations.

[3] Sambhâra-sedan ti nânâvidha-pa*nn*a-bhaṅga-seda*m* (B.). Apparently a poultice or fomentation in which various kinds of leaves or twigs are used.

[4] Mahâsedan ti mahanta*m* seda*m*: porisa-ppamâ*n*a*m* âvâ*t*am aṅgârâna*m* pûretvâ, pa*m*su-vâlikâdîhi pidahitvâ, tattha nânâvidhâni vâta-hara*n*a-pa*nn*âni santharitvâ tela-makkhitena gattena tattha nipa*gg*itvâ samparivattantena sarîra*m* sedetu*m* anu*g*ânâmîti attho (B.). A pit, six feet deep, is filled with charcoal, and covered with a coating of earth or sand. The leaves good for rheumatism are spread

'I allow you, O Bhikkhus, the use of hemp-water (bang)[1].'

(The disease) became no better.

'I allow you, O Bhikkhus, the use of hot baths in water in which medicinal herbs have been steeped[2].'

4. Now at that time the venerable Pilindava*kkh*a had intermittent ague.

'I allow, O Bhikkhus, the letting of blood.'

(The disease) became no better.

'I allow you, O Bhikkhus, to make use of a horn to let blood[3].'

Now at that time the feet of the venerable Pilindava*kkh*a were blistered.

'I allow, O Bhikkhus, the use of ointment for the feet.'

(The disease) became no better.

---

over the sand. The patient reposes on the leaves on the affected limb, which has been rubbed over with oil; and turns over and over until his whole body has been well steamed.

[1] Bhaṅgodakan ti nânâ-pa*nn*a-bhaṅga-kudhita-udaka*m*. Tehi pa*nn*ehi *k*a udakena *k*a siñ*k*itvâ sedetabbo (B.). Bhaṅga may here mean 'broken bits,' namely, of the leaves, just as sâkhâ-bhaṅga at *G*âtaka I, 158 means 'twig.' Compare uttari-bhaṅga, *G*âtaka I, 197, 349; Dhammapada 171; *K*ullavagga VIII, 4, 4; sarîra-bhaṅga, Mahâ-parinibbâna Sutta VI, 59; and bhaṅga alone at *G*âtaka I, 392; Mahâvagga I, 25, 10; Rh. D., 'Buddhist Suttas from the Pâli,' p. 241. For kudhita we should read kuthita.

[2] Dakako*tth*akan ti udaka-ko*tth*a*m* *k*â*ñ*m vâ do*n*i*m* vâ u*n*hodakassa pûretvâ tattha tattha pavisitvâ seda-kamma-kara*n*a*m* anu*g*ânâmîti attho (B.). Compare Dhammapada, p. 103.

[3] Wise, p. 176, says, 'The local accumulation of bad blood may be removed by means of cupping, which is performed by a horn, cut smooth and even at the large extremity, and with a small opening at the narrow end.' Compare Su*s*ruta, Sûtrasthâna, chap. 27, and *S*arîrasthâna, chap. 8 (at the end).

'I allow you, O Bhikkhus, to keep water ready for washing the feet (of travellers)[1].'

Now at that time a certain Bhikkhu had boils.

'I allow, O Bhikkhus, the use of the lancet.'

Decoctions of astringent herbs were required.

'I allow, O Bhikkhus, decoctions of astringent herbs[2].'

Sesamum salve was required.

'I allow, O Bhikkhus, the use of sesamum salve[3].'

5. Compresses were required.

'I allow, O Bhikkhus, the use of compresses[4].'

It was necessary to tie up the sore with cloth.

'I allow, O Bhikkhus, the use of bandages for tieing up wounds.'

The sore itched.

'I allow, O Bhikkhus, the sprinkling of a sore with mustard-powder[5].'

The sore became moist[6].

'I allow you, O Bhikkhus, to fumigate (the sore).'

Proud flesh formed on the wound[7].

'I allow you, O Bhikkhus, to cut off (proud flesh) with a lancet.'

---

[1] This would seem to be a preventive remedy. Water may be kept ready, so that the incoming Bhikkhus may use it, and their feet therefore may not become blistered. But perhaps pa*gg*a here means some curative application of water to the feet, such as cold water bandages, for example. Compresses (?poultices) are mentioned below (§ 5) for boils.

[2] Compare chapter 4.

[3] Buddhaghosa explains tila-kakka as ground sesamum seeds (pi*tth*ehi tilehi attho); but kalka is paste or salve. See Wise, p. 129.

[4] Kaba*l*ikan ti (MS. pakalikan) va*n*a-mukhe sattu-pi*ndam* pakkhipitu*m* (B.). Compare Böhtlingk-Roth, sub voce kavalikâ.

[5] Sâsapa-pi*tth*ena, says Buddhaghosa.

[6] Compare the quotations from Su*s*ruta in Böhtlingk-Roth under klidyati.

[7] Va*n*a- (MS. viddha*m*) ma*m*san ti adhika-ma*msam*: âni viya u*tth*ahati (B.).

The wound would not close up.

'I allow, O Bhikkhus, the use of oil for wounds.'

The oil ran over.

They told this thing to the Blessed One.

'I allow, O Bhikkhus, the use of fine rags[1], and of all kinds of ways of treating wounds.'

6. Now at that time a certain Bhikkhu was bitten by a snake.

They told this thing to the Blessed One.

'I allow, O Bhikkhus, the four kinds of filth to be given—dung, urine, ashes, and clay.'

Now the Bhikkhus thought: 'Are these things among those which may be taken even without being offered to us by others, or among things which cannot be taken unless they are offered?'

They told this thing to the Blessed One.

'I allow these things, O Bhikkhus, to be accepted if any one be there to offer them[2], and if not, then that you may take them yourselves and use them.'

Now at that time a certain Bhikkhu had drunk poison.

'I allow you, O Bhikkhus, to give (as an emetic) a decoction of dung.'

Then the Bhikkhus thought: 'Is this among those things which may be taken even without being offered to us by others, or is it among things which cannot be taken unless they are offered?'

They told this thing to the Blessed One.

'I rule, O Bhikkhus, that there is a proper taking when a man takes what he himself has made; and

[1] Vikâsikan ti tela-ruddhana-pilotika*m* (B.). See VIII, 2.

[2] A kappiya-kâraka is one who by offering a thing to a Bhikkhu, makes that thing kappiya, allowable, to the Bhikkhu.

that such a thing need not be received again from others.'

7. Now at that time a certain Bhikkhu suffered from the ghara-dinnaka[1] disease.

'I allow you, O Bhikkhus, to give him to drink a decoction of soil turned up by the plough[2].'

Now at that time a certain Bhikkhu had constipation[3].

'I allow you, O Bhikkhus, to give him a decoction of the ashes of burnt rice[4].'

Now at that time a certain Bhikkhu had the jaundice.

'I allow you, O Bhikkhus, to give to drink a decoction made with (cows') urine[5].'

Now at that time a certain Bhikkhu had skin disease.

'I allow, O Bhikkhus, the anointing with perfumes.'

Now at that time a certain Bhikkhu had a superfluity of humors in his body[6].'

'I allow you, O Bhikkhus, to give a purgative.'

Clarified gruel was required.

---

[1] Ghara-dinnakan ti vasikara*n*a-pâna-samu*tth*ita-rogo, 'a disease arising from a philter, which when given brings another into one's power' (B.). He was bewitched, was suffering from the results of sorcery.

[2] Sîtâlo*l*in ti nangalena kasantassa phâle lagga-mattika*m* udakena alo*l*etvâ pâyetu*m* anu*g*ânâmîti attho (B.).

[3] Du*tth*agaha*n*iko 'ti vipanna-gaha*n*iko. Ki*kkh*ena u*kk*âro nikkhamatîti. Compare Rh. D., 'Buddhist Suttas from the Pâli,' p. 260 note.

[4] Âmisakhâran ti sukkhodana*m* *gh*âpetvâ tâya *kh*arikâya paggharita*m* khârodaka*m* (B.).

[5] Mutta-harîtakan ti gomutta-paribhâvita*m* harîtaka*m* (B.).

[6] Abhisannakâyo 'ti ussanna-dosa-kâyo (B.). Dosa is a disturbance of the so-called humors in the body. Compare VIII, 1, 30.

'I allow, O Bhikkhus, the use of clarified gruel.'

Natural juice was required[1].

'I allow, O Bhikkhus, the use of natural juice.'

Artificial and natural juice was required[2].

'I allow, O Bhikkhus, the use of artificial and natural juice.'

Meat broth was required[3].

'I allow, O Bhikkhus, the use of meat broth.'

15.

1. Now at that time the venerable Pilindavakkha had a mountain cave at Râgagaha cleared out, with the object of making it into a cave dwelling-place. And the Mâgadha king Seniya Bimbisâra went to the place where the venerable Pilindavakkha was; and when he had come there, he saluted the venerable Pilindavakkha, and took his seat on one side.

And when he was so seated the Mâgadha king Seniya Bimbisâra said to the venerable Pilindavakkha, 'What is it that my Lord, the Thera, is having done?'

'I am having a cave cleared out, with the object of making it into a cave dwelling-place.'

'Do you then, Sir, require an ârâmika (a park-keeper)?'

'Not so, great king! A park-keeper has not been prescribed by the Blessed One.'

'Then, Sir, enquire of the Blessed One (concerning this matter), and let me then know.'

---

[1] Akata-yûsan ti asiniddho mugga-pakita-pâriyo (B.).

[2] Katâkatan ti so ka baddhoka-siniddho (B.).

[3] Compare chap. 23. 1–8.

'Very well, O King!' said the venerable Pilindava*kkh*a in assent to the Mâgadha king Seniya Bimbisâra.

2. Then the venerable Pilindava*kkh*a taught and incited and roused and gladdened the Mâgadha king Seniya Bimbisâra with religious discourse. And the Mâgadha king Seniya Bimbisâra, when he had been taught &c. by the religious discourse, rose from his seat, and bowed down before the venerable Pilindava*kkh*a, and passing round him with his right side towards him, departed thence.

Then the venerable Pilindava*kkh*a sent a message to the Blessed One, saying, 'Lord! the Mâgadha king Seniya Bimbisâra desires to present me with a park-keeper. What am I, therefore, Lord, to do?'

Then the Blessed One, in that connection, after delivering a religious discourse, said to the Bhikkhus:

'I allow you, O Bhikkhus, the accepting of a park-keeper.'

3. And a second time the Mâgadha king Seniya Bimbisâra went to the place where the venerable Pilindava*kkh*a was; and when he had come there he saluted the venerable Pilindava*kkh*a, and took his seat on one side.

And when he was so seated the Mâgadha king Seniya Bimbisâra said to the venerable Pilindava*kkh*a, 'Has the Blessed One allowed a park-keeper?'

'Yes, O King!'

'Then, Sir, I will present a park-keeper to you.'

Now the Mâgadha king Seniya Bimbisâra, after he had (thus) promised a park-keeper to the venerable Pilindava*kkh*a, forgot it. And after a time he recovered recollection of it, and addressed a certain minister who had charge of general affairs, and said: 'The park-keeper whom I promised to the venerable one, has he been given to him?'

'No, your Majesty!'

'How long is it then, good Sir, since that was determined?'

4. Then that minister, counting up the nights, said to the Mâgadha king Seniya Bimbisâra, 'Five hundred nights, your Majesty.'

'Give then, my good Sir, five hundred park-keepers to the venerable one!'

'As your Majesty commands,' said that minister in assent to the Mâgadha king Seniya Bimbisâra; and he gave over to the venerable Pilindava*kkh*a five hundred park-keepers, and (for their use) a distinct village grew up. And they called it Ârâmika-gâma, and they called it also Pilinda-gâma. Thenceforward the venerable Pilindava*kkh*a depended upon the families living in that village (for alms, &c.). And the venerable Pilindava*kkh*a robed himself early in the morning, and entered into Pilinda-gâma, duly bowled and robed for alms.

5. Now at that time there was a feast in that village, and the children were celebrating it, with their ornaments on, and decked with garlands. And the venerable Pilindava*kkh*a, when he was going his rounds for alms, straight on from house to house, came to the dwelling-place of a certain park-keeper; and when he had come there he sat down on a seat prepared for him.

And at that time the daughter of that park-keeper's wife, seeing the other children with their ornaments on, and decked with garlands, began to cry (saying), 'Give me too a garland, give me an ornament!'

And the venerable Pilindava*kkh*a said to that park-keeper's wife: 'Why does that girl cry?'

'This girl, venerable Sir, seeing the other children with their ornaments on, and decked with garlands, is crying (and saying), "Give me too a garland, give me too an ornament!" But whence should we, who have become so poor, get garlands or ornaments?'

6. Then the venerable Pilindava*kkh*a took a grass chumbat[1], and said to the park-keeper's wife: 'Bind, I pray you, this grass chumbat round the child's head.'

And the park-keeper's wife took the grass chumbat, and bound it round the girl's head. And that became a chaplet of gold, beautiful, lovely, and pleasing, such that there was no chaplet of gold in the king's seraglio like it.

And people told the Mâgadha king Seniya Bimbisâra, 'There is a chaplet of gold, your Majesty, in the house of such and such a park-keeper, such that there is no chaplet of gold in the king's seraglio like it. How could he, poor as he is, have got (such a thing)? For a certainty he must have procured it by theft.'

Then the Mâgadha king Seniya Bimbisâra had (the whole of) that park-keeper's family thrown into bonds.

7. Now the venerable Pilindava*kkh*a robed himself again early in the morning, and went, duly bowled and robed, into Pilinda-gâma for alms. And going his round for alms straight on from house to house he came to the dwelling-place of that park-keeper; and

[1] A circular roll of grass, or cloth, to be placed on the head when a pot of oil or water was being carried on the head. Compare *k*umba*t*aka, and Rh. D.'s 'Buddhist Birth Stories,' p. 295.

when he had come there he asked the neighbours, 'Where is the family of this park-keeper gone to?'

'The king, Sir, has had them thrown into bonds on account of that chaplet of gold.'

Then the venerable Pilindava*kkh*a went on to the residence of the Mâgadha king Seniya Bimbisâra: and when he had come there he sat down on the seat prepared for him. And the Mâgadha king Seniya Bimbisâra went to the place where the venerable Pilindava*kkh*a was; and when he had come there, he bowed down before the venerable Pilindava*kkh*a, and took his seat on one side. And when he was so seated the venerable Pilindava*kkh*a said to the Mâgadha king Seniya Bimbisâra:

8. 'Why, O King, has the park-keeper's family been thrown into bonds?'

'That park-keeper, Sir, has in his house a chaplet of gold, such that there is no chaplet of gold in the king's seraglio like it. Whence should he, poor as he is, have got (such a thing)? For a certainty he has procured it by theft.'

Then the venerable Pilindava*kkh*a determined that the palace of the Mâgadha king Seniya Bimbisâra should be gold. And it became all of gold.

'Now, your Majesty, whence have you this so great quantity of gold?'

'I understand, Lord. This is your miraculous power' (said the king. And so saying) he set that park-keeper's family free.

9. When the people, glad at heart and full of satisfaction, saw that so great a miracle had been shown by the venerable Pilindava*kkh*a to the king and his royal retinue, they brought to the venerable Pilindava*kkh*a the five kinds of medicine,—that is to

say, ghee, butter, oil, honey, and molasses. Now (besides this) the venerable Pilindava*kkh*a was accustomed to receive the five kinds of medicine; and whatever he received he distributed among his attendant (Bhikkhus). So the retinue became abounding therein, and as they received it they laid it aside, filling vessels and pots; and filling water-strainers and bags with it they laid them in the windows, and they remained there clinging and adhering together, and the Vihâras became sprinkled and scattered all over with them through the (gnawing of) rats. People who saw this, when they went round the Vihâras, were annoyed, murmured, and became indignant (saying), 'These Sakyaputtiya Sama*n*as are becoming storers up of goods like the Mâgadha king Seniya Bimbisâra.'

10. The Bhikkhus heard the people thus murmuring, &c. And those Bhikkhus who were moderate were indignant, &c., saying,

'How can Bhikkhus think (of possessing) such abundance?'

And those Bhikkhus told the matter to the Blessed One.

'Is it true, Bhikkhus, as they say, that Bhikkhus think (of possessing) such abundance?'

'It is true, Lord.'

The Blessed One rebuked them, and after delivering a religious discourse, he addressed the Bhikkhus: 'Whatsoever kinds of medicine are meet for the use of sick Bhikkhus,—that is to say, ghee, butter, oil, honey, and molasses,—when such are received they must be used within a period of seven days during which they may be stored up. Whosoever goes beyond that limit shall be dealt with according to law[1].'

End of the first Bhâ*n*avâra on the law of medicines.

16.

1. Now after the Blessed One had remained at Sâvatthi as long as he thought fit, he went forth on his journey towards Râ*g*agaha. And on the way the venerable Kaṅkhâ-revata saw a sugar factory, and on stepping aside to it (he saw the men) putting flour and cane-dust into the molasses. When he saw that he thought: 'Molasses mixed with food is not permitted: it is not permitted to take such molasses (at a time) beyond the time (for the daily meal).' And fearing to offend he ate not of it, and his attendant Bhikkhus ate not, and such as held him worthy to be heard, they ate not.

They told this thing to the Blessed One.

'Why, O Bhikkhus, do they put flour and cane-dust into molasses?'

'In order, Lord, to make it firm.'

'If, O Bhikkhus, they put flour and cane-dust into molasses to make it firm, but it is still (nevertheless) considered to be molasses, I allow you, O Bhikkhus, such molasses as much as you like.'

2. Now the venerable Kaṅkhâ-revata saw on the way a kidney bean growing out of a dung heap. And when he had seen it, he thought: 'Beans are not permitted (to us, for) beans grow ready ripe[2].' And

[1] Compare the 23rd Nissaggiya.

[2] Pakkâ pi muggâ *g*âyanti, the meaning of which is not quite clear. Buddhaghosa says, yathâsukha*m* paribhu*ñg*itabbâ, pakkattâ

he did not eat, fearing to offend, and his attendant Bhikkhus did not eat, and such as held him worthy to be heard, they also did not eat the beans.

They told this thing to the Blessed One.

'Though, Bhikkhus, beans grow ready ripe, yet I allow you, O Bhikkhus, to eat beans as much as you like.'

3. Now at that time a certain Bhikkhu suffered from wind in the stomach. He drank salt sour gruel; and thereby his sickness abated.

They told this thing to the Blessed One.

'I allow, O Bhikkhus, to one who is sick the use of salt sour gruel, to one who is not sick the use thereof mixed with water[1] as a beverage.'

17.

1. Now the Blessed One journeying on in due course came to Râgagaha. And there at Râgagaha the Blessed One stayed at the Veluvana in the Kalandaka-nivâpa.

Now at that time the Blessed One was troubled with wind in his stomach. And the venerable Ânanda thinking, 'Now formerly the Blessed One when suffering from wind in the stomach had ease from Teka*t*ula[2] gruel,' made ready of his own accord tila seeds, and rice, and beans; and kept

---

hi te kappiyâ. Perhaps the doubt was supposed to have arisen because the beans required no cooking, but grew, ready to eat, of themselves.

[1] Compare asambhinna-pâyâsa at *G*âtaka, vol. i, p. 55, l. 32.

[2] That is, gruel containing the three pungent (ka*t*u) substances, which are explained to be ginger and two kinds of pepper.

them indoors; and cooked them indoors of his own accord, and offered them to the Blessed One, saying, 'Let the Blessed One drink this Teka*t*ula gruel.'

2. Now the Tathâgatas sometimes ask about what they know (&c., as usual, as, for instance, in I, 31, 5, down to the end).

And the Blessed One said to the venerable Ânanda, 'Whence, Ânanda, is this gruel?'

Then the venerable Ânanda told this thing to the Blessed One.

3. The Blessed Buddha rebuked him, saying, 'This is improper, Ânanda, unbecoming, unsuitable, unworthy of Sama*n*as, not allowable, and ought to be avoided. How can you, Ânanda, think (of permitting yourself) such abundance? Whatever, Ânanda, is kept indoors, is not allowed; whatever is cooked indoors, is not allowed; and whatever is cooked of your own accord, is not allowed. This will not redound, Ânanda, to the conversion of the unconverted.'

And when he had rebuked him, and delivered a religious discourse, he said to the Bhikkhus: 'Whatsoever is kept indoors, O Bhikkhus, or cooked indoors, or cooked of your own accord, is not to be eaten. Whosoever shall eat thereof, is guilty of a dukka*t*a offence.

4. 'And if, O Bhikkhus, there be food kept indoors, or cooked indoors, or cooked of your own accord, and one shall eat thereof, he is guilty of three dukka*t*a offences. If, O Bhikkhus, food kept indoors, and cooked indoors, shall have been so cooked by others, and one eat thereof, he is guilty of two dukka*t*a offences. If, O Bhikkhus, food kept indoors, shall have been cooked out of doors, and

so cooked of your own accord, and one eat thereof, he is guilty of two dukka*t*a offences.

5. 'If, O Bhikkhus, food kept out of doors shall have been cooked indoors, and of your own accord, and one eat thereof, he is guilty of two dukka*t*a offences. If, O Bhikkhus, food kept indoors, shall have been cooked out of doors, and by others, and one eat thereof, he is guilty of a dukka*t*a offence. If, O Bhikkhus, food kept out of doors shall have been cooked indoors, and by others, and one eat thereof, he is guilty of a dukka*t*a offence. If, O Bhikkhus, food kept out of doors, shall have been cooked out of doors, and of your own accord, and one shall eat thereof, he is guilty of a dukka*t*a offence. If, O Bhikkhus, food kept out of doors, shall have been cooked out of doors, and by others, and one shall eat thereof, he is not guilty.'

6. Now at that time, the Bhikkhus, thinking, 'Food cooked of one's own accord has been disallowed by the Blessed One,' feared to offend by cooking a second time food (already cooked once).

They told this thing to the Blessed One.

'I allow you, O Bhikkhus, to cook food a second time.'

7. Now at that time there was a scarcity of food in Râ*g*agaha. People brought salt, and oil, and rice, and hard food to the Ârâma. These the Bhikkhus kept out of doors; and vermin [1] ate them, and thieves carried them off.

They told this thing to the Blessed One.

---

[1] Buddhaghosa says, ukkapi*nd*akâ pi khâdantîti bilâla-mûsika-godha-muṅgûsâ khâdanti. The expression recurs in VI, 33, 5.

'I allow you, O Bhikkhus, to keep food indoors.'

When they kept it indoors, and cooked it out of doors, those men who practised self-mortification by living on the remains of offered food[1] crowded round them; and the Bhikkhus ate in fear.

They told this thing to the Blessed One.

'I allow you, O Bhikkhus, to cook indoors.'

In the time of scarcity, those who (by offering food, inviting Bhikkhus to their houses, &c.) made (the accepting or eating of food) allowable (to the Bhikkhus), used to take more (for themselves), and give less to the Bhikkhus.

'I allow you, O Bhikkhus, to cook of your own accord. I allow you, O Bhikkhus, to cook indoors, and of your own accord, food kept indoors.'

8. Now at that time a number of Bhikkhus who had spent the rainy season in the land of Kâsi, and were journeying to Râ*g*agaha to visit the Blessed One, did not receive on the way as full a supply as they required of food, either bitter or sweet. And there was plenty of eatable fruit, but there was no one to make it allowable for them[2]. And those Bhikkhus went on in weariness to Râ*g*agaha, to the Veluvana, in the Kalandaka-nivâpa, where the Blessed One was. And when they had come there, they bowed down before the Blessed One, and took their seats on one side.

Now it is the custom of the Blessed Buddhas to exchange courteous greetings with Bhikkhus who

[1] Buddhaghosa says, damakâ ti vighâsâdâ. The same explanation is given in Abhidhânappadîpikâ, verse 467, where the Sinhalese expression is indul kannâ, and the English 'one who eats orts.'

[2] See the last section.

arrive. And the Blessed One said to those Bhikkhus:

'Do things go well with you, O Bhikkhus? Do you get enough to support yourselves with? Have you accomplished your journey without too much fatigue? And whence, O Bhikkhus, have you come?'

9. 'Things go well with us, Lord. We have spent the rainy season in the land of Kâsi; and as we were journeying to Râ*g*agaha to visit the Blessed One, we did not receive on the way as full a supply as we required of food, either bitter or sweet. And there was plenty of eatable fruit, but there was no one to make it allowable for us. And we came on our way in weariness.'

Then the Blessed One, in that connection, after having delivered a religious discourse, said to the Bhikkhus: 'I allow you, O Bhikkhus, wherever edible fruit is seen and there is no one to make it allowable, to pick it of your own accord, and take it away. And when you see one who can make it allowable, you are to place it on the ground, and (only) eat it after you have received it again. I allow you, O Bhikkhus, to take whatever (fruit) you have picked up[1].'

18.

1. Now at that time a certain Brâhman had received some fresh tila seeds, and some fresh honey. Now it occurred to that Brâhman: 'What if I were to give these fresh tila seeds, and this

[1] Compare below, 21. 1.

fresh honey to the Bhikkhu-samgha with the Buddha at their head.' And that Brâhman went to the place where the Blessed One was, and when he had come there, he exchanged courteous greetings with the Blessed One. And after he had exchanged with the Blessed One the greetings and compliments of friendship and civility, he stood on one side. And, so standing, that Brâhman said to the Blessed One:

'May the venerable Gotama grant me that the venerable Gotama shall take his morrow's meal at my home to-morrow with the Bhikkhu-samgha.'

The Blessed One consented by remaining silent. And when that Brâhman perceived that the Blessed One had consented he went away.

2. And that Brâhman, at the end of that night, when he had made ready sweet food, both hard and soft, had the time announced to the Blessed One (in the words), 'It is time, O Gotama, and the meal is prepared.'

And the Blessed One, early in the morning, having put on his under robe, went duly bowled and robed to that Brâhman's residence. And when he had come there, he sat down on a seat prepared for him, and with him the Bhikkhu-samgha.

And that Brâhman satisfied with the sweet food, hard and soft, the Bhikkhu-samgha with the Buddha at their head, and waited on them with his own hand. And when the Blessed One had finished his meal, and had washed his hands and his bowl, the Brâhman took his seat on one side. And as he so sat the Blessed One instructed, and roused, and incited, and gladdened that Brâhman with religious discourse, and rose from his seat, and went away.

3. Now not long after the Blessed One had gone

it occurred to that Brâhman: 'The things for the sake of which I invited the Bhikkhu-sa*m*gha with the Buddha at their head, thinking, "I will give them the fresh tila seeds and the fresh honey,"—those I have neglected to give. What if I were now to have the fresh tila seeds and the fresh honey taken, in pots and vessels, to the Ârâma!'

And that Brâhman had the fresh tila seeds and the fresh honey taken in pots and vessels, and went to the place where the Blessed One was. And when he had come there, he stood on one side; and so standing that Brâhman said to the Blessed One:

4. 'The things for the sake of which I invited the Bhikkhu-sa*m*gha with the Buddha at their head, thinking, "I will give them the fresh tila seeds and the fresh honey,"—those I have neglected to give. May the venerable Gotama receive of me the fresh tila seeds and the fresh honey.'

'Very well then, Brâhman; give them to the Bhikkhus.'

Now at that time, during the scarcity, people invited Bhikkhus to a slender meal, and they, counting the number (of those invited), refused (the invitation). And the whole Sa*m*gha was (once) invited; but the Bhikkhus, fearing to offend, did not accept the invitation [1].

'Accept it, O Bhikkhus, and eat. I allow, O Bhikkhus, that a Bhikkhu who has eaten and who has refused food still offered may nevertheless eat food, if it be brought from within, even if it has not been left over [2].

[1] Compare Pâtimokkha, Pâ*k*ittiya 32.

[2] This is an exception to Pâ*k*ittiya 35. A Bhikkhu who has

19.

1. Now at that time a family who were devoted to the venerable Upananda, of the Sakya clan, sent hard food for the Sa*m*gha, saying, 'This is to be given to the Sa*m*gha with especial reference to the venerable Upananda.'

Now at that time the venerable Upananda of the Sakya clan had gone forth to the village for alms. And those men went to the Ârâma, and asked the Bhikkhus:

'Where, Sirs, is the venerable Upananda?'

'The venerable Upananda of the Sakya clan has gone forth to the village for alms.'

'This hard food, Sirs, is to be given to the Sa*m*gha, with especial reference to the venerable Upananda.'

They told this thing to the Blessed One.

'In that case, O Bhikkhus, receive it, and put it aside till Upananda returns.'

2. And the venerable Upananda, after having attended on the families in the forenoon, returned during the (after-part of the) day.

Now at that time, during the scarcity, people invited the Bhikkhus to a slender meal; and they,

finished, and has declared himself to have done so by declining further food, can still take 'leavings' without offending. By this rule he is also allowed to take food tato nîhata*m*, literally, 'brought out thence,' which seems to mean 'out of the store of the giver.' The expression recurs in VI, 32, 1, and again in VI, 32, 2 (at the end), where the exceptions to Pâ*k*ittiya 35 laid down in this and the following rules are again, the scarcity having passed away, put aside by 'the Blessed One.'

counting the numbers (of those invited, refused) the invitation. And the whole Samgha was (once) invited; but the Bhikkhus, fearing to offend, did not accept the invitation.

'Accept it, O Bhikkhus, that a Bhikkhu who has eaten, and who has refused food still offered, may nevertheless eat food, if it have been received before meal-time (in the forenoon), even if it has not been left over[1].'

20.

1. Now the Blessed One having remained at Râgagaha as long as he thought fit, proceeded on his way to Sâvatthi. And wandering straight on from place to place he arrived at Sâvatthi. And there, at Sâvatthi, the Blessed One stayed at the *G*etavana, Anâtha-pi*nd*ika's Grove.

Now at that time the venerable Sâriputta suffered from fever. And the venerable Mahâ Moggallâna went to the place where the venerable Sâriputta was; and when he had come there he said to the venerable Sâriputta:

'You have lately had fever, friend Sâriputta. By what means has it got well?'

'By lotus stalks, my friend, of various kinds.'

Then the venerable Mahâ Moggallâna, as quickly as a strong man would stretch forth his arm, or draw it in again when it had been stretched forth, vanished from the *G*etavana and appeared on the bank of the Mandâkinî lake.

2. And a certain Nâga saw the venerable Mahâ

[1] See the last note.

Moggallâna coming from afar: and on seeing him he said to the venerable Mahâ Moggallâna:

'May my lord, the venerable Mahâ Moggallâna, approach. Welcome to my lord, the venerable Mahâ Moggallâna. What may my lord have need of? What shall I give to him?'

'I want the edible stalks of the various lotuses.'

Then that Nâga gave command to another Nâga, saying, 'Very well then, good friend, give the venerable one edible stalks of the lotuses.'

And that Nâga plunged into the Mandâkinî lake, and plucked with his trunk edible stalks of the lotuses, and washed them thoroughly, and bound them in a bundle, and went to the place where the venerable Mahâ Moggallâna was.

3. Then the venerable Mahâ Moggallâna as quickly (&c., as in § 1) vanished from the bank of the Mandâkinî lake, and appeared in *G*etavana. Then that Nâga also vanished from the bank of the Mandâkinî lake, and appeared in the *G*etavana. And when that Nâga had caused the venerable Mahâ Moggallâna to receive those edible stalks of the lotuses he vanished from the *G*etavana, and appeared on the shore of the Mandâkinî lake.

Then the venerable Mahâ Moggallâna presented those edible stalks of the lotuses to the venerable Sâriputta. And the fever abated on the venerable Sâriputta when he had eaten the edible stalks of the lotuses. And many of them remained over.

4. Now at that time, during the scarcity (&c., as above, in chap. 18. 4, down to:) did not accept the invitation.

'Accept it, O Bhikkhus, and eat. I allow a Bhikkhu who has eaten, and has refused food still offered, to eat things growing in woods and ponds, even if they are not the leavings of the meal of one who has eaten[1].'

21.

1. Now at that time edible fruit was very plentiful in Sâvatthi, but there was no one to make it allowable[2]. And the Bhikkhus, fearing to offend, would not eat of it.

They told that thing to the Blessed One.

'I allow you, O Bhikkhus, to eat fruit which has not yet had any seed in it, or which has no more seed in it, even without any one being there to make it allowable[3].'

22.

1. Now when the Blessed One had remained at Sâvatthi as long as he thought fit, he went forth on his journey to Râ*g*agaha. And wandering straight on he arrived at Râ*g*agaha: and there at Râ*g*agaha he stayed at the Veluvana in the Kalandaka-nivâpa.

Now at that time a certain Bhikkhu was suffering from fistula[4]. And the physician (named) Âkâsagotta lanced it. And the Blessed One when he

[1] See the note above, on VI, 18, 4.

[2] See above, VI, 17, 7.

[3] Buddhaghosa says, abî*g*an ti taru*n*a-phala*m*; yassa bî*g*a*m* aṅkura*m* na *g*aneti. Nibbatta-bî*g*an (nivatta-bî*g*an?) ti bî*g*a*m* nibbattetva (nivattetvâ?) apanetvâ.

[4] Compare VIII, 1, 14.

was going round through the sleeping-places came to the place where that Bhikkhu dwelt.

2. Âkâsa-gotta, the physician, saw the Blessed One coming from afar; and when he saw him he said to the Blessed One: 'Let the venerable Gotama come and look at this Bhikkhu's orifice; it is like the mouth of an iguana!' And the Blessed One thinking, 'This foolish fellow is making fun of me,' kept silence and turned away. And in that connection, and on account of that, he called a meeting of the Bhikkhu-sa*m*gha, and asked the Bhikkhus: 'Is there, O Bhikkhus, in that Vihâra a Bhikkhu who is sick?'

'There is, Lord.'

'What is the matter, O Bhikkhus, with that Bhikkhu?'

'That venerable one, Lord, has a fistula, and Âkâsa-gotta, the physician, has been lancing it.'

3. The Blessed Buddha rebuked (that Bhikkhu), saying, 'This is improper, O Bhikkhus, for that foolish one, unbecoming, indecent, unworthy of Sama*n*as, not allowable, and ought not to be done. How can this foolish fellow, O Bhikkhus, allow a surgical operation to be performed in that part of his body[1]? The skin there, O Bhikkhus, is tender, the wound is difficult to treat, the knife is difficult to guide. This will not redound, O Bhikkhus, to the conversion of the unconverted.'

And having rebuked him, the Blessed One, after delivering a religious discourse, said to the Bhikkhus: 'You are not, O Bhikkhus, to allow a surgical operation to be performed upon you in that part

[1] Sambâdhe.

of your bodies. Whosoever allows that, is guilty of a thullakkaya offence.'

4. Now at that time the *Kh*abbaggiya Bhikkhus, since a surgical operation had been forbidden by the Blessed One, used a clyster[1].

They told this thing to the Blessed One.

'Is it true, as they say, O Bhikkhus, that the *Kh*abbaggiya Bhikkhus use a clyster?'

'It is true, Lord.'

He rebuked them, and having delivered a religious discourse, said to the Bhikkhus: 'No surgical operation is to be performed within a distance of two inches round the anus, and a clyster is not to be used. Whosoever does so, is guilty of a thullakkaya offence[2].'

23.

1. And the Blessed One, after having dwelt at Râgagaha as long as he thought fit, went forth to Benares. Wandering from place to place he came to Benares. There the Blessed One dwelt near Benares, in the deer-park Isipatana.

At that time there were at Benares a devout layman Suppiya and a devout laywoman Suppiyâ who showed their faith in both ways: they were givers and doers, and devoted themselves to the service of the fraternity. And Suppiyâ, the lay-devotee, went to the Ârâma, and going around from Vihâra to Vihâra, and from cell to cell, she asked

[1] Vatthikamma. See Wise, 'Hindu Medicine,' pp. 143 and following.

[2] Surgical operations are allowed in 14. 5 and below.

the Bhikkhus: 'Who is sick, venerable Sirs? For whom, and what shall I procure?'

2. At that time a certain Bhikkhu had taken a purgative. And that Bhikkhu said to Suppiyâ, the lay-devotee: 'I have taken a purgative, sister, and I want some broth[1].'

(She replied): 'Well, reverend Sir, it shall be procured for you,'—and went to her house and gave order to a pupil[2]: 'Go, my good Sir, and see if there is any meat to be had[3].'

That man accepted this order of Suppiyâ, the lay-devotee (by saying), 'Yes, Madam,' and searched through the whole of Benares, but did not find any meat on hand[3]. Then that man went to Suppiyâ, the lay-devotee; having approached her he said to Suppiyâ, the lay-devotee: 'There is no meat to be had, Madam; the killing of cattle is interdicted to-day.'

3. Then Suppiyâ, the lay-devotee, thought: 'If that sick Bhikkhu does not get the broth his sickness will increase, or he will die. It would be unbecoming indeed for me to promise something, and not to procure it;'—(thinking thus) she took a knife, cut a piece of flesh from her thigh, and gave it to her maid-servant (saying), 'Go, my girl,

---

[1] Pa*ikkh*âdaniya. See Abhidhânappadîpikâ, verse 468, and above, chap. 14. 7, at the end.

[2] Of her husband's?

[3] Pavattama*m*sa, which Buddhaghosa explains, 'matassa ma*m*sa*m*.' Pavatta means 'already existing,' opposed to what is brought into existence for a special purpose, and pavattama*m*sa is said here, therefore, in order to exclude uddissa-kata-ma*m*sa (meat of animals killed especially for them), which Bhikkhus were not allowed to partake of (see chap. 31. 14). Compare also pavatta-phala-bhogana at *G*âtaka I, p. 6.

and get the strength out of this meat. In such and such a Vihâra is a sick Bhikkhu; give it to that (Bhikkhu). And should anybody call for me, tell him that I am sick;'—(speaking thus), she veiled her thigh with her upper garment, went into her inner room, and lay down on her bed.

4. And Suppiya, the lay-devotee, came to his house and asked the maid-servant: 'Where is Suppiyâ?'

'She lies in the inner room, Sir.' Then Suppiya, the lay-devotee, went to the place where Suppiyâ, the lay-devotee, was; having approached her he said to Suppiyâ, the lay-devotee: 'Why are you lying down?'

'I am sick.'

'What is the matter with you?'

Then Suppiyâ, the lay-devotee, told the whole matter to Suppiya, the lay-devotee. And Suppiya, the lay-devotee, said: 'Oh wonderful! oh astonishing! How believing and how pious is this Suppiyâ who gives even her own flesh (to the indigent). What else can there be which she would not give?' (Speaking thus), joyful and elated he went to the place where the Blessed One was; having approached him, and respectfully saluted the Blessed One, he sat down near him.

5. Sitting near him, Suppiya, the lay-devotee, said to the Blessed One: 'Might the Blessed One, Lord, consent to take his meal with me to-morrow, together with the fraternity of Bhikkhus.'

The Blessed One expressed his consent by remaining silent. Then Suppiya, the lay-devotee, when he understood that the Blessed One had accepted his invitation, rose from his seat, respectfully saluted the Blessed One, and passing round him with his right side towards him, went away.

And when the night had elapsed, Suppiya, the lay-devotee, ordered excellent food, both hard and soft, to be prepared, and had the meal-time announced to the Blessed One in the words: 'It is time, Lord, the meal is ready.' And in the forenoon the Blessed One, having put on his under-robes, took his alms-bowl, and, with his *k*îvara on, went to the house of Suppiya, the lay-devotee. When he had arrived there, he sat down with the Bhikkhus who followed him, on seats laid out for them.

6. And Suppiya, the lay-devotee, went to the place where the Blessed One was; having approached him and respectfully saluted the Blessed One, he stationed himself near him. When he was standing near him, the Blessed One said to Suppiya, the lay-devotee: 'Where is Suppiyâ?'

'She is sick, Lord.'

'Well, let her come here.'

'She is not able to do so, Lord.'

'Well then you must take her and carry her (to me).'

Then Suppiya, the lay-devotee, took Suppiyâ, the lay-devotee, and carried her (to the Buddha). And in the moment the Blessed One saw her, that great wound was healed; and there was good skin there, with the tiny hairs thereon.

7. And Suppiya, the lay-devotee, and Suppiyâ, the lay-devotee (thought): 'Oh wonderful! oh astonishing! What high power and great faculties the Tathâgata possesses, in that in the moment the Blessed One has seen (Suppiyâ), that great wound has been healed; and there is good skin there,

with the tiny hairs thereon;'—(thinking thus), joyful and elated they served and offered with their own hands excellent food, both hard and soft, to the fraternity of Bhikkhus with the Buddha at its head. And when the Blessed One had finished his meal, and cleansed his bowl and his hands, they sat down near him. And the Blessed One, after having taught, incited, animated, and gladdened Suppiya, the lay-devotee, and Suppiyâ, the lay-devotee, by religious discourse, rose from his seat and went away.

8. In consequence of that, and on this occasion, the Blessed One, having ordered the fraternity of Bhikkhus to assemble, questioned the Bhikkhus: 'Who was it, O Bhikkhus, who asked Suppiyâ, the lay-devotee, for meat?'

When he had spoken thus, that Bhikkhu said to the Blessed One: 'It is I, Lord, who asked Suppiyâ, the lay-devotee, for meat.'

'Has it been brought to you, O Bhikkhu?'

'It has been brought, Lord.'

'Have you eaten it, O Bhikkhu?'

'I have eaten it, Lord.'

'And did you enquire, O Bhikkhus, (what) meat it was?'

'Lord! I did not enquire about that.'

9. Then the blessed Buddha rebuked him: 'How can you, O foolish one, eat meat without having enquired (what it is)? It is man's flesh, O foolish one, which you have eaten. This will not do, O foolish one, for converting the unconverted,' (&c.)

Having rebuked him and delivered a religious discourse, he thus addressed the Bhikkhus: 'There are, O Bhikkhus, believing, pious people who give up even their own flesh. Let no one, O Bhikkhus, eat man's flesh. He who does, commits a thullak*k*aya (or, grave) offence. And let no one, O Bhikkhus, eat meat without having enquired (what it is). He who does, commits a dukka*t*a offence.'

10. At that time the king's elephants died. During a famine the people ate that elephants' flesh, and when the Bhikkhus came and asked for alms, they gave them elephants' flesh. The Bhikkhus ate that elephants' flesh. People were annoyed, murmured, and became angry: 'How can the Sakyaputtiya Sama*n*as eat elephants' flesh? Elephants are an attribute of royalty. If the king knew that, they would not be in his favour.'

They told this thing to the Blessed One.

'Let no one, O Bhikkhus, eat elephants' flesh. He who does, commits a dukka*t*a offence.'

11. At that time the king's horses died. During a famine (&c., as in § 10, down to:)

'Let no one, O Bhikkhus, eat horse-flesh. He who does, commits a dukka*t*a offence.'

12. At that time the people, during a famine, ate dogs' flesh, and when the Bhikkhus came and asked for alms, they gave them dogs' flesh. The Bhikkhus ate that dogs' flesh. People were annoyed, murmured, and became angry: 'How can the Sakyaputtiya Sama*n*as eat dogs' flesh? Dogs are disgusting and loathsome animals.'

They told this thing to the Blessed One.

'Let no one, O Bhikkhus, eat dogs' flesh. He who does, commits a dukka*t*a offence.'

13. At that time the people, during a famine, ate serpents' flesh (&c., as in § 12, down to:) 'How can

the Sakyaputtiya Samanas eat serpents' flesh? Serpents are disgusting and loathsome animals.'

And the serpent king Supassa went to the place where the Blessed One was; having approached him and respectfully saluted the Blessed One, he stationed himself near him. Standing near him the serpent king Supassa said to the Blessed One: 'There are, Lord, unbelieving serpents who are disinclined (to the faith); these might do harm to the Bhikkhus even on trifling occasions. Pray, Lord, let their reverences not eat serpents' flesh. Then the Blessed One taught, incited, animated, and gladdened the serpent king Supassa by religious discourse (&c., down to:), and passing round him with his right side towards him, went away.'

In consequence of that the Blessed One, after having delivered a religious discourse, thus addressed the Bhikkhus: 'Let no one, O Bhikkhus, eat serpents' flesh. He who does, commits a dukkata offence.'

14. At that time hunters had killed a lion and eaten his flesh, and when the Bhikkhus came and asked for alms, they gave them lions' flesh. The Bhikkhus, having eaten that lions' flesh, sojourned in the forest. Then the lions, (attracted) by the smell of lions' flesh, fell upon the Bhikkhus.

They told this thing to the Blessed One.

'Let no one, O Bhikkhus, eat lions' flesh. He who does, commits a dukkata offence.'

15. At that time hunters had killed a tiger, &c., a panther, &c., a bear, &c., a hyena (&c., as in § 14, down to:)

'Let no one, O Bhikkhus, eat a hyena's flesh. He who does, commits a dukkata offence.'

24.

1. And the Blessed One, after having dwelt at Benares as long as he thought fit, went forth to Andhakavinda, accompanied by a great number of Bhikkhus, by twelve hundred and fifty Bhikkhus. At that time the people in the country, after having loaded their carts with much salt and oil and rice and hard food, followed from behind the fraternity of Bhikkhus with the Buddha at its head (thinking), 'When our turn comes, we will make a meal for them;' and five hundred people who ate the remains of (the Bhikkhus') food (followed on their way). And the Blessed One, wandering from place to place, came to Andhakavinda.

2. Now a certain Brâhma*n*a, whose turn did not come, thought: 'Two months have elapsed while I have been following the fraternity of Bhikkhus with the Buddha at its head, in order to make a meal for them when my turn comes, but my turn does not come. I am alone here, and many household affairs of mine are going to ruin. What if I were to look into the provision-room, and what I should not see in the provision-room, to prepare that (for the Bhikkhus)!' Then that Brâhma*n*a looked into the provision-room and did not see there two (sorts of food), rice-milk and honey-lumps.

3. And that Brâhma*n*a went to the place where the venerable Ânanda was; having approached him, he said to the venerable Ânanda: 'As my turn did not come, my dear Ânanda, I thought: "Two months have elapsed (&c., down to:). What if I were to look into the provision-room, and what I should not

see in the provision-room, to prepare that!" Thus, my dear Ânanda, I looked into the provision-room and did not see there two (sorts of food), rice-milk and honey-lumps. If I were to prepare, my dear Ânanda, rice-milk and honey-lumps (for the Bhikkhus), would the reverend Gotama accept it from me?'

'Well, my good Brâhma*n*a, I will ask the Blessed One.'

4. And the venerable Ânanda told this thing to the Blessed One.

'Well, Ânanda, let him prepare (those dishes).'

'Well, my good Brâhma*n*a, you may prepare (those dishes).'

And when the night had elapsed, that Brâhma*n*a had abundant rice-milk and honey-lumps prepared, and offered them to the Blessed One (in the words): 'May the reverend Gotama accept from me this rice-milk and honey-lumps.'

'Well, my good Brâhma*n*a, give it to the Bhikkhus.'

The Bhikkhus, fearing to offend, did not accept it.

'Accept it, O Bhikkhus, and eat it.'

Then that Brâhma*n*a with his own hands served and offered abundant rice-milk and honey-lumps to the fraternity of Bhikkhus with the Buddha at its head; and when the Blessed One had washen his hands, when he had cleansed his bowl and his hands, he sat down near him.

5. When he was seated near him, the Blessed One said to that Brâhma*n*a: 'Tenfold, O Brâhma*n*a, is the merit attached to rice-milk. In what way is it tenfold? He who gives rice-milk, gives life; he gives colour; he gives joy; he gives strength; he gives readiness of mind; rice-milk when it is drunk removes hunger; dispels thirst;

sets right the humors of the body; purifies the bladder; and promotes the digestion. This tenfold merit, O Brâhma*n*a, is attached to rice-milk.

6. 'He who attentively at the right time gives rice-milk to the self-possessed, who live on what others give to them, will benefit them in ten ways: life and colour, joy and strength (he gives to them);—

'Readiness of mind arises from it; it dispels hunger and thirst, and sets the humors right; it purifies the bladder, and brings the food to digestion. As medicine the Perfect One has praised it.

'Therefore should rice-milk be continually given by a man who is longing for joy, who is desirous of heavenly joy, or who aspires to human prosperity.'

7. And the Blessed One, having gladdened that Brâhma*n*a by these stanzas, rose from his seat and went away.

And in consequence of this event the Blessed One, after having delivered a religious discourse, thus addressed the Bhikkhus: 'I allow you, O Bhikkhus, (to partake of) rice-milk and honey-lumps.'

25.

1. Now the people heard: 'The Blessed One has allowed (to the Bhikkhus to partake of) rice-milk and honey-lumps.' They prepared early in the morning solid rice-milk[1] and honey-lumps. The Bhikkhus, having satiated themselves in the

[1] Bho*gg*a-yâgu, literally, eatable rice-milk, which seems opposed to the ordinary rice-milk which was drunk. Yâgu is the Pâli word for what is called in Anglo-Indian terminology 'congey.' Bho*gg*a-yâgu is 'rice pudding made with milk.'

morning with solid rice-milk and with honey-lumps, (afterwards) did not dine in the dining-hall with good appetite. At that time a certain minister, who was but newly converted, had invited the fraternity of Bhikkhus with the Buddha at its head for the next day. Now this newly converted minister thought: 'What if I were to prepare for these twelve hundred and fifty Bhikkhus twelve hundred and fifty dishes of meat, and offer to each Bhikkhu one dish of meat!'

2. And when that night had elapsed, that newly converted minister ordered excellent food, both hard and soft, and twelve hundred and fifty dishes of meat to be prepared, and had meal-time announced to the Blessed One in the words: 'It is time, Lord, the meal is ready.' And in the forenoon the Blessed One, having put on his under-robes, took his alms-bowl, and, with his *k*îvara on, went to the house of that newly converted minister. When he had arrived there, he sat down with the Bhikkhus who followed him, on seats laid out for them.

3. Then that newly converted minister in his dining-hall waited on the Bhikkhus. The Bhikkhus said to him: 'Give us little, friend; give us little, friend.'

'Do not take little, reverend Sirs, because you think: "This minister is but newly converted." Much food, both hard and soft, has been prepared by me, and twelve hundred and fifty dishes of meat; I will offer to each Bhikkhu one dish of meat. Take, reverend Sirs, as much as you want.'

'This is not the reason, friend, for which we take little. But we have satiated ourselves in the morning with solid rice-milk and with honey-lumps; therefore we take little.'

4. And that newly converted minister was annoyed, murmured, and became angry: 'How can their reverences, when I have invited them, partake of solid rice-milk with other people, as if I were unable to give them as much as they want.' (Thinking thus), he went around angry, displeased, and in an offensive temper, filling the bowls of the Bhikkhus (and saying), 'Eat or take it away!' And that newly converted minister served and offered with his own hands excellent food, both hard and soft, to the fraternity of Bhikkhus with the Buddha at its head; and when the Blessed One had finished his meal and cleansed his bowl and his hands, he sat down near him. And the Blessed One, after having taught, incited, animated, and gladdened that newly converted minister, who was sitting near him, by religious discourse, rose from his seat and went away.

5. And soon after the Blessed One was gone, scruples and remorse befell that newly converted minister: 'Alas, it is evil to me, it is not good to me! Alas, it is loss to me, it is not gain to me that I went around (among the Bhikkhus) angry, displeased, and in an offensive temper, filling their bowls (and saying), "Eat or take it away!" What have I produced thereby, more merit or more demerit?'

And that newly converted minister went to the place where the Blessed One was; having approached him and respectfully saluted the Blessed One, he sat down near him. Sitting near him, that newly converted minister said to the Blessed One: 'Lord, soon after the Blessed One was gone, scruples and remorse have befallen me: "Alas, it is evil to me

(&c., down to:) more merit or more demerit?" Lord, what have I produced thereby, more merit or more demerit?'

6. 'The moment, friend, in which you invited the fraternity of Bhikkhus with the Buddha at its head for the next day, that moment you acquired much merit. And the moment in which each Bhikkhu received one lump of rice from you, that moment you acquired much merit. You gained the inheritance of heaven.'

Then that newly converted minister thought: 'Oh, it is good to me! Oh, it is gain to me! I have acquired much merit! I have gained the inheritance of heaven!'—and glad and joyful he rose from his seat, respectfully saluted the Blessed One, and passing round him with his right side towards him, went away.

7. In consequence of that, and on this occasion, the Blessed One, having ordered the fraternity of Bhikkhus to assemble, questioned the Bhikkhus: 'Is it true, O Bhikkhus, that the Bhikkhus, having been invited to one place, partake of solid rice-milk with other persons?'

'It is true, Lord.'

Then the blessed Buddha rebuked those Bhikkhus: 'How can these foolish persons, O Bhikkhus, having been invited to one place, partake of solid rice-milk with other persons? This will not do, O Bhikkhus, for converting the unconverted,' &c. Having rebuked them and delivered a religious discourse, he thus addressed the Bhikkhus: 'Let no one, O Bhikkhus, when he is invited to one place, partake of solid rice-milk with other persons. He who does, is to be treated according to the law.'

26[1].

1. And the Blessed One, after having dwelt at Andhakavinda as long as he thought fit, went forth to Râ*g*agaha, accompanied by a great number of Bhikkhus, by twelve hundred and fifty Bhikkhus. At that time Bela*tth*a Ka*kk*âna was travelling on the road from Râ*g*agaha to Andhakavinda with five hundred carts all full of pots of sugar. And the Blessed One saw Bela*tth*a Ka*kk*âna coming from afar; when he saw him, he left the road, and sat down at the foot of a tree.

2. And Bela*tth*a Ka*kk*âna went to the place where the Blessed One was; having approached him and respectfully saluted the Blessed One, he stationed himself near him. Standing near him, Bela*tth*a Ka*kk*âna said to the Blessed One: 'I wish, Lord, to give to each Bhikkhu one pot of sugar.'

'Well, Ka*kk*âna, bring here one pot of sugar.'

Bela*tth*a Ka*kk*âna accepted this order of the Blessed One (by saying), 'Yes, Lord,' took one pot of sugar and went to the place where the Blessed One was; having approached him, he said to the Blessed One: 'I have brought here, Lord, the pot of sugar; what shall I do with it, Lord?'

'Well, Ka*kk*âna, give the sugar to the Bhikkhus.'

3. Bela*tth*a Ka*kk*âna accepted this order of the Blessed One (by saying), 'Yes, Lord,' gave the

[1] See the 33rd Pâ*k*ittiya Rule about parampara-bhogana (taking food in turn).

sugar to the Bhikkhus, and said to the Blessed One: 'I have given the sugar to the Bhikkhus, Lord, but there is much sugar left over; what shall I do with it, Lord?'

'Well, Ka*kk*âna, give the Bhikkhus as much sugar as they want.'

Bela*tth*a Ka*kk*âna accepted this order of the Blessed One (by saying), 'Yes, Lord,' gave the Bhikkhus as much sugar as they wanted, and said to the Blessed One: 'I have given, Lord, the Bhikkhus as much sugar as they want, but there is much sugar left over; what shall I do with it, Lord?'

'Well, Ka*kk*âna, let the Bhikkhus eat their fill with sugar.'

Bela*tth*a Ka*kk*âna accepted this order of the Blessed One (by saying), 'Yes, Lord,' and let the Bhikkhus eat their fill with sugar; some Bhikkhus filled their bowls and filled their water strainers and bags with it.

4. And Bela*tth*a Ka*kk*âna, having let the Bhikkhus eat their fill with sugar, said to the Blessed One: 'The Bhikkhus, Lord, have eaten their fill with sugar, but there is much sugar left over; what shall I do with it, Lord?'

'Well, Ka*kk*âna, give the sugar to the people who eat the remains of (the Bhikkhus') food,' &c.

'Well, Ka*kk*âna, give the people who eat the remains of (the Bhikkhus') food as much sugar as they want,' &c.

5. 'Well, Ka*kk*âna, let the people who eat the remains of (the Bhikkhus') food, eat their fill with sugar' (&c., down to:); some of the people who ate the remains of (the Bhikkhus') food, filled their

pots and jars, and filled their baskets and the folds of their dress with it.

6. And Bela*tth*a Ka*kk*âna, having let the people who ate the remains of (the Bhikkhus') food, eat their fill with sugar, said to the Blessed One: 'The people, Lord, who eat the remains of (the Bhikkhus') food, have eaten their fill with sugar, but there is much sugar left over; what shall I do with it, Lord?'

'I see no one, Ka*kk*âna, in the world of men and gods, in Mâra's and Brahma's world, among all beings, Sama*n*as and Brâhma*n*as, gods and men, by whom that sugar, when he has eaten it, can be fully assimilated, save by the Tathâgata or by a disciple of the Tathâgata. Therefore, Ka*kk*âna, throw that sugar away at a place free from grass, or sink it into water in which there are no living things.'

Bela*tth*a Ka*kk*âna accepted this order of the Blessed One (by saying), 'Yes, Lord,' and sunk that sugar into water in which there were no living things.

7. And that sugar, when thrown into the water, hissed and bubbled, and steamed, and sent forth smoke. As a ploughshare, which has been heated through the whole day and is thrown into water, hisses and bubbles, and steams, and sends forth smoke, so that sugar, when thrown into the water, hissed and bubbled, steamed, and sent forth smoke. And Bela*tth*a Ka*kk*âna, terrified and having his hair erect with fear, went to the place where the Blessed One was; having approached him and respectfully saluted the Blessed One, he sat down near him.

8. When Bela*tth*a Ka*kk*âna was sitting near him,

the Blessed One preached to him in due course; that is to say, he talked about the merits obtained by alms-giving, about the duties of morality, about heaven, about the evils, the vanity, and the defilement of lusts, and about the blessings of the abandonment of lusts. When the Blessed One saw that the mind of Bela*tth*a Ka*kk*âna was prepared, impressible, free from obstacles (to understanding the Truth), elated, and believing, then he preached what is the principal doctrine of the Buddhas, namely, Suffering, the Cause of suffering, the Cessation of suffering, the Path. Just as a clean cloth free from black specks properly takes the dye, thus Bela*tth*a Ka*kk*âna, even while sitting there, obtained the pure and spotless Eye of the Truth (that is, the knowledge): 'Whatsoever is subject to the condition of origination is subject also to the condition of cessation.'

9. And Bela*tth*a Ka*kk*âna, having seen the Truth, having mastered the Truth, having understood the Truth, having penetrated the Truth, having overcome uncertainty, having dispelled all doubts, having gained full knowledge, dependent on nobody else for the knowledge of the doctrine of the Teacher, said to the Blessed One: 'Glorious, Lord! glorious, Lord! Just as if one should set up, Lord, what had been overturned, or should reveal what had been hidden, or should point out the way to one who had lost his way, or should bring a lamp into the darkness, in order that those who had eyes might see visible things, thus has the Blessed One preached the doctrine in many ways. I take my refuge, Lord, in the Blessed One, and in the Dhamma, and in the fraternity of Bhikkhus; may

the Blessed One receive me from this day forth while my life lasts as a disciple who has taken his refuge in him.'

27.

And the Blessed One, wandering from place to place, came to Râ*g*agaha. There the Blessed One dwelt near Râ*g*agaha, in the Ve*l*uvana, at Kalanda-kanivâpa. At that time the Bhikkhus at Râ*g*agaha had plenty of sugar. The Bhikkhus feared to offend (and thought): 'The Blessed One has allowed the eating of sugar only to the sick and not to the healthy,' and therefore they did not eat sugar.

They told this thing to the Blessed One.

'I allow, O Bhikkhus, to the sick the eating of sugar, and to the healthy the drinking of sugar-water.'

28[1]

1. And the Blessed One, after having dwelt at Râ*g*agaha as long as he thought fit, went forth to Pâ*t*aligâma, accompanied by a great number of Bhikkhus, by twelve hundred and fifty Bhikkhus. Wandering from place to place the Blessed One came to Pâ*t*aligâma.

[1] Chaps. 28–30 are, with a few unimportant variations, word for word the same as Mahâparinibbâna Sutta I, 19–II, 3; II, 16–24. See Rh. D.'s Introduction to his translation of the Mahâparinibbâna Sutta, pp. xxxiv seq., and his note there at II, 16.

Now the lay-devotees at Pâtaligâma heard: 'The Blessed One has arrived at Pâtaligâma.' And the Pâtaligâma lay-devotees went to the place where the Blessed One was; having approached him and respectfully saluted the Blessed One, they sat down near him. When they were seated near him, the Blessed One taught, incited, animated, and gladdened the Pâtaligâma lay-devotees by religious discourse.

2. And the Pâtaligâma lay-devotees, having been taught, incited, animated, and gladdened by the Blessed One by religious discourse, said to the Blessed One: 'Might the Blessed One, Lord, consent to come to our rest house together with the fraternity of Bhikkhus.' The Blessed One expressed his consent by remaining silent. Then the Pâtaligâma lay-devotees, when they understood that the Blessed One had accepted their invitation, rose from their seats, respectfully saluted the Blessed One, and passing round him with their right side towards him, went away to the rest house. When they had arrived there, they strewed the whole floor of the rest house[1], placed seats in it, set up a water-pot, and fixed an oil lamp. Then they went to the place where the Blessed One was; having approached him and respectfully saluted the Blessed One, they stationed themselves near him.

3. Standing near him the Pâtaliputta lay-devotees said to the Blessed One: 'We have strewn the whole floor of the rest house, Lord, (with sand), we have placed seats in it, set up a water-pot, and

[1] Perhaps we are to supply 'with sand.' Comp. Dîpavamsa VI, 64; XII, 71, &c.

fixed an oil lamp. May the Blessed One, Lord, do now what he thinks fit.'

And in the forenoon the Blessed One, having put on his under-robes, took his alms-bowl, and, with his *k*ivara on, went to the rest house together with the Bhikkhus who followed him. When he had arrived there, he washed his feet, entered the rest house, and took his seat against the centre pillar, with his face towards the east. And the Bhikkhus also washed their feet, entered the rest house, and took their seats against the western wall, with their faces towards the east, having the Blessed One before their eyes. And the Pâ*t*aligâma lay-devotees also washed their feet, entered the rest house, and took their seats against the eastern wall, with their faces towards the west, having the Blessed One before their eyes.

4. Then the Blessed One thus addressed the Pâ*t*aligâma lay-devotees: 'Fivefold, O householders, is the loss of the wrong-doer through his want of rectitude. And which is this fivefold loss? In the first place, O householders, the wrong-doer, devoid of rectitude, falls into great poverty through sloth; this is the first loss of the wrong-doer through his want of rectitude. And again, O householders, of the wrong-doer, devoid of rectitude, evil repute gets noised abroad; this is the second &c. And again, O householders, whatever society the wrong-doer, devoid of rectitude, enters—whether of noblemen, Brâhma*n*as, heads of houses, or Sama*n*as—he enters shyly and confused; this is the third &c. And again, O householders, the wrong-doer, devoid of rectitude, is full of anxiety when he dies; this is the fourth &c. And again, O householders, the

wrong-doer, devoid of rectitude, on the dissolution of his body, after death, is reborn into some state of distress and punishment, a state of woe, and hell; this is the fifth &c. This is the fivefold loss, O householders, of the wrong-doer through his want of rectitude.

5. 'Fivefold, O householders, is the gain of the well-doer through his practice of rectitude. And which is this fivefold gain? In the first place, O householders, the well-doer, strong in rectitude, acquires great wealth through his industry; this is the first gain of the well-doer through his practice of rectitude. And again, O householders, of the well-doer, strong in rectitude, good reports are spread abroad; this is the second &c. And again, O householders, whatever society the well-doer, strong in rectitude, enters—whether of noblemen, Brâhma*n*as, heads of houses, or Sama*n*as—he enters confident and self-possessed; this is the third &c. And again, O householders, the well-doer, strong in rectitude, dies without anxiety; this is the fourth &c. And again, O householders, the well-doer, strong in rectitude, on the dissolution of his body, after death, is reborn into some happy state in heaven; this is the fifth &c. This is the fivefold gain, O householders, of the well-doer through his practice of rectitude.'

6. When the Blessed One had thus taught, incited, animated, and gladdened the Pâ*t*aligâma lay-devotees far into the night with religious discourse, he dismissed them, saying, 'The night is far spent, O householders. May you do now what you think fit.' The Pâ*t*aligâma lay-devotees accepted the Blessed One's word by saying, 'Yes, Lord,' rose from their

seats, respectfully saluted the Blessed One, and passing round him with their right side towards him, went away.

7. And the Blessed One, not long after the Pâtaligâma lay-devotees had departed thence, went to an empty place[1] (in order to give himself to meditation).

At that time Sunîdha and Vassakâra, two ministers of Magadha, were building a (fortified) town at Pâtaligâma in order to repel the Vaggis. And the Blessed One, rising up early in the morning, at dawn's time, saw with his divine and clear vision, surpassing that of ordinary men, great numbers of fairies who haunted the ground there at Pâtaligâma. Now, wherever ground is occupied by powerful fairies, they bend the hearts of powerful kings and ministers to build dwelling-places there. Wherever ground is occupied by fairies of middling power, &c.; of inferior power, they bend the hearts of middling kings and ministers, &c., of inferior kings and ministers to build dwelling-places there.

8. And the Blessed One said to the venerable Ânanda: 'Who are they, Ânanda, who are building a town at Pâtaligâma?'

'Sunîdha and Vassakâra, Lord, the two ministers of Magadha, are building a town at Pâtaligâma in order to repel the Vaggis.'

'As if they had consulted, Ânanda, with the Tâvatimsa gods, so (at the right place), Ânanda, the Magadha ministers Sunîdha and Vassakâra build this town at Pâtaligâma in order to repel the Vaggis. When I had risen up early in the morning, Ânanda, at dawn's time, I saw with my divine

[1] Suññâgâra. Comp. I, 78, 5; Suttavibhanga, Pârâg. IV, 4, 1.

and clear vision (&c., as in § 7, down to:) they bend the hearts of inferior kings and ministers to build dwelling-places there. As far, Ânanda, as Aryan people dwell, as far as merchants travel, this will become the chief town, the city of Pâ*t*aliputta. But danger of destruction, Ânanda, will hang over Pâ*t*aliputta in three ways, by fire, or by water, or by internal discord[1].'

9. And the Magadha ministers Sunîdha and Vassakâra went to the place where the Blessed One was; having approached him, they exchanged greeting with the Blessed One; having exchanged with him greeting and complaisant words, they stationed themselves near him; then standing near him the Magadha ministers Sunîdha and Vassakâra said to the Blessed One: 'Might the reverend Gotama consent to take his meal with us to-day together with the fraternity of Bhikkhus.'

The Blessed One expressed his consent by remaining silent. Then the Magadha ministers Sunîdha and Vassakâra, when they understood that the Blessed One had accepted their invitation, went away.

---

[1] The event prophesied here, Pâ*t*aliputta's becoming the capital of the Magadha empire, is placed by the various authorities under different kings. Hwen Thsang and the Burmese writer quoted by Bishop Bigandet ('Legend of the Burmese Buddha,' third edition, vol. ii, p. 183) say that it was Kâlâsoka who removed the seat of the empire to Pâ*t*aliputta. The *G*ains, on the other hand, state that it was Udâyi, the son of A*g*âtasattu. Most probably the latter tradition is the correct one, as even king Mu*nd*a is mentioned in the Aṅguttara Nikâya as having resided at Pâ*t*aliputta. Comp. Rh. D.'s 'Buddhist Suttas,' Introd. pp. xv seq.; H. O.'s Introduction to the Mahâvagga, p. xxxvii; and the remarks of Professor Jacobi and of H. O. in Zeitschrift der Deutschen Morg. Gesellschaft, vol. xxxiv, pp. 185, 751, 752, note 2.

10. And the Magadha ministers Sunîdha and Vassakâra ordered excellent food, both hard and soft, to be prepared, and had meal-time announced (&c.[1], down to:) on seats laid out for them. And the Magadha ministers Sunîdha and Vassakâra with their own hands served and offered excellent food, both hard and soft, to the fraternity of Bhikkhus with the Buddha at its head; and when the Blessed One had finished his meal and cleansed his bowl and his hands, they sat down near him. When they were sitting near him, the Blessed One gladdened the Magadha ministers Sunîdha and Vassakâra by these stanzas:

11. 'Wheresoe'er the prudent man shall take up his abode, let him support there good and upright men of self-control.

'Let him make offerings to all such deities as may be there. Revered, they will revere him; honoured, they honour him again;

'Are gracious to him as a mother to the son of her womb. And a man who has the grace of the gods, good fortune he beholds.'

And the Blessed One, having gladdened the Magadha ministers Sunîdha and Vassakâra by these stanzas, rose from his seat and went away.

12. And the Magadha ministers Sunîdha and Vassakâra followed the Blessed One from behind, saying, 'The gate the Samaṇa Gotama goes out by to-day shall be called Gotama's gate, and the ferry at which he crosses the river Ganges shall be called Gotama's ferry.' And the gate the Blessed One went out by

[1] See chap. 23. 5, &c. Instead of 'Lord,' read here, 'Reverend Gotama.'

was called Gotama's gate. And the Blessed One went on to the river. At that time the river Ganges was brimful and overflowing[1]; and wishing to cross to the opposite bank, some began to seek for boats, some for rafts of wood, while some made rafts of basket-work.

13. And the Blessed One saw those people who wished to cross to the opposite bank, some seeking for boats, some for rafts of wood, and some making rafts of basket-work. When he saw them, he vanished as quickly as a strong man might stretch his bent arm out, or draw back his outstretched arm, from this side of the river Ganges, and stood on the further bank with the company of the Bhikkhus.

And the Blessed One, perceiving all this, on this occasion, pronounced this solemn utterance:

'They who cross the ocean's floods making a solid path across the pools—

'Whilst the vain world ties its basket rafts: these are the wise, these are the saved indeed.'

29.

1. And the Blessed One went to Ko*t*igâma. There at Ko*t*igâma the Blessed One resided. And the Blessed One thus addressed the Bhikkhus:

'It is through not understanding and grasping four Noble Truths, O Bhikkhus, that we have had to run so long, to wander so long in this weary path of transmigration, both you and I. And what are

[1] Samatitthikâ. This word is replaced by samatîrthikâ at Lal. Vist. pp. 501, 528. Compare, however, Rh. D.'s note on Tevigga Sutta I, 24 ('Buddhist Suttas,' p. 178).

these four? By not understanding and grasping the Noble Truth of Suffering, O Bhikkhus; by not understanding and grasping the Noble Truth of the Cause of suffering; by not understanding and grasping the Noble Truth of the Cessation of suffering; by not understanding and grasping the Noble Truth of the Path which leads to the cessation of suffering: thereby we have had to run so long, to wander so long in this weary path of transmigration, both you and I.

2. 'But now, O Bhikkhus, the Noble Truth of Suffering is understood and grasped; the Noble Truth of the Cause of suffering, &c., of the Cessation of suffering, &c., of the Path which leads to the cessation of suffering is understood and grasped. The craving for existence is rooted out; that which leads to renewed existence is destroyed; and there is no more birth!

'By not seeing the four Noble Truths as they really are, long is the path that is traversed through many a birth.

'Now these are grasped; the cause of birth is removed, the root of sorrow rooted out, and there is no more birth.'

30.

1. Now the courtezan Ambapâlî heard that the Blessed One had arrived at Ko*t*igâma. And the courtezan Ambapâlî ordered a number of magnificent vehicles to be made ready, mounted one of these vehicles, and left Vesâli with her magnificent vehicles in order to visit the Blessed One. She

went in the carriage as far as the ground was passable for carriages; there she alighted; and she proceeded on foot to the place where the Blessed One was. Having approached him and respectfully saluted the Blessed One, she sat down near him.

2. When she was sitting near him, the Blessed One taught, incited, animated, and gladdened the courtezan Ambapâlî by religious discourse. And the courtezan Ambapâlî, having been taught, &c., by the Blessed One by religious discourse, said to the Blessed One: 'Might the Blessed One, Lord, consent to take his meal with me to-morrow together with the fraternity of Bhikkhus.'

The Blessed One expressed his consent by remaining silent.

Then the courtezan Ambapâlî, when she understood that the Blessed One had accepted her invitation, rose from her seat, respectfully saluted the Blessed One, and, passing round him with her right side towards him, went away.

3. Now the Li*kkh*avis of Vesâli heard that the Blessed One had arrived at Ko*t*igâma. And the Li*kkh*avis of Vesâli ordered a number of magnificent vehicles to be made ready, mounted these vehicles, and left Vesâli with their magnificent vehicles in order to visit the Blessed One. Some of the Li*kkh*avis were dark, dark in colour, and wearing dark clothes and ornaments; some of them were fair, fair in colour, and wearing light clothes and ornaments; some of them were red, ruddy in colour, and wearing red clothes and ornaments; some of them were white, pale in colour, and wearing white colours and ornaments. And the courtezan Ambapâlî drove up against the young

Li*kkh*avis, pole to pole, yoke to yoke, wheel to wheel, axle to axle. [4.] And those Li*kkh*avis said to the courtezan Ambapâlî: 'How is it, Ambapâlî, that you drive up against the young Li*kkh*avis, pole to pole, &c.?'

'My Lords, I have just invited the Blessed One with the fraternity of Bhikkhus for their morrow's meal.'

'Ambapâlî! give up this meal to us for a hundred thousand.'

'My Lords, were you to offer all Vesâli with its subject territory, I would not give up this meal.'

Then the Li*kkh*avis snapped their fingers (exclaiming), 'We are outdone by this woman[1]! we are out-reached by this woman[1]!'

4. Then the Li*kkh*avis went to the place where the Blessed One was. And the Blessed One saw the Li*kkh*avis coming from afar; when he saw them, he addressed the Bhikkhus and said: 'O Bhikkhus, let those of the Bhikkhus who have never seen the Tâvati*m*sa gods, gaze upon this company of the Li*kkh*avis, behold this company of the Li*kkh*avis, compare this company of the Li*kkh*avis, even as a company of Tâvati*m*sa gods!'

And the Li*kkh*avis went in the carriages as far as the ground was passable for carriages (&c., as in §§ 1, 2, down to:) 'Might the Blessed One, Lord, consent to take his meal with us to-morrow together with the fraternity of Bhikkhus.'

---

[1] Ambakâya, which Buddhaghosa explains by itthikâya, comp. the well-known Mantra, Vâ*g*asaneyi Sa*m*hitâ 23. 18: Ambe ambike 'mbâlike, &c. Probably the word ambakâ is a contemptuous form intended here at the same time to convey an allusion to the mango-(amba-) gardens which Ambapâlî possessed, and from which she was named. Comp. Rh. D.'s note at Mahâparinibbâna Sutta II, 19.

'I have promised, O Li*kkh*avis, to dine to-morrow with Ambapâlî the courtezan.'

5. And the Blessed One, after having dwelt at Ko*t*igâma as long as he thought fit, went to *Ñ*âtikâ. There the Blessed One dwelt at *Ñ*âtikâ, in the Brick Hall (Gi*ñg*akâvasatha). And when the night had elapsed, the courtezan Ambapâlî ordered in her park excellent food (&c., as in chap. 28. 10[1], down to:) she sat down near him. Sitting near him the courtezan Ambapâlî said to the Blessed One: 'I give up this Ambapâlî grove, Lord, to the fraternity of Bhikkhus with the Buddha at its head.' The Blessed One accepted the Ârâma. Then the Blessed One, after having taught, incited, animated, and gladdened the courtezan Ambapâlî by religious discourse, rose from his seat and went to the Mahâvana. There the Blessed One dwelt at Vesâli, in the Mahâvana, in the Kû*t*âgâra-sâlâ.

End of the Li*kkh*avi Bhâ*n*avâra.

31.

1. At that time many distinguished Li*kkh*avis were sitting together assembled in the town-hall and spoke in many ways in praise of the Buddha, of the Dhamma, and of the Sa*m*gha. At that time Sîha, the general-in-chief (of the Li*kkh*avis), a disciple of the Niga*nth*a sect, was sitting in that assembly. And Sîha, the general, thought: 'Truly

[1] Replace 'the Magadha ministers Sunîdha and Vassakâra' by 'the courtezan Ambapâlî,' and instead of 'Reverend Gotama,' read 'Lord.'

he, the Blessed One, must be the Arahat Buddha, since these many distinguished Li*kkh*avis, who are sitting here together assembled in the town-hall, speak in so many ways in praise of the Buddha, of the Dhamma, and of the Sa*m*gha. What if I were to go and visit him, the Arahat Buddha.'

2. And Sîha, the general, went to the place where the Niga*nth*a Nâtaputta[1] was; having approached him, he said to the Niga*nth*a Nâtaputta: 'I wish, Lord, to go and visit the Sama*n*a Gotama.'

'Why should you, Sîha, who believe in the result of actions[2] (according to their moral merit), go to visit the Sama*n*a Gotama, who denies the result of actions? For the Sama*n*a Gotama, Sîha, denies the result of actions; he teaches the doctrine of non-action; and in this doctrine he trains his disciples.'

Then the desire to go and to visit the Blessed One, which had arisen in Sîha, the general, abated in him.

3. And a second time many distinguished Li*kkh*avis were sitting together (&c., as in §§ 1, 2, down to the end).

And a third time many distinguished Li*kkh*avis were sitting together, &c. And a third time Sîha, the general, thought: 'Truly he, the Blessed One, must be the Arahat Buddha, since these many distinguished Li*kkh*avis, who are sitting here together assembled in the town-hall, speak in so many ways

[1] The founder of the Niga*nth*a sect, who is, according to the important discovery of Professors Bühler and Jacobi, identical with the Mahâvîra of the *G*ain legends. See Jacobi's Preface to the Kalpasûtra, pp. 1 seq.

[2] Kiriyavâda.

in praise of the Buddha, of the Dhamma, and of the Sa*m*gha. What are the Niga*nth*as to me, whether they give their consent or not? What if I were to go without asking the Niga*nth*as for their consent, to visit him, the Blessed One, the Arahat Buddha.'

4. And Sîha, the general, went out of Vesâli with five hundred vehicles at broad daylight in order to visit the Blessed One. He went in the carriage as far as the ground was passable for carriages; there he alighted; and he proceeded on foot to the place where the Blessed One was. Having approached him, and respectfully saluted the Blessed One, he sat down near him. When he was sitting near him, Sîha, the general, said to the Blessed One: 'I have heard, Lord, that the Sama*n*a Gotama denies the result of actions; he teaches the doctrine of non-action, and in this doctrine he trains his disciples. Now, Lord, those who speak thus: "The Sama*n*a Gotama denies the result of actions," &c.—do they say the truth of the Blessed One, and do they not bear false witness against the Blessed One and pass off a spurious Dhamma as your Dhamma? And there is nothing blameworthy in a discourse and dispute like this regarding matters of the Dhamma; for it is our intention, Lord, to avoid bringing false accusations against the Blessed One.'

5[1]. 'There is a way, Sîha, in which one speaking truly could say of me: "The Sama*n*a Gotama denies action[2]; he teaches the doctrine of non-action; and in this doctrine he trains his disciples."

[1] A part of the following discourse is the same as Suttavibhaṅga, Pârâ*g*. I, 1, 3.

[2] 'The doctrine of non-action,' and 'the doctrine of action,'

'And again, Sîha, there is a way in which one speaking truly could say of me: "The Samana Gotama maintains action [1]; he teaches the doctrine of action; and in this doctrine he trains his disciples."

'And again, Sîha, there is a way in which one speaking truly could say of me: "The Samana Gotama maintains annihilation [2]; he teaches the doctrine of annihilation; and in this doctrine he trains his disciples."

'And again, Sîha, there is a way in which one speaking truly could say of me: "The Samana Gotama proclaims contemptibleness [3]; he teaches the doctrine of contemptibleness; and in this doctrine he trains his disciples."

'And again, &c.: "The Samana Gotama proclaims Vinaya [4]; he teaches the doctrine of Vinaya; and in this doctrine he trains his disciples."

'And again, &c.: "The Samana Gotama proclaims Tapas [5], &c."

'And again, &c.: "The Samana Gotama is apagabbha [6]; he teaches the doctrine of apagabbhatâ, &c."

---

taken in the ordinary sense of the words, are the doctrines that the actions of sentient beings receive not, or receive, their reward according to the law of moral retribution. In this discourse, however, a peculiar meaning is attached to these two terms; see § 6.

[1] See note 2, p. 110.

[2] Ukkhedavâda ('the doctrine of annihilation') is the doctrine that death is the annihilation of existence ('ukkhedavâdâ sato sattassa ukkhedam vinâsam vibhavam paññâpenti.' Brahmagâla-sutta). But in this discourse the word is taken in a peculiar sense; comp. § 7.

[3] Gegukkhitâ. See § 7.

[4] 'Right conduct.' But in this discourse it is also taken in the sense of 'putting away' (scil. evil); see § 8.

[5] 'Self-mortification,' literally, 'burning,' in which sense the word is taken in § 8.

[6] Apagabbha (apragalbha) and apagabbhatâ ordinarily mean

'And again, &c.: "The Samana Gotama is confident[1]; he teaches the doctrine of confidence, &c."

6. 'And in which way is it, Sîha, that one speaking truly could say of me: "The Samana Gotama denies action; he teaches the doctrine of non-action; and in this doctrine he trains his disciples?" I teach, Sîha, the not-doing of such actions as are unrighteous, either by deed, or by word, or by thought; I teach the not bringing about of the manifold conditions (of heart) which are evil and not good. In this way, Sîha, one speaking truly could say of me: "The Samana Gotama, &c."

'And in which way is it, Sîha, that one speaking truly could say of me: "The Samana Gotama maintains action; he teaches the doctrine of action; and in this doctrine he trains his disciples?" I teach, Sîha, the doing of such actions as are righteous, by deed, by word, and by thought; I teach the bringing about of the manifold conditions (of heart) which are good and not evil. In this way, &c."

7. 'And in which way is it, Sîha, that one speaking truly could say of me: "The Samana Gotama maintains annihilation; he teaches the doctrine of annihilation; and in this doctrine he trains his disciples?" I proclaim, Sîha, the annihilation of lust, of ill-will, of delusion; I proclaim the annihilation of the manifold conditions (of heart) which are evil and not good. In this way, &c."

'And in which way is it, Sîha, that one speaking truly could say of me: "The Samana Gotama

---

'irresolute' and 'irresolution.' But here the words are taken in quite another sense, with a pun that cannot be rendered in English; see § 9.

[1] See § 9.

proclaims contemptibleness, &c.?" I deem, Sîha, unrighteous actions contemptible, whether they be performed by deed, or by word, or by thought; I proclaim the doctrine of the contemptibleness of falling into the manifold conditions (of heart) which are evil and not good. In this way, &c.

8. 'And in which way is it, Sîha, that one speaking truly could say of me: "The Samana Gotama proclaims Vinaya, &c.?" I teach, Sîha, the doing away[1] with lust, with ill-will, with delusion; I teach the doing away with the manifold conditions (of heart) which are evil and not good. In this way, &c.

'And in which way is it, Sîha, that one speaking truly could say of me: "The Samana Gotama proclaims Tapas, &c.?" I teach, Sîha, that all the conditions (of heart) which are evil and not good, unrighteous actions by deed, by word, and by thought must be burnt away[2]. He who has freed himself, Sîha, from all conditions (of heart) which are evil and not good, which ought to be burnt away, who has rooted them out, and has done away with them as a palm tree is rooted out[3], so that they are destroyed[4] and cannot grow up again—such a

---

[1] Vinayâya.

[2] Tapanîya, connected with tapas.

[3] Tâlâ vatthukatâ. See Buddhaghosa's explanation of this phrase in Vinaya Pitaka, vol. iii, p. 267.

[4] Anabhâvam gatâ (see the correction, Vinaya Pitaka, vol. ii, p. 363), literally, 'They are gone to non-existence.' Buddhaghosa takes great pains in explaining anabhâva; and he quotes also a various reading anubhâva; see Vinaya Pitaka, vol. iii, p. 267. But anabhâva is correct, and must be understood as a synonym of abhâva. As to ana-, equal to a-, compare S. Goldschmidt, Zeitschr. der Deutschen Morg. Ges. vol. xxxii, pp. 100 seq.; Weber, Hâla, p. 16; Pischel's note on Hemakandra II, 190; Curtius, Griechische

person do I call accomplished in Tapas. Now the Tathâgata, Sîha, has freed himself from all conditions, &c. In this way, &c.

9. 'And in which way is it, Sîha, that one speaking truly could say of me: "The Samana Gotama is apagabbha (irresolute[1]), &c.?" He who has freed himself, Sîha, from the necessity of returning in future into a mother's womb[2], and of being reborn into new existences, who has rooted out (his being subject to) rebirth, and has done away with it as a palm tree is rooted out, so that it is destroyed and cannot grow up again—such a person do I call apagabbha. Now the Tathâgata, Sîha, has freed himself, &c. In this way, &c.

'And in which way is it, Sîha, that one speaking truly could say of me: "The Samana Gotama is confident, &c.?" I am confident, Sîha, by the highest confidence; and thus I teach the doctrine of confidence and train my disciples in it. In this way, &c.'

10. When he had spoken thus, Sîha, the general, said to the Blessed One: 'Glorious, Lord! glorious, Lord! (&c., as in chap. 26. 9, down to:) may the Blessed One receive me from this day forth while my life lasts as a disciple who has taken his refuge in him.'

'Consider first, Sîha, what you are doing. It is becoming that well-known persons like you should do nothing without due consideration.'

Etymologie, 5th edition, p. 306 (ἀνάεδνος, &c.). Another Pâli word containing this prefix ana- is anamata, anamatagga; see, for instance, *G*âtaka II, p. 56.

[1] See § 5 with our note.

[2] Into a 'gabbha.' 'Apagabbha' is taken here as 'not subject to returning to a gabbha.'

'By this, Lord, my joy and my faith in the Blessed One has still increased, in that the Blessed One says to me: "Consider first, &c." Had the other Titthiya teachers, Lord, got me as their disciple, they would carry around their banners through the whole of Vesâli (and cry): "Sîha, the general, has become our disciple!" But the Blessed One says to me: "Consider first, &c." For the second time, Lord, I take my refuge in the Blessed One, and in the Dhamma, and in the Bhikkhu-sa*m*gha: may the Blessed One receive me from this day forth while my life lasts as a disciple who has taken his refuge in him.'

11. 'For a long time, Sîha, drink has been offered to the Niga*nth*as in your house[1]. You should therefore deem it right (also in the future) to give them food when they come (to you on their alms-pilgrimage).'

'By this, Lord, my joy and my faith in the Blessed One has still increased, in that the Blessed One says to me: "For a long time, &c." I have been told, Lord: "The Sama*n*a Gotama says: 'To me alone gifts should be given; to nobody else gifts should be given. To my pupils alone gifts should be given; to no one else's pupils gifts should be given. Only what is given to me has great reward; what is given to others has not great reward. Only what is given to my pupils has great reward; what is given to the pupils of others has not great reward.'" But the Blessed One exhorts me to give also to the Niga*n*-*th*as. Well, Lord, we will see what will be season-

[1] Literally, 'your house has been an opâna to the Niga*nth*as.' Opâna may be either avapâna or, as Buddhaghosa seems to understand it, udapâna (compare oka = udaka).

able. For the third time, Lord, I take my refuge in the Blessed One, &c.'

12. And the Blessed One preached to Sîha, the general, in due course; that is to say, he talked about the merits obtained by almsgiving, about the duties of morality (&c., in the usual way; see, for instance, I, 8, 2, 3, down to:) dependent on nobody else for knowledge of the doctrine of the Teacher, he said to the Blessed One: 'Lord, may the Blessed One consent to take his meal with me to-morrow, together with the fraternity of Bhikkhus.'

The Blessed One expressed his consent by remaining silent. Then Sîha, the general, when he understood that the Blessed One had accepted his invitation, rose from his seat, respectfully saluted the Blessed One, and, passing round him with his right side towards him, went away.

And Sîha, the general, gave order to a certain man (among his subalterns, saying), 'Go, my friend, and see if there is any meat to be had[1].' And when that night had elapsed, Sîha, the general, ordered excellent food (&c., as in chap. 23. 5, down to the end).

13. At that time a great number of Niga*nth*as (running) through Vesâli, from road to road and from cross-way to cross-way[2], with outstretched arms, cried: 'To-day Sîha, the general, has killed a great ox and has made a meal for the Sama*n*a Gotama; the Sama*n*a Gotama knowingly eats this meat of an animal killed for this very purpose, and has thus become virtually the author of that deed (of killing the animal)!'

Then a certain man went to the place where Sîha,

[1] About pavattama*m*sa, see the note at chap. 23. 2.

[2] See X, 1, 9.

the general, was. Having approached him he said to Sîha, the general, into his ear: 'Please, Lord, have you noticed that a great number of Niga*nth*as (running) through Vesâli, &c.?'

'Do not mind it, my good Sir. Long since those venerable brethren are trying to discredit the Buddha, the Dhamma, and the Sa*m*gha; and those venerable brethren do not become tired of telling false, idle, vain lies of the Blessed One. Not for our life would we ever intentionally kill a living being.'

14. And Sîha, the general, served and offered with his own hands excellent food, both hard and soft, to the fraternity of Bhikkhus with the Buddha at its head; and when the Blessed One (&c., as in chap. 23. 7, down to the end).

In consequence of that the Blessed One, having delivered a religious discourse, addressed the Bhikkhus and said:

'Let no one, O Bhikkhus, knowingly eat meat (of an animal) killed for that purpose. Whosoever does so, is guilty of a dukka*t*a offence.

'I prescribe, O Bhikkhus, that fish is pure to you in three cases: if you do not see, if you have not heard, if you do not suspect (that it has been caught specially to be given to you).'

32.

1. Now at that time Vesâli was well provided with food, the harvest was good, alms were easy to obtain, one could very well get a living[1] by gleaning, or through favour.

[1] Literally, 'keep oneself going.' Compare the use of yâpetu*m* at Mahâ-parinibbâna Sutta II, 32.

And when the Blessed One had retired into solitude this consideration presented itself to his mind: 'The things which I have prescribed for the Bhikkhus in a time of scarcity, when the harvest is bad, and alms are difficult to obtain—keeping food indoors, cooking it indoors, cooking it of one's own accord, taking what they can pick up, eating food brought from within, or received before meal-time, eating things found in woods or in pools[1], those things the Bhikkhus enjoy also now.'

And the Blessed One, in the evening, when he had left his solitude, said to the venerable Ânanda: 'The things which (&c., as above, down to:) or in pools—do the Bhikkhus enjoy those things now also?'

'They enjoy them, Lord.'

2. Then the Blessed One, in that connection, and on that account, after having delivered a religious discourse, said to the Bhikkhus:

'The things which I have prescribed (&c., as in § 1, down to:) or in pools—those I do not allow from this day forth. You are not, O Bhikkhus, to eat food kept indoors, or cooked indoors, or cooked of your own accord; nor to take things (to eat) which you have picked up. Whosoever shall do so, is guilty of a dukka*t*a offence. And you are not, O Bhikkhus—after you have once finished eating, and have refused food still offered—to eat food brought from within, or received before meal-time, or found in the woods or pools, even if it be food which is not the leavings of the meal of one who has eaten on invitation. Whosoever shall so eat, shall be dealt with according to law[2].'

[1] For these rules, see above, VI, 17–19.

[2] See the 35th Pâ*k*ittiya Rule, and our note upon it.

33.

1. Now at that time the country people loaded much salt, and oil, and rice, and hard food on their carts, and making a laager in the outer enclosure of the Ârâma, they waited there, saying, 'When it comes to our turn, we will provide a meal.' And a great storm-cloud arose.

Then those people went to the place where the venerable Ânanda was; and when they had come there they said to the venerable Ânanda: 'We loaded a quantity of salt, and oil, and rice, and hard food on to our carts; and they stand there. Now a great storm-cloud has arisen. What are we now, Ânanda, Sir, to do with them?'

Then the venerable Ânanda told this thing to the Blessed One.

2. 'In that case, Ânanda, let the Sa*m*gha decide upon some outside building as a kappiya-bhûmi (that is to say, a site, outside the actual dwelling, in which provisions can be kept or cooked without breaking the rule laid down in the last chapter) and keep the stores there (in a building) of any shape the Sa*m*gha chooses, such as vihâra, a*ddh*ayoga, pâsâda, hammiya, guhâ[1].

'And thus, O Bhikkhus, should it be resolved upon. A discreet and able Bhikkhu should proclaim the following *ñ*atti before the Sa*m*gha: "Let the Sa*m*gha, reverend Sirs, hear me. If the Sa*m*gha is ready, let the Sa*m*gha appoint the Vihâra called N. N. to be our kappiya-bhûmi. This is the *ñ*atti. Let the Sa*m*gha, reverend Sirs, hear me.

[1] On these five kinds of buildings, see above, I, 30, 4; II, 8, 1.

The Sa*m*gha appoints the Vihâra called N. N. to be our kappiya-bhûmi. Let any one of the venerable brethren who is in favour of appointing the Vihâra (&c., down to:) thus I understand."'

3. Now at that time men in that place—the kappiya-bhûmi duly chosen by resolution (of the Sa*m*gha)—boiled congey, and boiled rice, and mixed curries, and cut up meat, and split fire-wood. And when the Blessed One, as the night was passing away, rose up, he heard a great and loud noise, as of the cawing of crows. On hearing this he asked the venerable Ânanda: 'What now, Ânanda, may be this great and loud noise, as of the cawing of crows?'

4. 'In that place, Lord,—the kappiya-bhûmi duly chosen by resolution (of the Sa*m*gha),—men are now boiling congey, and boiling rice, and mixing curries, and cutting up meat, and splitting fire-wood. Thence, Lord, comes that great and loud noise, as of the cawing of crows.'

Then the Blessed One, in that connection, and on that account, after he had delivered a religious discourse, said to the Bhikkhus:

'A kappiya-bhûmi, O Bhikkhus, duly chosen, is not to be made use of. Whosoever shall so use it, is guilty of a dukka*t*a offence. I allow you, O Bhikkhus, a kappiya-bhûmi of three kinds, one that has become so by means of a proclamation[1],

[1] Buddhaghosa says on this word: 'When a Vihâra is to be erected on piles, or the foundations of its walls are to be dug out, and the stones on which it is to rest are already laid, then when the first pile or the first stone of the walls is put upon them, the men standing round in a body proclaim, "Let us make a kappiya-ku*t*î."' The proclamation cannot be made after the building has got further than the actual stage here described. Ussâvanâ is

an ox-stall[1], and a building belonging to laymen[2].'

5. Now at that time the venerable Yasoga was sick, and drugs were brought for his use, and these the Bhikkhus put out of doors. Vermin ate them, and thieves carried them away[3].

They told this thing to the Blessed One.

'I allow you, O Bhikkhus, to use a duly chosen kappiya-bhûmi (to keep drugs in). I allow you, O Bhikkhus, a kappiya-bhûmi of four kinds, one that has become so by means of a proclamation, an ox-stall, a building belonging to laymen, and a duly chosen one.'

End of the twenty-fourth Bhânavâra.

34.

1. Now at that time in Bhaddiya-nagara there dwelt a householder named Mendaka (the Goat), who was possessed of this miraculous power: When he had bathed his head, and had had his granary swept out, he could sit outside and fill the granary

---

therefore from ussâveti, 'to proclaim;' and antika is used here, as below in VII, 1, 7.

[1] Gonisâdika. Compare Buddhaghosa's explanation of gonisâdi-nivittho gâmo at Sutta-vibhaṅga, Pâr. II, 3, as given by Minayeff, 'Prâtimoksha,' p. 66, lines 7, 8. Here Buddhaghosa says simply, 'There are two kinds of ox-stalls; ârâma ox-stalls and vihâra ox-stalls. Of these, when neither the ârâma nor the dwellings are fenced in (parikkhittâni honti), that is an ârâma ox-stall; when all or some of the dwellings are fenced in, and not the ârâma, that is a vihâra ox-stall. So both kinds depend upon the fencing in of the ârâma.'

[2] This seems to mean that stores could be kept for the Samgha on laymen's premises.

[3] Compare above, VI, 17, 7.

by making showers of grain fall down from the sky. His wife was possessed of this miraculous power: When she sat down beside a pint[1] pot and vessel for curry and sauce she could serve the serving men with food; and so long as she did not get up, it was not exhausted. Their son was possessed of this miraculous power: He could take a bag containing a thousand[2], and give to each serving man six months' wages; and so long as he held it in his hand, it was not exhausted.

2. Their daughter-in-law was possessed of this miraculous power: When she sat down beside a four-bushel[3] basket she could give six months' rice to the serving men; and so long as she did not get up, it was not exhausted. Their slave was possessed of this miraculous power: When he ploughed with one plough-share seven furrows were formed.

3, 4. Now the Mâgadha king Seniya Bimbisâra heard: 'In Bhaddiya-nagara in our kingdom there dwells, they say, a householder named Me*nd*aka, who is possessed (&c., as in §§ 1, 2, down to the end).'

5. Then the Mâgadha king Seniya Bimbisâra said to a certain minister who had charge of general affairs: 'They say, good Sir, that in Bhaddiya-nagara (&c., as above). Go, good Sir, and find out about this. When you have seen it, it shall be the same as if I myself had seen it.'

'Even so, Lord,' said that minister, in assent, to the Mâgadha king Seniya Bimbisâra, and he set out for Bhaddiya-nagara with his fourfold host.

6. And proceeding straight on he came to Bhaddiya-nagara, and to the place where the householder

[1] A*lh*aka. See Rh. D., 'Ancient Coins and Measures,' p. 18.

[2] Ibid. p. 9 and note 4.

[3] Do*n*a. Ibid. p. 18.

Me*nd*aka was; and when he had come there, he said to the householder Me*nd*aka: 'I have received command from the king, "They say, good Sir (&c., as above, § 5)." Let us behold, O householder, your miraculous power.'

Then Me*nd*aka the householder bathed his head, and had his granary swept out, and sat down outside it. And showers of grain fell down from the sky and filled the granary.

'I have seen, O householder, your miraculous power. Let us see that of your wife.'

7. Then Me*nd*aka the householder gave command to his wife, 'Serve then the fourfold host with food.'

And the wife of Me*nd*aka the householder took her seat beside a pint pot and a vessel of sauces and curry, and served the fourfold host with food; and until she rose up it was not exhausted.

'I have seen, O householder, the miraculous power of your wife. Let us see that of your son.'

8. Then Me*nd*aka the householder gave command to his son, 'Pay then, my dear boy, six months' wages to the fourfold host.'

And the son of Me*nd*aka the householder took one bag containing a thousand, and paid the fourfold army six months' wages. And so long as he held it in his hand, it was not exhausted.

'I have seen, O householder, the miraculous power of your son. Let us see that of your daughter-in-law.'

9. Then Me*nd*aka the householder gave command to his daughter-in-law, 'Give, then, six months' rice to the fourfold host.'

And the daughter-in-law of Me*nd*aka the householder sat down beside one four-bushel basket, and provided the fourfold host with six months' rice. And so long as she did not get up, it was not exhausted.

'I have seen, O householder, the miraculous power of your daughter-in-law. Let us see that of your slave.'

'The miraculous power of my slave, Sir, must be seen in the field.'

'It is enough, O householder. I have seen the miraculous power of your slave.'

Then that minister returned again to Râ*g*agaha with his fourfold host, and went to the place where the Mâgadha king Seniya Bimbisâra was, and when he had come there he told the matter to the Mâgadha king Seniya Bimbisâra.

10. Now the Blessed One, when he had remained at Vesâli as long as he thought fit, went on his way to Bhaddiya with a great company of Bhikkhus, with one thousand two hundred and fifty Bhikkhus. And the Blessed One wandering straight on arrived at Bhaddiya. And there the Blessed One stayed in the *G*âtiyâvana.

11. And Me*nd*aka the householder heard: 'Behold, that Sama*n*a Gotama, of the Sakya clan, who left the Sakya tribe to adopt the religious life, is now arrived at Bhaddiya and is staying in the *G*âtiyâvana. Now regarding that venerable Gotama, such is the high reputation that has been noised abroad that he is said to be a fully-enlightened one, blessed, and worthy, abounding in wisdom and goodness, happy, with knowledge of the worlds, unsurpassed, who guides men as a driver curbs a bullock, a teacher of gods and men, a blessed Buddha. He by himself thoroughly understands, and sees, as it

were face to face, this universe, the world with its Devas, and with its Brahmas, and with its Mâras, and all creatures, Sama*n*as and Brâhma*n*as, gods and men: and he then makes that knowledge known to others. The truth doth he make known, both in the spirit and in the letter: lovely in its origin, lovely in its progress, lovely in its consummation. The higher life doth he proclaim, in all its purity and all its perfectness. Blessed is the sight of Arahats like that.'

12. Then Me*nd*aka the householder had a number of splendid carriages made ready, and mounting one of them he set out from Bhaddiya with the train of splendid carriages to visit the Blessed One.

And many Titthiyas saw Me*nd*aka the householder as he was coming from afar; and when they had seen him, they said to Me*nd*aka the householder:

'Whither, O householder, are you going?'

'I am going, Sirs, to visit the Blessed One, the Sama*n*a Gotama.'

'But why, O householder, do you, being a Kiriya-vâda, go out to visit the Blessed One who is an Akiriya-vâda? For, O householder, the Sama*n*a Gotama, who is an Akiriya-vâda, teaches Dhamma without the doctrine of action[1], and in this Dhamma he instructs his hearers.'

13. Then thought Me*nd*aka the householder: 'For a certainty that Blessed One must be an Arahat Buddha: since these Titthiyas are so jealous of him.' And he went on to the place where the Blessed One was, proceeding in the carriage as far

[1] See above, VI, 31, 5.

as the ground was passable for carriages, and then dismounting from the carriage, and going on foot. And when he had come there, he bowed down before the Blessed One, and took his seat on one side.

And when he was so seated the Blessed One preached (&c., as usual, for instance, I, 8, 2, 3, down to:) 'taken his refuge in him.'

'May the Blessed One consent to take his meal, together with the Bhikkhu-sa*m*gha, at my house to-morrow.'

The Blessed One consented by remaining silent.

14. Then Me*nd*aka the householder when he saw that the Blessed One had consented (&c., as usual, see VI, 18, 1, 2, down to:) sat down on the seat prepared for him.

15. Then the wife, and the son, and the daughter-in-law, and the slave of Me*nd*aka the householder went to the place where the Blessed One was: and when they had come there they bowed down before the Blessed One and took their seats on one side.

And the Blessed One preached to them (&c., as in § 13, down to:) 'taken their refuge in him.'

16. Then Me*nd*aka the householder served the Bhikkhu-sa*m*gha with the Buddha at their head (&c., as usual, down to:) sat down on one side.

And when he was so seated Me*nd*aka the householder said to the Blessed One: 'So long as the Blessed One shall stay at Bhaddiya, so long will I provide the Bhikkhu-sa*m*gha with the Buddha at their head with food every day.'

Then the Blessed One gladdened (&c., as usual, down to:) the Blessed One rose from his seat, and went away.

17. Now when the Blessed One had remained

at Bhaddiya as long as he thought fit, he went on, without informing Me*nd*aka the householder, to Aṅguttarâpa with a great company of Bhikkhus, with one thousand two hundred and fifty Bhikkhus.

And Me*nd*aka the householder heard: 'The Blessed One, they say, has gone on to Aṅguttarâpa with (&c., down to:) Bhikkhus.' And Me*nd*aka the householder gave command to his slaves and servants: 'Load then, my men, a quantity of salt and oil, and rice, and hard food, and come: and let one thousand two hundred and fifty cow-keepers come with one thousand two hundred and fifty cows. Wherever we find the Blessed One there will we supply him with fresh milk.'

18. And Me*nd*aka the householder came up with the Blessed One in a desert place on the way. And Me*nd*aka the householder went up to the place where the Blessed One was: and when he had come he stood on one side. And so standing, Me*nd*aka the householder said to the Blessed One: 'May the Blessed One consent to take his meal (&c., as usual, down to:) 'The time has come, and the meal is ready.'

19. And the Blessed One early in the morning (&c., down to:) sat down on the seat prepared for him.

Then Me*nd*aka the householder gave command to those thousand two hundred and fifty cow-keepers: 'Take then, my men, each of you a cow, and wait each of you upon a Bhikkhu, and provide him with fresh milk.'

And Me*nd*aka the householder waited upon the Bhikkhu-sa*m*gha with the Buddha at their head with his own hand, and satisfied them with sweet food, hard and soft, and with fresh milk.

The Bhikkhus, fearing to offend, would not take the milk:

'Take it, Bhikkhus, and drink it.'

20. And Me*nd*aka the householder, when he had waited with his own hand upon the Bhikkhu-sa*m*gha with the Buddha at their head, and had satisfied them with sweet food, hard and soft, and with fresh milk; and when the Blessed One had finished his meal, and had washed his hands and his bowl, took his seat on one side.

And, so sitting, Me*nd*aka the householder said to the Blessed One: 'There are desert ways, Lord, waterless and foodless, where it is not easy to travel without supplies for the journey. It would be well if the Blessed One were to allow the Bhikkhus to take supplies with them.'

Then the Blessed One gladdened (&c., as usual, down to:) rose from his seat, and went away.

21. And the Blessed One, in that connection, and on that account, after having delivered a religious discourse, said to the Bhikkhus:

'I allow you, O Bhikkhus, the five products of the cow;—milk, curds, ghee, buttermilk, and butter. There are, O Bhikkhus, desert ways, waterless and foodless, where it is not easy to travel without supplies for the journey. I allow you, O Bhikkhus, to provide yourselves with supplies for a journey;—rice for him who wants rice, beans for him who wants beans[1], salt for him who wants salt, molasses for him who wants molasses, oil for him who wants oil, ghee for him who wants ghee. There are, O Bhikkhus, faithful and converted men who deposit

[1] Two kinds of beans are mentioned, **mugga** and **mâsa**.

gold with a kappiya-kâraka[1], saying, "Provide whatever is allowable for this Bhikkhu." I allow you, O Bhikkhus, to accept whatever is allowable. But I do not say by that, O Bhikkhus, that you may, on any pretext whatsoever, accept or seek for gold.'

35.

1. Now the Blessed One proceeded straight on, on his alms-pilgrimage, to Âpa*n*a. And Keniya the ascetic[2] heard the saying, 'Behold! the Sama*n*a Gotama, who was born in the Sâkya clan, and who went forth from the Sâkya clan (to adopt the religious life), has arrived at Âpa*n*a, and is staying at Âpa*n*a. Now regarding that venerable Gotama, such is the high reputation that has been noised abroad that he is said to be a fully-enlightened one, blessed and worthy, abounding in wisdom and goodness, happy, with knowledge of the worlds, unsurpassed, who guides men as a driver curbs a bullock, a teacher of gods and men, a blessed Buddha. He by himself thoroughly understands, and sees, as it were face to face, this universe, the world with its Devas, and with its Brahmas, and with its Mâras, and all creatures, Sama*n*as and Brâhma*n*as, gods and men: and he then makes his knowledge known to others. The truth doth he make known, both in the spirit and in the letter:

[1] See above, chap. 17. 8.

[2] In Pâli *Ga*t*ila*; that is, 'one with long matted hair.' See our note on Mahâvagga I, 15, 1; and compare also Dîpava*m*sa I, 38; *G*âtaka I, 15, 84; Dhammapada, v. 141, and the passages quoted by Professor Oldenberg in his edition of the *K*ullavagga, p. 350, and by Dr. Rhys Davids in his 'Buddhist Birth Stories,' p. 185.

lovely in its origin, lovely in its progress, lovely in its consummation. The higher life doth he proclaim, in all its purity and all its perfectness. Blessed is the sight of Arahats like that[1]!' And Keniya the ascetic thought: 'What now should I have taken[2] to the Samana Gotama.'

2. And Keniya the ascetic thought: 'They who are the ancient *Ri*shis of the Brâhmans, the authors of the sacred verses, the utterers of the sacred verses, whose ancient form of words, so uttered chaunted or composed, the Brâhmans of to-day chaunt over again and repeat, intoning or reciting exactly as had been intoned or recited—to wit, A*tth*aka, Vâmaka, Vâmadeva, Vessâmitta, Yamataggi, Angirasa, Bhâradvâ*g*a, Vâse*tth*a, and Bhagu[3]—they were abstainers from food at night, and abstainers from food at the wrong time, yet they used to receive such things as drinks. (3.) Now the Samana Gotama is also an abstainer from food

[1] This is a stock phrase. Compare above VI, 34, 11, and the Tevi*gg*a Sutta I, 7, 46, and the passages quoted on the last by Rh. D., 'Buddhist Suttas,' p. 287.

[2] That is, as a present, the usual tribute of respect.

[3] The names of these *Ri*shis, and the above phrases from 'They who' &c. downwards, recur several times in the Tevi*gg*a Sutta. See Rh. D., 'Buddhist Suttas,' p. 172, &c. Most of these names are easily to be identified, being in Sanskrit Vâmadeva, Vi*s*vâmitra, *G*amadagni (who is only mentioned in this list in reference to Rig-veda III, 62, quoted from below. See also Oldenberg's note to *S*ânkhâyana's G*ri*hya-sûtra IV, 10 in Indische Studien XV, 153), Ângirasa, Bhâradvâ*g*a, Vasish*th*a, Ka*s*yapa, and Bh*ri*gu. The only doubtful names are Vâmaka and A*tth*aka. The latter must be Ash*t*aka, mentioned as the author of Rig-veda X, 104, unless it be supposed to be a corrupt reading under which some representation of Atri may lurk. Vâmaka is the only unintelligible form, for it would be difficult to see how that word could come to stand for the Vamra to whom Rig-veda X, 99 is ascribed.

at night, an abstainer from food at the wrong time[1]. It will be worthy of him too to receive such things as drinks. And when he had had a quantity of drinkables made ready he had them carried on pin-goes and went up to the place where the Blessed One was. And when he had come there, he greeted him; and after exchanging with him the greetings of friendship and civility, he stood by on one side. And so standing Keniya the ascetic spake thus to the Blessed One:

'May the Blessed One accept at my hands these drinkables.'

'Very good then, Keniya; give them to the Bhikkhus.'

The Bhikkhus, fearing to offend, would not receive them.

'Receive them, O Bhikkhus, and make use of them.'

4. Then Keniya the ascetic having, with his own hand, satisfied the Bhikkhu-sa*m*gha with the Buddha at their head with many drinkables until they refused any more, took his seat, when the Blessed One had washed his hands, and had laid aside the bowl, on one side. And when he was so seated the Blessed One taught and incited and aroused and gladdened Keniya the ascetic with religious discourse: and Keniya the ascetic, when he had been taught and incited and aroused and gladdened by the Blessed One with religious discourse, spake thus to the Blessed One:

'May the venerable Gotama grant to me the privilege of providing the to-morrow's meal for him, together with the company of the Bhikkhus.'

[1] See the eighth section of the *K*ûla-sîla.

5. 'Great, O Keniya, is the company of the Bhikkhus. Two hundred and fifty are the Bhikkhus in number. And thou art greatly devoted to the Brâhmans.'

Yet a second time spake Keniya the ascetic to the Blessed One thus:

'What though the company of the Bhikkhus, O Gotama, be great; and though two hundred and fifty be the number of the Bhikkhus. May the venerable Gotama grant to me the privilege of providing the to-morrow's meal for him, together with the company of the Bhikkhus.'

'Great, O Keniya (&c., as before).'

Yet a third time spake Keniya the ascetic to the venerable Gotama thus:

'What though the company of the Bhikkhus (&c., as before).'

Then the Blessed One granted, by remaining silent, his consent. And when Keniya the ascetic perceived that the Blessed One had granted his consent, he arose from his seat, and departed thence.

6. Then the Blessed One on that occasion, and in that connection, after he had delivered a religious discourse, addressed the Bhikkhus, and said:

'I allow you, O Bhikkhus, eight kinds of drinkable things: mango-syrup, and jambu-syrup, and plantain-syrup[1], and mo*k*a-syrup, and honey, and

[1] So Buddhaghosa; but it may also be cocoa-nut or cinnamon, according to Böhtlingk-Roth sub voce. Buddhaghosa's words are *Ko*k*a*-pânan ti a*tth*ika-kadali-phalehi kata-pâna*m*; and he explains mo*k*a by ana*tth*ikehi kadali-phalehi kata-pâna*m*. As kadali is the ordinary plantain or banana, which has no seeds, the meaning of the difference he makes between the two kinds is not clear. The expression eka*tth*ithâlapakka, at *G*âtaka I, 70, evidently rests on the same meaning of the word a*tth*i, which there also

grape-juice, and syrup made from the edible root of the water-lily[1], and phârusaka[2]-syrup. I allow you, O Bhikkhus, the juice of all fruits, except the juice prepared from corn[3]. I allow you, O Bhikkhus, drinks prepared from all leaves, except drinks prepared from potherbs[4]. I allow you, O Bhikkhus, drinks prepared from all flowers, except liquorice-juice[5]. I allow you, O Bhikkhus, the use of the juice of the sugar cane.'

7. And Keniya the ascetic, at the end of the night, had sweet food, both hard and soft, made ready at his hermitage: and he had the time announced to the Blessed One, saying, 'It is time, O Gotama, and the meal is ready.'

And the Blessed One, having put on his under robes early in the morning, went, duly bowled and robed, to the place where the hermitage of Keniya the ascetic was. And when he had arrived there, he sat down on the seat spread out for him, and with him the company of the Bhikkhus. Then

---

cannot be, as usual, seed; for there is no such thing as a palmyra fruit with one seed. See Rh. D.'s note on p. 94 of the 'Buddhist Birth Stories.'

[1] In the text read sâlûka.

[2] This is the Grewia Asiatica of Linnaeus. See Bohtlingk-Roth under parûsaka.

[3] Toddy and arrack are so prepared. The use of toddy was one of the famous Ten Points of the heretics at the Council of Vesâli. See below, *K*ullavagga XII, 1, 11. Buddhaghosa explains this as 'drink made from any one of the seven kinds of corn;' where the seven kinds referred to must be those mentioned in the Abhidhâna-ppadîpikâ, verses 450, 451.

[4] *D*âka = sâka. Compare our note below on VI, 36, 8, and *G*âtaka, ed. Fausböll, I, 308.

[5] Madhuka-puppha-rasa*m*; Madhuka is the Bassia Latifolia of Linnaeus.

Keniya the ascetic, with his own hand, offered to the company of the Bhikkhus with the Buddha at their head, and satisfied them with the sweet food, both hard and soft. And when the Blessed One had finished his meal and had washed his hands and his bowl, he (Keniya) took his seat on one side.

8. And when he was so seated the Blessed One pronounced the benediction on Keniya the ascetic in these verses:

'Of the offerings[1] the fire sacrifice is the chief, of sacred verses the chief is the Sâvitthi[2];

'Among men the king is chief, and of waters the ocean,

'Of constellations the moon is chief, and of heat-givers the sun,

'But of them, the conquering ones, who long after good, the Saṁgha, verily, is chief.'

And when the Blessed One had, in these verses, pronounced the benediction[3] on Keniya the ascetic, he rose from his seat, and departed thence[4].

36.

1. Now when the Blessed One had stayed at Âpana as long as he thought fit, he went on, on his pilgrimage, to Kusinârâ, with a great company

---

[1] Yaññâ. Compare above, I, 22, 4, and our note there (p. 138).

[2] This is of course the well-known verse Rig-veda III, 62, 10. The argumentum ad hominem here is a fresh confirmation of the view already expressed above in our note on I, 15, 1, that by the Gatilas are to be understood the orthodox Brâhman ascetics.

[3] Compare the Book of the Great Decease I, 31, and Gâtaka I, 119.

[4] §§ 7, 8 recur in the Sela Sutta (Sutta Nipâta, III, 7, 21, 22), where they stand in a much more appropriate context.

of Bhikkhus, with two hundred and fifty Bhikkhus. And the Mallas of Kusinârâ heard, saying, 'The Blessed One, they say, is coming to Kusinârâ with a great company of Bhikkhus, with two hundred and fifty Bhikkhus.' And they established a compact to the effect that whosoever went not forth to welcome the Blessed One, should pay a fine of five hundred (pieces[1]).

Now at that time there was a certain Malla, by name Roga, who was a friend of the venerable Ânanda's. And the Blessed One, continuing in due course his pilgrimage, arrived at Kusinârâ.

2. Then the Mallas of Kusinârâ went forth to welcome the Blessed One. And Roga the Malla, having gone forth to welcome the Blessed One, went on to the place where the venerable Ânanda was: and when he had come there, he saluted the venerable Ânanda, and stood by on one side. And to him, so standing, the venerable Ânanda spake thus:

'This is most excellent of thee, friend Roga, that thou hast come forth to welcome the Blessed One!'

'It is not I, O Ânanda, who am much moved[2] by the Buddha, or the Dhamma, or the Samgha. But by the clansmen a compact was made to the effect that whosoever went not forth to welcome the Blessed One should pay a fine of five hundred (pieces). So that it was through fear of being fined

[1] That is, the square kahâpânas of copper or bronze, figured in the Bârhut bas-reliefs, and mentioned in the Dhammapada. See Rh. D.'s 'Ancient Coins and Measures,' p. 4, § 5.

[2] Bahukato; only found in this passage. Buddhaghosa says, Nâham bhante Ânanda bahukato ti nâham Buddhâdi-gata-pasâda-bahumânena idhâgato ti dassetî ti. Here Buddhâdi means the Buddha, the Dhamma, and the Samgha.

by my clansmen that even I went forth to welcome the Blessed One.'

Then the venerable Ânanda was filled with sorrow, thinking, 'How can Roga the Malla speak thus?'

3. And the venerable Ânanda went up to the place where the Blessed One was: and when he had come there, he saluted the Blessed One, and took his seat on one side, and so sitting the venerable Ânanda spake to the Blessed One thus:

'This Roga the Malla, Lord, is a very distinguished and well-known person. Great would be the efficacy[1] of the adherence given by well-known persons like him to this doctrine and discipline. May the Blessed One be pleased so to act, that Roga the Malla shall become devoted to this doctrine and discipline.'

'Now that, Ânanda, is not a hard thing for the Tathâgata—so to act that Roga the Malla should become devoted to this doctrine and discipline.'

4. Then the Blessed One suffused Roga the Malla with the feeling of his love[2], and rising from his seat he entered into his dwelling-place. And Roga the Malla, overcome by the Blessed One by the sense of his love, just as a young calf follows the kine, so did he go on from dwelling-place to dwelling-place, and from apartment to apartment, asking the Bhikkhus:

'Where then, Sirs, is that Blessed One dwelling now, the Arahat Buddha? For we desire to visit that Blessed One, the Arahat Buddha.'

[1] Mahiddhiyo, where, as so often elsewhere, Iddhi has no supernatural connotation. Compare the passages quoted above in our note on I, 15, 2.

[2] Compare Rh. D., 'Buddhist Birth Stories, p. 112.

'This, friend, is his dwelling-place, the door of which is shut. Go up therefore quietly, and without crossing the threshold, enter into the verandah, and knock at the cross-bar. The Blessed One will open the door to thee.'

5. So Ro*g*a the Malla did so, and the Blessed One opened the door. And Ro*g*a the Malla entered into the dwelling-place, and saluted the Blessed One and took his seat on one side. And to Ro*g*a the Malla sitting there the Blessed One preached in due course: that is to say, he talked to him of giving; of moral conduct; of heaven; of the danger of vanity, of the corruption of lusts; and of the advantages of renunciation. When the Blessed One saw that the mind of Ro*g*a the Malla was prepared, impressible, free from obstacles to understanding the truth, elated, and believing, then he preached that which is the principal doctrine of the Buddhas, namely, Suffering, the Cause of suffering, the Cessation of suffering, and the Path. And just as a clean cloth, free from black specks, properly takes the dye, thus did Ro*g*a the Malla, even while sitting there, obtain the pure and spotless eye of the truth (that is, the knowledge that), 'Whatsoever is subject to the condition of beginning, that is subject also to the condition of cessation.' And Ro*g*a the Malla, having seen the truth, having mastered the truth, having understood the truth, having penetrated the truth, having overcome uncertainty, having dispelled all doubts, having gained full knowledge, dependent on no one else for knowledge of the doctrine of the Teacher, thus spake to the Blessed One:

'May the venerable one be pleased, Lord, to

receive from me alone, and not from others, the requisites of the Order: that is to say, robes, and food, and dwelling-places, and medicine for the use of the sick.'

'Whosoever, Roga, with the knowledge of a disciple, and with the insight of a disciple[1], has perceived the Truth, even as thou hast, they also will think, "Oh! that the venerable ones would be pleased to receive from me alone, and not from others, the requisites of the order." Therefore, Roga, they shall receive them from you, indeed, but also from others.'

6. Now at that time a certain succession had been fixed, in which the inhabitants of Kusinârâ should each in succession provide food for the Samgha. And it occurred to Roga the Malla, who had not received a place in the succession, thus: 'What if I were to inspect the Samgha's storehouse, and provide whatever I found wanting in the storehouse?' And on inspecting the storehouse, he found there no potherbs, and no meal[2].

Then Roga the Malla went up to the place where the venerable Ânanda was, and when he had come there, he spake to the venerable Ânanda thus:

'It occurred to me (&c., as before, down to:) and no meal. If, Ânanda, I were to provide potherbs and meal, would the Blessed One accept them at my hands?'

7. The venerable Ânanda told this thing to the Blessed One.

---

[1] Sekhena, as opposed to asekhena. That is, with the knowledge of one who is not himself an Arahat. See our note on Mahâvagga I, 7, 13.

[2] See the note at the end of § 8.

'Very good, then, Ânanda. Let him provide them.'

'Very good, then, Roga. Provide them accordingly.'

Then Roga the Malla at the end of the night, after he had had a quantity of potherbs and meal made ready, offered them to the Blessed One, saying, 'May the Blessed One accept at my hands the potherbs and the meal.'

'Very good, then, Roga. Present them to the Bhikkhus.'

The Bhikkhus, fearing to offend, did not accept them.

'Accept them, O Bhikkhus, and make use of them.'

8. Then Roga the Malla, with his own hand, offered to the company of the Bhikkhus with the Buddha at their head, and satisfied them with the potherbs and the meal. And when the Blessed One had finished his meal, and had cleansed his hands and the bowl, he (Roga) took his seat on one side. And when he was so seated the Blessed One taught, and incited, and conversed, and gladdened Roga the Malla with religious discourse. And Roga the Malla, when he had been taught, &c., rose from his seat and departed thence.

And the Blessed One, on that occasion, and in that connection, when he had delivered a religious discourse, addressed the Bhikkhus, and said:

'I allow you, O Bhikkhus, all kinds of potherbs[1], and all kinds of meal[2].'

---

[1] Sabbañ *k*a *t*âkan (sic) ti sappi-âdîhi pakka*m* vâ apakka*m* vâ ya*m* kiñ*k*i *t*âka*m* (B.)

[2] Pi*tth*a-khâdaniyan ti pi*tth*amaya*m* khâdaniya*m* (B.)

37.

1. Now the Blessed One, when he had stayed at Kusinârâ as long as he thought fit, went on, on his pilgrimage to Âtumâ, with a great company of the Bhikkhus, with two hundred and fifty Bhikkhus. And at that time there was dwelling at Âtumâ a certain man, who had entered the Order in his old age, and who had previously been a barber[1]. He had two sons, handsome[2], skilled in discourse[3], able, fully educated in all the arts which belonged to the barbers' craft handed down to them by their teachers[4].

2. Now this dotard[5] heard the news: 'The Blessed One, they say, is coming to Âtumâ with

[1] This man is identified by the tradition with the Subhadda mentioned in the accounts of the Great Decease, and of the First Council. See Rh. D.'s note on Mahâ-parinibbâna Sutta VI, 40.

[2] Buddhaghosa understands this word, which he reads differently, as meaning 'sweet-voiced.' Mañkukâ (sic) ti madhura-vakanâ. We follow the ordinary meaning of mañgu.

[3] Here again Buddhaghosa gives a technical meaning to the word, unsupported by the derivation. He says, Patibhâneyyakâ ti sake sippe patibhâna-sampannâ. This agrees with Childers's rendering (sub voce) of Gâtaka I, 60; but compare Sigâlovâda Sutta, ed. Grimblot, p. 309.

[4] On the idiomatic phrase sakam âkariyakam, compare Mahâparinibbâna Sutta III, 7, 8 (text ed. Childers, pp. 24 and following).

[5] Literally, 'this man who had gone forth (from the household state into the homeless life of the Order) in his old age.' But it is impossible to repeat this long phrase throughout the narrative as is done in the Pâli, where the meaning of the phrase is expressed by one compound. As the Pâli word vuddha-pabbagito connotes contempt, and even censure (men entering the Order in their old age being often represented as incapable of appreciating even the simplest principles of the 'doctrine and discipline'), the use of the word 'dotard' in our translation seems to retain the spirit of the Pâli epithet, while avoiding the inconvenient length of a literal version.

a great company of the Bhikkhus, with two hundred and fifty Bhikkhus.' Then that dotard spake thus to his sons: 'They say the Blessed One is coming, my children[1], to Âtumâ with a great company of Bhikkhus, with two hundred and fifty Bhikkhus. Go, therefore, my children, and taking your barbers' lad[2] with you, collect in quart pots from house to house, salt, and oil, and rice, and meal. And we will prepare congey for the Blessed One when he has arrived.'

3. Very good, Father, said they, and (did so). And when people saw those young men, of pleasing appearance, and skilful in discourse, so acting, then even those who were not willing to be led into joining in the act were led to join in it; and being so led, they gave abundantly. So the young men collected a great quantity of salt, and oil, and rice, and meal.

4. And the Blessed One in due course arrived in his journey at Âtumâ; and there at Âtumâ the Blessed One stayed at the Threshing-floor. And that dotard, when the night was far spent, had much congey made ready, and offered it to the Blessed One, saying, 'May the Blessed One accept the congey at my hands.'

Now the Tathâgatas sometimes ask about what they know; sometimes they do not ask about what they know. They understand the right time when to ask, and they understand the right time when not to ask. The Tathâgatas put questions full of

---

[1] Tâta, not tâtâ. It will be seen that Childers is wrong in supposing that the plural form is always used when more than one person is addressed.

[2] Khura-bha*n*da*m*; not 'shaving materials;' compare hatthi-bha*n*d*o* and assa-bha*n*d*o* at Mahâvagga I, 61, and below, § 5.

sense, not void of sense: to what is void of sense, the bridge is pulled down for the Tathâgatas. For two purposes the blessed Buddhas put questions to the Bhikkhus—when they intend to preach the Truth, and when they intend to institute a rule of conduct to their disciples[1]. And the Blessed One spake thus to that dotard, 'Whence, O Bhikkhu, is this congey?'

Then that dotard informed the Blessed One of the whole matter.

5. The Blessed Buddha rebuked him, saying, 'This is improper, O foolish one, not according to rule, unsuitable, unworthy of a Sama*n*a, unbecoming, and ought not to be done. How can you, O foolish one, having gone forth (from the world into the Order), instigate others to do what is unlawful. This will not conduce, O foolish one, to the conversion of the unconverted.'

And when he had rebuked him, and had delivered a religious discourse, he addressed the Bhikkhus, and said: 'One who has gone forth ought not, O Bhikkhus, to instigate others to an unlawful act[2]. Whosoever does so, is guilty of a dukka*t*a. And one, O Bhikkhus, who has formerly been a barber is not to keep a barber's boy. Whosoever does so, is guilty of a dukka*t*a.'

38.

1. And when the Blessed One had tarried at Âtumâ as long as he thought fit, he went on his

[1] See Mahâvagga I, 31, 5.

[2] Unlawful, because one Bhikkhu may not beg for others, and it is unlawful for those others to accept things thus procured.

journey towards Sâvatthi. And in due course, journeying straight on, he arrived at Sâvatthi, and there, at Sâvatthi, the Blessed One stayed in the Ârama of Anâtha-pi*nd*ika.

Now at that time there was in Sâvatthi great abundance of solid food in the shape of fruits. And the question arose among the Bhikkhus, 'Has, now, the Blessed One permitted the use of fruits as solid food, or has he not?'

They told this thing to the Blessed One.

'I allow you, O Bhikkhus, all solid food in the shape of fruits.'

39.

1. Now at that time, seedlings belonging to the Sa*m*gha grew upon private ground, and seedlings belonging to private persons grew upon ground which was the property of the Sa*m*gha.

They told this thing to the Blessed One.

'Of seedlings belonging to the Sa*m*gha, grown upon private ground, half the produce, O Bhikkhus, you may have, when you have given a part to the private owner. Of seedlings belonging to a private person, grown upon ground the property of the Sa*m*gha, you may have the use, when you have given a part to the private owner[1].'

40.

1. Now at that time there used to arise among the Bhikkhus a fear lest they should offend in

[1] Buddhaghosa explains the 'part' (bhâga*m*) as the twelfth part, which, he says, is in accordance with the ancient custom of India. Used absolutely, as in this passage, bhâga usually means 'half.'

some particular or other, they thinking, 'Has this been permitted by the Blessed One, or has it not?'

They told this thing to the Blessed One.

'Whatsoever, O Bhikkhus, has not been disallowed by me in the words, "This beseems you not," then, if that thing is in accord with what is unlawful, and is contrary to what is lawful, that is not lawful. Whatsoever has not been disallowed by me with the words, "This beseems you not," then, if that thing is in accord with what is lawful, and is contrary to what is unlawful, that is lawful.

'And whatsoever, O Bhikkhus, has not been allowed by me with the words, "This beseems you," then, if that thing is in accord with what is lawful, and is contrary to what is unlawful, that is not lawful. Whatsoever has not been allowed by me with the words, "This beseems you," then, if that thing is in accord with what is lawful, and is contrary to what is unlawful, that is lawful[1].'

2. Then the Bhikkhus thought: 'Is food that may be eaten till the first watch of the night[2] lawful, or not, when mixed with food that ought to be eaten before noon on the same day? Is food that may be eaten at any time within seven days[3] lawful, or not, when mixed with food that ought to be eaten before noon on the same day? Is food that may be eaten at any time during life[4] lawful, or not, when mixed with food that ought to be eaten

[1] The formal expressions referred to in these two paragraphs are precisely the expressions to which, in the Book of the Great Decease VI, 40, and in the *K*ullavagga XI, 1, 1, Subhadda is stated to have taken such serious objection.

[2] This refers to certain medicines; see Mahâvagga VI, 1, 5.

[3] This also refers to certain medicines; see the 23rd Nissaggiya.

[4] What this refers to is unknown to us.

before noon on the same day? Is food that may be eaten at any time within seven days lawful, or not, when mixed with food that may be eaten at any time during life? Is food that may be eaten at any time during life lawful, or not, when mixed with food that may be eaten at any time within seven days?'

They told this thing to the Blessed One.

3. 'Food that may be eaten up to the first watch of the night, or food that may be eaten at any time within seven days, or food that may be eaten at any time during life, is lawful, O Bhikkhus, when mixed with food that ought to be eaten before noon on the same day, up till noon-time, and it is not lawful after noon-time. Food that may be eaten at any time within seven days, or food that may be eaten at any time during life, is lawful, O Bhikkhus,—when it has been mixed with food that may be eaten up to the first watch of the night,—up till the first watch of the night, and is not lawful after the first watch of the night. Food that may be eaten at any time during life, is lawful, O Bhikkhus,—when it has been mixed with food that may be eaten at any time within seven days,—at any time within seven days, and is not lawful beyond seven days[1].'

Here ends the sixth Khandhaka on Medicaments.

[1] Buddhaghosa says that this holds good if the two are so mixed that the taste (rasu) has become one (sambhinna). If the two are not so mixed, then they may be divided, and the part allowable during the longer period may be enjoyed up to the end of that period. See I, 20, 9; V, 2, 1; VI, 16, 3; VIII, 1, 24, and the notes there.

SEVENTH KHANDHAKA.

(THE KA*TH*INA CEREMONIES.)

1.

1. Now at that time the Blessed One was staying at Sâvatthi, in the *G*etavana, Anâthapi*nd*ika's Grove. And at that time about thirty Pâ*th*eyyaka Bhikkhus[1],

---

[1] Buddhaghosa says, 'Pâ*th*eyya (the Berlin MS. reads Pâveyya) is the name of a kingdom situated to the west of the Kosala country. This passage refers to Bhikkhus who dwelt there. The Bhatta-vaggiya Theras (so the Berlin MS.; query Satta-vaggiya), who were brothers of the Kosala king, sons of the same father, are here alluded to.'

But with which of the many kingdoms 'to the west of the Kosala country' are we to identify Pâ*th*eyya? The word does not occur in the stock list, found in different parts of the Pâli Pi*t*akas, of the sixteen Mahâ-*g*anapadâ; that is to say, Aṅga, Magadha, Kâsi, Kosala, Va*gg*i, Malla, *K*etiya, Va*m*sa, Kuru, Pañ*k*âla, Ma*kkh*a, Sûrasena, Assaka, Avanti, Gandhâra, Kambo*g*a. The account of the Council at Vesâli gives us a hint as to the right answer to the above question; for the Thera Sambhûta, who took part in that Council, is called a Pâ*th*eyyaka in *K*ullavagga XII, 2, 7, and is also said at *K*ullavagga XII, 1, 8 to have lived Ahogaṅge Pabbate. The position of this hill is further described in the Mahâva*m*sa as being on the upper Ganges—uddhagaṅgâya .... Ahogaṅgamhi pabbate (p. 39, ed. Turnour). Then again in *K*ullavagga XII, 1, 7 the Thera Yasa, when wishing to put himself in communication with the Bhikkhus in Pâ*th*eyya and in other places, goes to Kosambî as the most convenient meeting-place for Bhikkhus coming from the East. The other places mentioned in that passage in juxta-position with Pâ*th*eyya would seem to show that Pâ*th*eyya, with Pâ*k*îna, Avanti, and Dakkhi*n*âpatha, is one of the principal divisions into which India, as then known, was divided; and that it includes most, if not all, of the great westerly kingdoms of

who were all dwellers in the forest, all living on alms, all dressed in rags from the dust heap, all having only three robes each, when they were on the way to Sâvatthi to visit the Blessed One, at the time when the period for entering upon Vassa was at hand, were unable to reach Sâvatthi in time to spend the Vassa there, and stayed at Sâketa on the way for the Vassa. And they spent the period of Vassa in discomfort, thinking, 'Our Blessed One is staying near us, six leagues from here, and we are not able to visit the Blessed One.'

And when, after three months, those Bhikkhus had completed their Vassa residence, and had held their Pavâranâ, they went on to the place where the Blessed One was, at Sâvatthi, in the Getavana, Anâthapindika's Grove, while the rain was falling, and the waters were gathering[1], and the swamps were forming, and their robes were all drenched, and they were weary. And when they had arrived, they saluted the Blessed One, and took their seats on one side.

2. Now it is the custom of the blessed Buddhas to greet kindly Bhikkhus who have just arrived. And the Blessed One said to those Bhikkhus[2]:

'Do things go well with you, O Bhikkhus? Do

Kuru, Pañkâla, &c., which are the last eight of the sixteen kingdoms in the stock list above referred to. Probably the literal meaning of Pâtheyya is 'western' (Sans. pratyañk). In the Suttavibhanga (Pâkittiya 34) merchants are mentioned who are travelling from Râgagaha to the Patiyâloka, which must mean 'the western country,' just as Patiyârâma (Dîpav. 17, 11) means 'the western Ârâma.'

[1] Udaka-samgahe 'ti udakena samgahite ghatite samsatthe thale ka ninne ka ekodakibhûte 'ti attho (B.).

[2] Compare IV, 1, 8, and foll.

you get enough to support yourselves with? Have you kept Vassa well, in unity, and in concord, and without quarrel, and have you not suffered from want of food?'

'Things go well with us, Lord; we get enough to support ourselves with, Lord; we have kept Vassa, Lord, in unity, and in concord, and without quarrel, and have not suffered from want of food. When we were on our way, Lord, about thirty Pâ*th*eyyaka Bhikkhus, to Sâvatthi to visit the Blessed One, we were unable to reach Sâvatthi in time (&c., as in § 1, down to:). And when, after three months. Lord, we had completed our Vassa residence, and had held our Pavâra*n*â, we have made our way, while the rain was falling, and the waters were gathering, and the swamps were forming; and our robes were all drenched; and we have become weary.'

3. Then the Blessed One in that connection, having delivered a religious discourse, addressed the Bhikkhus, and said[1]:

[1] As has been remarked in a previous note (to the first Nissaggiya Pâ*k*ittiya Rule) some of the details of these Ka*th*ina ordinances are at present difficult to understand. But the general meaning of them is already clear. Immediately after the Pavâra*n*â, the ceremony by which the Vassa residence is closed, there follows a distribution of the robes belonging to the local Sa*m*gha, (that is, the portion of the Order dwelling within one boundary,) to the particular Bhikkhus composing the Sa*m*gha. This distribution commences with the ka*th*in-atthâra, atthâra, 'spreading out,' not being used here literally for spreading out on the ground or otherwise, but in a secondary, juristic sense. And the act performed receives the technical name atthâra by a process of putting a part for the whole, the spreading out in the sun (see our note, p. 18) for the whole ceremony. We translate the term according to the context, sometimes by 'spreading out,' sometimes by 'ceremony,' sometimes by 'dedication.'

'I prescribe, O Bhikkhus, that the Ka*th*ina ceremony shall be performed by Bhikkhus when

---

The Ka*th*ina, literally 'hard,' is the stock of cotton cloth provided by the faithful to be made up into robes for the use of the Sa*m*gha during the ensuing year. The whole of this cotton cloth must be dyed, sewn together, and made into robes, and then formally declared to be (not only common property, Sa*m*ghika, but) available for immediate distribution—all on one and the same day. The object of this was that the Sa*m*gha, or at least a quorum of the Sa*m*gha, being able to be present throughout, there would be less chance of any mistake by which what was intended equally for all might come to be unequally divided among a few. All the Brethren who have kept their Vassa within the limits of the district within which the particular Sa*m*gha lives (and therefore technically called an âvâsa, 'residence'), and who have taken part in the Pavâra*n*â, are entitled to share in the distribution.

(Buddhaghosa says, 'Ettha kathinatthâra*m* ke labhanti ke na labhanti. Ga*n*avasena tâva pa*kkh*ima-ko*n*yâ pa*ñk*a *g*anâ (for at least five must be present to make a Pavâra*n*â legal, Mahâvagga IX, 4, 1) . . . . vu*tth*avassavasena purimikâya vassa*m* upagantvâ pa*th*ama-pavâra*n*âya pavâritâ labhanti.')

There can of course be no ka*th*in-atthâra if there is no ka*th*ina; and, under certain restrictions laid down in the Nissaggiya Pâ*k*ittiya Rules, laymen were allowed to give robes for the special use of a particular Bhikkhu. If, however, a layman was desirous of giving the much more meritorious gift of a Ka*th*ina to the whole community, then he is to present the cloth in the early morning to a properly constituted meeting of the Sa*m*gha, and the Ka*th*ina ceremony has to be gone through. All the Brethren living within the boundary have to be present, and to take part in the work of making the cotton cloth up into robes; and if there is any danger of the work not being concluded before the day is over, even the most senior Bhikkhus, or the most revered for their learning or insight, must lend a hand. Then follows the distribution so far only as is set forth in the next section (§ 4) and in the note to it.

Now it would often happen that, at the end of the rainy season of Vassa, the last year's robes of some of the Bhikkhus would be worn out. And yet no laymen would come forward to give a Ka*th*ina until some time after the Vassa residence had closed. But

they have completed their Vassa. And five things are allowable to you, O Bhikkhus, after the Ka*th*ina ceremony has been held—going for alms to the houses of people who have not invited you[1], going

if any one did offer a Ka*th*ina, and the ceremony was duly performed, then each Bhikkhu had a right to supply his actual needs from the robes made out of the Ka*th*ina. He need not do so at once. His want might not be pressing, or might not even arise till afterwards. During such an interval the five privileges (Ânisa*m*sâ) mentioned in this section (§ 3) are accorded to the Bhikkhus, though they would be against the rules in force during the rest of the year.

But if the Bhikkhu kept on postponing his choice would the privileges accorded by this section hold good even during the whole year? Could the Bhikkhu, by his mere abstention, thus bring about a practical abrogation of the general rules? Not so, for the five privileges are in their turn suspended by any one of the eight things mentioned below in § 7.

We may add that at the present time in Burma and Ceylon, the robes for the Bhikkhus are usually provided in accordance with the rules regulating gifts to particular Bhikkhus. But the gift of a Ka*th*ina is still by no means uncommon. See Spence Hardy's 'Eastern Monachism,' pp. 121 and foll. There is probably, however, very seldom any necessity for the Bhikkhus to avail themselves of any of the five privileges, except the last.

[1] This privilege is one of the exceptions allowed, in the Pâtimokkha, to the 46th Pâ*k*ittiya. Bhikkhus were allowed, as a general rule, to pass through a village, with their alms-bowls in their hands, in order to give any disciple who wished to do so the opportunity of giving them food. (To describe this procedure by our word 'begging,' as is so often done, is, to say the least, misleading.) The 46th Pâ*k*ittiya lays down, in certain circumstances, a restriction on this general rule. The present section removes that restriction during the period of Ka*th*in-atthâra; in order, according to Buddhaghosa (see the note on Pâ*k*. 46), to prevent the stock of robes falling short. That is, apparently, with the hope that a freer intercourse than usual between Bhikkhus and laity might lead to a gift of a Ka*th*ina when it was urgently required.

Here Buddhaghosa says simply, 'Anâmanta-*k*âro 'ti yâva ka*th*ina*m* na uddhariyati tâva anâmantetvâ.' Âmanteti must be equal to âpu*kkh*ati. Compare Böhtlingk-Roth under âmantra*n*a.

for alms without wearing the usual set of three robes[1], going for alms in a body of four or more[2], possessing as many robes as are wanted[3], and whatever number of robes shall have come to hand, that shall belong to them (that is, to the Bhikkhus entitled, by residence and otherwise, to share in the distribution[4]).

'And thus, O Bhikkhus, is the Ka*th*ina to be dedicated.

4. 'Let a learned, competent Bhikkhu proclaim

[1] This privilege is granted as a relaxation of the 2nd Nissaggiya. Buddhaghosa says, 'Asamâdâna-*k*âro 'ti ti-*k*ivara*m* asamâdâya *k*ara-*nam* *k*ivara-vippavâso kappissatiti attho.' Compare Mahâvagga VIII, 23, 3. It will be seen that the wording of the Pâtimokkha Rule is not inconsistent with the rule laid down here.

[2] This is a relaxation of the 32nd Pâ*k*ittiya, and is mentioned in that rule.

[3] This would seem to be a relaxation of the 1st Pâ*k*ittiya. Though it is not referred to there in terms, it is implied in the clause by which the operation of the rule is postponed till after the Ka*th*ina has been 'taken up,' i. e. till each Bhikkhu has actually received his share, or otherwise lost his claim to it. Till that has taken place, a Bhikkhu may use (temporarily, and without actually appropriating them) as many robes as he likes. B. says, 'Yâvadattha-*k*ivaran ti yâvatâ *k*ivarena attho tâvatakam anadhi*tth*ita*m* avi-kappita*m* (compare Sutta-vibhaṅga Niss. I, 3, 1) kappissatîti attho.'

[4] That is, according to Buddhaghosa, either those belonging to a Bhikkhu who has died, or those belonging to the Sa*m*gha in any way. This shows that at the division not only the robes made out of the gift of a Ka*th*ina were to be included, but whatever robes had not been given as intended specially for some one Bhikkhu. As to the actual practice now in Ceylon, compare Spence Hardy, loc. cit. Buddhaghosa says here: 'Yo *k*a tattha *k*ivar-uppâdo tattha ka*th*inatthata-simâya mataka-*k*ivara*m* vâ hotu sa*m*gha*m* uddissa dinna*m* vâ sa*m*ghikena tatr' uppâdena âbhata*m* vâ yena kena*k*i âkârena ya*m* sa*m*ghika*m* *k*ivara*m* uppaggati ta*m* tesa*m* bhavissatiti attho.' The use of the pronoun nesa*m* at the end of the rule is awkward, following after vo; but the meaning as translated is not open to doubt.

the following ñatti before the Samgha: "This Kathina-cloth has become the property of the Samgha. If the Samgha is ready, let the Samgha hand over the Kathina-cloth to such and such a Bhikkhu to spread out the Kathina. This is the ñatti. Let the Samgha, reverend Sirs, hear me. This Kathina-cloth has become the property of the Samgha. The Samgha hands it over to such and such a Bhikkhu to spread out the Kathina. If the Samgha approves of the handing over of the Kathina to such and such a Bhikkhu for spreading it out, let it remain silent. The Samgha approves thereof. Therefore does it remain silent. Thus I understand[1]."

5. 'Now thus, O Bhikkhus, has the Kathina ceremony been duly held; and thus has it not been duly held[2].

[1] This formula is one of those included in the collection entitled Kammavâkam. It appears from Minayeff (Prâtimoksha, pp. 75, 76) that the Bhikkhu so appointed superintends the processes of dyeing, sewing, &c. When the new robes are ready for wear, he lays aside one of his old robes which has been worn out (pakkuddharitvâ), and chooses for himself one of the new ones (navam adhitthahitvâ), saying as he does so, 'imâya samghâtiyâ (or, as the case may be, uttarâsangena, antaravâsakena) kathinam attharâmi.' This speech shows the technical application of the verb attharati in this connection. He then points out the remaining robes to the Bhikkhus there present, specifying which he thinks fit for the elder, and which for the younger members of the Order (Theras and Navakas); but not assigning further any particular robes to particular Bhikkhus. Finally he calls upon the Samgha for their formal approval of his procedure (compare the closing words of §§ 5, 6). But when they have given it, the distribution is not at an end. The time has only come when each of the Bhikkhus can transmute his claim to an undivided share into the actual possession of a divided share. Until he does so, the Kathina privileges set out in § 3 are allowed to him.

[2] The formal permission to each Bhikkhu to take his share is

'When, O Bhikkhus, has it not been duly held?'

'The Ka*th*ina ceremony has not been duly held when the stuff has only been marked (for the purposes of measurement)[1]: when it has only been washed: when it has only been calculated (to see how many robes it will make): when it has only been cut out: when it has only been pieced together[2]: when it has only been sewn in lengths[3]: when it has only been marked[4]: when it has only been made strong (in the seams)[5]: when it has only

---

not completed by any one of the following acts having been performed. The technical terms of the tailor's craft are, as will be seen, by no means easy to follow.

[1] Ullikhita-mattenâ 'ti dighato *k*a puthulato *k*a pamâ*n*a-gaha*n*a-mattena. Pamâ*n*a*m* hi ga*n*hanto tassa tassa padesassa sa*ñg*ânanattha*m* nakhâdîhi vâ pari*kkh*eda*m* dassento ullikhati, nalâ*t*âdisu vâ gha*m*sati. Tasmâ ta*m* pamâ*n*a-gaha*n*a*m* ullikhita-mattan ti vu*kk*ati (B.).

[2] Bandhana-mattenâ 'ti mogha-suttak-âropana-mattena (B.). Mogha-suttakâni, 'false threads,' are threads put in the cloth to show where it is to be cut or sewn. See Buddhaghosa on *K*ullavagga V, 11, 3 (p. 317 of H. O.'s edition). Our clause therefore means temporarily pieced together as the commencement of the tailoring work.

[3] Ova*tt*iya (sic) -kara*n*a-mattenâ 'ti mogha-suttakânusârena dîgha-sibbita-mattena (B.). Sewn in lengths along the lines of the false threads mentioned in the last note. The word occurs also in Mahâvagga VIII, 14, 2; and in *K*ullavagga V, 1, 2 we are told that the *Kh*abbaggiya Bhikkhus ova*tt*ika*m* dhârenti. Buddhaghosa says there vigg*h*ita-kara*n*a*m* ova*tt*ikâ.

[4] By joining on a little piece of cloth. Ka*n*d*u*sa-kara*n*a-mattenâ 'ti muddiya-pa*tt*a bandhana-mattena, says Buddhaghosa.

[5] Da*l*h*i-kara*n*a-mattenâ 'ti dve *k*imilikâyo (MS. *k*ilimikâyo) ekato katvâ sibbita-mattena: athavâ pa*th*ama-*k*imilikâ gha*tt*etvâ *th*apitâ hoti, ka*th*ina-sâ*t*aka*m* tassâ ku*kkh*i-*k*imilika*m* katvâ sappita- (read sibbita-) mattenâ 'ti pi attho. Mahâ-pa*kk*ariya*m* pakati-*k*ivarassa upassaya-dânenâ 'ti vutta*m*. Kurundiya*m* pakatipa*tt*a-*k*ivara*m* dupa*tt*a*m* kâtum ku*kkh*i-*k*imilika*m* alliyâpana-mattenâ 'ti vutta*m* (B.). On *k*imilikâ compare Minayeff's 'Prâtimoksha,' p. 87.

been strengthened by a braid[1] or by a binding[2] along the back, or by being doubled in parts[3]: when it has only been put into the dye[4]: when the decision (by the presiding Bhikkhu, as to which robes he will take for himself) has been made (but not been carried out[5]): when there has been talk (about the merit acquired by presenting the Samgha with cloth, and the donor has been induced thereby to show his liberality[6]): when the gift is only a temporary one[7]: when the ceremony has been postponed[8]:

[1] Anuvâta-karana-mattenâ 'ti pitthi-anuvâta-âropana-mattena (B.). Compare VIII, 21, 1.

[2] Paribhanda-karana-mattenâ 'ti kukkhi-anuvâta-âropana-mattena (B.). Compare VIII, 21, 1.

[3] Ovattheyya (sic) -karana-mattenâ 'ti âgantuka-patt'-âropana-mattena: kathina-kivarato vâ pattam gahetvâ aññasmim akathina-kivare patt'-âropana-mattena (B.).

[4] Kambala-maddana-mattenâ 'ti ekavâram yeva ragane pakkhittena danta-vannena pandu-palâsa-vannena vâ: sake pana sakim vâ dvikkhattum vâ rattam (MS. ratthum) pi saruppam hoti vattati (B.).

[5] Or perhaps, according to some commentators, when it has been decided to accept the gift as a Kathina, that is, when it has been decided that the cloth is of a suitable kind to make robes out of. Buddhaghosa says: Nimitta-katenâ 'ti iminâ dussena kathinam attharissâmiti evam nimittakatena. Ettakam eva Parivâre vuttam. Atthakathâsu pana ayam sâtako sundaro, sakkâ iminâ kathinam attharitun ti evam nimittakatam katvâ laddhenâ 'ti attho. Compare below, § 6, for this and the two following words, the meaning of which is very doubtful.

[6] Buddhaghosa: Parikathâ-katenâ 'ti kathinam nâma dâtum vattati, kathina-dâyako bahu-puññam pasavatiti evam parikathâya uppâditena. Kathinam nâma ati-ukkattham vattati: mâtaram pi na viññâpetum vattati: âkâsato otinna-sadisam eva vattati.

[7] Buddhaghosa simply says: kukku-katenâ 'ti tâvakâlikena. The last word means 'only for a time, temporary, on loan;' see Gâtaka I, 121, 393, and Kullavagga X, 16, 1; but the explanation is not clear. According to the Abhidhâna-ppadipikâ kukku is a measure of length.

[8] Sannidhi-katenâ 'ti ettha duvidho sannidhi; karana-sannidhi

when the ceremony has had to be abandoned (because it has lasted through the night)[1]: when the ceremony has fallen through (from other causes)[2]: when (in the formal choice by the presiding Bhikkhu) the upper robes have been left out, or the under robes, or the waist-cloths: when any one of the five parts of the robe have been omitted in the cutting out[3]: when the ceremony has been presided over by more than one Bhikkhu[4]. And even when the Ka*th*ina ceremony has (otherwise) been normally performed, if (the Sa*m*gha) ratifying the distribution, be other than the (whole Sa*m*gha) dwelling within the boundary, then also the Ka*th*ina ceremony has not been duly held[5].

'In these cases, O Bhikkhus, the Ka*th*ina ceremony has not been duly held.

6. 'And when, O Bhikkhus, has the Ka*th*ina ceremony been duly held?'

'When the robes have been made out of new

---

*k*a ni*k*aya-sannidhi *k*a. Tattha tadah' eva akatvâ *th*apetvâ karana*m* karana-sannidhi; sa*m*gho a*gg*a ka*th*ina-dussa*m* labhitvâ puna-divase deti aya*m* ni*k*aya-sannidhi (B.).

[1] Nissaggiyenâ 'ti ratti-nissaggiyena. Parivâre pi vutta*m* nissaggiya*m* nâma kayiramâne aruna*m* udriyatîti (B.).

[2] Akappa-katenâ 'ti anâdinna-kappa-bindhunâ (B.), which we do not understand. Perhaps we should read bindunâ.

[3] Aññatra pañ*k*akena vâ atireka-pañ*k*akena vâ 'ti pañ*k*a vâ atirekâni vâ kha*nd*âni katvâ mahâ-ma*nd*ala-a*ddh*a-ma*nd*alâni dassetvâ katen' eva va*tt*ati. Eva*m* hi sama*nd*ali-kata*m* hoti. Ta*m* *th*apetvâ aññena a*kkh*innakena vâ dvi-tti-*k*atu-kha*nd*ena vâ na va*tt*ati (B.). On these five parts of the robe compare below, Mahâvagga VIII, 12, 2.

[4] Aññatra puggalassa atthârâ 'ti puggalassa atthâra*m* *th*apetvâ na aññena sa*m*ghassa vâ ga*n*assa vâ atthârena atthata*m* hoti (B.). The official 'distributor' (atthâraka) must be a single person, not a ga*n*a, or the Sa*m*gha.

[5] See the note on § 4, and below, VIII, 23.

cotton-cloth, or as good as new, or out of cloth[1], or out of (rags) taken from the dust-heap[2], or out of odd bits picked up in the bazaar[3]: when the decision (by the presiding Bhikkhu as to which robes he will take for himself) has not (merely) been made (but carried out): when there has been no talk about (the merit acquired by offering a Ka*th*ina): when the gift is not merely a temporary one: when the ceremony has not been postponed: when it has not been necessary to abandon the ceremony: when the ceremony has not fallen through: when (in the choice made by the presiding Bhikkhu) the upper robes have not been left out, nor the under robes, nor the waist-cloths: when not one of the five parts of the robe have been omitted in the cutting out: when (the ceremony has been presided over) by one Bhikkhu. And also when, after the Ka*th*ina ceremony has been (otherwise) normally performed, the ratification has been given by the (whole Sa*m*gha) dwelling within the boundary.

'In these cases, O Bhikkhus, the Ka*th*ina ceremony has been duly held.'

2[4].

1. 7. 'Now when, O Bhikkhus, is the Ka*th*ina (that is to say, the privileges allowed after the Ka*th*ina ceremony) suspended?

---

[1] Pilo*t*ikâyâ 'ti hata-vatthaka-sâ*t*akena (B.).

[2] Pa*m*sukulenâ 'ti te-visatiyâ khettesu uppanna-pa*m*sukulena.

[3] Pâpa*n*ikenâ 'ti âpana-dvâre patita-pilo*t*ika*m* gahetvâ ka*th*in-atthâya deti, tenâpi va*tt*atîti attho (B.). Compare VIII, 14, 2.

[4] The new chapter should have begun here, and not with the next section as printed in the text.

'There are, O Bhikkhus, these eight grounds[1] for the suspension of the Ka*th*ina (privileges)[2]—the ground depending on (the Bhikkhus) having gone away, on (his robe being ready) finished, on his resolve (not to have it finished), on (his robe) having been destroyed, on his having heard (of the general suspension of the privileges of the whole Sa*m*gha), on the lapse of expectation (that a special gift of a robe would be made to him), on his having gone beyond the boundary (of the Sa*m*gha to whom the Ka*th*ina was given), on the common suspension (of the Ka*th*ina privileges of the whole Sa*m*gha).

[1] Mâtikâ 'ti mâtaro *g*anettiyo 'ti attho (B.). So also in VIII, 14.

[2] The discussion of these eight grounds of the suspension of the five Ka*th*ina privileges is closely connected with the description in the 13th chapter of the two so-called Palibodhas. Palibodha seems to mean the continued existence of a claim on the Bhikkhu's side to a share in the distribution of the Ka*th*ina. Two conditions are necessary to the validity of this claim; the first touching the Bhikkhu's domicile (âvâsa), the second the state of his wardrobe (*k*ivara). He must remain within the boundary (sîmâ) of the Sa*m*gha to whom the Ka*th*ina has been given; or if he has left it, then he must have the intention of returning, the animus revertendi. And secondly, he must be in actual want of robes. If either of these conditions fail, then the Bhikkhu is apalibodha in respect of the âvâsa or the *k*îvara respectively. If he is apalibodha in both respects, then there follows the suspension of the Ka*th*ina privileges, the ka*th*in-uddhâra, or ka*th*in-ubbhâra, so far as he is concerned.

So the eight grounds of the suspension of the privileges referred to in our present section (chap. 1. 7) either refer to the Bhikkhu's domicile or to the state of his robes, or to ways in which his case falls within the general suspension of privileges of the whole Sa*m*gha. Each of the eight cases is explained in detail in the following sections, except the sixth ground, which is specially treated of afterwards in chapters 8 and 9. See the note on the title at the end of this chapter, and compare further our note on the first Nissaggiya Pâ*k*ittiya.

2. 1. 'A Bhikkhu, after the Ka*th*ina ceremony has been held[1], takes a robe ready for wear, and goes away, thinking, "I will come back."

'That Bhikkhu's Ka*th*ina privileges are suspended on the ground of his having gone away.

'A Bhikkhu, after the Ka*th*ina ceremony has been held, takes a robe and goes away. And when he had got beyond the boundary he thinks, "I will have the robe made up here, and will never go back." And he gets the robe made up.

'That Bhikkhu's Ka*th*ina privileges are suspended on the ground of his having a robe ready for wear.

'A Bhikkhu, after the Ka*th*ina ceremony has been held, takes a robe and goes away. And when he has got beyond the boundary he thinks, "I will neither have the robe made up, nor will I go back."

'That Bhikkhu's Ka*th*ina privileges are suspended on the ground of his having so decided.

'A Bhikkhu, after the Ka*th*ina ceremony has been held, takes a robe and goes away. And when he has got beyond the boundary he thinks, "I will have the robe made up here, and will never go back." And he has the robe made up. And as the robe is being made up for him, it is spoilt.

'That Bhikkhu's Ka*th*ina privileges are suspended on the ground of the robe being so spoilt.

2. 'A Bhikkhu, after the Ka*th*ina ceremony has been held, takes a robe and goes away, thinking, "I will come back." When he has got beyond the boundary he has that robe made up. When his robe has thus been made up he bears the news, "The Ka*th*ina, they say, has been suspended in that district[1]."

[1] Literally, 'whose Ka*th*ina has been spread out.'

'That Bhikkhu's Ka*th*ina privileges are suspended on the ground of his having heard that news.

'A Bhikkhu, after the Ka*th*ina ceremony has been held, takes a robe and goes away, thinking, "I will come back." And when he has got beyond the boundary he has that robe made up. And then, after it has been made up, he postpones his return until the (general) suspension of privileges has taken place.

'That Bhikkhu's Ka*th*ina privileges are suspended on the ground of his being beyond the boundary.

'A Bhikkhu, after the Ka*th*ina ceremony has been held, takes a robe and goes away, thinking, "I will come back." And when he has got beyond the boundary he has that robe made up. And then, when it has been made up, he postpones his return until the very moment when the (general) suspension of privileges takes place[1].

'That Bhikkhu's Ka*th*ina privileges are suspended on the ground of the common suspension (of the privileges of the whole Sa*m*gha).'

End of the section entitled Âdâya-sattaka[2].

3.

'A Bhikkhu, after the Ka*th*ina ceremony has been

---

[1] In the table of contents (p. 266) sambhu*n*âti is replaced by sambhoti. Abhisambhu*n*eyya*m* occurs in Burnouf's 'Lotus,' &c., p. 313.

[2] That is, 'the seven cases in which he takes a robe away.' The eighth case is explained below in chapters 8, 9.

held, takes with him a robe ready for wear, and goes away, &c.[1]'

End of the section entitled Samâdâya-sattaka[2].

4.

'A Bhikkhu, after the Ka*th*ina ceremony has been held, takes a robe not ready, and goes away. And when he has got beyond the boundary he thinks, "I will have the robe made up here, and will never go back;" and he gets the robe made up, &c.[3]'

End of the section entitled Âdâya-*kh*akka[4].

5.

'A Bhikkhu, after the Ka*th*ina ceremony has been held, takes with him a robe not ready, and goes away, &c.[5]'

End of the section entitled Samâdâya-*kh*akka[6].

[1] This chapter is word for word identical with chap. 2: only instead of 'takes' (âdâya) read 'takes with him' (samâdâya). We cannot say what different meaning these two words are intended to convey.

[2] That is, 'the seven cases in which he takes a robe with him.'

[3] Six of the seven cases specified in chap. 2 (with the exception of the first of the seven) are repeated here in the same words, with the only difference that instead of 'takes a robe' it is said here 'takes a robe not ready.' The first case is necessarily omitted, because it is essential to that case, that the Bhikkhu going away takes with him a robe ready for wear.

[4] 'The six cases in which he takes a robe away.'

[5] As in chap. 4. For 'takes' read 'takes with him.' See the note at chap. 3.

[6] 'The six cases in which he takes a robe with him.'

6.

1. 'A Bhikkhu, after the Ka*th*ina ceremony has been held, takes a robe, and goes away. And when he has got beyond the boundary he thinks, "I will have the robe made up here, and will never go back." And he gets the robe made up.

'That Bhikkhu's Ka*th*ina privileges are suspended on the ground of his having a robe ready for wear, &c.[1]

2. 'A Bhikkhu, after the Ka*th*ina ceremony has been held, takes a robe and goes away, thinking, "I will never come back." And when he has got beyond the boundary he thinks, "I will have the robe made up here." And he gets the robe made up, &c.[2]

3. 'A Bhikkhu, after the Ka*th*ina ceremony has been held, takes a robe and goes away, without taking a resolution; he neither thinks "I will come back," nor does he think "I will not come back." And when he has got beyond the boundary, &c.[3]

4. 'A Bhikkhu, after the Ka*th*ina ceremony has been held, takes a robe and goes away, thinking,

[1] This case is word for word identical with the second case in chap. 2. 1. After it follow the third and fourth case of chap. 2. 1, which it is unnecessary to print here again in full extent. The triad of these cases is repeated here in order to serve as a basis for the variations which are to follow in §§ 2, 3.

[2] The triad of § 1 is repeated here, with the difference, as is seen from the opening clauses which we have fully printed, that the Bhikkhu, before he has got beyond the boundary, and not afterwards as in § 1, resolves upon not returning to the âvâsa.

[3] The whole triad as in § 1. The only difference between § 3 and § 1 consists in the following words being added in § 3 in each of the three cases, 'without taking a resolution; he neither thinks "I will come back," nor does he think "I will not come back."'

"I will come back." And when he has got beyond the boundary, &c.[1]'

7.

'A Bhikkhu, after the Ka*th*ina ceremony has been held, takes a robe with him and goes away, &c.[2]'

End of the Âdâya- ('Taking away') Bhâ*n*avâra.

8.

1. 'A Bhikkhu, after the Ka*th*ina ceremony has been held, goes away with the expectation of getting a robe (presented). And when he has got beyond the boundary, &c. And he adopts such a course of action as may lead to his expectation being realised. But he obtains a robe where he had not expected it, and does not obtain it where he had expected it. And he thinks, "I will have the robe made up here, and will never go back." And he gets the robe made up.

'That Bhikkhu's Ka*th*ina privileges are suspended on the ground of his having a robe ready for wear.

'A Bhikkhu, after the Ka*th*ina ceremony has been

[1] Supply here the whole triad as in § 1, the words 'thinking "I will come back"' being constantly added. After this triad follow three other cases which are exactly identical with the three contained in chap. 2. 2.

[2] The whole chapter 6 is repeated here three times, the first time replacing the words 'takes a robe' by 'takes a robe with him' (comp. chap. 3); the second time replacing 'takes a robe' by 'takes a robe not ready' (comp. chap. 4); and the third time with these two modifications combined (comp. chap. 5).

held (&c., as in the preceding case). And he thinks, "I will neither have the robe made up, nor will I go back."

'That Bhikkhu's Ka*th*ina privileges are suspended on the ground of his having so decided.

'A Bhikkhu, after the Ka*th*ina ceremony has been held, &c. And he thinks, "I will have the robe made up here, and will never go back." And he has the robe made up. And as the robe is being made up for him, it is spoilt.

'That Bhikkhu's Ka*th*ina privileges are suspended on the ground of the robe being so spoilt.

'A Bhikkhu, after the Ka*th*ina ceremony has been held, goes away with the expectation of getting a robe (presented). And when he has got beyond the boundary, he thinks, "I will adopt here such a course of action as may lead to my expectation being realised, and will never go back." And he devotes himself to obtaining that expected gift, but his expectation comes to nothing.

'That Bhikkhu's Ka*th*ina privileges are suspended on the ground of the lapse of that expectation.'

2, 3[1].

End of the section entitled Anâsâ-do*l*asaka[2].

9.

1. 'A Bhikkhu, after the Ka*th*ina ceremony has been held, goes away with the expectation of getting

---

[1] §§ 2, 3 stand exactly in the same relation to § 1 in which chap. 6. 2, 3 stand to chap. 6. 1.

[2] 'The twelve cases (in which the robe is received) against expectation.'

a robe (presented), thinking, "I will come back." And when he has got beyond the boundary, he devotes himself to the realisation of his expectation, and he obtains a robe where he had expected it, and does not obtain one where he had not expected it. And he thinks, "I will have the robe made up here, and will never go back," &c.[1]

2. 'A Bhikkhu, after the Ka*th*ina ceremony has been held, goes away with the expectation of getting a robe (presented), thinking, "I will come back." And when he has got beyond the boundary, he hears the news: "The Ka*th*ina, they say, has been suspended in that district." And he thinks, "Since the Ka*th*ina has been suspended in that district, I will devote myself here to obtaining the gift I am expecting." And he adopts such action as may lead to the realisation of his expectation, and he obtains a robe where he had expected it, and does not obtain one where he had not expected it. And he thinks, "I will have the robe made up here, and will never go back," &c.[2]

3. 'A Bhikkhu, after the Ka*th*ina ceremony has been held, goes away with the expectation of getting a robe (presented), thinking, "I will come back." And when he has got beyond the boundary, he adopts such action as may lead to the realisation of his expectation, and he obtains a robe where he had expected it, and does not obtain one where he had not expected it, and he has that robe made up.

---

[1] Here follows the same development into the four cases of ni*tth*ânantika, sanni*tth*ânantika, nâsanantika, and âsâva*kkh*edika ka*th*inuddhâra, as in chap. 8. 1.

[2] Supply here the same four cases as in the preceding paragraph or in chap. 8. 1.

When that robe has thus been made up he hears the news, "The Ka*th*ina, they say, has been suspended in that district."

'That Bhikkhu's Ka*th*ina privileges are suspended on the ground of his having heard that news.

'A Bhikkhu, after the Ka*th*ina ceremony has been held, goes away with the expectation of getting a robe, thinking, "I will come back." And when he has got beyond the boundary, he thinks, "I will devote myself to obtaining that expected gift, and will never go back." And he cares for that expected gift, but his expectation collapses.

'That Bhikkhu's Ka*th*ina privileges are suspended on the ground of the lapse of that expectation.

'A Bhikkhu, after the Ka*th*ina ceremony has been held, goes away with the expectation of getting a robe, thinking, "I will come back." And when he has got beyond the boundary, he devotes himself to the realisation of his expectation, and he obtains a robe where he had expected it, and does not obtain one where he had not expected it, and he has that robe made up. And then, after it has been made up, he postpones his return until the (general) suspension of privileges has taken place.

'That Bhikkhu's Ka*th*ina privileges are suspended on the ground of his being beyond the boundary.

'A Bhikkhu, after the Ka*th*ina ceremony has been held (&c., as in the preceding case, down to:) And then, after it has been made up, he postpones his return until the very moment when the (general) suspension of privileges takes place.

'That Bhikkhu's Ka*th*ina privileges are suspended on the ground of the common suspension.'

End of the section entitled Âsâ-do*l*asaka[1].

10.

'A Bhikkhu, after the Ka*th*ina ceremony has been held, goes away on some business. And when he has got beyond the boundary, he conceives the expectation of getting a robe (presented). And he devotes himself to the realisation of his expectation, and he obtains, &c.[2]'

End of the Kara*n*îya-do*l*asaka[3].

11.

1. 'A Bhikkhu, after the Ka*th*ina ceremony has been held, goes away travelling to the (four) quarters (of the world[4]), guarding[5] his claim to a share in the robes. When he is so travelling, the Bhikkhus ask him: "Where have you kept Vassa, friend, and where have you your share in the robes?"

'He replies: "I have kept Vassa in such and such

[1] 'The twelve cases (in which the robe is received) as expected.'

[2] See chap. 8. 1. The same three times four cases are specified here as in chap. 8; only the opening clauses of each case, which we have printed above, are different from those in chap. 8.

[3] 'The twelve cases of (the Bhikkhu's going away on) business.'

[4] Comp. II, 21, 1.

[5] Apa*k*inayamâna, comp. apa*k*iti, apa*k*ita.

a residence, and there I have my share in the robes."

'They say to him: "Go, friend, and bring your robe hither; we will make it up for you here."

'And he goes to that residence and asks the Bhikkhus: "Where is the portion of robes due to me, friends?"

'They reply: "Here it is, friend; where are you going?"

'He says: "I will go to such and such a residence; there the Bhikkhus will make up the robe for me."

'They answer: "Nay, friend, do not go; we will make up the robe for you here."

'And he thinks, "I will have the robe made up here, and will not go back (to that other place)," &c.[1]

2. 'A Bhikkhu, after the Ka*th*ina ceremony has been held, goes away travelling (&c., as in § 1, down to:) "Here it is, friend." And he takes that robe and sets out for that residence. On the way some Bhikkhus ask him: "Friend, where are you going?"

'He says: "I intend to go to such and such a residence; there the Bhikkhus will make up the robe for me."

'They answer: "Nay, friend, do not go; we will make up the robe for you here."

'And he thinks, "I will have the robe made up here, and will not go back (to that other place)," &c.[2]

3. 'A Bhikkhu, after the Ka*th*ina ceremony has been held, goes away travelling (&c., as in § 1, down to:) "Here it is, friend." And he takes that robe, and sets out for that residence. And when going

---

[1] Here follow the three cases as given in chap. 6. 1, in the usual way.

[2] The usual three cases; see the preceding note.

to that residence, he thinks, "I will have the robe made up here, and will not go back (to that place)," &c.[1]'

End of the Apa*k*inana-navaka[2].

12.

'A Bhikkhu intent on finding a comfortable place (to live in), after the Ka*th*ina ceremony has been held, takes a robe, and goes away, thinking, "I will go to such and such a residence; if it is comfortable there, I will remain there; if it is not, I will go to such and such a residence; if it is comfortable there, I will remain there; if it is not, I will go to such and such a residence; if it is comfortable there, I will remain there; if it is not, I will go back."

'When he has got beyond the boundary, he thinks, "I will have the robe made up here, and will never go back," &c.[3]'

End of the five cases of the Bhikkhu intent on comfort.

13.

1. 'On two conditions, O Bhikkhus, the claim (of a Bhikkhu to a share in the distribution) of the

---

[1] The same three cases as before.

[2] 'The nine cases in which he guards (his claim).'

[3] The usual three cases as before, and then the two cases of the sîmâtikkantika ka*th*inuddhâra and the saha bhikkhûhi ka*th*inuddhâra, which run as may be seen from chap. 2. 2 (the two last cases there) or from chap. 9. 3.

Ka*th*ina continues to exist, and on the failing of these two conditions it is lost[1].

'And which are the two conditions, O Bhikkhus, for the continued existence of that claim? The condition regarding the residence, and the condition regarding the robe.

'And which, O Bhikkhus, is the condition regarding the residence? A Bhikkhu, O Bhikkhus, goes away (for a time), when it is raining or storming, with the intention of returning to that residence. In this case, O Bhikkhus, the condition regarding the residence is fulfilled. And which, O Bhikkhus, is the condition that regards the robe? A Bhikkhu's robe, O Bhikkhus, is not made up, or not ready, or his expectation of getting a robe has ceased. In this case, O Bhikkhus, the condition regarding the robe is fulfilled. These, O Bhikkhus, are the two conditions for the continued existence of the claim.

2. 'And which, O Bhikkhus, is the failing of the two conditions by which the claim is lost? The failing of the condition regarding the residence, and the failing of the condition regarding the robe.

'And in which case, O Bhikkhus, does the condition regarding the residence fail?

'A Bhikkhu, O Bhikkhus, goes away from the residence, giving it up, turning away from it with contempt, abandoning it, with the intention of not returning. In this case, O Bhikkhus, the condition regarding the residence fails. And in which case, O Bhikkhus, does the condition regarding the robe

[1] Literally, there are two Palibodhas of the Ka*th*ina and two Apalibodhas. On the subject discussed in this chapter—the Palibodhas—see the note on chap. 1. 7.

fail? A Bhikkhu's robe, O Bhikkhus, has been made up, or spoilt, or lost, or burnt, or his expectation of getting a robe has ceased. In these cases, O Bhikkhus, the condition regarding the robe fails. This is the failing of the two conditions, O Bhikkhus, by which the claim is lost.'

End of the seventh Khandhaka, the Ka*th*ina-khandhaka.

EIGHTH KHANDHAKA.

(THE DRESS OF THE BHIKKHUS.)

1.

1. At that time the blessed Buddha dwelt at Râgagaha, in the Veluvana, in the Kalandaka-nivâpa. At that time Vesâlî was an opulent, prosperous town, populous, crowded with people, abundant with food[1]; there were seven thousand seven hundred and seven storeyed buildings, and seven thousand seven hundred and seven pinnacled buildings, and seven thousand seven hundred and seven pleasure grounds (Ârâmas), and seven thousand seven hundred and seven lotus-ponds. There was also the courtezan Ambapâlikâ[2], who was beautiful, graceful, pleasant, gifted with the highest beauty of complexion, well versed in dancing, singing, and lute-playing, much visited by desirous people. She asked fifty (kahâpanas) for one night. Through that person Vesâlî became more and more flourishing.

2. Now a merchant from Râgagaha went to Vesâlî on a certain business. That Râgagaha merchant saw what an opulent, prosperous town Vesâlî was, how populous, crowded with people, and abundant with food, and the seven thousand seven

[1] Compare Mahâ-sudassana Sutta I, 3, and Mahâ-parinibbâna Sutta V, 42.

[2] See above, VI, 30, 6; Mahâ-parinibbâna Sutta II, 16 seq.

hundred and seven storeyed buildings . . . . and the courtezan Ambapâlî, who was beautiful . . . . and through whom Vesâlî became more and more flourishing. And the Râgagaha merchant, after having done his business in Vesâlî, returned to Râgagaha and went to the place where the Mâgadha king Seniya Bimbisâra was. Having approached him, he said to the Mâgadha king Seniya Bimbisâra: 'Vesâlî, Your Majesty, is an opulent, prosperous town (&c., as in § 1, down to :) Through that person Vesâlî becomes more and more flourishing. May it please Your Majesty, let us also install a courtezan.'

(The king replied), 'Well, my good Sir, look for such a girl whom you can install as courtezan.'

3. Now at that time there was at Râgagaha a girl Sâlavatî by name, who was beautiful, graceful, pleasant, and gifted with the highest beauty of complexion. That girl Sâlavatî the Râgagaha merchant installed as courtezan. And before long the courtezan Sâlavatî was well versed in dancing, singing, and lute-playing, and much visited by desirous people, and she asked one hundred (kahâpa*n*as) for one night. And before long the courtezan Sâlavatî became pregnant. Now the courtezan Sâlavatî thought: 'Men do not like a pregnant woman. If anybody should find out regarding me that "The courtezan Sâlavatî is pregnant," my whole position will be lost. What if I were to have the people told that I am sick.'

And the courtezan Sâlavatî gave orders to the door-keeper (saying), 'Let no man enter here, my good door-keeper, and if a man calls for me, tell him that I am sick.' The door-keeper accepted this order of the courtezan Sâlavatî (by saying), 'Yes, Madam.'

4. And the courtezan Sâlavatî, when the child in her womb had reached maturity, gave birth to a boy. And the courtezan Sâlavatî gave orders to her maid-servant (saying), 'Go, my girl, put this boy into an old winnowing basket, take him away, and throw him away on a dust-heap.' The servant accepted this order of the courtezan Sâlavatî (by saying), 'Yes, Madam,' put that boy into an old winnowing basket, took him away, and threw him away on a dust-heap.

At that time a royal prince, Abhaya by name[1], went betimes to attend upon the king, and saw that boy, around whom crows were gathering. When he saw that, he asked the people: 'What is that, my good Sirs, around which the crows are gathering?'

'It is a boy, Your Highness[2].'

'Is he alive, Sirs?'

'He is alive, Your Highness.'

'Well, my good Sirs, bring that boy to our palace and give him to the nurses to nourish him.'

And those people accepted that order of the royal prince Abhaya (by saying), 'Yes, Your Highness,' brought that boy to the palace of the royal prince Abhaya, and gave him to the nurses (saying), 'Nourish (this boy).'

[1] This 'royal prince Abhaya' (Abhaya kumâra) is mentioned by the *G*ainas under the name of Abhayakumâra as the son of Se*n*iya, i. e. Bimbisâra. See Jacobi, Zeitschrift der Deutschen Morg. Gesellschaft, vol. xxxiv, p. 187.

[2] The word which we have translated 'Your Highness' (deva, lit. 'God') is the same which is used by all persons except by Sama*n*as in addressing a king.

Because (the people had said about this boy to Abhaya), 'He is alive' (*g*îvati), they gave him the name of *G*îvaka; because he had been caused to be nourished by the royal prince (kumârena posâpito), they gave him the name of Komârabhak*k*a[1].

5. And ere long *G*îvaka Komârabhak*k*a came to the years of discretion. And *G*îvaka Komârabhak*k*a went to the place where the royal prince Abhaya was; having approached him he said to the royal prince Abhaya: 'Who is my mother, Your Highness, and who is my father?'

'I do not know your mother, my good *G*îvaka, but I am your father, for I have had you nourished.'

Now *G*îvaka Komârabhak*k*a thought: 'In these royal families it is not easy to find one's livelihood without knowing an art. What if I were to learn an art.'

6. At that time there lived at Takkasilâ (Τάξιλα) a world-renowned physician. And *G*îvaka Komârabhak*k*a without asking leave of the royal prince Abhaya set out for Takkasilâ. Wandering from place to place he came to Takkasilâ and to the place where

[1] Evidently the redactors of this passage referred the first part of the compound Komârabhak*k*a to the royal prince (kumâra) Abhaya, and intended Komârabhak*k*a to be understood as 'a person whose life is supported by a royal prince.' So also the name Kumâra-Kassapa is explained in the *G*âtaka commentary (Rh. D., 'Buddhist Birth Stories,' p. 204). The true meaning of the name, however, appears to have been different, for in Sanskrit kumârabh*ri*tyâ and kaumârabh*ri*tya are technical terms for the part of the medical science which comprises the treatment of infants (see Wise, 'Commentary on the Hindu System of Medicine,' p. 3). We believe, therefore, that this surname Komârabhak*k*a really means, 'Master of the kaumârabh*ri*tya science.'

that physician was. Having approached him he said to that physician, 'I wish to learn your art, doctor.'

'Well, friend *G*îvaka, learn it.'

And *G*îvaka Komârabha*kk*a learnt much, and learnt easily, and understood well, and did not forget what he had learnt. And when seven years had elapsed, *G*îvaka Komârabha*kk*a thought: 'I learn much, and learn easily, and I understand well, and I do not forget what I have learnt. I have studied now seven years, and I do not see the end of this art. When shall I see the end of this art?'

7. And *G*îvaka Komârabha*kk*a went to the place where that physician was; having approached him he said to that physician: 'I learn much, doctor, and I learn easily; I understand well, and do not forget what I have learnt. I have studied now seven years, and I do not see the end of this art. When shall I see the end of this art?'

'Very well, my dear *G*îvaka, take this spade, and seek round about Takkasilâ a yo*g*ana on every side, and whatever (plant) you see which is not medicinal, bring it to me.'

*G*îvaka Komârabha*kk*a accepted this order of that physician (saying), 'Yes, doctor,' took a spade, and went around about Takkasilâ a yo*g*ana on every side, but he did not see anything that was not medicinal. Then *G*îvaka Komârabha*kk*a went to the place where that physician was; having approached him he said to that physician: 'I have been seeking, doctor, all around Takkasilâ a yo*g*ana on every side, but I have not seen anything that is not medicinal.'

(The physician replied), 'You have done your learning, my good *G*îvaka; this will do for acquiring your livelihood.' Speaking thus he gave to *G*îvaka

Komârabha*kk*a a little (money) for his journey (home).

8. And *G*îvaka Komârabha*kk*a took that little money, given to him for his journey, and set out for Râ*g*agaha. And on the way at Sâketa that little money of *G*îvaka Komârabha*kk*a was spent. Now *G*îvaka Komârabha*kk*a thought: 'These ways are wild, and there is but little water and little food; it is difficult to travel here without money for the journey. What if I were to try to get some money for my journey.'

At that time the se*tth*i's[1] wife at Sâketa had been suffering for seven years from disease in the head; many very great and world-renowned physicians came, but they could not restore her to health; they received much gold, and went away.

And *G*îvaka Komârabha*kk*a, when he had entered Sâketa, asked the people: 'Who is sick here, my good Sirs? Whom shall I cure?'

'That se*tth*i's wife, doctor, has been suffering for seven years from a disease in the head; go, doctor, and cure that se*tth*i's wife.'

9. Then *G*îvaka Komârabha*kk*a went to the house of that householder, the se*tth*i; and when he had reached it, he gave orders to the door-keeper (saying), 'Go, my good door-keeper, and tell the se*tth*i's wife: "A physician has come in, Madam, who wants to see you."'

That door-keeper accepted this order of *G*îvaka Komârabha*kk*a (saying), 'Yes, doctor,' went to the place where the se*tth*i's wife was, and having approached her, he said to the se*tth*i's wife: 'A physician has come in, Madam, who wants to see you.'

[1] See the note at I, 7, 1.

'What sort of man is that physician, my good door-keeper?'

'He is a young man, Madam.'

'Nay, my good door-keeper, what can a young physician help me? Many very great and world-renowned physicians have come and have not been able to restore me to health; they have received much gold, and have gone away.'

10. Thus that door-keeper went to *G*îvaka Komârabha*kk*a; having approached him he said to *G*îvaka Komârabha*kk*a: 'The se*tth*i's wife has said, doctor: "Nay, my good door-keeper (&c., as in § 9)."'

(*G*îvaka replied), 'Go, my good door-keeper, and tell the se*tth*i's wife: "The physician, Madam, says: 'Do not give me anything beforehand, Madam; when you shall have been restored to health, then you may give me what you like.'"'

The door-keeper accepted this order of *G*îvaka Komârabha*kk*a (saying), 'Yes, doctor,' went to the place where the se*tth*i's wife was, and having approached her he said to the se*tth*i's wife: 'The physician, Madam, says (&c., as above).'

'Well, my good door-keeper, let the physician enter.'

The door-keeper accepted this order of the se*tth*i's wife (saying), 'Yes, Madam,' went to the place where *G*îvaka Komârabha*kk*a was, and having approached him he said to *G*îvaka Komârabha*kk*a: 'The se*tth*i's wife calls you, doctor.'

11. Then *G*îvaka Komârabha*kk*a went to the place where the se*tth*i's wife was; having approached her, and having carefully observed the change in the appearance of the se*tth*i's wife, he said to the

se*tth*i's wife: 'We want one pasata[1] of ghee, Madam.' Then the se*tth*i's wife ordered one pasata of ghee to be given to *G*îvaka Komârabha*kk*a. And *G*îvaka Komârabha*kk*a boiled up that pasata of ghee with various drugs, ordered the se*tth*i's wife to lie down on her back in the bed, and gave it her through her nose. And the butter given through the nose came out through the mouth. And the se*tth*i's wife spat it out into the spittoon, and told the maid-servant: 'Come, my girl, take this ghee up with a piece of cotton.'

12. Then *G*îvaka Komârabha*kk*a thought: 'It is astonishing how niggardly this house-wife is, in that she has this ghee, which ought to be thrown away, taken up with a piece of cotton. I have given her many highly precious drugs. What sort of fee will she give me?'

And the se*tth*i's wife, when she observed the change of demeanour in *G*îvaka Komârabha*kk*a, said to *G*îvaka Komârabha*kk*a: 'Why are you perplexed, doctor?'

'I thought: "It is astonishing, &c."'

'Householders like us, doctor, know why to economize thus; this ghee will do for the servants or workmen to anoint their feet with, or it can be poured into the lamp. Be not perplexed, doctor, you will not lose your fee.'

---

[1] One pras*ri*ta or pras*ri*ti ('handful') is said by the Sanskrit lexicographers to be equal to two palas. About the pala, which according to the ghee measure (gh*ri*tapramâ*n*a) of Magadha was the thirty-second part of a prastha, see the Atharva-pari*s*ish*t*a 35, 3, ap. Weber, Ueber den Vedakalender namens Jyotisham, p. 82. Compare also Rh. D., 'Ancient Coins and Measures of Ceylon,' pp. 18, 19.

13. And *G*îvaka Komârabha*kk*a drove away the disease in the head which the se*tth*i's wife had had for seven years, by once giving her medicine through the nose. Then the se*tth*i's wife, who had been restored to health, gave four thousand (kâhâpa*n*as) to *G*îvaka Komârabha*kk*a; her son (thinking), 'My mother stands there restored,' gave him four thousand; her daughter-in-law (thinking), 'My mother-in-law stands there restored,' gave him four thousand; the se*tth*i, the householder, (thinking), 'My wife stands there restored,' gave him four thousand and a man-servant and a maid-servant and a coach with horses.

Then *G*îvaka Komârabha*kk*a took those sixteen thousand (kâhâpa*n*as) and the man-servant, the maid-servant, and the coach with the horses, and set out for Râ*g*agaha. In due course he came to Râ*g*agaha, and to the place where the royal prince Abhaya was; having approached him he said to the royal prince Abhaya: 'This, Your Highness, (have I received for) the first work I have done, sixteen thousand and a man-servant and a maid-servant and a coach with horses; may Your Highness accept this as payment for my bringing up.'

'Nay, my dear *G*îvaka, keep it, but do not get a dwelling for yourself elsewhere than in our residence.'

*G*îvaka Komârabha*kk*a accepted this order of the royal prince Abhaya (saying), 'Yes, Your Highness,' and got himself a dwelling in the residence of the royal prince Abhaya.

14. At that time the Magadha king Seniya Bimbisâra suffered from a fistula; his garments were stained with blood. When the queens saw that,

they ridiculed (the king, and said): 'His Majesty is having his courses. His Majesty will bring forth!' The king was annoyed at that. And the Magadha king Seniya Bimbisâra said to the royal prince Abhaya: 'I am suffering, my dear Abhaya, from such a disease that my garments are stained with blood; and the queens, when they see it, ridicule (me by saying), "His Majesty is, &c." Pray, my dear Abhaya, find a physician for me, able to cure me.'

'This excellent young physician of ours, Sire, *G*îvaka, he will cure Your Majesty.'

'Then pray, my dear Abhaya, give orders to the physician *G*îvaka, and he shall cure me.'

15. Then the royal prince Abhaya gave orders to *G*îvaka Komârabha*kk*a (saying), 'Go, my dear *G*îvaka, and cure the king.'

*G*îvaka Komârabha*kk*a accepted this order of the royal prince Abhaya (by saying), 'Yes, Your Highness,' took some medicament in his nail, and went to the place where the Magadha king Seniya Bimbisâra was. Having approached him, he said to the Magadha king Seniya Bimbisâra: 'Let us see your disease, Your Majesty.' And *G*îvaka Komârabha*kk*a healed the fistula of the Magadha king Seniya Bimbisâra by one anointing.

Then the Magadha king Seniya Bimbisâra, having been restored to health, ordered his five hundred wives to put on all their ornaments; then he ordered them to take their ornaments off and to make a heap of them, and he said to *G*îvaka Komârabha*kk*a: 'All these ornaments, my dear *G*îvaka, of my five hundred wives shall be thine.'

'Nay, Sire, may Your Majesty remember my office.'

'Very well, my dear *G*îvaka, you can wait upon me and my seraglio and the fraternity of Bhikkhus with the Buddha at its head.'

*G*îvaka Komârabha*kk*a accepted this order of the Magadha king Seniya Bimbisâra (by saying), 'Yes, Your Majesty.'

16. At that time the se*tth*i at Râ*g*agaha had been suffering for seven years from a disease in the head. Many very great and world-renowned physicians came, and were not able to restore him to health; they received much gold and went away. And a prognostication had been made by the physicians to him, to wit: Some of the physicians said: 'The se*tth*i, the householder, will die on the fifth day:' other physicians said: 'The se*tth*i, the householder, will die on the seventh day.'

Now (a certain) Râ*g*agaha merchant thought: 'This se*tth*i, this householder, does good service both to the king and to the merchants' guild. Now the physicians have made prognostication to him (&c., as above). There is *G*îvaka, the royal physician, an excellent young doctor. What if we were to ask the king for his physician *G*îvaka to cure the se*tth*i, the householder?'

17. And the Râ*g*agaha merchant went to the place where the Magadha king Seniya Bimbisâra was; having approached him, he said to the Magadha king Seniya Bimbisâra: 'That se*tth*i, Sire, that householder, does good service both to Your Majesty and to the merchants' guild. Now the physicians have made prognostication to him, &c. May it please Your Majesty to order the physician *G*îvaka to cure the se*tth*i, the householder.'

Then the Magadha king Seniya Bimbisâra gave

orders to *G*îvaka Komârabha*kk*a (saying), 'Go, my dear *G*îvaka, and cure the se*tth*i, the householder.'

*G*îvaka Komârabha*kk*a accepted this order of the Magadha king Seniya Bimbisâra (by saying), 'Yes, Your Majesty,' went to the place where the se*tth*i, the householder, was, and having approached him, and having carefully observed the change in his appearance, he said to the se*tth*i, the householder: 'If I restore you to health, my good householder, what fee will you give me?'

'All that I possess shall be yours, doctor, and I will be your slave.'

18. 'Well, my good householder, will you be able to lie down on one side for seven months?'

'I shall be able, doctor, to lie down on one side for seven months.'

'And will you be able, my good householder, to lie down on the other side for seven months?'

'I shall be able, doctor, to lie down on the other side for seven months.'

'And will you be able, my good householder, to lie down on your back for seven months?'

'I shall be able, doctor, to lie down on my back for seven months.'

Then *G*îvaka Komârabha*kk*a ordered the se*tth*i, the householder, to lie down on his bed, tied him fast to his bed, cut through the skin of the head, drew apart the flesh on each side of the incision, pulled two worms out (of the wound), and showed them to the people (saying), 'See, Sirs, these two worms, a small one and a big one. The doctors who said, "On the fifth day the se*tth*i, the householder, will die," have seen this big worm, and how it would penetrate on the fifth day to the brain of the se*tth*i, the householder, and that when it had penetrated to the brain, the se*tth*i, the householder, would die. Those doctors have seen it quite rightly. And the doctors who said, "On the seventh day the se*tth*i, the householder, will die," have seen this small worm, and how it would penetrate on the seventh day to the brain of the se*tth*i, the householder, and that when it had penetrated to the brain, the se*tth*i, the householder, would die. Those doctors have seen it quite rightly.' (Speaking thus) he closed up the sides of the wound, stitched up the skin on the head, and anointed it with salve.

19. And when seven days had elapsed, the se*tth*i, the householder, said to *G*îvaka Komârabha*kk*a: 'I am not able, doctor, to lie down on one side for seven months.'

'Did you not tell me, my good householder: "I shall be able, doctor, to lie down on one side for seven months?"'

'It is true, doctor, I told you so indeed, but I shall die (if I do); I cannot lie down on one side for seven months.'

'Well, my good householder, then you must lie down on the other side for seven months.'

And when seven days had elapsed, the se*tth*i, the householder, said to *G*îvaka Komârabha*kk*a: 'I am not able, doctor, to lie down on the other side for seven months.'

'Did you not tell me, &c.'

'It is true, doctor, I told you so indeed, &c.'

'Well, my good householder, then you must lie down on your back for seven months.'

And when seven days had elapsed, the se*tth*i, the householder, said to *G*îvaka Komârabha*kk*a: 'I am not able, doctor, to lie down on my back for seven months.'

'Did you not tell me, &c.?'

'It is true, doctor, I told you so indeed, &c.'

20. 'If I had not spoken thus to you, my good householder, you would not have lain down even so long a time. But I knew beforehand, "After three times seven days the se*tth*i, the householder, will be restored to health." Arise, my good householder, you are restored; look to it what fee you give me.'

'All that I possess shall be yours, doctor, and I will be your slave.'

'Nay, my good householder, do not give me all that you possess, and do not be my slave; give one hundred thousand (kâhâpa*n*as) to the king, and one hundred thousand to me.'

Then the se*tth*i, the householder, having regained his health, gave a hundred thousand (kâhâpa*n*as) to the king, and a hundred thousand to *G*îvaka Komârabha*kk*a.

21. At that time the son of the se*tth*i at Benares, who used to amuse himself by tumbling (mokkha*k*ikâ[1]), brought upon himself an entanglement of his

[1] Mokkha*k*ikâ is explained in a passage quoted by Childers sub voce and taken from the Sumangala Vilâsinî on the 4th Mag*gh*ima Sîla. (Compare Rh. D., 'Buddhist Suttas from the Pâli,' p. 193.) The passage from Buddhaghosa is however not devoid of ambiguity. He says: 'Mokkha*k*ikâ is the feat of turning over and over. One gets hold of a staff in the air, and places his head on the ground; turning himself upside down. This is what is meant (by the word mokkha*k*ikâ).' It is not clear whether the performer suspends himself by his feet from a horizontal bar fixed at a height above the ground; or whether he turns a sommersault, holding at the same time a stick in his hands. The latter seems

intestines, in consequence of which he could digest neither the rice-milk which he drank, nor the food of which he partook, nor was he able to ease himself in the regular way. In consequence of that he grew lean, he looked disfigured and discoloured, (his complexion became) more and more yellow, and the veins stood out upon his skin.

Now the se*tth*i of Benares thought: 'My son is suffering from such and such a disease: he neither can digest the rice-milk which he drinks (&c., as above, down to:) and the veins stand out upon his skin. What if I were to go to Râ*g*agaha and to ask the king for his physician *G*îvaka to cure my son.'

And the se*tth*i of Benares went to Râ*g*agaha and repaired to the place where the Magadha king Seniya Bimbisâra was; having approached him he said to the Magadha king Seniya Bimbisâra: 'My son, Your Majesty, is suffering from such and such a disease: he neither can digest the rice-milk which he drinks (&c., as above, down to:) and the veins stand out upon his skin. May it please Your Majesty to order the physician *G*îvaka to cure my son.'

22. Then the Magadha king Seniya Bimbisâra gave orders to *G*îvaka Komârabha*kk*a (saying), 'Go, my dear *G*îvaka; go to Benares, and cure the se*tth*i's son at Benares.'

*G*îvaka Komârabha*kk*a accepted this order of the Magadha king Seniya Bimbisâra (by saying), 'Yes, Your Majesty,' went to Benares, and repaired to the place where the son of the Benares se*tth*i was; having approached him, and having carefully

---

more in accordance with the phrase 'holding a stick in the air' (âkâse da*nd*a*m* gahetvâ) and with the phrase 'turning over and over' (samparivat*t*ana*m*).

observed the change in his appearance, he ordered the people to leave the room, drew the curtain, tied him fast to a pillar, placed his wife in front of him, cut through the skin of the belly, drew the twisted intestines out, and showed them to his wife (saying), 'Look here what the disease was, from which your husband was suffering. This is the reason why he neither can digest the rice-milk which he drinks, nor can digest the food of which he partakes, nor is able to ease himself in the regular way, and why he has grown lean, and looks disfigured and discoloured, and (why his complexion has become) more and more yellow, and the veins have stood out upon his skin.' (Speaking thus), he disentangled the twisted intestines, put the intestines back (into their right position), stitched the skin together, and anointed it with salve. And before long the Benares se*tth*i's son regained his health.

Then the se*tth*i of Benares (saying to himself), 'My son stands here restored to health,' gave sixteen thousand (kâhâpa*n*as) to *G*îvaka Komârabha*kk*a. And *G*îvaka Komârabha*kk*a took those sixteen thousand (kâhâpa*n*as), and went back again to Râ*g*agaha.

23. At that time king Pa*gg*ota (of U*gg*enî) was suffering from jaundice. Many very great and world-renowned physicians came and were not able to restore him to health; they received much gold and went away. Then king Pa*gg*ota sent a messenger to the Magadha king Seniya Bimbisâra (with the following message): 'I am suffering from such and such a disease; pray, Your Majesty[1], give

[1] This passage in which king Pa*gg*ota is represented as addressing king Bimbisâra by the respectful expression 'deva' may in our

orders to the physician *G*îvaka; he will cure me.' Then the Magadha king Seniya Bimbisâra gave orders to *G*îvaka Komârabha*kk*a (saying), 'Go, my dear *G*îvaka; go to U*gg*enî, and cure king Pa*gg*ota.'

*G*îvaka Komârabha*kk*a accepted this order of the Magadha king Seniya Bimbisâra (by saying), 'Yes, Your Majesty,' went to U*gg*enî and to the place where king Pa*gg*ota was, and having approached him, and having carefully observed the change in his appearance, he said to king Pa*gg*ota:

24. 'I will boil up some ghee, Sire, which Your Majesty must drink.'

'Nay, my good *G*îvaka; do what you can for restoring me without giving me ghee; I have an aversion and a distaste for ghee.'

Then *G*îvaka Komârabha*kk*a thought: 'The disease of this king is such a one that it cannot be cured without ghee. What if I were to boil up ghee so that it takes the colour, the smell, and the taste of an astringent decoction[1].'

Then *G*îvaka Komârabha*kk*a boiled some ghee with various drugs so as to give it the colour, the smell, and the taste of an astringent decoction. And *G*îvaka Komârabha*kk*a thought: 'When this king shall have taken the butter and digested it, it will make him vomit. This king is cruel; he might have me killed. What if I were to take leave before-

opinion be brought forward against Professor Jacobi's conjecture (Zeitschrift der Deutschen Morg. Gesellschaft, vol. xxxiv, p. 188) that Bimbisâra was merely a feudal chief under the supreme rule of king Pa*gg*ota. The Pi*t*aka texts are always very exact in the selection of the terms of respect in which the different persons address each other.

[1] See, about the decoctions used in medicine, VI, 4.

hand.' And *G*îvaka Komârabha*kk*a went to the place where king Pa*gg*ota was; having approached him he said to king Pa*gg*ota:

25. 'We physicians, Sire, draw out roots and gather medical drugs at such an hour as this. May it please Your Majesty to send the following order to the (royal) stables, and to the gates (of the town): "Let *G*îvaka ride out on what animal he likes; let him leave (the town) by what gate he likes; let him leave at what hour he likes; let him enter again at what hour he likes."'

And king Pa*gg*ota sent the following order to the (royal) stables and to the gates (of the town): 'Let *G*îvaka ride out on what animal he likes, &c.'

At that time king Pa*gg*ota had a she-elephant, called Bhaddavatikâ, which could travel fifty yo*g*anas (in one day). And *G*îvaka Komârabha*kk*a gave the ghee to king Pa*gg*ota (saying), 'May Your Majesty drink this decoction.' Then, having made king Pa*gg*ota drink the ghee, *G*îvaka Komârabha*kk*a went to the elephant stable, and hasted away from the town on the she-elephant Bhaddavatikâ.

26. And when king Pa*gg*ota had drunk that ghee and was digesting it, it made him vomit. Then king Pa*gg*ota said to his attendants: 'That wicked *G*îvaka, my good Sirs, has given me ghee to drink. Go, my good Sirs, and seek the physician *G*îvaka.'

(The attendants answered), 'He has run away from the town on the she-elephant Bhaddavatikâ.'

At that time king Pa*gg*ota had a slave, Kâka by name, who could travel sixty yo*g*anas (in one day), who had been begotten by a non-human being. To this slave Kâka, king Pa*gg*ota gave the order: 'Go, my good Kâka, and call the physician *G*îvaka back (saying), "The king orders you to return, doctor." But those physicians, my good Kâka, are cunning people; do not accept anything from him.'

27. And the slave Kâka overtook *G*îvaka Komârabha*kk*a on his way, at Kosambî, when he was taking his breakfast. And the slave Kâka said to *G*îvaka Komârabha*kk*a: 'The king orders you to return, doctor.'

(Gîvaka replied), 'Wait, my good Kâka, until we have taken our meal; here, my good Kâka, eat.'

(Kâka said), 'Nay, doctor, the king has told me, "Those physicians, my good Kâka, are cunning people; do not accept anything from him."'

At that time *G*îvaka Komârabha*kk*a, who had cut off some drug with his nail, was eating an emblic myrobalan fruit and drinking water. And *G*îvaka Komârabha*kk*a said to the slave Kâka: 'Here, my good Kâka, eat of this myrobalan fruit and take some water.'

28. Then the slave Kâka thought: 'This physician eats the myrobalan and drinks the water; there cannot be any harm in it;' so he ate half of the myrobalan and drank some water. And that half myrobalan which (*G*îvaka) had given him to eat, opened his bowels on the spot.

Then the slave Kâka said to *G*îvaka Komârabha*kk*a: 'Can my life be saved, doctor?'

(*G*îvaka replied), 'Be not afraid, my good Kâka, you will be quite well. But the king is cruel; that king might have me killed; therefore do I not return.'

Speaking thus he handed over to Kâka the she-elephant Bhaddavatikâ and set out for Râ*g*agaha. Having reached Râ*g*agaha in due course, he went to the place where the Magadha king Seniya Bimbisâra was; having approached him he told the whole thing to the Magadha king Bimbisâra.

(Bimbisâra said), 'You have done right, my good *G*îvaka, that you have not returned; that king is cruel; he might have had you killed.'

29. And king Pa*gg*ota, being restored to health, sent a messenger to *G*îvaka Komârabha*kk*a (with this message), 'May *G*îvaka come to me; I will grant him a boon.'

(*G*îvaka replied), 'Nay, Sir, may His Majesty remember my office.'

At that time king Pa*gg*ota had a suit of Siveyyaka cloth[1], which was the best, and the most excellent, and the first, and the most precious, and the noblest of many cloths, and of many suits of cloth, and of many hundred suits of cloth, and of many thousand suits of cloth, and of many hundred thousand suits of cloth. And king Pa*gg*ota sent this suit of Siveyyaka cloth to *G*îvaka Komârabha*kk*a. Then *G*îvaka Komârabha*kk*a thought: 'This suit of Siveyyaka cloth which king Pa*gg*ota has sent me, is the best and the most excellent (&c., down to :) and of many hundred thousand suits of cloth. Nobody else is worthy to receive it but He the blessed, perfect

[1] Buddhaghosa gives two explanations of Siveyyaka*m* dussayuga*m*. 'Either Siveyyaka cloth means the cloth used in the Uttarakuru country for veiling the dead bodies when they are brought to the burying-ground (sivathikâ). (A certain kind of birds take the bodies to the Himavat mountains in order to eat them, and throw the cloths away. When eremites find them there, they bring them to the king.) Or Siveyyaka cloth means a cloth woven from yarn which skilful women in the Sivi country spin.' No doubt the latter explication is the right one.

Arahat-Buddha, or the Magadha king Seniya Bimbisâra.'

30. At that time a disturbance had befallen the humors of the Blessed One's body. And the Blessed One said to the venerable Ânanda: 'A disturbance, Ânanda, has befallen the humors of the Tathâgata's body; the Tathâgata wishes to take a purgative.' Then the venerable Ânanda went to the place where *G*îvaka Komârabha*kk*a was; having approached him he said to *G*îvaka Komârabha*kk*a:

'My good *G*îvaka, a disturbance has befallen the humors of the Tathâgata's body; the Tathâgata wishes to take a purgative.'

(*G*îvaka replied), 'Well, venerable Ânanda, you ought to rub the Blessed One's body with fat for a few days.'

And the venerable Ânanda, having rubbed the Blessed One's body with fat for some days, went to the place where *G*îvaka Komârabha*kk*a was; having approached him he said to *G*îvaka Komârabha*kk*a: 'I have rubbed, my good *G*îvaka, the Tathâgata's body with fat; do you now what you think fit.'

31. Then *G*îvaka Komârabha*kk*a thought: 'It is not becoming that I should give a strong purgative to the Blessed One.' (Thinking thus), he imbued three handfuls of blue lotuses with various drugs and went therewith to the place where the Blessed One was; having approached him he offered one handful of lotuses to the Blessed One (saying), 'Lord, may the Blessed One smell this first handful of lotuses; that will purge the Blessed One ten times.' Thus he offered also the second handful of lotuses to the Blessed One (saying), 'Lord, may the Blessed One smell this second handful of lotuses;

that will purge the Blessed One ten times.' Thus he offered also the third handful of lotuses to the Blessed One (saying), 'Lord, may the Blessed One smell this third handful of lotuses; that will purge the Blessed One ten times. Thus the Blessed One will have purged full thirty times.' And *G*îvaka Komârabha*kk*a, having given to the Blessed One a purgative for full thirty times, bowed down before the Blessed One, and passed round him with his right side towards him, and went away.

32. And *G*îvaka Komârabha*kk*a, when he was out of doors, thought: 'I have given indeed to the Blessed One a purgative for full thirty times, but as the humors of the Tathâgatha's body are disturbed, it will not purge the Blessed One full thirty times; it will purge the Blessed One only twenty-nine times. But the Blessed One, having purged, will take a bath; the bath will purge the Blessed One once; thus the Blessed One will be purged full thirty times.'

And the Blessed One, who understood by the power of his mind this reflection of *G*îvaka Komârabha*kk*a, said to the venerable Ânanda: '*G*îvaka Komârabha*kk*a, Ânanda, when he was out of doors, has thought: "I have given indeed (&c., as above, down to:) thus the Blessed One will be purged full thirty times." Well, Ânanda, get warm water ready.'

The venerable Ânanda accepted this order of the Blessed One (saying), 'Yes, Lord,' and got warm water ready.

33. And *G*îvaka Komârabha*kk*a went to the place where the Blessed One was; having approached him and respectfully saluted the Blessed One, he sat down near him; sitting near him *G*îvaka Komârabha*kk*a said to the Blessed One: 'Lord, has the

Blessed One purged?' (Buddha replied), 'I have purged, *G*îvaka.' (*G*îvaka said), 'When I was out of doors, Lord, I thought: "I have given indeed, &c." Lord, may the Blessed One take a bath, may the Happy One take a bath.' Then the Blessed One bathed in that warm water; the bath purged the Blessed One once; thus the Blessed One was purged full thirty times.

And *G*îvaka Komârabha*kk*a said to the Blessed One: 'Lord, until the Blessed One's body is completely restored, you had better abstain from liquid food.' And ere long the Blessed One's body was completely restored.

34. Then *G*îvaka Komârabha*kk*a took that suit of Siveyyaka cloth and went to the place where the Blessed One was; having approached him, and having respectfully saluted the Blessed One, he sat down near him. Sitting near him, *G*îvaka Komârabha*kk*a said to the Blessed One: 'Lord, I ask one boon of the Blessed One.' (Buddha replied), 'The Tathâgatas, *G*îvaka, are above granting boons (before they know what they are).' (*G*îvaka said), 'Lord, it is a proper and unobjectionable demand.'—'Speak, *G*îvaka.'

'Lord, the Blessed One wears only pa*m*sukûla robes (robes made of rags taken from a dust heap or a cemetery[1]), and so does the fraternity of Bhikkhus. Now, Lord, this suit of Siveyyaka cloth has been sent to me by king Pa*gg*ota, which is the best, and the most excellent, and the first, and the most precious, and the noblest of many cloths and of

[1] Buddhaghosa: 'To the Blessed One during the twenty years from his Sambodhi till this story happened no one had presented a lay robe.'

many suits of cloth, and of many hundred suits of cloth, and of many thousand suits of cloth, and of many hundred thousand suits of cloth. Lord, may the Blessed One accept from me this suit of Siveyyaka cloth, and may he allow to the fraternity of Bhikkhus to wear lay robes[1].'

The Blessed One accepted the suit of Siveyyaka cloth. And the Blessed One taught, incited, animated, and gladdened *G*îvaka Komârabha*kk*a by religious discourse. And *G*îvaka Komârabha*kk*a, having been taught, incited, animated, and gladdened by the Blessed One by religious discourse, rose from his seat, respectfully saluted the Blessed One, passed round him with his right side towards him, and went away.

35. And the Blessed One, after having delivered a religious discourse in consequence of that, thus addressed the Bhikkhus:

'I allow you, O Bhikkhus, to wear lay robes. He who likes may wear pa*m*sukûla robes; he who likes may accept lay robes. Whether you are pleased with the one or with the other sort[2] of robes, I approve it.'

Now the people at Râ*g*agaha heard, 'The Blessed One has allowed the Bhikkhus to wear lay robes.' Then those people became glad and delighted (because they thought), 'Now we will bestow gifts (on the Bhikkhus) and acquire merit by good works,

[1] Gahapati*k*îvara may be translated also, as Buddhaghosa explains it, 'a robe presented by lay people.'

[2] Itarîtara ('the one or the other') clearly refers to the two sorts of robes mentioned before, not, as Childers (s.v. itarîtaro) understands it, to whether the robes are good or bad. Compare also chap. 3, § 2.

since the Blessed One has allowed the Bhikkhus to wear lay robes.' And in one day many thousands of robes were presented at Râgagaha (to the Bhikkhus).

And the people in the country heard, 'The Blessed One has allowed the Bhikkhus to wear lay robes.' Then those people became glad (&c., as above, down to:) And in one day many thousands of robes were presented through the country also (to the Bhikkhus).

36. At that time the Samgha had received a mantle. They told this thing to the Blessed One.

'I allow you, O Bhikkhus, to wear a mantle.'

They had got a siik mantle.

'I allow you, O Bhikkhus, to wear a silk mantle.'

They had got a fleecy counterpane [1].

'I allow you, O Bhikkhus, to use a fleecy counterpane.'

End of the first Bhânavâra.

2.

At that time the king of Kâsi [2] sent to Gîvaka Komârabhakka a woollen garment made half of Benares cloth . . . [3]. Then Gîvaka Komârabhakka

---

[1] See Abhidhânapp. v. 312.

[2] Buddhaghosa: 'This king was Pasenadi's brother, the same father's son.' He appears to have been a sub-king of Pasenadi, for in the Lohikka-sutta it is stated that Pasenadi's rule extended both over Kâsi and Kosala ('Râgâ Pasenadi Kosalo Kâsikosalam agghâvasati').

[3] Our translation of addhakâsikam kambalam is merely

took that woollen garment made half of Benares cloth and went to the place where the Blessed One was; having approached him, and respectfully saluted the Blessed One, he sat down near him. Sitting near him, *G*îvaka Komârabha*kk*a said to the Blessed One: 'Lord, this woollen garment made half of Benares cloth. . . .[1] has been sent to me by the king of Kâsi. May the Blessed One, Lord, accept this woollen garment, which may be to me a long time for a good and a blessing.' The Blessed One accepted that woollen garment.

And the Blessed One taught (&c., as in chap. 1, § 34, down to:) and went away.

And the Blessed One, after having delivered a religious discourse in consequence of that, thus addressed the Bhikkhus:

'I allow you, O Bhikkhus, to use woollen garments.'

3.

1. At that time the fraternity got robes of different kinds. Now the Bhikkhus thought: 'What robes are allowed to us by the Blessed One, and what robes are not allowed?'

They told this thing to the Blessed One.

'I allow you, O Bhikkhus, six kinds of robes, viz.

---

conjectural. Buddhaghosa has the following note: 'A*ddh*akâsiya*m*, here kâsi means one thousand; a thing that is worth one thousand, is called kâsiya. This garment was worth five hundred; therefore it is called a*ddh*akâsiya. And for the same reason it is said, upa*ddh*akâsina*m* khamamâna*m*.' Perhaps vikâsika*m* at VI, 15, 5 may have some connection with the word used here.

[1] See last note.

those made of linen, of cotton, of silk, of wool, of coarse cloth, and of hempen cloth.'

2. At that time the Bhikkhus accepted lay robes, but did not get pa*m*sukûla robes, because they had scruples (and thought): 'The Blessed One has allowed us either kind of robes only, not both kinds[1].'

They told this thing to the Blessed One.

'I allow, O Bhikkhus, that he who accepts lay robes, may get also pa*m*sukûla robes. If you are pleased with those both sorts of robes, I approve that also.'

4.

1. At that time a number of Bhikkhus were travelling on the road in the Kosala country. Some of these Bhikkhus went off (the road) to a cemetery in order to get themselves pa*m*sukûla robes; some (other) Bhikkhus did not wait. Those Bhikkhus who had gone to the cemetery for pa*m*sukûla robes, got themselves pa*m*sukûlas; those Bhikkhus who had not waited, said to them: 'Friends, give us also a part (of your pa*m*sukûlas).' They replied, 'We will not give you a part, friends; why have you not waited?'

They told this thing to the Blessed One.

'I prescribe, O Bhikkhus, that you are not obliged to give a part against your will to Bhikkhus who have not waited.'

2. At that time a number of Bhikkhus were travelling on the road in the Kosala country. Some

---

[1] See chap. 1, § 35.

of these Bhikkhus went off (the road) to a cemetery in order to get themselves pa*m*sukûla robes; some (other) Bhikkhus waited for them. Those Bhikkhus who had gone to the cemetery for pa*m*sukûla robes, got themselves pa*m*sukûlas; those Bhikkhus who had waited, said to them: 'Friends, give us also a part (of your pa*m*sukûlas).' They replied, 'We will not give you a part, friends; why did you not also go off (to the cemetery)?'

They told this thing to the Blessed One.

'I prescribe, O Bhikkhus, that you give a part (even) against your will to Bhikkhus who have waited.'

3. At that time a number of Bhikkhus were travelling on the road in the Kosala country. Some of these Bhikkhus went aside first from (the road) to a cemetery in order to get themselves pa*m*sukûla robes; some (other) Bhikkhus went aside later. Those Bhikkhus who had gone first to the cemetery for pa*m*sukûla robes, got themselves pa*m*sukûlas; those Bhikkhus who had got off later, did not get any, and said (to the other ones): 'Friends, give us also a part.' They replied, 'We will not give you a part, friends; why did you get off (to the cemetery) after us?'

They told this thing to the Blessed One.

'I prescribe, O Bhikkhus, that you are not obliged to give a part against your will to Bhikkhus who have gone (to the cemetery) later (than yourselves).'

4. At that time a number of Bhikkhus were travelling on the road in the Kosala country. They went altogether off (the road) to a cemetery in order to get themselves pa*m*sukûla robes; some of the Bhikkhus got pa*m*sukûlas, other Bhikkhus did not

get any. The Bhikkhus who had got nothing, said: 'Friends, give us also a part (of your pa*m*sukûlas).' They replied, 'We will not give you a part, friends; why did you not get (them yourselves)?'

They told this thing to the Blessed One.

'I prescribe, O Bhikkhus, that you give a part (even) against your will to Bhikkhus who have gone (to the cemetery) together with yourselves.'

5. At that time a number of Bhikkhus were travelling on the road in the Kosala country. They went off (the road) to a cemetery in order to get themselves pa*m*sukûla robes, after having made an agreement (about the distribution of what they were to find). Some of the Bhikkhus got themselves pa*m*sukûlas, other Bhikkhus did not get any. The Bhikkhus who had got nothing, said: 'Friends, give us also a part (of the pa*m*sukûlas).' They replied, 'We will not give you a part, friends; why did you not get (them yourselves)?'

They told this thing to the Blessed One.

'I prescribe, O Bhikkhus, that you give a part, (even) against your will, to Bhikkhus who have gone (with you to the cemetery) after having made with you an agreement (about the distribution of the pa*m*sukûlas).'

5.

1. At that time people went to the Ârâma with robes[1] (which they intended to present to the

[1] It will be as well to remind the reader that here and in the following chapters *k*îvara can mean both 'a robe' and 'cloth for making robes.'

Bhikkhus). They found there no Bhikkhu who was to receive the robes; so they took them back again. (In consequence of that) few robes were given (to the Bhikkhus).

They told this thing to the Blessed One.

'I prescribe, O Bhikkhus, that you appoint a Bhikkhu possessed of the following five qualities, to receive the robes (presented to the Bhikkhus): (a person) who does not go in the evil course of lust, in the evil course of hatred, in the evil course of delusion, in the evil course of fear, and who knows what has been received and what has not.

2. 'And you ought, O Bhikkhus, to appoint (such a Bhikkhu) in this way: First, that Bhikkhu must be asked (to accept that commission). When he has been asked, let a learned, competent Bhikkhu proclaim the following *ñatti* before the Sa*m*gha: "Let the Sa*m*gha, reverend Sirs, hear me. If the Sa*m*gha is ready, let the Sa*m*gha appoint the Bhikkhu N. N. to receive the robes (presented to the Bhikkhus). This is the *ñatti*. Let the Sa*m*gha, reverend Sirs, hear me. The Sa*m*gha appoints the Bhikkhu N. N. to receive the robes (presented). Let any one of the venerable brethren who is in favour of our appointing the Bhikkhu N. N. to receive the robes (presented), be silent, and any one who is not in favour of it, speak. The Bhikkhu N. N. has been appointed by the Sa*m*gha to receive the robes (presented). The Sa*m*gha is in favour of it, therefore are you silent; thus I understand."'

6.

1. At that time the Bhikkhus who had to receive the robes (presented), after having received them, left them there (in the Vihâras) and went away; the robes were spoilt.

They told this thing to the Blessed One.

'I prescribe, O Bhikkhus, that you appoint a Bhikkhu possessed of the following five qualities, to lay by the robes (received): (a person) who does not go in the evil course of lust, in the evil course of hatred, in the evil course of delusion, in the evil course of fear, and who knows what is laid by and what is not.

2. 'And you ought, O Bhikkhus, to appoint (&c., see chap. 5, § 2).'

7.

At that time the Bhikkhus appointed to lay the robes by, laid the robes by in an open hall, or at the foot of a tree, or in the hollow of a Nimba tree[1]; thus they were eaten by rats and white ants.

They told this thing to the Blessed One.

'I prescribe, O Bhikkhus, that you appoint what the Sa*m*gha chooses, a Vihâra, or an A*ddh*ayoga[2], or a storied building, or an attic, or a cave, to be the store-room[3] (of the Sa*m*gha).

---

[1] Compare III, 12, 5. [2] Compare I, 30, 4.

[3] The word bha*nd*âgâra does not imply any special reference to robes more than to any other articles belonging to the Sa*m*gha. A good many things which were usually kept in the bha*nd*âgâra are mentioned at *K*ullav. VI, 21, 3.

'And you ought, O Bhikkhus, to appoint it in this way: Let a learned, competent Bhikkhu proclaim the following *ñatti* before the Saṁgha: "Let the Saṁgha, reverend Sirs, hear me. If the Saṁgha is ready, let the Saṁgha appoint the Vihâra called N. N. to be the store-room (of the Saṁgha), (&c., the usual formula of a *ñattidutiya kamma*)."'

8.

1. At that time the cloth in the Saṁgha's store-room was not protected (from rain, mice, &c.)

They told this thing to the Blessed One.

'I prescribe, O Bhikkhus, that you appoint a Bhikkhu possessed of the following five qualities, to take charge of the store-room: (a person) who does not go in the evil course of lust (&c., as in chap. 5, § 1), and who knows what is protected and what is not.

'And you ought, O Bhikkhus, to appoint (&c., see chap. 5, § 2).'

2. At that time the *Kh*abbaggiya Bhikkhus expelled a Bhikkhu, who had charge of a store-room, from his place.

They told this thing to the Blessed One.

'Let no one, O Bhikkhus, expel a Bhikkhu, who has charge of a store-room, from his place. He who does so, commits a *dukkaṭa* offence.'

9.

1. At that time the Saṁgha's store-room was over-full of clothes.

They told this thing to the Blessed One.

'I prescribe, O Bhikkhus, that they should be distributed by the assembled Samgha.'

At that time the whole Samgha, when distributing the clothes, made a bustle.

They told this thing to the Blessed One.

'I prescribe, O Bhikkhus, that you appoint a Bhikkhu possessed of the following five qualities, to distribute the clothes: (a person) who does not go in the evil course of lust . . . . and who knows what is distributed and what is not.

'And you ought, O Bhikkhus, to appoint (&c., see chap. 5, § 2).'

2. Now the Bhikkhus appointed to distribute the clothes thought: 'In what way are we to distribute the clothes?'

They told this thing to the Blessed One.

'I prescribe, O Bhikkhus, that you first assort the clothes, estimate them, share them according to their higher or lower value[1], then count the Bhikkhus, divide them into troops[2], and divide the portions of cloth (accordingly).'

Now the Bhikkhus, who were to distribute the clothes, thought: 'What portion of cloth shall be given to the Sâmaneras?'

They told this thing to the Blessed One.

'I prescribe, O Bhikkhus, that you give to the Sâmaneras half a portion.'

---

[1] Buddhaghosa: 'If there are robes of the same quality, for instance, each worth ten (kâhâpanas), for all Bhikkhus, it is all right; if they are not, they must take together the robes which are worth nine or eight, with those which are worth one or two, and thus they must make equal portions.'

[2] 'In case the day should not suffice for distributing the robes to the Bhikkhus one by one' (Buddhaghosa).

3. At that time a certain Bhikkhu wished to go across (a river or a desert) with the portion that should come to him.

They told this thing to the Blessed One.

'I prescribe, O Bhikkhus, that you give to a Bhikkhu who is going across (a river or a desert), the portion that should come to him.'

At that time a certain Bhikkhu wished to go across (a river or a desert) with a greater portion (of cloth than fell to his share).

They told this thing to the Blessed One.

'I prescribe, O Bhikkhus, that you give more than the due portion (to a Bhikkhu who desires it), if he gives a compensation.'

4. Now the Bhikkhus, who were to distribute the clothes, thought: 'How are we to assign the portions of cloth (to the single Bhikkhus), by turns as they arrive (and ask for cloth), or according to their age (i. e. the time elapsed since their ordination)?'

They told this thing to the Blessed One.

'I prescribe, O Bhikkhus, that you cast lots, made of grass-blades, after having made every defective portion even.'

10.

1. At that time the Bhikkhus dyed cloth with (cow-)dung or with yellow clay. The robes were badly coloured.

They told this thing to the Blessed One.

'I prescribe, O Bhikkhus, that you use the following six kinds of dye, viz. dye made of roots, dye made of trunks of trees, dye made of bark, dye made of leaves, dye made of flowers, dye made of fruits.'

2. At that time the Bhikkhus dyed cloth with unboiled dye; the cloth became ill-smelling.

They told this thing to the Blessed One.

'I prescribe, O Bhikkhus, that you boil the dye (and use) little dye-pots.'

They spilt the dye.

'I prescribe, O Bhikkhus, that you put basins (under the dye-pots) to catch the spilt (dye).'

At that time the Bhikkhus did not know whether the dye was boiled or not.

They told this thing to the Blessed One.

'I prescribe, O Bhikkhus, that you let a drop of dye fall into water, or on to your nail (in order to try if the dye is duly boiled).'

3. At that time the Bhikkhus, when pouring the dye out (of the pot), upset the pot; the pot was broken.

They told this thing to the Blessed One.

'I prescribe, O Bhikkhus, that you use a dye-ladle or a scoop with a long handle.'

At that time the Bhikkhus did not possess vessels for keeping dye.

They told this thing to the Blessed One.

'I prescribe, O Bhikkhus, that you get jars and bowls for keeping the dye.'

At that time the Bhikkhus rubbed the cloth against the vessels and the bowls (in which they dyed it); the cloth was rent.

They told this thing to the Blessed One.

'I prescribe, O Bhikkhus, that you use a (large) trough for dying (cloth) in.'

11.

1. At that time the Bhikkhus spread the cloth on the floor (when they had dyed it); the cloth became dusty.

They told this thing to the Blessed One.

'I prescribe, O Bhikkhus, that you spread grass (and put the cloth on it).'

The grass they had spread was eaten by white ants.

They told this thing to the Blessed One.

'I prescribe, O Bhikkhus, that you get a bambû peg or rope to hang the cloth on.'

They hung it up in the middle; the dye dropped down on both sides.

They told this thing to the Blessed One.

'I prescribe, O Bhikkhus, that you tie it fast at the corner.'

The corner wore out.

They told this thing to the Blessed One.

'I prescribe, O Bhikkhus, the use of a clothes-line.'

The dye dropped down on one side.

They told this thing to the Blessed One.

'I prescribe, O Bhikkhus, that you turn the cloth, when dying it, whenever required, and that you do not go away before the dye has ceased to drop.'

2. At that time the cloth had become stiff[1].

They told this thing to the Blessed One.

---

[1] Buddhaghosa: Patthinan ti (this is the reading of the Berlin MS.) atira*g*itattâ thaddha*m*, i. e. 'Patthina*m* means that it had become stiff from too much dye.' Thîna or thinna is Sanskrit styâna.

'I prescribe, O Bhikkhus, that you dip (the cloth) into water (in order to remove the excessive dye).'

At that time the cloth became rough.

They told this thing to the Blessed One.

'I prescribe, O Bhikkhus, (that you smooth it by) beating it with your hands.'

At that time the Bhikkhus possessed a*kkh*innaka[1] robes of yellowish colour like ivory. The people were annoyed, murmured, and became angry: '(The Bhikkhus dress) like those who still live in the pleasures of the world.'

They told this thing to the Blessed One.

'You ought not, O Bhikkhus, to possess a*kkh*innaka robes. He who does, commits a dukka*t*a offence.'

12.

1. Now when the Blessed One had remained at Râ*g*agaha as long as he thought fit, he set forth on his journey towards Dakkhi*n*â-giri (the Southern Hills[2]). And the Blessed One beheld how the Magadha rice fields were divided into short pieces[3],

[1] That is, made of untorn cloth. See VIII, 21, 2.

[2] These are always mentioned in connection with Râ*g*agaha (Mahâvagga I, 53; *K*ullavagga XI, 1–10), and are probably the name of the mountainous district immediately south of Râ*g*agaha.

[3] A*kk*ibaddhan (sic) ti *k*aturassakedârakabaddha*m* (B.). I have never seen a field divided 'ray-fashion,' which would apparently be the literal translation of the term, and it is difficult to see how the necessary water could be conducted from strip to strip of a field so divided. Buddhaghosa also, though his explanation is insufficient, evidently does not take a*kk*i in the ordinary sense (Rh. D.).

and in rows[1], and by outside boundaries[2] (or ridges), and by cross boundaries[3].

On seeing this the Blessed One spake thus to the venerable Ânanda: 'Dost thou perceive, Ânanda, how the Magadha rice fields are divided into short pieces, and in rows, and by outside boundaries, and by cross boundaries?'

'Even so, Lord.'

'Could you, Ânanda, provide[4] robes of a like kind for the Bhikkhus?'

'I could, Lord.'

Now when the Blessed One had remained in the Southern Hills as long as he thought fit, he returned again to Râgagaha.

Then Ânanda provided robes of a like kind for many Bhikkhus; and going up to the place where the Blessed One was, he spake thus to the Blessed One: 'May the Blessed One be pleased to look at the robes which I have provided.'

2. Then the Blessed One on that occasion addressed the Bhikkhus and said: 'An able man, O Bhikkhus, is Ânanda; of great understanding, O Bhikkhus, is Ânanda, inasmuch as what has been spoken by me in short that can he understand in full, and can make the cross seams[5], and the

---

[1] Pa*l*ibaddhan (sic) ti âyâmato *k*a vitthârato *k*a dîghamariyâdabaddha*m* (B.).

[2] Mariyâdabaddhan (sic) ti antarantarâya mariyâdâya mariyâdabaddha*m* (B.).

[3] Singhâ*t*akabaddhan (sic) ti mariyâdâyâ (sic) mariyâda*m* viniviggh*itvâ gata*tth*âne singhâ*t*akabaddha*m*. *K*atukkasa*nth*ânan ti attho (B.).

[4] Sa*m*vidahitun ti kâtu*m* (B.).

[5] Kusi*m* pî 'ti âyâmato *k*a vitthârato *k*a anuvâtâdîna*m* dîghapa*tt*âna*m* eta*m* adhiva*k*ana*m* (B.).

intermediate cross seams[1], and the greater circles[2], and the lesser circles[3], and the turning in[4], and the lining of the turning in[5], and the collar piece[6], and the knee piece[7], and the elbow piece[8]. And it shall be of torn pieces[9], roughly sewn together[10], suitable for a Samana, a thing which his enemies cannot covet[11]. I enjoin upon you, O Bhikkhus, the use of an under robe of torn pieces, and of an upper robe of torn pieces, and of a waist cloth of torn pieces[12].'

---

[1] *Addh*akusî ti antarantarâ rassa-pa*tt*ânam nâmam (B.).

[2] Ma*nd*alan ti pañ*k*a-kha*nd*ika-*k*îvarassa ekekasmim kha*nd*e mahâ-ma*nd*alam (B.).

[3] A*ddh*ama*nd*alan ti khuddaka-ma*nd*alam (B.).

[4] Viva*tt*an ti ma*nd*alañ *k*a *addh*a-ma*nd*alañ *k*a ekato katvâ sibbitam mag*gh*ima-kha*nd*am (B.).

[5] Anuviva*tt*an ti tassa ubhosu passesu dve kha*nd*âni. Athavâ viva*tt*assa ekekapassato dvinnam pi *k*atunnam pi kha*nd*ânam etam nâmam (B.).

[6] Gîveyyakan ti gîva-*tth*âne da*lh*i-karan-attham aññam suttam sibbitam âgantuka-pa*tt*am (B.).

[7] *G*aṅgheyyakan ti *g*aṅgha-pâpuna-*tth*âne tatth' eva samsibbita-pa*tt*am. Gîva-*tth*âne *k*a *g*aṅgha-*tth*âne *k*a pa*tt*ânam ev' etam nâman ti pi vadanti (B.).

[8] Bâhantan ti anuviva*tt*ânam bahi ekekakha*nd*am. Athavâ suppamâ*n*am *k*îvaram pârupentena samharitâ bâhâya upari *th*apitâ ubho anto-bahi-mukhâ ti*tth*anti. Tesam etam nâmam. Ayam eva hi nayo Mahâ-atthakathâyam vutto ti (B.). This latter explanation from bâhâ seems evidently more correct than the other one from bahi; and we accordingly follow it.

[9] See the end of the last chapter.

[10] Satta-lûkha; in which compound the signification of satta is by no means clear. Buddhaghosa has no note upon it. Now it is curious that in chapter 21, below, it is laid down that the robe is to be sutta-lûkha, the meaning of which would fit this passage excellently. We have accordingly adopted that reading here.

[11] Compare the similar expressions at *G*âtaka I, 8 and 9.

[12] The general sense of this chapter is clear enough. As an Indian field, the common property of the village community, was

13.

1. Now when the Blessed One had remained at Râgagaha as long as he thought fit, he went forth on his journey towards Vesâli. And the Blessed One, when on the high road between Râgagaha and Vesâli, saw a number of Bhikkhus smothered up in robes[1], they went along with robes made up into a roll[2] on their heads, or on their backs, or on their waist. And when the Blessed One saw them, he thought: 'With too great celerity have these foolish persons given themselves up to superfluity[3] in the matter of dress. It would be well were I to confine the dress of the Bhikkhus within limits, and were to fix a bound thereto.'

2. And the Blessed One, proceeding in due course on his journey toward Vesâli, arrived at that place. And there, at Vesâli, the Blessed One stayed at the Gotamaka shrine[4]. And at that time in the cold

divided, for the purposes of cultivation, across and across, so must also the Bhikkhu's robe be divided. That some, both of the agricultural and of the tailoring terms, should now be unintelligible to us is not surprising. Buddhaghosa himself, as the extracts from his commentary show, was not certain of the meaning of them all.

[1] Ubbhandite *k*îvarehi. The former word is of course applied to the Bhikkhus. Compare Childers, under Bhan*d*ikâ, and *G*âtaka I, 504 (last line but one).

[2] Bhisî = Sanskrit B*r*isî. Compare the 14th Pâ*k*ittiya, where we ought to have rendered the word 'bolster.' Childers is incorrect in translating it by 'mat.'

[3] Mentioned also, as being near to Vesâli, in the 'Book of the Great Decease,' III, 2.

[4] Bâhullâya âvattâ. This phrase occurs in Mahâvagga I, 31, 5.

winter nights, in the period between the Ash*t*akâ festivals when the snow falls[1], the Blessed One sat at night in the open air with but one robe on, and the Blessed One felt not cold. As the first watch of the night was coming to its end, the Blessed One felt cold; and he put on a second robe, and felt not cold. As the middle watch of the night was coming to its end, the Blessed One felt cold; and he put on a third robe, and felt not cold. As the last watch of the night was coming to an end, when the dawn was breaking and the night was far spent[2], the Blessed One felt cold; and he put on a fourth robe, and felt not cold.

3. Then this thought sprang up in the Blessed One's mind: 'Those men of good birth[3] in this doctrine and discipline who are affected by cold, and are afraid of cold, they are able to make use of three robes[4]. It were well if in confining within limits the dress of the Bhikkhus, and in fixing a bound thereto, I were to allow the use of three robes.' And on that occasion the Blessed One, when he had

---

[1] See our note on the same phrase at Mahâvagga I, 20, 15.

[2] Nandimukhiyâ rattiyâ. The derivation of this phrase is uncertain, though the general meaning is not subject to doubt. The Sanskrit form of the whole phrase will be found in the Lalita Vistara at p. 447. Comp. *S*âṅkhâyana-g*ri*hya, ed. Oldenberg, IV, 4, where the word nândîmukho occurs in a different connection.

[3] In the text read Ye pi kho kulaputtâ. The idea is that men of lower grade, being accustomed to cold, would not want so many robes. But there must be one rule for all; and the rule is accordingly made to suit the comfort of the weaker brethren—early Buddhism, contrary to an erroneous opinion still frequently expressed, being opposed to asceticism.

[4] Or, 'to get on with the three robes.' Compare the use of yâpetu*m* in the 'Book of the Great Decease,' II, 32.

delivered a religious discourse, addressed the Bhikkhus, and said:

4, 5. 'When on the high road, &c. . . . I saw, &c. . . . and I thought, &c. . . . (all the chapter is repeated down to ". . . . I were to allow the use of three robes"). I allow you, O Bhikkhus, the use of three robes, (to wit), a double waist cloth, and a single[1] upper robe, and a single under garment[2].'

---

[1] Ekakkiyam. Compare Gâtaka I, 326. Buddhaghosa says dvigunam dupatta-samghâtim ekakkiyam ekapattam. Though 'single,' the lengths of cotton cloth, pieced together, of which the robes were made, were allowed to be doubled at the seams, the collar, the elbows, and the knees. See above, VII, 1, 5.

[2] The waist cloth (samghâti) was wrapped round the waist and back, and secured with a girdle. The under garment (antaravâsaka; see also the end of this note) was wrapped round the loins and reached below the knee, being fastened round the loins by an end of the cloth being tucked in there; and sometimes also by a girdle. The upper robe (uttarâsamga) was wrapped round the legs from the loins to the ankles, and the end was then drawn, at the back, from the right hip, over the left shoulder, and either (as is still the custom in Siam, and in the Siamese sect in Ceylon) allowed to fall down in front, or (as is still the custom in Burma, and in the Burmese sect in Ceylon) drawn back again over the right shoulder, and allowed to fall down on the back. From the constant reference to the practice of adjusting the robe over one shoulder as a special mark of respect (for instance, Mahâvagga I, 29, 2; IV, 3, 3), the Burmese custom would seem to be in accordance with the most ancient way of usually wearing the robe. The oldest statues of the Buddha, which represent the robe as falling over only one shoulder, are probably later than the passages just referred to.

The ordinary dress of laymen, even of good family, in Gotama's time was much more scanty than the decent dress thus prescribed for the Bhikkhus. See Rh. D.'s note on the 'Book of the Great Decease,' VI, 26. But it consisted also, like that of the Bhikkhus, not in garments made with sleeves or trousers, to fit the limbs, but in simple lengths of cloth.

The antara-vâsaka corresponds, in the dress of the monks, to

6. Now at that time the *Kh*abbaggiya Bhikkhus, on the ground that three robes had been allowed by the Blessed One, used to frequent the village in one suit of three robes, and in another suit to rest in the Ârâma, and in another to go to the bath. Then those Bhikkhus who were modest were annoyed, murmured, and became indignant, saying, 'How can the *Kh*abbaggiya Bhikkhus wear extra suits of robes.'

And those Bhikkhus told the matter to the Blessed One. Then the Blessed One on that occasion, when he had delivered a religious discourse, addressed the Bhikkhus, and said:

'You are not, O Bhikkhus, to wear an extra suit of robes. Whosoever does so, shall be dealt with according to law[1].'

7. Now at that time the venerable Ânanda had acquired an extra suit of robes, and the venerable Ânanda was desirous of giving the extra suit to the venerable Sâriputta, but the venerable Sâriputta was staying at Sâketa. Then the venerable Ânanda thought: 'It hath been laid down by the Blessed One that we are not to keep an extra suit of robes. Now I have received one, and I want to give it to the venerable Sâriputta; but he is staying at Sâketa. What now shall I do?'

---

the sâ*t*ika in the dress of ordinary women, and was of the same shape as the udaka-sâ*t*ika, or bathing dress, prescribed for the use both of monks (below, chapter 15) and of nuns (Bhikkhunî-vibhaṅga, Pâ*k*ittiya XXII). The latter was, however, somewhat shorter.

The ordinary dress of the Bhikkhunîs or Sisters consisted of the same three garments as that of the Bhikkhus.

[1] That is, according to the first Nissaggiya. The first section of the Sutta-vibhaṅga on that r e is identical with this section.

And the venerable Ânanda told this thing to the Blessed One.

'How long will it be, Ânanda, before the venerable Sâriputta returns?'

'He will come back, Lord, on the ninth or the tenth day from now.'

Then the Blessed One on that occasion, when he had delivered a religious discourse, addressed the Bhikkhus, and said:

'I allow you, O Bhikkhus, to keep an extra suit of robes up to the tenth day[1].'

8. Now at that time the Bhikkhus used to get extra suits of robes given to them. And these Bhikkhus thought: 'What now should we do with extra suits of robes?'

They told this thing to the Blessed One.

'I enjoin upon you, O Bhikkhus, to make over an extra suit of robes (to other Bhikkhus who have no robes[2]).'

14.

1. Now when the Blessed One had remained at Vesâli as long as he thought fit, he went onwards on his journey towards Benares. And in due course he arrived at Benares, and there, at Benares, he stayed in the hermitage in the Migadâya.

Now at that time a certain Bhikkhu's under robe was torn. And that Bhikkhu thought: 'The Blessed

[1] So the first Nissaggiya; the second section of the Sutta-vibhaṅga on which rule is identical with this section 7.

[2] On vikappetum, compare our note above, the 59th Pâkittiya, and below, chapters 20, 22.

One has ordained the use of three robes, a double waist cloth, and a single upper robe, and a single under-garment [1], and this under-garment of mine is torn. What if I were to insert a slip of cloth [2] so that the robe shall be double all round and single in the middle.'

2. So that Bhikkhu inserted a slip of cloth. And the Blessed One on his way round the sleeping apartments saw him doing so, went up to the place where he was, and said to him:

'What are you doing, O Bhikkhu?'

'I am inserting a slip of cloth, Lord.'

'That is very good, O Bhikkhu. It is quite right of you, O Bhikkhu, to insert a slip of cloth.'

And the Blessed One on that occasion, when he had delivered a religious discourse, addressed the Bhikkhus, and said:

'I allow you, O Bhikkhus, to use a double waist cloth, and a single upper robe, and a single under-garment, of cloths which are new, or as good as new [3]; and the use of a fourfold waist cloth, and of a double upper robe, and of a double under robe of cloth which has been worn for a long time. You are to make endeavour to get sufficient material from rags taken from the dust-heap [4], or from bits picked up in the bazaar [4]. I allow you, O Bhikkhus, slips of cloth inserted bolt-like to hold a torn robe

[1] See above, VIII, 13, 5.

[2] Buddhaghosa says, Aggala*m* a*kkh*âdeyyan (sic) ti *kh*inna*tth*â*n*e pilotika-kha*nd*a*m* laggâpeyya*m*. The word occurs at Gâtaka I, 8, where the liability to want such an insertion is given as one of the nine disadvantages of a robe from the ascetic's point of view.

[3] Ahata-kappâna*m*. See above, VII, 1, 6.

[4] See our notes on these expressions above, VII, 1, 6.

together, patches[1], darns[2], and small pieces of cloth sewn on by way of marking[2], or of strengthening[2] the robe.'

15.

1. Now when the Blessed One had remained at Benares as long as he thought fit, he went onwards on his journey toward Sâvatthi. And in due course journeying straight on he arrived at Sâvatthi; and there, at Sâvatthi, he stayed at the *G*etavana, Anâtha-pi*nd*ika's Ârâma. And Visâkhâ the mother of Migâra went up to the place where the Blessed One was; and when she had come there, she saluted the Blessed One, and took her seat on one side. And the Blessed One taught Visâkhâ the mother of Migâra seated thus: and incited, and aroused, and gladdened her with religious discourse. And Visâkhâ the mother of Migâra when she had been thus taught, &c., spake thus to the Blessed One: 'Will my Lord the Blessed One consent to accept his morrow's meal at my hands, together with the company of the Bhikkhus?' The Blessed One, by remaining silent, granted his consent; and Visâkhâ the mother of Migâra, perceiving that the Blessed One had consented, rose from her seat, and saluted the Blessed One, and keeping him on her right side as she passed him, she departed thence.

[1] This liability to have to be patched is given, in connection with the previous phrase, as one of the nine disadvantages of robes at *G*âtaka I, 8; and **tunnavâya** occurs as the expression for a mender of old clothes at *K*ullavagga VI, 5, 1.

[2] See our notes on these expressions above, VII, 1, 5.

2. Now at that time, when the night was far spent, there was a great storm of rain over the whole world[1]. And the Blessed One said to the Bhikkhus:

'Just as it is raining in the Getavana, O Bhikkhus, so is it raining over the whole world. Let yourselves, O Bhikkhus, be rained down upon, for this is the last time there will be a mighty storm of rain over the whole world.'

'Even so, Lord,' said those Bhikkhus in assent to the Blessed One; and throwing off their robes they let themselves be rained down upon.

3. And Visâkhâ the mother of Migâra having provided sweet food, both hard and soft, gave command to a slave girl, saying,

'Go thou[2] to the Ârâma; and when you are there, announce the time, saying, "The time, Sirs, has arrived, and the meal is ready."'

'Even so, my Lady,' said the slave girl in assent to Visâkhâ, the mother of Migâra; and going to the Ârâma she beheld there the Bhikkhus, with their robes thrown off, letting themselves be rained down upon. Then thinking, 'These are not Bhikkhus in the Ârâma, they are naked ascetics letting the rain fall on them,' she returned to the place where Visâkhâ the mother of Migâra was, and said to her:

'There are no Bhikkhus in the Ârâma; there are

---

[1] *K*âtuddîpiko, literally, 'over the four continents,' into which the world was supposed to be divided. Compare Genesis vii. 44.

[2] Ga*kkh*a *ge*; where *ge* is the appropriate form of address invariably used to a female slave or maid-servant. Compare Childers, in the 'Dictionary,' p. 617.

naked ascetics there, letting the rain fall on themselves.'

Then it occurred to Visâkhâ the mother of Migâra—she being learned, expert, and wise—'For a certainty the venerable ones must have thrown off their robes in order to let themselves be rained down upon, and this foolish girl thinks therefore that there are no Bhikkhus in the Ârâma, but only naked ascetics letting the rain fall on them.' And she again gave command to the slave girl, saying,

'Go thou to the Ârâma; and when you are there, announce the time, saying, "The time, Sirs, has arrived, and the meal is ready."'

4. Now the Bhikkhus when they had cooled their limbs, and were refreshed in body, took their robes, and entered each one into his chamber. When the slave girl came to the Ârâma, not seeing any Bhikkhus, she thought: 'There are no Bhikkhus in the Ârâma. The Ârâma is empty.' And returning to Visâkhâ the mother of Migâra she said so.

Then it occurred to Visâkhâ the mother of Migâra—she being learned, expert, and wise—'For a certainty the venerable ones, when they had cooled their limbs and were refreshed in body, must have taken their robes, and entered each one into his chamber.' And she again gave command to the slave girl, saying,

'Go thou to Ârâma; and when you are there announce the time, saying, "The time, Sirs, has arrived, and the meal is ready."'

5. And the Blessed One said to the Bhikkhus: 'Make yourselves ready, O Bhikkhus, with bowl and robe; the hour for the meal has come.'

'Even so, Lord,' said the Bhikkhus in assent to

the Blessed One. And in the morning the Blessed One, having put on his under-garment, and being duly bowled and robed, vanished from the *G*etavana as quickly as a strong man would stretch forth his arm when it was drawn in, or draw it in again when it was stretched forth, and appeared in the mansion[1] of Visâkhâ the mother of Migâra. And the Blessed One took his seat on the seat spread out for him, and with him the company of the Bhikkhus.

6. Then said Visâkhâ the mother of Migâra: 'Most wonderful, most marvellous is the might and the power of the Tathâgata, in that though the floods are rolling on knee-deep, and though the floods are rolling on waist-deep, yet is not a single Bhikkhu wet, as to his feet, or as to his robes.' And glad and exalted in heart she served and offered with her own hand to the company of the Bhikkhus, with the Buddha at their head, sweet food, both hard and soft. And when the Blessed One had finished his meal, and had cleansed his hands and the bowl, she took her seat on one side. And, so sitting, she spake thus to the Blessed One:

'Eight are the boons, Lord, which I beg of the Blessed One.'

'The Tathâgatas, O Visâkhâ, are above granting boons (before they know what they are)[2].'

'Proper, Lord, and unobjectionable are the boons I ask.'

'Speak then, O Visâkhâ.'

7. 'I desire, Lord, my life long to bestow robes

---

[1] Ko*tth*aka does not only mean a room, as given by Childers: it signifies here, as at *G*âtaka I, 227, a battlemented dwelling, the house of a person of rank.

[2] See our note on this phrase at I, 54, 4.

for the rainy season on the Saṁgha, and food for in-coming Bhikkhus, and food for out-going Bhikkhus, and food for the sick, and food for those who wait upon the sick, and medicine for the sick, and a constant supply of congey, and bathing robes for the nuns.'

'But what circumstance is it, O Visâkhâ, that you have in view in asking these eight boons of the Tathâgata?'

'I gave command, Lord, to my slave girl, saying, "Go thou to the Ârâma; and when you are there, announce the time, saying, 'The time, Sirs, has arrived, and the meal is ready.'" And the slave girl went, Lord, to the Ârâma; but when she beheld there the Bhikkhus with their robes thrown off, letting themselves be rained down upon, she thought: "These are not Bhikkhus in the Ârâma, they are naked ascetics letting the rain fall on them," and she returned to me and reported accordingly. Impure, Lord, is nakedness, and revolting. It was this circumstance, Lord, that I had in view in desiring to provide the Saṁgha my life long with special garments for use in the rainy season[1].

8. 'Moreover, Lord, an in-coming Bhikkhu, not being able to take the direct roads, and not knowing the places where food can be procured, comes on his way wearied out by seeking for an alms. But when he has partaken of the food I shall have provided for in-coming Bhikkhus, he will come on his way without being wearied out by seeking for an alms, taking the direct road, and knowing the place where food can be procured. It was this circumstance

[1] See below, the note on § 15.

that I had in view in desiring to provide the Sa*m*gha my life long with food for in-coming Bhikkhus.

'Moreover, Lord, an out-going Bhikkhu, while seeking about for an alms for himself, may be left behind by the caravan[1], or may arrive too late at the place whither he desires to go, and will set out on the road in weariness. But when he has partaken of the food I shall have provided for out-going Bhikkhus, he will not be left behind by the caravan; he will arrive in due time at the place whither he desires to go, and he will set out on the road when he is not weary. It was this circumstance, Lord, that I had in view in desiring to provide the Sa*m*gha my life long with food for out-going Bhikkhus.

9. 'Moreover, Lord, if a sick Bhikkhu does not obtain suitable foods his sickness may increase upon him, or he may die. But if a Bhikkhu have taken the diet that I shall have provided for the sick, neither will his sickness increase upon him, nor will he die. It was this circumstance, Lord, that I had in view in desiring to provide the Sa*m*gha my life long with diet for the sick.

'Moreover, Lord, a Bhikkhu who is waiting upon the sick, if he has to seek out food for himself, may bring in the food (to the invalid) when the sun is already far on his course[2], and he will lose his

---

[1] Compare sukhâ vihâyati in the Sigâlovâda Sutta at p. 302 of Grimblot's 'Sept Suttas Pâlis.'

[2] Compare Ussûra-seyyo in the Sigâlovâda Sutta at p. 302 of Grimblot's 'Sept Suttas Pâlis;' and Böhtlingk-Roth, under utsûra.

opportunity of taking his food[1]. But when he has partaken of the food I shall have provided for those who wait upon the sick, he will bring in food to the invalid in due time, and he will not lose his opportunity of taking his food. It was this circumstance, Lord, that I had in view in desiring to provide the Sa*m*gha my life long with food for those who wait upon the sick.

10. 'Moreover, Lord, if a sick Bhikkhu does not obtain suitable medicines his sickness may increase upon him, or he may die. But if a Bhikkhu have taken the medicines which I shall have provided for the sick, neither will his sickness increase upon him, nor will he die. It was this circumstance, Lord, that I had in view in desiring to provide the Sa*m*gha my life long with medicines for the sick.

'Moreover, Lord, the Blessed One when at Andhakavinda, having in view the ten advantages thereof, allowed the use of congey[2]. It was those advantages I had in view, Lord, in desiring to provide the Sa*m*gha my life long with a constant supply of congey.

11. 'Now, Lord, the Bhikkhunîs are in the habit of bathing in the river A*k*iravatî with the courtesans, at the same landing-place, and naked. And the courtesans, Lord, ridiculed the Bhikkhunîs, saying, "What is the good, ladies, of your maintaining[3] chastity when you are young? are not the

[1] Bhatta*kkh*eda*m* karissati, because he may not eat solid food after sun-turn.

[2] See Mahâvagga VI, 24. The ten advantages are enumerated in § 5 there.

[3] In the text read *k*in*n*ena. Compare Bhikkhunî-vibhaṅga, Pâ*k*ittiya XXI, 1, where the whole passage recurs. The first sentence also recurs ibid., Pâ*k*ittiya II.

passions things to be indulged? When you are old, maintain chastity then; thus will you be obtainers of both ends." Then the Bhikkhunîs, Lord, when thus ridiculed by the courtesans, were confused. Impure, Lord, is nakedness for a woman, disgusting, and revolting. It was this circumstance, Lord, that I had in view in desiring to provide the Bhikkhunî-sa*m*gha my life long with dresses to bathe in.'

12. 'But what was the advantage you had in view for yourself, O Visâkhâ, in asking these eight boons of the Tathâgata?'

'Bhikkhus who have spent the rainy seasons in various places will come, Lord, to Sâvatthi, to visit the Blessed One. And on coming to the Blessed One they will ask, saying, "Such and such a Bhikkhu, Lord, has died. Where has he been re-born, and what is his destiny?" Then will the Blessed One explain that he had attained to the fruits of conversion, or of the state of the Sakadâgâmins, or of the state of the Anâgâmins, or of Arahatship[1]. And I, going up to them, shall ask, "Was that brother, Sirs, one of those who had formerly been at Sâvatthi?"

13. 'If they should reply to me, "He had formerly been at Sâvatthi," then shall I arrive at the conclusion, "For a certainty did that brother enjoy either the robes for the rainy season, or the food for the in-coming Bhikkhus, or the food for the out-going Bhikkhus, or the food for the sick, or the food for those that wait upon the sick, or the

[1] A conversation of the kind here referred to is related, as having actually taken place at Nâdika, in the 'Book of the Great Decease,' II, 5–8.

medicine for the sick, or the constant supply of congey." Then will gladness spring up within me on my calling that to mind; and joy will arise to me thus gladdened; and so rejoicing all my frame will be at peace; and being thus at peace I shall experience a blissful feeling of content; and in that bliss my heart will be at rest; and that will be to me an exercise of my moral sense, an exercise of my moral powers, an exercise of the seven kinds of wisdom[1]! This, Lord, was the advantage I had in view for myself in asking those eight boons of the Blessed One.'

14. 'It is well, it is well, Visâkhâ. Thou hast

[1] The succession of ideas in this paragraph is very suggestive, and throws much light both upon the psychological views and upon the religious feelings of the early Buddhists. The exact rendering of course of the abstract terms employed in the Pâli text is no doubt, as yet, beset with difficulty, for the reasons pointed out in Rh. D.'s 'Buddhist Suttas from the Pâli,' pp. xxv, xxvi; but the general sense of the passage is already sufficiently clear. For one or two words we have no real and adequate equivalent.

Kâya is neither 'body' nor 'faculties;' it is the whole frame, the whole individuality, looked at rather objectively than subjectively, and rather from the outward and visible than from the inner, metaphysical, stand-point. Compare the use of Sakkâya-di*tth*i and of Kâyena passati.

Sukha is not so much 'happiness,' simply and vaguely, as the serenity of the bliss which follows on happiness. It is contrasted with, and follows after, pâmo*gg*a and pîti, in the same way as in this passage, in the standing description of the *Gh*ânas (translated by Rh. D. in the Mahâ-sudassana Sutta II, 5–8, in the 'Buddhist Suttas,' p. 272). Its opposite, Dukkha, is a positive state of pain, and in comparison with this, sukha is negative, the absence of pain.

*K*itta is always more emotional than intellectual. It has the connotation, not of 'mind,' as is usually and erroneously supposed, but of 'heart.'

done well in asking eight boons of the Tathâgata with such advantages in view.'

And the Blessed One gave thanks to Visâkhâ the mother of Migâra in these verses;

'Whatsoever woman, upright in life, a disciple of the Happy One, gives, glad at heart and overcoming avarice, both food and drink—a gift, heavenly, destructive of sorrow, productive of bliss,—

'A heavenly life does she attain, entering upon the Path that is free from corruption and impurity;

'Aiming at good, happy does she become, and free from sickness, and long does she rejoice in a heavenly body.'

And when the Blessed One had given thanks to Visâkhâ the mother of Migâra in these verses, he arose from his seat, and departed thence.

15. Then the Blessed One on that occasion, after he had delivered a religious discourse, addressed the Bhikkhus, and said:

'I allow you, O Bhikkhus, garments for the rainy season[1], and food for in-coming Bhikkhus, and food for out-going Bhikkhus, and diet for the sick, and food for those that wait upon the sick, and medicine for the sick, and a constant supply of congey, and bathing robes for the sisterhood.'

Here ends the chapter called the Visâkhâ-bhâ*n*avâra.

[1] The size of such a garment is limited by the 91st Pâ*k*ittiya to six spans by two-and-a-half—that is just enough to go round the loins from the waist half down to the knee. It would be decent, and yet avoid the disadvantage of wearing the robes in the rain, where they would become wet and heavy in the manner described, for instance, at Mahâvagga VII, 1, 1.

16.

1, 2. Now at that time Bhikkhus who had eaten sweet foods went to sleep unmindful and unthoughtful. And they who had thus gone to sleep, dreamed[1]. . . . .

3. . . . . 'I allow, O Bhikkhus, for the protection of the body, and of the robe, and of the sleeping-place, the use of a mat.'

4. Now at that time the mat, being too short[2], did not protect the whole of the sleeping-place.

'I allow you, O Bhikkhus, to have a covering made as large as you like.'

17[3].

1. Now at that time the venerable Bela*tth*asîsa, the superior of the venerable Ânanda, had a disease of thick scabs; and by reason of the discharge thereof his robes stuck to his body. The Bhikkhus moistened those robes with water, and loosened them (from his body).

The Blessed One, as he was going on his rounds through the sleeping-places, saw them [doing so], and going up to the place where they were, he asked them:

[1] The remainder of this introductory story scarcely bears translation. The first sentences recur in the Sutta-vibhaṅga, Sa*m*ghâdisesa I, 2, 1, and Pâ*k*ittiya V, 1, 1.

[2] The length of a mat (nisidana*m*) was limited by the 89th Pâ*k*ittiya to two spans by one.

[3] This introductory story is also given as the introduction to Mahâvagga VI, 9.

'What is the matter, O Bhikkhus, with this Bhikkhu?'

'The venerable one has the disease of thick scabs; and by reason of the discharge thereof his robes stick to his body. So we are moistening those robes thoroughly with water, to loosen them (from his body).'

2. Then the Blessed One on that occasion, after having delivered a religious discourse, addressed the Bhikkhus, and said:

'I allow, O Bhikkhus, to whomsoever has the itch, or boils, or a discharge, or scabs, the use of an itch-cloth[1].'

18.

1. Now Visâkhâ the mother of Migâra took a cloth for wiping the face, and went up to the place where the Blessed One was. And on arriving there, she saluted the Blessed One, and took her seat on one side, and, so sitting, Visâkhâ the mother of Migâra spake thus to the Blessed One:

'May the Blessed One be pleased to accept of me this cloth for wiping the face, that that may be to me for a long time for a blessing and for good.'

And the Blessed One accepted the cloth for wiping the face. And he taught, and incited, and aroused, and gladdened Visâkhâ the mother of Migâra with religious discourse. And she, so taught &c., rose from her seat, and saluted the

[1] According to the 90th Pâkittiya such a cloth must not be more than four spans in length, and two in breadth.

Blessed One, and passing him on her right side, she departed thence.

Then the Blessed One on that occasion, after having delivered a religious discourse, addressed the Bhikkhus, and said:

'I allow you, O Bhikkhus, a cloth to wipe your faces with.'

19.

1. Now at that time Roga the Malla was a friend of the venerable Ânanda's[1]. And a linen cloth belonging to Roga the Malla had been deposited in the keeping of the venerable Ânanda; and the venerable Ânanda had need of a linen cloth.

They told this matter to the Blessed One.

'I allow you, O Bhikkhus, to take a thing on trust (that it would be given to you) when it belongs to a person possessed of these five qualifications—he must be an intimate and familiar friend who has been spoken to (about it)[2] and is alive, (and the Bhikkhu taking the thing) must know "He will remain pleased with me after I have taken it." I allow you, O Bhikkhus, to take a thing on trust (that it would be given to you)[3] when it belongs to a person possessed of these five qualifications.'

---

[1] He is also mentioned as such in Mahâvagga VI, 36.

[2] Buddhaghosa says, Âlapito ti mama santaka*m* ga*n*hâhi ya*m* i*kkh*eyyâsîti eva*m* vutto.

[3] Vissâsa*m* gahetu*m*, on which phrase compare vissâsâ ga*n*hâti in chapter 31, below, where the context leaves no doubt as to its meaning.

20.

1. Now at that time the Bhikkhus were fully provided with the three robes, but they had need of water-strainers[1] and of bags (to carry their bowls and other things in)[2].

They told this matter to the Blessed One.

'I allow you, O Bhikkhus, pieces of cloth requisite (for those purposes).'

2. Then it occurred to the Bhikkhus: 'The things allowed by the Blessed One—the three robes, and the robes for the rainy season, and the mat, and the bed-covering, and the cloth to cover boils &c. with, and to wipe the face with, and required (for water-strainers and bags)—are all these things things which ought to be kept to ourselves[3], or things which ought to be handed over[4] (from time to time by one Bhikkhu to another)?'

They told this matter to the Blessed One.

'I allow you, O Bhikkhus, to keep in hand the three robes, and not to assign them—to keep to yourselves the robes for the rainy season during the four months of the rains, but beyond that time to hand them over—to keep to yourselves the mats and the bed coverings, and not to hand them over—to keep to yourselves the coverings for the itch &c. while the disease lasts, but beyond that time to

[1] Compare *K*ullavagga VI, 13.

[2] Compare the passages given in the index to the text of the *K*ullavagga, p. 355, s. v. thavikâ.

[3] Compare below, VIII, 24, 3.

[4] Compare above, VIII, 8, 3.

hand them over—to keep to yourselves the cloths to wipe the face with, and those required for water-strainers and bags, and not to hand them over.'

21.

1. Now the Bhikkhus thought: 'What is the limit for the size of a robe up to which it ought to be handed over to another Bhikkhu[1]?'

They told this matter to the Blessed One.

'I prescribe, O Bhikkhus, to hand over any robe which is in length eight inches according to the accepted inch[2].'

Now at that time a robe belonging to the venerable Mahâ Kassapa, which had been made of cast-off pieces of cloth became heavy (by reason of the weight of the new pieces tacked on to it[3]).

They told this matter to the Blessed One.

'I allow you, O Bhikkhus, to darn it roughly together with thread[4].'

It was uneven at the end[5].

They told this thing to the Blessed One.

'I allow you, O Bhikkhus, to remove the unevenness[6].'

---

[1] See VIII, 13, 8, and our note on the 59th Pâkittiya.

[2] See our note on this word in the 92nd Pâkittiya.

[3] So explains the commentary, *Kh*inna-*tth*âne aggalâropanena garuko hoti.

[4] Suttalûkha*m* kâtun ti sutten' eva aggala*m* kâtun ti attho (B.). Compare above, chapter 12. 2.

[5] Vika*nn*o ti suttam a*ñk*itvâ sibbantâna*m* eko sa*m*ghâ*t*i-ko*n*o digho hoti, says Buddhaghosa. Vika*nn*aka in the 233rd *G*âtaka seems to mean 'harpoon.'

[6] Vika*nn*am uddharitun ti dîgha-ko*n*a*m* *kh*indidu*m* (B.).

The threads frayed out[1].

They told this matter to the Blessed One.

'I allow you, O Bhikkhus, to put a braiding or a binding along or round (the edge)[2].'

Now at that time the ribbons[3] of the under garment gave way[4].

They told this matter to the Blessed One.

'I allow you, O Bhikkhus, to make an eight-footed . . . [5].'

2. Now at that time when a set of robes was being made for a certain Bhikkhu it was impossible to make it entirely from torn pieces of cloth[6].

'I allow you, O Bhikkhus, to have two of the robes made of torn pieces of cloth, and one of cloth not torn.'

It was impossible to make two of the robes of torn pieces of cloth, and one of cloth not torn.

'I allow you, O Bhikkhus, to make two robes

---

[1] Okiratî (sic) ti *kh*inna-ko*n*ato ga*l*ati (B.). Ga*l*ati at VI, 13, 1, is 'ran over,' whereas okiriyanti at the corresponding passages VI, 12, 1, 2, is 'were spilt.' Probably the above rendering is the real meaning here, as the threads could not be literally spilt or sprinkled.

[2] On these difficult technical terms Buddhaghosa provokingly says, anuvâta*m* paribha*nd*am anuvâtañ *k*' eva paribha*nd*am. Childers, under the first, has merely 'with the wind,' and under the second, 'girdle.' The same expressions occur also above, at VII, 1, 5, where Buddhaghosa again only explains the words by the words themselves.

[3] We probably ought to read pa*tt*â, not pattâ; but what is meant by the ribbons of the sa*m*ghâ*t*i is very doubtful. Buddhaghosa says nothing.

[4] For lu*gg*ati compare palu*gg*ati.

[5] What this is is again uncertain, and Buddhaghosa gives no help.

[6] See above, chapter 11, at the end.

(out of the set) of untorn pieces, and one of torn pieces.'

Even this was impossible.

'I allow you, O Bhikkhus, to make (each robe out of the set) half (from torn pieces) and half[1] (from untorn pieces). But a set of robes made entirely from untorn pieces is not to be worn. Whosoever shall wear (a set of robes so made) is guilty of a dukka*t*a.'

22.

1. Now at that time a quantity of robes had come into the possession of a certain Bhikkhu, and he was desirous of giving those robes to his father and mother.

They told this matter to the Blessed One.

'Since they are his father and mother, what can we say, O Bhikkhus, though he give them to them. I allow you, O Bhikkhus, to give (robes, in such a case,) to your parents. And a gift of faith is not to be made of no avail. Whosoever shall make it of no avail, he is guilty of a dukka*t*a[2].'

23.

1. Now at that time a certain Bhikkhu who had deposited his robes[3] in Andhavana entered the

[1] Anvâdhika*m*, on which Buddhaghosa says nothing.

[2] Compare the 1st and 3rd Nissaggiyas, and above, VIII, 13, 8, as to the rules concerning extra robes, and what is to be done with them.

[3] For the rule as to such depositing, see the 29th Nissaggiya.

village for alms (clad only) in his waist cloth and nether garment[1]. Thieves carried off that robe. That Bhikkhu became ragged and ill-clad.

The Bhikkhus spake thus: 'How is it, friend, that you have become ragged and ill-clad?'

'I had deposited my robe in Andhavana, and entered the village in my waist cloth and nether garment. Thieves carried off that robe. Thence am I become ragged and ill-clad.'

They told this matter to the Blessed One.

'You are not, O Bhikkhus, to enter the village (clad only) in your waist cloth and nether garment. Whosoever shall do so is guilty of a dukka*t*a[2].'

2. Now at that time the venerable Ânanda through thoughtlessness went into the village for alms in his waist cloth and nether garment.

The Bhikkhus spake to him thus: 'Hath it not been laid down by the Blessed One that we are not to enter the village in our waist cloth and nether garment. Why have you, O friend, gone so into the village?'

'It is true, my friends, that it has been laid down by the Blessed One that we are not to enter the village so, but I did it out of thoughtlessness.'

They told this matter to the Blessed One.

3. 'There are five reasons, O Bhikkhus, for laying

---

*K*îvara (robe) must here be used for Sa*m*ghâ*t*i. See our note on VIII, 13, 5, and section 2, below, where sa*m*ghâ*t*i occurs.

[1] On Santaruttara, see the 7th Nissaggiya. It is clear from this passage that Buddhaghosa was right in his limitation of the word as used in that rule; and we should have done better, therefore, to follow it in our translation of the rule.

[2] Compare the 1st, 2nd, 3rd, and 4th Sekhiyas, and the 2nd Nissaggiya; and also above, VII, 1, 3.

aside the robe[1]—when he (the Bhikkhu) is sick, when it is the appointed time for keeping the rainy season[2], when it is necessary to go to the other side of a river, when the vihâra has been securely fastened with a bolt[3], when the Ka*th*ina ceremony has been performed[4]. These, O Bhikkhus, are the five reasons for laying aside the robe (Sa*m*ghâ*t*i).

'There are five reasons, O Bhikkhus, for laying aside the waist cloth and the nether garment. [The reasons are the same as in the last paragraph.] These, O Bhikkhus, are the five reasons, &c.

'There are five reasons for laying aside the garment for use in the rainy season—when he is sick, when it is necessary to go beyond the boundary (?)[5], when it is necessary to go to the other side of a river, when the vihâra has been securely fastened with a bolt, when the garment for use in the rainy

---

[1] Here the word used is Sa*m*ghâ*t*i.

[2] On sa*m*keta, compare II, 8, 1. Buddhaghosa merely says here, Vassika-sa*m*ketan ti *k*attâro mâse. As sa*m*keta implies a mutual agreement, the 'appointed time' here probably means, not the time fixed by the Buddha, but the time agreed upon by the Sa*m*gha as that to which the rule laid down by the Buddha should apply. There may easily have arisen questions as to the exact day on which the four months should properly begin; and there were even differences of opinion as to the exact length of the period itself, some making it three, and some four months. See on these points Childers, under Vassa and Vassûpanâyikâ.

[3] From fear of thieves.

[4] See the 2nd Nissaggiya, and above, VII, 1, 3.

[5] Buddhaghosa has nothing on this reason. It would seem that the garment in question might be left behind when the Bhikkhu had to go on a journey, if that journey would take him beyond the boundary of the technical 'residence.' On the use of the word, see the passages collected by H. O. in the Index to the Pâli Text (vol. ii. p. 349, s. v. sîmâ).

season has not been made, or has been left unfinished[1].

'These, O Bhikkhus, are the five reasons,' &c.

24.

1. Now at that time a certain Bhikkhu kept Vassa[2] alone. The people then gave him robes, saying, 'We give them to the Sa*m*gha.'

Then that Bhikkhu thought: 'It has been laid down by the Blessed One that the lowest number which can constitute a Sa*m*gha is four[3]. Now I am by myself, and these people have given the robes, saying, "We give them to the Sa*m*gha." I had better take these robes, which are the property of a Sa*m*gha, to Sâvatthi.'

So that Bhikkhu did so, and told the matter to the Blessed One.

'These robes are your own, O Bhikkhu, until the Ka*th*ina ceremony shall have been performed[4].'

2. 'Now in case, O Bhikkhus, a Bhikkhu keep Vassa alone, and the people of the place give

---

[1] It is evident from this last reason that the reasons are not such as would justify a Bhikkhu in laying aside the garment in such a way as to remain naked, but such as would justify him in not using the rainy-season garment when he might otherwise have done so. In the five cases mentioned he might wear the nether garment only reaching from above the navel to below the knees, instead of the garment for the rainy season, which was smaller in size. See our note above on VIII, 13, 5, and VIII, 15, 15.

[2] That is, spent the rainy season.

[3] This is laid down in Mahâvagga IX, 4, 1.

[4] And thereby the Ka*th*ina license suspended. Compare the 1st, 2nd, and 3rd Nissaggiyas, and our note on p. 18.

him robes, intending them for the Sa*m*gha,—I prescribe, O Bhikkhus, that those robes shall be his until the Ka*th*ina ceremony shall have been performed.'

3. Now at that time a certain Bhikkhu spent the rest of the year (besides the rainy season)[1] alone. The people there (&c., as before, in the first paragraph of 24. 1, down to the end).

So that Bhikkhu did so, and told the matter to the Bhikkhus. They told the matter to the Blessed One.

'I prescribe, O Bhikkhus, that you are to divide such robes with the Sa*m*gha (whether large or small in number) that may be present there.

4. 'Now in case, O Bhikkhus, a Bhikkhu spend the rest of the year (besides the rainy season) alone, and the people of the place give him robes, intending them for the Sa*m*gha,—I allow, O Bhikkhus, that that Bhikkhu should appropriate those robes to himself[2], saying, "These robes are for me." If another Bhikkhu should arrive before those robes have been appropriated to that Bhikkhu, an equal share is to be given (to the in-coming Bhikkhu). If while the robes are being divided by those Bhikkhus, and before the lot has been cast, another Bhikkhu should arrive, an equal share is to be given to him. If while the robes are being divided by those Bhikkhus, and after the lot has been cast, another Bhikkhu

[1] Buddhaghosa says, Utukâlan ti vassânato *aññam* kâla*m*, where vassâna means the rainy season. See Abhidhânappadîpikâ, verse 79.

[2] On this sense of adhi*tth*âtu*m*, see above, Mahâvagga VIII, 20, 2.

should arrive, an equal share need not, if they do not wish it [1], be given to him.'

5. Now at that time two Theras, who were brothers, the venerable Isidâsa and the venerable Isibhatta, having spent the rainy season in Sâvatthi, went to take up their abode in a certain village. The people there, thinking, 'It is long since these Theras have arrived here,' made gifts of both food and robes.

The Bhikkhus who resided there asked the Theras, saying, 'These robes, Sirs, which are the property of the Sa*m*gha, have come to us through the Theras' arrival [2]. Will the Theras accept a share?'

The Theras answered: 'As we understand the rule laid down by the Blessed One, these robes belong to you alone until the Ka*th*ina ceremony shall have been performed [3].'

6. Now at that time three Bhikkhus spent the rainy season at Râ*g*agaha. The people there made gifts of robes, saying, 'We give them to the Sa*m*gha.'

Then those Bhikkhus thought thus: 'It has been laid down by the Blessed One that the smallest Sa*m*gha shall consist of four persons, and we are only three, and these people have made gifts of robes, intending to give them to the Sa*m*gha. What now ought we to do with them?'

Now at that time there were staying in Pâ*t*ali-

---

[1] Akâmâ; on which compare II, 27, 15, and especially II, 34, 3, and IV, 17, 6.

[2] Âgamma, which is here nearly the same as uddissa. To give the full import of the expression it would be necessary to say, 'have come to us in consequence of the inducement offered to the givers by the presence of the Theras here.'

[3] See our note above on § 1.

putta, at the kukku*t*ârâma, a number of Theras—the venerable Nilavâsi, and the venerable Sâ*n*avâsi[1], and the venerable Gopaka, and the venerable Bhagu, and the venerable Phalika-sandâna. And those Bhikkhus went to Pâ*t*aliputta, and asked the Theras what they should do.

The Theras answered: 'As we understand the rule laid down by the Blessed One, these robes belong to you alone until the Ka*th*ina ceremony shall have been performed.'

25.

1. Now at that time the venerable Upananda of the Sakya race, having spent the rainy season at Sâvatthi, went to take up his abode in a certain village. The Bhikkhus in that place assembled together with the object of dividing the robes. They said to him:

'These robes, friend, which are the property of the Sa*m*gha, are about to be divided. Will you accept a share of them?'

'Yes, friends, I will,' said he; and taking his share, departed thence and took up his abode elsewhere.

[The same thing happened there, and] he departed thence and took up his abode elsewhere.

[The same thing happened there, and so] he returned to Sâvatthi with a great bundle of robes.

2. The Bhikkhus said to him: 'What a merito-

[1] There is a Sâ*n*avâsi who takes a prominent part at the Council of Vesâli (*K*ullavagga XII, 1, 8; XII, 2, 4). He is probably meant to be considered the same as this one.

rious person you are, friend Upananda. Plenty of robes have come into your possession!'

'Where is my merit, friends?' said he, and [told them all that had happened][1].

3. 'How then, friend Upananda, have you spent the rainy season in one place, and accepted a share of robes in another place?'

'Yes, friends, that is so.'

Those Bhikkhus who were moderate were indignant, murmured, and became annoyed, saying, 'How can the venerable Upananda spend the rainy season in one place, and accept a share of robes in another place?'

They told the matter to the Blessed One.

'Is it true, Upananda, as they say, that you have spent the rainy season in one place, and have accepted a share of robes in another place?'

'It is true, Lord.'

The Blessed Buddha rebuked him, saying, 'How can you, O foolish one, act so? This will not redound to the conversion of the unconverted, or to the increase of the converted!'

And after having rebuked him, and delivered a religious discourse, he addressed the Bhikkhus, saying, 'Whosoever, O Bhikkhus, has spent the rainy season in one place, is not to accept a share of the robes in another place. Whosoever does so shall be guilty of a dukka*t*a.'

4. Now at that time the venerable Upananda of the Sakya race spent the rainy season alone in two residences, thinking thus to obtain many robes. And the Bhikkhus thought: 'How should his portion

---

[1] Section 1 repeated, with the necessary change of person, &c.

of the robes be assigned to Upananda of the Sakya race?'

They told the matter to the Blessed One.

'Give, O Bhikkhus, to that foolish one but one portion[1]. In case, O Bhikkhus, a Bhikkhu spend the rainy season alone in two residences, thinking thus to obtain many robes, then, if he have spent exactly half the season in one place and half in another, a half portion of the robes due to him shall be given to him in one place, and a half in the other; but in whichever place of the two he have spent a greater part of the rainy season, thence shall the portions of robes due to him be given.'

26.

1. Now at that time a certain Bhikkhu had a disturbance in his bowels, and he lay fallen in his own evacuations. And the Blessed One on going round the sleeping-places accompanied by the venerable Ânanda came to that Bhikkhu's abode, and saw him so. And he went up to him, and asked him, 'What is the matter with you, O Bhikkhu?'

'I have a disturbance, Lord, in my bowels.'

'Then have you, O Bhikkhu, any one to wait upon you?'

'No, Lord.'

'Why do not the Bhikkhus wait upon you?'

'Because I am of no service, Lord, to the Bhikkhus.'

2. Then the Blessed One said to the venerable

[1] Buddhaghosa says, Ekâdhippâyan ti eka*m* adhippâya*m*. Eka-puggala-pa*t*ivisa*m* eva dethâ ti attho.

Ânanda: 'Go, Ânanda, and fetch some water. Let us bathe this Bhikkhu.'

'Even so, Lord,' said the venerable Ânanda, in assent to the Blessed One, and fetched the water. And the Blessed One poured the water over that Bhikkhu; and the venerable Ânanda wiped him down. And the Blessed One taking hold of him at the head, and the venerable Ânanda at the feet, they lifted him up, and laid him down upon his bed.

3. Then the Blessed One, on that occasion and in that connection, convened a meeting of the Bhikkhu-sa*m*gha, and asked the Bhikkhus, 'Is there, O Bhikkhus, in such and such an apartment, a Bhikkhu who is sick?'

'There is, Lord.'

'Then what, O Bhikkhus, is the matter with that Bhikkhu?'

'He has a disturbance, Lord, in his bowels.'

'And is there any one, O Bhikkhus, to wait upon him?'

'No, Lord.'

'Why, then, do not the Bhikkhus wait upon him?'

'That Bhikkhu, Lord, is of no service to the Bhikkhus; therefore do they not wait upon him.'

'Ye, O Bhikkhus, have no mothers and no fathers who might wait upon you! If ye, O Bhikkhus, wait not one upon the other, who is there indeed who will wait upon you? Whosoever, O Bhikkhus, would wait upon me, he should wait upon the sick.

4. 'If he have an upa*ggh*âya, his upa*ggh*âya should wait upon him as long as his life lasts, and wait until he has recovered; and so if he have an â*k*ariya, a saddhi-vihârika, an antevâsika, a fellow

saddhi-vihârika, or a fellow antevâsika[1]. And if he have neither of all these, then should the Sa*m*gha wait upon him; and whosoever does not do so, shall be guilty of a dukka*t*a.

5. 'There are five qualities, O Bhikkhus, which, when a sick man has, he is difficult to wait upon—when he does not do what is good for him; when he does not know the limit (of the quantity of food) that is good for him[2]; when he does not take his medicine; when he does not let a nurse who desires his good know what manner of disease he has, or when it is getting worse that that is so, or when it is getting better that that is so, or when it is stationary that that is so; and when he has become unable to bear bodily pains that are severe, sharp, grievous, disagreeable, unpleasant, and destructive to life[3]. These are the five qualities, O Bhikkhus, which, when a sick man has, he is difficult to wait upon.

6. 'There are five qualities, O Bhikkhus, which, when a sick man has, he is easy to wait upon—when he does' (&c., the contrary of the last section).

7. 'There are five qualities, O Bhikkhus, which, when one who waits upon the sick has, he is incompetent to the task—when he is not capable of prescribing medicines; when he does not know what (diet) is good and what is not good for the patient, serving what is not good, and not serving what is good for him; when he waits upon the sick out of

---

[1] On all except the last two this duty has already been enjoined above in the passages on the mutual duties of masters and pupils (Mahâvagga I, 24, 25; I, 26, 11; I, 32, 3; I, 33, 1).

[2] Compare *G*âtaka II, 293, 294.

[3] This last clause occurs also above, at I, 49, 6.

greed, and not out of love; when he revolts from removing evacuations, saliva or vomit; when he is not capable from time to time of teaching, inciting, arousing, and gladdening the patient with religious discourse. These are the five qualities, O Bhikkhus, which, when one who waits upon the sick has, he is incompetent to the task.

8. 'There are five qualities, O Bhikkhus, which, when one who waits upon the sick has, he is competent to the task—when he is capable' (&c., the contrary of the last section).

27.

1. Now at that time two Bhikkhus were journeying along a high road in the country of Kosala. And they came to a certain residence, and there one of the two fell ill. Then the Bhikkhus there thought: 'Waiting upon the sick has been highly spoken of by the Blessed One. Let us then, friends, now wait upon this Bhikkhu.' And they waited upon him, and while he was being nursed by them, he completed his time[1]. Then those Bhikkhus took that Bhikkhu's bowl and his robes, and went to Sâvatthi, and told the matter to the Blessed One.

2. 'On the death of a Bhikkhu, O Bhikkhus, the Sa*m*gha becomes the owner of his bowl and of his robes. But, now, those who wait upon the sick are of much service. I prescribe, O Bhikkhus, that the bowl and the set of robes are to be assigned by the

[1] That is, he died.

Sa*m*gha to them who have waited upon the sick. And thus, O Bhikkhus, are they to be assigned. The Bhikkhu who has waited upon the sick ought to go before the Sa*m*gha, and to say thus: "Such and such a Bhikkhu, Sirs, has completed his time. These are his set of robes and his bowl." Then a discreet and able Bhikkhu ought to lay the proposition before the Sa*m*gha, saying, "Let the Sa*m*gha hear me. Such and such a Bhikkhu has completed his time. These are his set of robes and his bowl. If it is convenient to the Sa*m*gha, let the Sa*m*gha assign this set of robes and this bowl to those who have waited upon the sick." 'This is the *ñ*atti.' [Here follow the usual formal words of a kammavâ*k*â[1].]

3. Now at that time a certain Sâma*n*era had completed his time.

They told this matter to the Blessed One.

[The decision and the kammavâ*k*â are the same as in § 2.]

4. Now at that time a certain Bhikkhu and a Sâma*n*era waited upon a sick Bhikkhu; and while he was being waited upon by them he completed his time. And the Bhikkhu who had waited upon the sick thought: 'How now ought the due portion of robes be given to the Sâma*n*era who waited upon the sick?'

They told this matter to the Blessed One.

'I prescribe, O Bhikkhus, that you are to give an equal portion to a Sâma*n*era who waits upon the sick.'

5. Now at that time a certain Bhikkhu who was

[1] There is only one, not three Kammavâ*k*âs, given in the text.

possessed of much property, and of a plentiful supply of a Bhikkhu's requisites, completed his time.

They told this matter to the Blessed One.

'On the death of a Bhikkhu, O Bhikkhus, the Samgha becomes the owner of his bowl and of his robes. But, now, those who wait upon the sick are of much service. I prescribe, O Bhikkhus, that the set of robes and the bowl are to be assigned by the Samgha to them who have waited upon the sick. And whatever little property and small supply of a Bhikkhu's requisites there may be, that is to be divided by the Samgha that are present there; but whatever large quantity of property and large supply of a Bhikkhu's requisites there may be, that is not to be given away[1] and not to be apportioned[2], but to belong to the Samgha of the four directions[3], those who have come in, and those who have not[4].'

28.

1. Now at that time a certain Bhikkhu came naked up to the place where the Blessed One was, and said:

'The Blessed One, Lord, has praised in many ways the moderate man and the contented who has eradicated (evil), who has shaken off his passions, who is gracious, reverent, energetic[5]. Now this

---

[1] See *K*ullavagga VI, 15, 2. [2] See *K*ullavagga VI, 16, 2.

[3] That is, 'of all the world.'

[4] This description of the totality of the Samgha is constantly found in dedicatory inscriptions. See Rh. D.'s paper in the Indian Antiquary, May, 1872.

[5] So, for example, in *K*ullavagga I, 1, 3.

nakedness, Lord, is in many ways effectual to moderation and content, to the eradication of evil, to the suppressions of the passions, to graciousness, reverence, and zeal. It were well, Lord, if the Blessed One would enjoin nakedness upon the Bhikkhus.'

The Blessed Buddha rebuked him, saying, 'This would be improper, O foolish one, crooked, unsuitable, unworthy of a Sama*n*a, unbecoming, and it ought not to be done. How can you, O foolish one, adopt nakedness as the Titthiyas do? This will not conduce, O foolish one, to the conversion of the unconverted.'

And when he had rebuked him, and had delivered a religious discourse, he addressed the Bhikkhus, and said:

'You are not, O Bhikkhus, to adopt nakedness, as the Titthiyas do[1]. Whosoever does so, shall be guilty of a grave offence (Thulla*kk*aya).'

2. [The whole section repeated respectively in the case of a Bhikkhu clad in a garment of grass, clad in a garment of bark[2], clad in a garment of phalaka cloth[3], clad in a garment of hair[4], clad in the skin of a wild animal, clad in the feathers of

---

[1] Compare above, VIII, 15, 7 and 11.

[2] This is several times referred to in the *G*âtakas; for instance, pp. 6, 9, 12.

[3] Perhaps made of leaves. Compare Böhtlingk-Roth's, No. 5, sub voce; and *G*âtaka I, 304 (phalakattharasayana). Perhaps also *G*âtaka I, 356, 'making a man his phalaka,' may be a figure of speech founded on this use of the word, and mean 'making him his covering.'

[4] Like the well-known Titthiya Agita, one of the six great heretics (Sâmañña-phala Sutta, ed. Grimblot, p. 114, = Book of the Great Decease, V, 60).

an owl, clad in antelope skins (with the hoofs left on)[1]. But instead of 'adopt nakedness as the Titthiyas do' substitute respectively 'wear a garment of grass, &c., which is the symbol[2] the Titthiyas use.']

3. Now at that time a certain Bhikkhu came up to the place where the Blessed One was, clad in cloth made of the stalks of the akka plant[3].

[All as before in § 1, down to:]

And when he had rebuked him, and had delivered a religious discourse, he addressed the Bhikkhus, and said:

'You are not, O Bhikkhus, to dress yourselves in the stalks of the akka plant. Whosoever does so, shall be guilty of a dukka*t*a.'

[§ 3 is then repeated of a Bhikkhu clad in cloth made of the maka*k*i fibre[4].]

29.

1. Now at that time the *Kh*abbaggiya Bhikkhus wore robes that were all of a blue, light yellow, crimson, brown, black, brownish yellow, or dark

---

[1] Buddhaghosa, at Suttavibhaṅga, Pârâ*g*ika I, 10, 3, where this word occurs, says on it, A*g*inakkhikan (sic) ti saloma*m* sakhura*m* a*g*ina-miga-*k*amma*m*. Compare also above, Mahâvagga V, 2, 4.

[2] Titthiya-dha*g*a. Compare *G*âtaka I, 65, and *K*ullavagga I, 27.

[3] Akkanâ*l*an ti akkanâ*l*amaya*m* (B.). Compare Böhtlingk-Roth, under arka.

[4] Potthako ti maka*k*imayo vu*kk*ati (B.). So also Childers, sub voce

yellow colour[1]; they wore robes with skirts to them which were not made of torn pieces of cloth, or were long, or had flowers on them, or cobras' hoods on them; they wore jackets, and dresses of the Tirîtaka plant[2], and turbans.

The people were indignant, murmured, and became annoyed, saying, 'This is like those still living in the enjoyments of the world.'

They told the matter to the Blessed One.

'Robes that are all of a blue colour [&c.; all the things mentioned in the first paragraph being here repeated] are not to be worn. Whosoever wears them shall be guilty of a dukkata[3].'

30.

1. Now at that time Bhikkhus, after having spent the rainy season, but before a gift of robes had fallen to the Samgha, went away (from the place); left the Order; died; admitted that they were Sâmaneras; or that they had abandoned the precepts; or that they had become guilty of an extreme

---

[1] See Buddhaghosa's explanations of all these colours in the note on V, 2, 1.

[2] Buddhaghosa says on this word, Tirîtan (sic) ti pana rukkhakhallimayam, tam pâda-punkhanam kâtum vattati. *Khalli* is 'bark.'

[3] Buddhaghosa says that the robes of the colours mentioned in this chapter may be worn if they have first been dyed, or may be used as coverlets, or may be cut up and used as parts of robes. So the robes with skirts to them may be worn if the forbidden skirts have first been torn or cut off.

offence; or that they were mad; or that their minds were unhinged; or that they suffered bodily pain; or that suspension had been pronounced against them for their refusal to acknowledge an offence they had committed, or to atone for such an offence, or to renounce a false doctrine; or that they were eunuchs; or that they had furtively attached themselves (to the Sa*m*gha); or that they had gone over to the Titthiyas; or that they were an animal; or that they had been guilty of matricide, or of parricide; or that they had murdered an Arahat; or that they had violated a Bhikkhunî; or that they had caused a schism in the Sa*m*gha; or that they had shed (a Buddha's) blood; or that they were hermaphrodites[1].

They told this matter to the Blessed One.

2. 'In case, O Bhikkhus, a Bhikkhu, after having spent the rainy season, goes away before a gift of robes has fallen to the Sa*m*gha—then they are nevertheless to be allotted to him if there be any person present proper to receive them on his behalf.

'Moreover in case, O Bhikkhus, a Bhikkhu, after having spent the rainy season, and before a gift of robes has fallen to the Sa*m*gha, leaves the Order, or dies, or acknowledges that he has become a Sâma*n*era, or that he has abandoned the precepts, or lastly that he has become guilty of an extreme offence,—then the Sa*m*gha becomes the owner (of the portion of robes that would have fallen to him).

[1] The above list of disqualifications has already occurred at II, 36; IV, 14.

'Moreover in case, O Bhikkhus, a Bhikkhu, after having spent the rainy season, and before a gift of robes has fallen to the Sa*m*gha, acknowledges that he has become mad, or unhinged in his mind, or in bodily pain, or that he has been suspended for refusal to acknowledge an offence he had committed, or to atone for such an offence, or to renounce a false doctrine—then (his portion of robes is nevertheless) to be allotted to him if there be any person present proper to receive them on his behalf.

'Moreover in case, O Bhikkhus, a Bhikkhu, after having spent the rainy season, and before a gift of robes has fallen to the Sa*m*gha, acknowledges that he is a eunuch, or that he had furtively attached himself to the Sa*m*gha, or that he had gone over to the Titthiyas, or that he is an animal, or that he had been guilty of matricide, or of parricide, or that he had murdered an Arahat, or that he had violated a Bhikkhunî, or that he had raised a schism in the Sa*m*gha, or that he had shed a Buddha's blood, or that he is a hermaphrodite—then the Sa*m*gha becomes the owner (of the portion of robes that would have fallen to him).

3. '[The same rules as in § 2, if he had gone away, &c., after the gift of robes had been made to the Sa*m*gha, but before the robes had been divided among the individual members of the Sa*m*gha belonging to the place where he had spent the rainy season.]

4. 'Moreover in case, O Bhikkhus, after the Bhikkhus have spent the rainy season, divisions arise among the Sa*m*gha before any robes have fallen to them, and the people there give the water (of

presentation[1]) to one party, and the robes to the other party, thinking, "We are giving to the Sa*m*gha"—then those (robes are the property) of the (whole) Sa*m*gha.

'The people there give the water of presentation to one party, and the robes to the same party, thinking, "We are giving to the Sa*m*gha"—then those robes are the property of the whole Sa*m*gha.

5. '[In the same two cases, if the people intend to give to the one party only, the robes are to be the property of that party.]

6. 'Moreover in case, O Bhikkhus, after the Bhikkhus have spent the rainy season, divisions arise among the Sa*m*gha after the gift of robes has been made to the Sa*m*gha, but before the division (of the robes to the individual members) has taken place—then at the division an equal share is to be given to all.'

31.

1. Now at that time the venerable Revata sent a robe to the venerable Sâriputta in charge of a certain Bhikkhu, saying, 'Give this robe to the Thera.' But that Bhikkhu, whilst on the way, took the robe himself in trust on the venerable Revata[2].

Now the venerable Revata, on meeting with the

---

[1] There is no doubt that this is the meaning here of udaka. Compare above, Mahâvagga I, 22, 18, and *G*âtaka I, 93; III, 286; Dîpava*m*sa XIII, 29.

[2] That is, in trust that the venerable Revata, if he knew that the Bhikkhu wanted it, would have given it to him. See above, Mahâvagga VIII, 19.

venerable Sâriputta, asked him, saying, 'I sent to the venerable Thera a robe. Did that robe come into his hands?'

'I know nothing, friend, about that robe.'

Then the venerable Revata said to that Bhikkhu: 'I sent a robe, my friend, in your charge to the Thera. Where is that robe?'

'I took the robe myself, Lord, in trust upon you.'

They told the matter to the Blessed One.

2. 'In case, O Bhikkhus, a Bhikkhu send a robe in charge of a Bhikkhu, saying, "Give this robe to such and such a Bhikkhu;" and he, whilst on the way, takes it himself in trust on the one who sends it—then it is rightly taken. But if he takes it himself in trust on the one to whom it was sent, it is wrongly taken.

'[The same repeated, the latter case being put first, and the former case last.]

'Moreover in case, O Bhikkhus, a Bhikkhu send a robe in charge of a Bhikkhu, saying, "Give this robe to such and such a Bhikkhu;" and he, whilst on the way, hears that that Bhikkhu who sent it is dead;—then if he keeps the robe himself[1] as the robe of a deceased Bhikkhu, it is rightly kept; if he takes it himself in trust on the one to whom it was sent, it is wrongly taken.

'[In the same case], if he, whilst on the way, hears that that Bhikkhu to whom it was sent is dead—then if he keeps the robe himself as the robe of a deceased Bhikkhu, it is wrongly kept; if he takes

[1] On this meaning of adhiti*tth*ati, see our note above, VIII, 20, 2; VIII, 24, 2.

it himself in trust on the one who sent it, it is rightly taken.

'[In the same case, if he hears, whilst on the way, that both are dead—then if he keeps it himself as the robe of a deceased Bhikkhu, to wit, the one who sent it, it is rightly kept; if he keeps it himself as the property of a deceased Bhikkhu, to wit, the one to whom it was sent, it is wrongly kept.]

3. 'Moreover in case, O Bhikkhus, a Bhikkhu send a robe in charge of a Bhikkhu, saying, "I give the robe to such and such a Bhikkhu"—then [in all the cases given in § 2 the decision is reversed][1].'

32.

1. There are, O Bhikkhus, these eight grounds[2] for the getting of a gift of robes—when he gives it to the boundary, when he gives it to (a Sa*m*gha which is) under agreement (with other Sa*m*ghas), when he gives it on a declaration of alms, when he gives it to the Sa*m*gha, when he gives it to both the Sa*m*ghas, when he gives it to the Sa*m*gha which has spent the rainy season (at the place), when he gives it to a specified number[3], when he gives it to a single Bhikkhu.

[1] The reason of all this is, that if the sender (A) says to the messenger (B), 'Give this robe to the sendee (C),' the property in the robe does not pass; if A says to B, 'I give this robe to C,' it does pass.

[2] Mâtikâ; used in the same sense here as at VII, 1, 7.

[3] That is, of monks and nuns—the Bhikkhu-sa*m*gha and the Bhikkhunî-sa*m*gha.

'When he gives it to the boundary, it is to be divided among all those Bhikkhus who have come within the boundary[1].

'When he gives it to a Sa*m*gha which is under agreement, there are a number of residences which hold in common whatever they get, and what is given in one residence is given in all.

'When he gives it on a declaration of alms (means when the givers say), "We give it at the place where constant supply of alms is kept up for the Sa*m*gha[2]."

'When he gives it to the Sa*m*gha, it is to be divided among the Sa*m*gha there present.

'When he gives it to both the Sa*m*ghas, though there be many Bhikkhus and only one Bhikkhunî, an equal half is to be given (to each of the two Sa*m*ghas), and though there be many Bhikkhunîs and only one Bhikkhu, an equal half is to be given (to each of the two Sa*m*ghas).

'When he gives it to the Sa*m*gha which has spent the rainy season, it is to be divided among as many Bhikkhus as have spent the rainy season at that particular residence.

'When he gives it to a specified number, it is the number present at the giving of congey, or

---

[1] See chapters II, 6 and following.

[2] Buddhaghosa says, Bhikkhâ-pa*ññ*attiyâ, ti attano pari*kk*âga-pa*ññ*apana-*tth*âne. Ten' ev' âha yattha sa*m*ghassa dhuvakârâ kariyantî ti. Tass' attho, yasmi*m* vihâre imassa *k*îvara-dâyakassa santaka*m* sa*m*ghassa pâkava*tt*a*m* vâ va*tt*ati, yasmi*m* vâ vihâre bhikkhû attano bhâra*m* katvâ sadâ gehe bhogesi. Yattha vârena âvâso vâ kârito, salâkabhattâdîni vâ nibaddhâni, yena pana sakalo pi vihâro pati*tth*âpito, tattha vattabba*m* eva n' atthi ime dhuvakârâ nâma.

rice, or hard food, or robes, or bedding, or medicine[1].

'When he gives it to a single Bhikkhu, he says, "I give a set of robes to such and such a one."'

Here ends the eighth Khandhaka, the *K*îvara-khandhaka.

---

[1] That is, he invites a number of Bhikkhus to partake of yâgu, and when the yâgu is served he says, 'I give robes to those who have partaken of the yâgu,' and so on in all the other cases except that of robes. In that case he says, 'I give robes to those who have previously received robes from me' (B.).

NINTH KHANDHAKA.

(VALIDITY AND INVALIDITY OF FORMAL ACTS OF THE SAMGHA.)

1.

1. At that time the blessed Buddha dwelt at *K*ampâ, on the brink of the lotus-pond Gaggarâ. At that time there was in the country of Kâsi (a village) called Vâsabha-gâma. There a Bhikkhu called Kassapa-gotta had his residence, who was bound (to that place) by the string (of the religious duties which he had to perform there[1]), and who exerted himself to the end that clever Bhikkhus from a distance might come to that place, and the clever Bhikkhus therein might live at ease, and that (religious life at) that residence might progress, advance, and reach a high state.

Now at that time a number of Bhikkhus, making their pilgrimage in the country of Kâsi, came to Vâsabha-gâma. And the Bhikkhu Kassapa-gotta saw those Bhikkhus coming from afar; when he saw them, he prepared seats for them, brought water for the washing of their feet, a foot-stool, and a towel[2]. Then he went forth to meet them, took their bowls and their robes, offered them (water) to drink, and provided a bath for them, and provided also rice-milk and food hard and soft.

---

[1] Tanti-baddha. Buddhaghosa says, Tanti-baddho 'ti tasmi*m* âvâse kâtabbatâ-tanti-pa*t*ibaddho.

[2] See our note at I, 6, 11.

Now those stranger Bhikkhus thought: 'The resident Bhikkhu here, O friends, is indeed good-natured; he provides a bath for us and provides also rice-milk, and food, hard and soft. What if we were to stay here, friends, at Vâsabha-gâma.' Thus those stranger Bhikkhus stayed there at Vâsabha-gâma.

2. Now the Bhikkhu Kassapa-gotta thought: 'These stranger Bhikkhus are rested now from their travel-weariness; they did not know their way here before, but now they know their way. It is troublesome indeed to be busy all one's life for people not related to one's self, and being asked[1] is disagreeable to men. What if I were to provide no longer rice-milk, and food, hard and soft (for those Bhikkhus).' Thus he did not provide any more (for them) rice-milk, and food, hard and soft.

Then those stranger Bhikkhus thought: 'Formerly, friends, this resident Bhikkhu used to provide baths for us, and to provide also rice-milk, and food, hard and soft. But now he does not provide any more rice-milk, and food, hard and soft. This resident Bhikkhu, friends, is in anger with us now. Well, friends, let us pronounce expulsion against this resident Bhikkhu.'

3. Then those stranger Bhikkhus assembled and said to the Bhikkhu Kassapa-gotta: 'Formerly, friend, you used to provide baths for us and to provide also rice-milk, and food, hard and soft. But now you do not provide any more rice-milk, and food, hard and soft. You have committed an offence, friend; do you see that offence?'

[1] As he was obliged to ask the people of Vâsabha-gâma for what the stranger Bhikkhus wanted.

'There is no offence, friends, for me to see.'

Then those stranger Bhikkhus pronounced expulsion against the Bhikkhu Kassapa-gotta for his refusal to see that (pretended) offence. Then the Bhikkhu Kassapa-gotta thought: 'I do not know indeed whether this is an offence or not, and whether I have made myself guilty of an offence or not, and whether I have been expelled or not, and whether that sentence is lawful or unlawful, objectionable or unobjectionable, valid or invalid. What if I were to go to *K*ampâ and to ask the Blessed One about this matter?'

4. And the Bhikkhu Kassapa-gotta put his resting-place in order, took up his alms-bowl and his robe, and went forth to *K*ampâ; and in due course he came to *K*ampâ and to the place where the Blessed One was. Having approached him and respectfully saluted the Blessed One, he sat down near him.

Now it is the custom of the blessed Buddhas to exchange greeting with incoming Bhikkhus. And the Blessed One said to the Bhikkhu Kassapa-gotta: 'Is it all well with you, O Bhikkhu? Do you find your living? Have you made your journey without too much fatigue? And from what place do you come, O Bhikkhu?'

'It is all well, Lord; I find my living, Lord; I have made the journey, Lord, without too much fatigue.

5. 'There is in the country of Kâsi, Lord, (a village) called Vâsabha-gâma. There I had my residence, Lord, (&c.[1], down to:) Then those

[1] See §§ 1–3. Instead of 'the Bhikkhu Kassapa-gotta' the

stranger Bhikkhus, Lord, pronounced against me expulsion for my refusal to see that offence. Then I thought, Lord: "I do not know indeed whether this is an offence or not, and whether I have made myself guilty of an offence or not, and whether I have been expelled or not, and whether that sentence is lawful or unlawful, objectionable or unobjectionable, valid or invalid. What if I were to go to *K*ampâ and to ask the Blessed One about this matter." Thus I have come here, Lord.'

6. (Buddha replied): 'This is no offence, O Bhikkhu; it is not an offence. You are innocent; you are not guilty of an offence. You are not expelled, and have not been expelled; the sentence by which you have been expelled is unlawful, objectionable, and invalid. Go, O Bhikkhu, and settle yourself again at Vâsabha-gâma.'

The Bhikkhu Kassapa-gotta expressed his assent to the Blessed One (by saying), 'Yes, Lord,' rose from his seat, and having respectfully saluted the Blessed One and walked round him with his right side towards him, he went on his way to Vâsabha-gâma.

7. Now those stranger Bhikkhus (at Vâsabha-gâma) were overcome by scruples and remorse: 'It is all loss to us indeed, it is no gain to us; we will fare ill indeed, we will not fare well, in this that we have expelled that pure, guiltless Bhikkhu without any cause and reason. Well, friends, let us go to *K*ampâ and let us confess there in the Blessed One's presence our sin in its sinfulness.'

pronoun of the first person is to be read; and the appellation 'Lord,' addressed to Buddha, is inserted several times.

And those stranger Bhikkhus put their resting-places in order, took up their alms-bowls and their robes, and went forth to *K*ampâ, and in due course they came to *K*ampâ and to the place where the Blessed One was. Having approached him and respectfully saluted the Blessed One, they sat down near him. Now it is the custom of the blessed Buddhas (&c.[1], down to:) 'It is all well, Lord; we find our living, Lord; we have made the journey, Lord, without too much fatigue. There is in the country of Kâsi, Lord, (a village) called Vâsabhagâma; from that place we come, Lord.'

8. 'So are you, O Bhikkhus, those who have expelled the resident Bhikkhu there?'

'We are, Lord.'

'For what cause, O Bhikkhus, and for what reason?'

'Without any cause and reason, Lord.'

Then the Blessed One rebuked those Bhikkhus: 'That is improper, O Bhikkhus, it is unbecoming, indecent, unworthy of Sama*n*as, unallowable, and to be avoided. How can you, O fools, expel a pure and guiltless Bhikkhu, without any cause and reason? This will not do, O Bhikkhus, for converting the unconverted.' Having thus rebuked them and delivered a religious discourse, he thus addressed the Bhikkhus: 'Let no one, O Bhikkhus, expel a pure and guiltless Bhikkhu without cause and reason. He who does, commits a dukka*t*a offence.'

9. Then those Bhikkhus rose from their seats, adjusted their upper robes so as to cover one

[1] See § 4. The alterations to be made ('those Bhikkhus' instead of 'the Bhikkhu Kassapa-gotta,' &c.) are obvious.

shoulder, prostrated themselves, inclining their heads to the feet of the Blessed One, and said to the Blessed One: 'Transgression, O Lord, has overcome us like the foolish, like the erring, like the unhappy, in this that we have expelled a pure, guiltless Bhikkhu without any cause and reason. May, O Lord, the Blessed One accept (the confession of) our sin in its sinfulness, and we will refrain from it in future.'

'Truly, O Bhikkhus, transgression has overcome you like the foolish, like the erring, like the unhappy, in that you have expelled a pure, guiltless Bhikkhu without any cause and reason. But as you see, O Bhikkhus, your sin in its sinfulness, and duly make amends for it, we accept it from you. For this, O Bhikkhus, is called progress in the discipline of the noble one, if one sees his sin in its sinfulness, and duly makes amends for it, and refrains from it in future.'

2.

1. At that time the Bhikkhus of *K*ampâ performed official acts in the following ways: they performed unlawful acts before an incomplete congregation; they performed unlawful acts before a complete congregation; they performed lawful acts before an incomplete congregation; they performed seemingly lawful acts before an incomplete congregation; they performed seemingly lawful acts before a complete congregation; a single Bhikkhu pronounced expulsion against a single one; a single Bhikkhu pronounced expulsion against two; a single Bhikkhu

pronounced expulsion against a number of Bhikkhus; a single Bhikkhu pronounced expulsion against a Sa*m*gha; two Bhikkhus pronounced expulsion against a single one . . . . against two . . . . . against a number of Bhikkhus . . . . against a Sa*m*gha; a number of Bhikkhus pronounced expulsion against a single one . . . . against two . . . . against another number . . . . against a Sa*m*gha; a Sa*m*gha pronounced expulsion against another Sa*m*gha[1].

2. Those Bhikkhus who were moderate, were annoyed, murmured, and became angry: 'How can the Bhikkhus of *K*ampâ perform official acts in the following ways: perform unlawful acts before an incomplete congregation (&c., down to:) how can a Sa*m*gha pronounce expulsion against another Sa*m*gha?'

These Bhikkhus told this thing to the Blessed One.

'Is it true, as they say, O Bhikkhus, that the Bhikkhus of *K*ampâ perform official acts in the following ways, &c.?'

'It is true, Lord.'

Then the blessed Buddha rebuked those Bhikkhus: 'It is improper, O Bhikkhus, what these foolish persons are doing; it is unbecoming, indecent, unworthy of Sama*n*as, unallowable, and to be avoided. How can these foolish persons, O Bhikkhus, perform official acts in the following ways, &c. This will not do, O Bhikkhus, for converting the unconverted.' Having thus rebuked them and delivered a religious discourse, he thus addressed the Bhikkhus:

3. 'If an official act, O Bhikkhus, is performed

[1] The cases of a Sa*m*gha's expelling a single Bhikkhu, or two Bhikkhus, or a number of Bhikkhus, are omitted, because such proceedings are lawful.

unlawfully by an incomplete congregation, it is no real act[1] and ought not to be performed. An official act performed unlawfully by a complete congregation is no real act and ought not to be performed (&c., as in § 1, down to :). A seemingly lawful act performed before a complete congregation is no real act and ought not to be performed. In case a single Bhikkhu pronounces expulsion against a single one,—this is no real act and ought not to be performed (&c., down to :). In case a Sa*m*gha pronounces expulsion against another Sa*m*gha,—this is no real act and ought not to be performed.

4. 'There are, O Bhikkhus, four kinds of official acts (which a Sa*m*gha can perform); an unlawful act performed by an incomplete congregation, an unlawful act performed by a complete congregation, a lawful act performed by an incomplete congregation, and a lawful act performed by a complete congregation.

'If, O Bhikkhus, an act is unlawful and performed by an incomplete congregation—such an act, O Bhikkhus, is objectionable and invalid on account of its unlawfulness and of the incompleteness (of the congregation). Such an act, O Bhikkhus, ought not to be performed, nor is such an act allowed by me.

'If, O Bhikkhus, an act is unlawful and performed by a complete congregation—such an act, O Bhikkhus, is objectionable and invalid on account of its unlawfulness. Such an act, &c.

'If, O Bhikkhus, an act is lawful and performed by an incomplete congregation—such an act, O Bhikkhus, is objectionable and invalid on account of

[1] I. e. it is null and void.

the incompleteness (of the congregation). Such an act, &c.

'If, O Bhikkhus, an act is lawful and performed by a complete congregation—such an act, O Bhikkhus, is unobjectionable and valid on account of its lawfulness and of the completeness (of the congregation). Such an act, O Bhikkhus, ought to be performed, and such an act is allowed by me.

'Therefore, O Bhikkhus, you ought to train yourselves thus: "Lawful acts which are performed by complete congregations—such acts will we perform[1]."'

3.

1. At that time the *Kh*abbaggiya Bhikkhus performed official acts in the following ways: they performed unlawful acts before an incomplete congregation (&c., as in chap. 2, § 1, down to:) they performed seemingly lawful acts before a complete congregation; they performed acts without a ñatti[2] and with the proclamation (of the kammavâ*k*â[2]); they performed acts without a proclamation (of the kammavâ*k*â) and with the ñatti; they performed acts without a ñatti and without a proclamation (of the kammavâ*k*â); they performed acts contrary to the Dhamma; they performed acts contrary to the Vinaya; they performed acts contrary to the doctrine of the Teacher; and they performed acts against which (the Bhikkhus present) protested, which were unlawful, objectionable, and invalid.

Those Bhikkhus who were moderate, were annoyed,

[1] A similar injunction is found at the close of chapter II, 14.

[2] See I, 28, &c.

&c. These Bhikkhus told this thing to the Blessed One.

'Is it true, as they say, O Bhikkhus, that the *Kh*abbaggiya Bhikkhus, &c.?'

'It is true, Lord, &c.'

Having thus rebuked them and delivered a religious discourse, he thus addressed the Bhikkhus:

2. 'If an official act, O Bhikkhus, is performed unlawfully by an incomplete congregation, it is no real act and ought not to be performed (&c.[1], down to:). If an official act, O Bhikkhus, is performed against which (the Bhikkhus present) protest, which is unlawful, objectionable, and invalid, this is no real act and ought not to be performed.

3. 'There are, O Bhikkhus, six kinds of official acts (which a Samgha can perform): an unlawful act, an act performed by an incomplete congregation, an act performed by a complete congregation, a seemingly lawful act performed by an incomplete congregation, a seemingly lawful act performed by a complete congregation, a lawful act performed by a complete congregation.

'And which, O Bhikkhus, is an unlawful act? If one performs, O Bhikkhus, a ñattidutiya act[2] with one ñatti, and does not proclaim a kammavâ*k*â, such an act is unlawful. If one performs, O Bhikkhus, a ñattidutiya act with two ñattis and does not proclaim a kammavâ*k*â . . . with one kammavâ*k*â and does not propose a ñatti . . . . with two

[1] Here the different categories of forbidden acts are enumerated one after the other, as in § 1.

[2] About ñatti, kammavâ*k*â, ñattidutiya, and ñatti*k*atuttha acts, see our note at I, 28, 3. 'Proposing a ñatti' and 'proclaiming a kammavâ*k*â' mean proposing a motion and putting a resolution to the assembled brethren.

kammavâ*k*âs and does not propose a ñatti, such an act is unlawful.

4. 'If one performs, O Bhikkhus, a ñatti*k*atuttha act with one ñatti and does not proclaim a kammavâ*k*â, such an act is unlawful. If one performs, O Bhikkhus, a ñatti*k*atuttha act with two (. . . . three, ... four) ñattis and does not proclaim a kammavâ*k*â, such an act is unlawful. If one performs, O Bhikkhus, a ñatti*k*atuttha act with one kammavâ*k*â (. . . . with two, ... three, ... four kammavâ*k*âs) and does not propose a ñatti, such an act is unlawful. Such acts, O Bhikkhus, are called unlawful acts.

5. 'And which, O Bhikkhus, is an act of an incomplete congregation?

'If, O Bhikkhus, at a ñattidutiya act not all Bhikkhus, as many as are entitled to vote, are present, if the *kh*anda[1] of those who have to declare their *kh*anda has not been conveyed (to the assembly), and if the Bhikkhus present protest, such an act is performed by an incomplete congregation.

'If, O Bhikkhus, at a ñattidutiya act as many Bhikkhus as are entitled to vote, are present, but if the *kh*anda of those who have to declare their *kh*anda has not been conveyed (to the assembly), and if the Bhikkhus present protest, such an act is performed by an incomplete congregation.

'If, O Bhikkhus, at a ñattidutiya act as many Bhikkhus as are entitled to vote, are present, if the *kh*anda of those who have to declare their *kh*anda has been conveyed, but if the Bhikkhus present protest, such an act is performed by an incomplete congregation.

[1] See II, 23.

'If, O Bhikkhus, at a ñattikatuttha act, &c.[1]

'Such acts, O Bhikkhus, are called acts performed by incomplete congregations.

6. 'And which, O Bhikkhus, is an act of a complete congregation?

'If, O Bhikkhus, at a ñattidutiya act as many Bhikkhus as are entitled to vote, are present. if the khanda of those who have to declare their khanda has been conveyed (to the assembly), and if the Bhikkhus present do not protest, such an act is performed by a complete congregation.

'If, O Bhikkhus, at a ñattikatuttha act (&c., as in last section).

'Such acts, O Bhikkhus, are called acts performed by complete congregations.

7. 'And which, O Bhikkhus, is a seemingly lawful act performed by an incomplete congregation?

'If, O Bhikkhus, at a ñattidutiya act the kammavâkâ is proclaimed first and the ñatti is proposed afterwards, if not all Bhikkhus, as many as are entitled to vote, are present, &c.[2]

8. 'And which, O Bhikkhus, is a seemingly lawful act performed by a complete congregation?

'If, O Bhikkhus, at a ñattidutiya act the kammavâkâ is proclaimed first and the ñatti is proposed afterwards, if as many Bhikkhus as are entitled to vote, are present, &c.[3]

---

[1] The identical three cases given before with regard to the ñattidutiya act are repeated here.

[2] The six cases given in this paragraph, of which three refer to ñattidutiya acts and three to ñattikatuttha acts, differ from those specified in § 5 only by the statement added in each of these cases regarding the inverted order of ñatti and kammavâkâ.

[3] This paragraph stands precisely in the same relation to § 6 in which the preceding one stands to § 5.

9. 'And which, O Bhikkhus, is a lawful act performed by a complete congregation?

'If, O Bhikkhus, at a *ñ*attidutiya act the *ñ*atti is proposed first and afterwards the act is performed with one kammavâ*k*â, if as many Bhikkhus as are entitled to vote, are present, if the *kh*anda of those who have to declare their *kh*anda has been conveyed (to the assembly), and if the Bhikkhus present do not protest, such an act is lawful and performed by a complete congregation.

'If, O Bhikkhus, at a *ñ*atti*k*atuttha act the *ñ*atti is proposed first and afterwards the act is performed with three kammavâ*k*âs, if as many Bhikkhus as are entitled to vote, &c., such an act is lawful and performed by a complete congregation.'

4.

1. 'There are five kinds of Sa*m*ghas: the Bhikkhu Sa*m*gha consisting of four persons, the Bhikkhu Sa*m*gha consisting of five persons . . . . of ten persons . . . . of twenty persons . . . . of more than twenty persons.

'In case, O Bhikkhus, the Bhikkhu Sa*m*gha consist of four persons, and acts lawfully, and is complete, it is entitled to perform all official acts except three acts, that is, the upasampadâ ordination, pavâra*n*â, and abbhâna[1].

'In case, O Bhikkhus, the Bhikkhu Sa*m*gha consist of five persons, and acts lawfully, and is complete, it is entitled to perform all official acts except

[1] See *K*ullavagga III, 2 seq.

two acts, that is, the upasampadâ ordination in the central countries[1] and abbhâna.

'In case, O Bhikkhus, the Bhikkhu Samgha consist of ten persons, and acts lawfully, and is complete, it is entitled to perform all official acts except one, namely, abbhâna.

'In case, O Bhikkhus, the Bhikkhu Samgha consist of twenty persons, and acts lawfully, and is complete, it is entitled to perform all official acts.

'In case, O Bhikkhus, the Bhikkhu Samgha consist of more than twenty persons, and acts lawfully, and is complete, it is entitled to perform all official acts.

2. 'An official act, O Bhikkhus, which requires the presence of four persons, if performed by a congregation in which a Bhikkhunî is the fourth, is no real act, and ought not to be performed. An official act, O Bhikkhus, which requires the presence of four persons, if performed by a congregation in which a sikkhamânâ is the fourth, ... in which a sâmanera, &c.[2], is the fourth, ... in which a person belonging to another communion is the fourth, ... in which a person staying within a different boundary[3] is the fourth, ... in which a person poised in the air by supernatural power is

[1] As regards the exceptional regulations referring to the upasampadâ ordination in the bordering countries, see above, V, 13, 12.

[2] Here follows the very frequent enumeration given, for instance, at II, 36, §§ 1-4.

[3] Generally speaking, the two categories of 'persons belonging to another communion,' and 'persons staying within another boundary,' can be considered as coincident. In certain cases, however, they could be distinguished; see X, 1, §§ 9, 10.

the fourth, ... in which a person against whom the Sa*m*gha institutes a proceeding is the fourth—is no real act and ought not to be performed.'

End of the regulations about acts performed by four persons.

3–5. 'An official act, O Bhikkhus, which requires the presence of five (. . . . ten, ... twenty) persons, if performed by a congregation in which a Bhikkhunî, &c.[1], is the fifth (. . . . tenth, ... twentieth), is no real act and ought not to be performed.'

End of the regulations about acts performed by five, (ten, twenty) persons.

6. 'If, O Bhikkhus, a congregation in which a person sentenced to the parivâsa discipline[2] is the fourth, institutes the proceedings of parivâsa, of mûlâya pa*t*ikassanâ, and of mânatta, or if a congregation in which such a person is the twentieth, confers abbhâna, this is no real act and ought not to be performed.

'If, O Bhikkhus, a congregation in which a person that ought to be sentenced to mûlâya pa*t*ikassanâ . . . . that ought to be sentenced to mânatta . . . . that is subject to the mânatta discipline . . . .

[1] Here the enumeration of § 2 is repeated.

[2] See about parivâsa, and the other Sa*m*ghakammas referred to in this paragraph, the details given in the second book of the *K*ullavagga.

on whom the abbhâna sentence ought to be conferred[1], institutes the proceedings of parivâsa, of mûlâya pa*t*ikassanâ, and of mânatta, or if a congregation in which such a person is the twentieth, confers abbhâna, this is no real act and ought not to be performed.

7. 'Of some persons, O Bhikkhus, the protest[2] raised in the assembly is effectual, of some persons it is ineffectual.

'And which are the persons, O Bhikkhus, whose protest raised in the assembly is ineffectual?

'The protest, O Bhikkhus, raised in the assembly by a Bhikkhunî is ineffectual. The protest, O Bhikkhus, raised in the assembly by a sikkhamânâ (&c.[3], down to:) by a person against whom the Sa*m*gha institutes a proceeding, is ineffectual. These are the persons, O Bhikkhus, whose protest raised in the assembly is ineffectual.

8. 'And which are the persons, O Bhikkhus, whose protest raised in the assembly is effectual?

'The protest, O Bhikkhus, of a Bhikkhu who is healthy (in mind), who belongs to the same communion[4], who stays within the same boundary[5], even

---

[1] But has not yet been conferred. An abbhita Bhikkhu is considered as fully rehabilitated.

[2] Against official acts which the Sa*m*gha is performing.

[3] This list of persons who cannot protest against official acts of the Sa*m*gha differs from that given in § 2 or at II, 36, §§ 1–4, only by three categories being here added after 'a person guilty of an extreme offence' (antimavatthu*m* ag*gh*âpannaka). These categories are the following: 'a madman,' 'a person whose mind is unhinged,' 'a person who suffers (bodily) pain.' See II, 22, 3, &c.

[4] That is, the Sa*m*gha which is going to perform the act in question.

[5] See the note at § 2.

if he have committed a sin which brings about immediate punishment in hell,—if he give notice of his protest at the meeting,—is effectual. This is the person, O Bhikkhus, whose protest raised in the assembly is effectual.

9. 'There are, O Bhikkhus, two cases of expulsion[1] (pronounced against a person). If expulsion, O Bhikkhus, had not been pronounced (before) against a person, and the Sa*m*gha pronounces expulsion against him, there are some against whom such expulsion has been pronounced duly, and others against whom it has been pronounced unduly.

'And which is a person, O Bhikkhus, against whom, if expulsion had not been pronounced before, and the Sa*m*gha pronounces expulsion against him, expulsion has been pronounced unduly? In case, O Bhikkhus, there be a pure, guiltless Bhikkhu,—if the Sa*m*gha pronounces expulsion against him, expulsion has been pronounced unduly. This, O Bhikkhus, is called a person against whom, if expulsion had not been pronounced before, and the Sa*m*gha pronounces expulsion against him, expulsion has been pronounced unduly.

'And which is a person, O Bhikkhus, against whom, &c., expulsion has been pronounced duly? In case, O Bhikkhus, there be an ignorant, unlearned Bhikkhu, a constant offender, who is unable to discern what is an offence[2], who lives in lay society, unduly

[1] Compare the rules regarding the pabbâ*g*aniyakamma, *K*ullavagga I, 13 seq., and our note at I, 79, 1.

[2] Anapadâna. Buddhaghosa: 'Anapadâno 'ti apa*t*âna- (read apadâna-) virahito. apadâna*m* vu*kk*ati pari*kkh*edo. âpatti-pari*kkh*eda-virahito 'ti attho.' Probably the word must not be derived from the root dâ, 'to give,' but from dâ, 'to cut.'

associating himself with lay people,—if the Samgha pronounces expulsion against him, expulsion has been pronounced duly. This, O Bhikkhus, is called a person, &c.

10. 'There are, O Bhikkhus, two cases of restoration (of an expelled Bhikkhu). If restoration, O Bhikkhus, had not been granted before to a person, and the Samgha grants restoration to him, there are some to whom such restoration will have been granted duly, and others to whom it will have been unduly granted.

'And which is a person, O Bhikkhus, to whom, &c., restoration has been granted unduly? A eunuch, O Bhikkhus, to whom restoration had not been granted before, and whom the Samgha restores, has been restored unduly. A person who has furtively attached himself (to the Samgha), &c.[1], to whom restoration had not been granted before, and whom the Samgha restores, has been restored unduly.

'This, O Bhikkhus, is called a person to whom, &c., restoration has been granted unduly. These, O Bhikkhus, are called persons to whom, &c., restoration has been granted duly.

11. 'And which is a person, O Bhikkhus, to whom, &c., restoration has been granted duly?' &c.[2]

End of the first Bhânavâra, called the Vâsabhagâma Bhânavâra.

---

[1] See the list of persons given at II, 36, 3.

[2] The formality and the repetitions are the same here as in § 10, and need not be repeated. The list of persons whose restoration is stated to be valid is the same as at I, 71, 1.

5.

1. 'In case, O Bhikkhus, there be no offence which a Bhikkhu should see (or, acknowledge as committed by himself), and if the Sa*m*gha, or a number of Bhikkhus, or a single person reprove him (and say): "You have committed an offence, friend; do you see that offence?"—and he replies: "There is no offence, friends, which I should see," and the Sa*m*gha pronounces expulsion against him for his refusal to see that offence,—this is an unlawful act.

'In case, O Bhikkhus, there be no offence which a Bhikkhu should atone for, &c.[1]

'In case, O Bhikkhus, there be no false doctrine which a Bhikkhu should renounce, &c.[2]

2. 'In case, O Bhikkhus, there be no offence which a Bhikkhu should see, and there be no offence which he should atone for, and if the Sa*m*gha, or a number of Bhikkhus, or a single person reprove him (and say): "You have committed an offence, friend; do you see that offence? Atone for that offence,"—and he replies: "There is no offence, friends, which I should see; there is no offence,

---

[1] The ukkhepaniyakamma âpattiyâ appa*t*inissagge (expulsion for a Bhikkhu's refusal to atone for an offence) is spoken of here exactly in the same terms as those in which the ukkhepaniyakamma âpattiyâ adassane (expulsion for a Bhikkhu's refusal to see an offence) is spoken of in the preceding clause. The brethren say to the pretended offender, 'You have committed an offence, friend; atone for that offence'—which he refuses to do.

[2] As above; the Bhikkhus institute the ukkhepaniyakamma pâpikâya di*tth*iyâ appa*t*inissagge (expulsion for a Bhikkhu's refusal to renounce a false doctrine).

friends, which I should atone for," and the Sa*m*gha pronounces expulsion against him for his refusal to see that offence, or for his refusal to atone for that offence,—this is an unlawful act.

3–5[1].

6–7. 'In case, O Bhikkhus, there be an offence which a Bhikkhu should see, and if the Sa*m*gha, or a number of Bhikkhus, or a single person reprove him (and say): 'You have committed an offence, friend; do you see that offence?"—and he replies: "Yes, friends, I see it," and the Sa*m*gha pronounces expulsion against him for his (pretended) refusal to see that offence,—this is an unlawful act.

'In case, O Bhikkhus, there be an offence which a Bhikkhu should atone for, &c.[2]

8–9. 'In case, O Bhikkhus, there be an offence which a Bhikkhu should see, and if the Sa*m*gha, or a number of Bhikkhus, or a single person reprove him (and say): "You have committed an offence, friend; do you see that offence?"—and he replies: "There is no offence, friends, which I should see," and the Sa*m*gha pronounces expulsion against him for his refusal to see that offence,—this is a lawful act[3].'

---

[1] As in § 2, the first and second of the three cases given in § 1 are combined, so follow now combinations of the first and third, the second and third, and of the first, second, and third cases respectively.

[2] Here follow again the cases of the ukkhepaniyakamma âpattiyâ appa*t*inissagge and pâpikâya di*tth*iyâ appa*t*inissagge, and the combinations of the three cases as above.

[3] Here follow the two other cases, together with the combinations of the three, exactly as above.

6.

1. And the venerable Upâli[1] went to the place where the Blessed One was. Having approached him and respectfully saluted the Blessed One, he sat down near him. Sitting near him the venerable Upâli said to the Blessed One: 'Lord, if a complete congregation performs an act at which the presence (of the accused Bhikkhu) is required, in his absence—is this act, Lord, performed lawfully according to Dhamma and Vinaya?'

'It is performed, Upâli, unlawfully against Dhamma and Vinaya.'

2. 'Lord, if a complete congregation performs an act at which (the accused Bhikkhu) ought to be called upon for an answer, without calling upon him for an answer—if it performs an act at which the confession (of the culprit) is required, without his confession—if it grants to a Bhikkhu to whom sati-vinaya[2] ought to be granted, an amû*lh*avinaya[3]—if it proceeds against a Bhikkhu to whom amû*lh*a-vinaya ought to be granted, with the tassapâpiyya-sikâkamma[4]—if it proceeds against a Bhikkhu against whom the tassapâpiyyasikâkamma ought

[1] That the redactors of this Pi*t*aka have chosen Upâli here and at X, 6, *K*ullavagga II, 2, 7, to question the Blessed One about the Vinaya regulations, stands evidently in connection with the tradition ascribing to Upâli an especial authority regarding the rules of the Order and styling him, as is said in the Dîpava*m*sa (IV, 3, 5; V, 7, 9), agganikkhittaka, i.e. original depositary, of the Vinaya tradition. See our Introduction, p. xii seq.

[2] See *K*ullavagga IV, 4, 10.

[3] See *K*ullavagga IV, 5.

[4] See *K*ullavagga IV, 11.

to be instituted, with the tagganiyakamma[1]—if it proceeds against a Bhikkhu against whom the tagganiyakamma ought to be instituted, with the nissayakamma—if it proceeds against a Bhikkhu against whom the nissayakamma ought to be instituted, with the pabbâganiyakamma—if it proceeds against a Bhikkhu against whom the pabbâganiyakamma ought to be instituted, with the patisâraniyakamma—if it proceeds against a Bhikkhu against whom the patisâraniyakamma ought to be instituted, with the ukkhepaniyakamma—if it sentences a Bhikkhu against whom the ukkhepaniyakamma ought to be instituted, to parivâsa[2]—if it sentences a Bhikkhu who ought to be sentenced to parivâsa, to mûlâya patikassanâ—if it sentences a Bhikkhu who ought to be sentenced to mûlâya patikassanâ, to mânatta—if it grants to a Bhikkhu who ought to be sentenced to mânatta, the decree of abbhâna—if it confers on a Bhikkhu to whom abbhâna ought to be granted, the upasampadâ ordination,—is this act, Lord, performed lawfully according to Dhamma and Vinaya?'

3. 'It is performed, Upâli, unlawfully against Dhamma and Vinaya. If a complete congregation, Upâli, performs an act at which the presence (of the accused Bhikkhu) is required, in his absence (&c., down to:) confers on a Bhikkhu to whom abbhâna ought to be granted, the upasampadâ ordination,—in such case, Upâli, this act is performed unlawfully against Dhamma and Vinaya, and in such case this Samgha trespasses against the law.'

---

[1] This Samghakamma and the following ones are explained in Kullavagga I, 1 seq.

[2] For this term and the next ones, see Kullavagga III, 1-7.

4. 'Lord, if a complete congregation performs an act at which the presence (of the accused Bhikkhu) is required, in his presence (&c., down to:) confers on a person, on whom the upasampadâ ordination ought to be conferred, the upasampadâ ordination,—is this act, Lord, performed lawfully according to Dhamma and Vinaya?'

'It is performed, Upâli, lawfully according to Dhamma and Vinaya. If a complete congregation performs an act (&c., down to:) the upasampadâ ordination,—in such case, Upâli, this act is performed lawfully according to Dhamma and Vinaya, and in such case this Samgha does not trespass against the law.'

5. 'Lord, if a complete congregation grants to a Bhikkhu to whom sativinaya ought to be granted, an amûlhavinaya, and to a Bhikkhu to whom amûlhavinaya ought to be granted, a sativinaya (&c.[1], down to:) confers on a Bhikkhu to whom abbhâna ought to be granted, the upasampadâ ordination, and grants to a person on whom the upasampadâ ordination ought to be conferred, the decree of abbhâna,—is this act, Lord, performed lawfully according to Dhamma and Vinaya?'

6. 'It is performed, Upâli, unlawfully against Dhamma and Vinaya. If a complete congregation grants to a Bhikkhu, &c.,—in such case, Upâli, this act is performed unlawfully against Dhamma and

[1] The Samghakammas enumerated in § 2, beginning with sativinaya, are arranged here in pairs, in direct and reverse order, in this way: sativinaya and amûlhavinaya, amûlhavinaya and sativinaya; then amûlhavinaya and tassapâpiyyasikâkamma, tassapâpiyyasikâkamma and amûlhavinaya, &c.

Vinaya, and in such case this Sa*m*gha trespasses against the law.'

7. 'Lord, if a complete congregation grants sativinaya to a Bhikkhu to whom sativinaya ought to be granted, and amû*lh*avinaya to a Bhikkhu to whom amû*lh*avinaya ought to be granted (&c.[1], down to:) grants abbhâna to a Bhikkhu to whom abbhâna ought to be granted, and confers the upasampadâ ordination on a person on whom the upasampadâ ordination ought to be conferred,—is this act, Lord, performed lawfully according to Dhamma and Vinaya?'

8. 'It is performed, Upâli, lawfully according to Dhamma and Vinaya (&c., down to:) and in such case this Sa*m*gha does not trespass against the law.'

9. And the Blessed One thus addressed the Bhikkhus: 'If a complete congregation, O Bhikkhus, grants to a Bhikkhu to whom sativinaya ought to be granted, an amû*lh*avinaya, in such case, O Bhikkhus, this act is performed unlawfully against Dhamma and Vinaya, and in such case this Sa*m*gha trespasses against the law. If a complete congregation, O Bhikkhus, institutes against a Bhikkhu to whom sativinaya ought to be granted, the tassapâpiyyasikâkamma (&c.[2], down to:) grants to a person on whom the

---

[1] The same dyads as in § 5.

[2] In this paragraph all possible combinations of two different Sa*m*ghakammas are formed in this way: first, sativinaya is combined with amû*lh*avinaya and all the rest, down to upasampadâ; then amû*lh*avinaya with all terms from tassapâpiyyasikâ down to sativinaya, and so on; the whole series ends thus with the combinations of upasampadâraha with all terms from sativinaya down to abbhâna.

upasampadâ ordination ought to be conferred, the decree of abbhâna,—in such case, O Bhikkhus, this act is performed unlawfully against Dhamma and Vinaya, and in such case this Samgha trespasses against the law.'

End of the second Bhânavâra, which contains the questions of Upâli.

7.

1. 'In case, O Bhikkhus, a Bhikkhu be litigious, contentious, quarrelsome, disputatious, and constantly raise questions before the Samgha. And the other Bhikkhus say among each other: "This Bhikkhu, friends, is indeed litigious, contentious, &c.; well, let us proceed against him with the tagganiyakamma[1]." And they proceed against him with the tagganiyakamma unlawfully[2] with an incomplete congregation[3], and he then goes from that district to another district. There the Bhikkhus say among each other: "Against this Bhikkhu, friends, the Samgha has proceeded with the tagganiyakamma unlawfully with an incomplete congregation; well, let us proceed against him with the tagganiyakamma." And they proceed against him with the tagganiya-kamma unlawfully with a complete congregation, and he then goes from that district again to another district. And there the Bhikkhus again say among each other (&c.,

[1] See *K*ullavagga I, 1–8. [2] See above, chap. 3, § 3 seq.
[3] See above, chap. 3, § 5.

down to:) and they proceed against him with the tagganiyakamma lawfully with an incomplete congregation . . . . seemingly lawfully[1] with an incomplete congregation . . . . seemingly lawfully with a complete congregation[2].

2–5. 'In case, O Bhikkhus, a Bhikkhu be litigious, &c.[3]

6. 'In case, O Bhikkhus, a Bhikkhu be ignorant, unlearned, a constant offender, unable to discern what is an offence[4], and lives in lay society, unduly associating himself with lay people. And the other Bhikkhus say among each other: "This Bhikkhu, friends, is indeed ignorant, unlearned, &c.; well, let us proceed against him with the nissayakamma[5]," and they proceed against him with the nissayakamma unlawfully with an incomplete congregation, &c.[6]

7. 'In case, O Bhikkhus, a Bhikkhu leads a life hurtful to the laity, and devoted to evil[7]. And the other Bhikkhus say among each other: "This

---

[1] See above, chap. 3, § 7.

[2] See above, chap. 3, § 8.

[3] As in § 1, but with a different arrangement of the five categories on which this exposition is based: unlawfully with an incomplete congregation, unlawfully with a complete congregation, lawfully with an incomplete congregation, seemingly lawfully with an incomplete congregation, seemingly lawfully with a complete congregation. In § 1 these categories are arranged in their natural order; in § 2 the second is placed at the head, then follow the third, fourth, fifth, and finally the first; in § 3 the exposition likewise begins with the third and ends with the second, &c. This arrangement is called 'a wheel' (*k*akka).

[4] See the note at chap. 4, § 9.

[5] See *K*ullavagga I, 9–12.

[6] The same five cases and the same *k*akka as in §§ 1–5.

[7] See the 13th Sa*m*ghâdisesa Rule.

Bhikkhu, friends, leads a life hurtful to the laity, and devoted to evil; well, let us proceed against him with the pabbâ*g*aniyakamma[1]," &c.[2]

8. 'In case, O Bhikkhus, a Bhikkhu abuses and reviles lay people. And the other Bhikkhus say among each other: "This Bhikkhu, friends, abuses and reviles lay people; well, let us proceed against him with the pa*t*isâra*n*iyakamma[3]," &c.[2]

9-11. 'In case, O Bhikkhus, a Bhikkhu, having committed an offence, refuses to see that offence (committed by himself)[4]. And the other Bhikkhus say among each other: "This Bhikkhu, friends, has committed an offence and refuses to see that offence; well, let us pronounce expulsion against him for his refusal to see that offence[5]," &c.[2]

12-13. 'In case, O Bhikkhus, a Bhikkhu, against whom the Sa*m*gha has proceeded with the ta*gg*aniyakamma, behaves himself properly, lives modestly, aspires to get clear of his penance, and asks for the revocation of the ta*gg*aniyakamma sentence. And the other Bhikkhus say among each other: "This Bhikkhu, friends, against whom the Sa*m*gha has proceeded with the ta*gg*aniyakamma, in truth behaves himself properly; he lives modestly, &c.; well, let us revoke the ta*gg*aniyakamma sentence pronounced against him." And they revoke the ta*gg*aniyakamma sentence

---

[1] See *K*ullavagga I, 13-17. [2] As in §§ 1-5 or in § 6.

[3] *K*ullavagga I, 18-24.

[4] § 10: A Bhikkhu, having committed an offence, refuses to atone for that offence. § 11: A Bhikkhu refuses to renounce a false doctrine.

[5] § 10: For his refusal to atone for that offence. § 11: For his refusal to renounce that false doctrine.

pronounced against him unlawfully with an incomplete congregation. And he then goes from that district to another district. There the Bhikkhus say among each other: "The *tagganiyakamma* sentence, friends, pronounced against this Bhikkhu has been revoked by the Samgha unlawfully with an incomplete congregation," &c.[1]

14. 'In case, O Bhikkhus, a Bhikkhu against whom the Samgha has proceeded with the nissayakamma .... with the pabbâganiyakamma .... with the patisâraniyakamma .... against whom the Samgha has pronounced expulsion for his refusal to see an offence .... for his refusal to atone for an offence .... for his refusal to renounce a false doctrine, behaves himself properly, &c.[2]

15. 'In case, O Bhikkhus, a Bhikkhu be litigious, contentious, quarrelsome, disputatious, and constantly raise questions before the Samgha. And the other Bhikkhus say among each other: "This Bhikkhu, friends, is indeed litigious, contentious, &c.; well, let us proceed against him with the tagganiyakamma." And they proceed against him with the tagganiyakamma, unlawfully with an incomplete congregation. Now among the Samgha residing in that district a contention is raised whether this is an act performed unlawfully with an incomplete congregation, or an act performed unlawfully with a complete congregation, or an act performed lawfully with an incomplete

[1] The analogous five cases with the *k*akka development as in §§ 1–5.

[2] As in §§ 12, 13.

congregation, or an act performed seemingly lawfully with an incomplete congregation, or an act performed seemingly lawfully with a complete congregation, or an act not performed, badly performed, to be performed again. In this case, O Bhikkhus, the Bhikkhus who say: "It is an act performed unlawfully with an incomplete congregation"—and the Bhikkhus who say: "It is an act not performed, badly performed, to be performed again"—these Bhikkhus are right herein.

16. 'In case, O Bhikkhus, a Bhikkhu be litigious (&c., as in § 15, down to:) and they proceed against him with the ta*gg*aniyakamma unlawfully with a complete congregation . . . . lawfully with an incomplete congregation . . . . seemingly lawfully with an incomplete congregation . . . . seemingly lawfully with a complete congregation. Now among the Sa*m*gha residing in that district (&c., as in § 15).

17–20. 'In case, O Bhikkhus, a Bhikkhu be ignorant, unlearned,' &c.[1]

End of the ninth Khandhaka, which treats of the events in *K*ampâ.

---

[1] The text treats here in §§ 17, 18 of the nissayakamma (see § 6) and of the Sa*m*ghakammas down to the expulsion for a Bhikkhu's refusal to renounce a false doctrine (see §§ 7–11) in the same manner as the ta*gg*aniyakamma is spoken of in §§ 15, 16. Then follows (§§ 19, 20) an exactly analogous exposition about the revocation of these Sa*m*ghakammas, which stands in the same relation to §§ 15–18 in which §§ 12–14 stand to §§ 1–11.

TENTH KHANDHAKA.

(SCHISMS AMONG THE SAMGHA.)

1.

1. At that time the blessed Buddha dwelt at Kosambî in the Ghositârâma.

At that time a certain Bhikkhu had committed an offence which he considered as an offence, while the other Bhikkhus considered that offence as no offence. Afterwards he began to consider that offence as no offence, and the other Bhikkhus began to consider that offence as an offence.

Now those Bhikkhus said to that Bhikkhu: 'You have committed an offence, friend; do you see that offence?'

(He replied): 'There is no offence, friends, which I should see.'

Then those Bhikkhus, bringing about unanimity (of the fraternity for their sentence) pronounced expulsion against that Bhikkhu for his refusal to see that offence.

2. Now that Bhikkhu was erudite; he had studied the Âgamas; he knew the Dhamma, the Vinaya, the Mâtikâ[1]; he was wise, learned, intelligent, modest, conscientious, anxious for training.

And that Bhikkhu went to his companions and friends among the Bhikkhus, and said to them: 'This is no offence, friends; this is not an offence.

[1] See *K*ullavagga I, 11, 1, with our note.

I am offenceless; I am not guilty of an offence; I am unexpelled and have not been expelled; the sentence by which I have been expelled is unlawful, objectionable, and invalid. May the venerable ones be my partisans according to Dhamma and Vinaya.'

Thus that Bhikkhu got his companions and friends among the Bhikkhus on his side.

And he sent also a messenger to his companions and friends among the Bhikkhus of the whole country (with the following message): 'This is no offence, friends; this is not an offence (&c., down to:). May the venerable ones be my partisans according to Dhamma and Vinaya.'

Thus that Bhikkhu got also his companions and friends among the Bhikkhus of the whole country on his side.

3. Now those Bhikkhus who were partisans of the expelled Bhikkhu, went to the place where those who had expelled him, were. Having approached them, they said to the Bhikkhus who had expelled him: 'This is no offence, friends; this is not an offence. This Bhikkhu is offenceless; this Bhikkhu is not guilty of an offence. This Bhikkhu is unexpelled; this Bhikkhu has not been expelled. The sentence by which he has been expelled is unlawful, objectionable, and invalid.'

When they had spoken thus, the Bhikkhus who had expelled that Bhikkhu, said to the partisans of the expelled one: 'This is an offence, friends; this is not no offence. This Bhikkhu is an offender; this Bhikkhu is not offenceless. This Bhikkhu is expelled; this Bhikkhu is not unexpelled. The sentence by which he has been expelled is lawful, unobjectionable, and valid. Do not stand, O venerable ones, on the side of this expelled Bhikkhu; do not follow him.'

But the partisans of the expelled Bhikkhu, though they were spoken to thus by the Bhikkhus who had expelled him, persevered nevertheless on the side of that expelled Bhikkhu and followed him.

4. And a certain Bhikkhu went to the place where the Blessed One was. Having approached him and respectfully saluted the Blessed One, he sat down near him. Sitting near him that Bhikkhu said to the Blessed One: 'A certain Bhikkhu, Lord, had committed an offence which he considered as an offence (&c., as in §§ 1-3, down to:). But the partisans, Lord, of the expelled Bhikkhu, though they were spoken to thus by the Bhikkhus who had expelled him, persevered nevertheless on the side of that expelled Bhikkhu and followed him.'

5. Then the Blessed One (exclaimed): 'The Bhikkhu Sa*m*gha is divided! The Bhikkhu Sa*m*gha is divided!'—and he rose from his seat and went to the place where the Bhikkhus were who had pronounced that sentence of expulsion. Having approached them, he sat down on the seat they had prepared. Sitting there the Blessed One said to the Bhikkhus who had pronounced expulsion against that Bhikkhu: 'Do not think, O Bhikkhus, that you are to pronounce expulsion against a Bhikkhu whatever be the facts of the case, saying, "It occurs to us to do so; it occurs to us to do so."

6. 'In case, O Bhikkhus, a Bhikkhu has committed an offence which he considers as no offence, while the other Bhikkhus consider it as an offence—if, O Bhikkhus, those Bhikkhus know with regard

to that Bhikkhu: "This venerable brother is erudite; he has studied the Âgamas; he knows the Dhamma, the Vinaya, the Mâtikâ; he is wise, learned, intelligent, modest, conscientious, anxious for training. Should we pronounce expulsion against this Bhikkhu for his refusal to see that offence, and should we not hold Uposatha with that Bhikkhu, but hold Uposatha without that Bhikkhu, this matter will cause among the Sa*m*gha altercations, contentions, discord, quarrels, divisions among the Sa*m*gha, disunion among the Sa*m*gha, separations among the Sa*m*gha, schisms among the Sa*m*gha,"—in that case, O Bhikkhus, let those Bhikkhus, standing in awe of causing divisions, not pronounce expulsion against that Bhikkhu for his refusal to see his offence.

7. 'In case, O Bhikkhus, a Bhikkhu has committed (&c., as above, down to:). "Should we pronounce expulsion against this Bhikkhu for his refusal to see that offence, and should we not hold Pavâra*n*â with that Bhikkhu, but hold Pavâra*n*â without that Bhikkhu, and not perform official acts with that Bhikkhu, but perform official acts without that Bhikkhu, and not sit down on our seats with that Bhikkhu, but sit down on our seats without that Bhikkhu, and not sit down to drink rice-milk with that Bhikkhu, but sit down to drink rice-milk without that Bhikkhu, and not sit down in the dining-hall with that Bhikkhu, but sit down in the dining-hall without that Bhikkhu, and not dwell under one roof with that Bhikkhu, but dwell under one roof without that Bhikkhu, and not perform with that Bhikkhu, according to seniority, the duties of respectfully saluting each other, rising from our seats, raising the joined hands before each other, and all

proper duties, but perform without that Bhikkhu, according to seniority, the duties, &c.,—this matter will cause among the Saṃgha (&c., as in § 6, down to the end).'

8. And the Blessed One, having spoken thus to the Bhikkhus who had pronounced that sentence of expulsion, rose from his seat, and went to the place where the partisans of the expelled Bhikkhu were. Having approached them, he sat down on the seat they had prepared. Sitting there the Blessed One said to the partisans of the expelled Bhikkhu: 'Do not think, O Bhikkhus, if you have committed an offence, that you need not atone for that offence, (saying to yourselves): "We are without offence." In case, O Bhikkhus, a Bhikkhu has committed an offence which he considers as no offence, while the other Bhikkhus consider it as an offence—if, O Bhikkhus, that Bhikkhu knows with regard to those Bhikkhus: "These venerable brethren are erudite (&c., down to:) anxious for training. It is impossible that they should, on my account, or on account of anybody else, abandon themselves to walking in longing, in malice, in delusion, in fear. Should these Bhikkhus pronounce expulsion against me for my refusal to see that offence, and should they not hold Uposatha with me, but hold Uposatha without me, and should they not hold Pavâraṇâ with me, but hold Pavâraṇâ without me (&c., as in § 7), this matter will cause, &c., schisms among the Saṃgha,"—in that case, O Bhikkhus, let that Bhikkhu, standing in awe of causing divisions, acknowledge that offence on the authority of his brethren[1].' And the

[1] In the text sandhâya must be corrected into saddhâya; see *K*ullavagga XI, 1, 10.

Blessed One, having spoken thus to the partisans of the expelled Bhikkhu, rose from his seat and went away.

9. At that time the Bhikkhus who were partisans of that expelled Bhikkhu, held Uposatha and performed official acts at that same place, within the boundary. On the other hand the Bhikkhus who had pronounced expulsion against him, went outside the boundary and there held Uposatha, and performed official acts.

Now a certain Bhikkhu of those who had expelled that Bhikkhu, went to the place where the Blessed One was; having approached him and having respectfully saluted the Blessed One, he sat down near him. Sitting near him that Bhikkhu said to the Blessed One: 'Lord, those Bhikkhus who are partisans of that expelled Bhikkhu, hold Uposatha, and perform official acts, at that same place, within the boundary. On the other hand, we who have pronounced expulsion against him, have gone outside the boundary and there hold Uposatha and perform official acts.'

(Buddha replied): 'If those Bhikkhus, O Bhikkhu, who are partisans of that expelled Bhikkhu, will hold Uposatha, and perform official acts, at that same place, within the boundary, according to the rules laid down by me about ñatti and anussâvanâ, these official acts which they perform will be lawful, unobjectionable, and valid. And if you, O Bhikkhus, who have expelled that Bhikkhu, will hold Uposatha, and perform official acts, at that same place, within the boundary (&c., down to :) and valid.

10. 'And why is this so? These Bhikkhus belong to another communion than that to which you

belong, and you belong to another communion than that to which they belong.

'There are two cases, O Bhikkhu, in which a Bhikkhu (though he dwell within the same boundary) is considered as belonging to another communion:—either he himself makes himself belong to another communion[1], or the Samgha in a complete congregation pronounces expulsion against him for his refusal to see (an offence committed by himself), or to atone (for such an offence), or to renounce (a false doctrine). These, O Bhikkhu, are the two cases in which a Bhikkhu is considered as belonging to another communion.

'There are two cases, O Bhikkhu, in which a Bhikkhu (belonging to either of the categories mentioned) reacquires the belonging to the same communion (with his brethren within the same boundary): either he himself makes himself belong (again) to that same communion[2], or the Samgha, having expelled him for his refusal to see (an offence), or to atone (for an offence), or to renounce (a false doctrine), restores him in a complete congregation. These, O Bhikkhu, are the two cases in which a Bhikkhu reacquires the belonging to the same communion.

2.

1. At that time the Bhikkhus, among whom altercations, contentions, and quarrels had arisen, in the dining-hall and amidst the houses, behaved

[1] By associating with expelled Bhikkhus.
[2] By giving up his connection with expelled Bhikkhus.

improperly towards each other in gesture and word, and came to blows.

The people were annoyed, murmured, and became angry (saying), 'How can these Sakyaputtiya Sama*n*as, when altercations, contentions, and quarrels have arisen among them, &c., and come to blows?' Some Bhikkhus heard those people that were annoyed, murmured, and had become angry. The moderate Bhikkhus were annoyed, murmured, and became angry (saying), 'How can the Bhikkhus, when altercations, &c.?'

These Bhikkhus told the thing to the Blessed One.

'Is it true, O Bhikkhus, &c.?'

'It is true, Lord.'

Having rebuked them, and delivered a religious discourse, he thus addressed the Bhikkhus: 'When divisions have arisen among the Sa*m*gha, O Bhikkhus, and when unlawful conduct and unfriendliness prevail among the Bhikkhus, then you ought to sit down on your seats (separately, saying to yourselves): "At least we will not behave improperly towards each other in gesture or word, and will not come to blows." When divisions have arisen among the Sa*m*gha, O Bhikkhus, and when lawful conduct and friendliness prevail among the Bhikkhus, then you may sit down (together), one by one from each side[1].'

2. At that time the Bhikkhus, among whom altercations, contentions, and quarrels had arisen, wounded each other with sharp words in the assemblies, and were unable to settle that question.

---

[1] Âsanantarikâya. Buddhaghosa: 'Ekeka*m* âsana*m* antara*m* katvâ nisîditabba*m*.'

Then a certain Bhikkhu went to the place where the Blessed One was; having approached him and respectfully saluted him, he stationed himself near him. Standing near him, that Bhikkhu said to the Blessed One: 'Lord, the Bhikkhus among whom altercations, contentions, and quarrels have arisen, wound each other with sharp words in the assemblies, and are unable to settle that question. Pray, Lord, may the Blessed One go to those Bhikkhus out of compassion towards them.'

And the Blessed One expressed his consent by remaining silent.

Then the Blessed One went to the place where those Bhikkhus were; having approached them, he sat down on the seat they had prepared. Sitting there the Blessed One thus addressed those Bhikkhus: 'Enough, O Bhikkhus, no altercations, no contentions, no disunion, no quarrel!'

When he had spoken thus, a certain Bhikkhu, an adherer of the party who were wrong, said to the Blessed One: 'Lord, may the Blessed One, the king of Truth, be patient! Lord, may the Blessed One quietly enjoy the bliss he has obtained already in this life! The responsibility for these altercations and contentions, for this disunion and quarrel will rest with us alone.'

And for the second time the Blessed One thus addressed those Bhikkhus: 'Enough, O Bhikkhus, &c.' And for the second time that Bhikkhu who adhered to the party who were wrong, said to the Blessed One: 'Lord, may the Blessed One, &c.' Then the Blessed One spoke thus to those Bhikkhus:

3. 'In former times, O Bhikkhus, there lived at

Benares a king of Kâsi, Brahmadatta by name, wealthy, rich in treasures, rich in revenues, rich in troops and vehicles, the lord over a great realm, with full treasuries and storehouses. And there was also a king of Kosala, Dîghîti by name, not wealthy, poor in treasures, poor in revenues, poor in troops and vehicles, the lord over a small realm, with empty treasuries and storehouses.

'And king Brahmadatta, O Bhikkhus, of Kâsi, having set the four hosts of his army in array, went out to war with king Dîghîti of Kosala.

'And king Dîghîti of Kosala heard, O Bhikkhus: "King Brahmadatta of Kâsi, having set the four hosts of his army in array, has gone out to war with me." Then king Dîghîti of Kosala thought, O Bhikkhus: "King Brahmadatta of Kâsi is wealthy, rich in treasures, &c.; and I am not wealthy, poor in treasures, &c. I am not able to stand against even one attack of king Brahmadatta of Kâsi. What if I were to flee from the town beforehand."

'And king Dîghîti of Kosala, O Bhikkhus, took his queen-consort with him and fled from the town beforehand.

'Then king Brahmadatta of Kâsi, O Bhikkhus, conquered the troops and vehicles, the realm, the treasuries and storehouses of king Dîghîti of Kosala, and took possession of them.

'And king Dîghîti of Kosala, O Bhikkhus, together with his consort, went forth to Benares. Wandering from place to place he came to Benares, and there at Benares, O Bhikkhus, king Dîghîti of Kosala dwelt, together with his consort, at a certain place near the town, in a potter's dwelling, in disguise, in the guise of a wandering ascetic.

4. 'And ere long, O Bhikkhus, the queen-consort of king Dîghîti of Kosala became pregnant. And there came upon her the longing of pregnant women; and she desired, at sunrise, to see an army, with its four hosts set in array, clad in armour, standing on auspicious ground, and to drink the water in which the swords were washed.

'And the queen-consort, O Bhikkhus, of king Dîghîti of Kosala said to king Dîghîti of Kosala: "I am pregnant, Lord, and the longing of pregnancy has come upon me; and I desire, at sunrise, &c."

'(The king replied): "Whence shall come, O queen, to people in distress like us, an army with four hosts set in array, clad in armour, standing on auspicious ground, and the water in which the swords are washed?"

'(The queen said): "If I do not obtain it, Lord, I shall die."

5. 'Now at that time, O Bhikkhus, the Brâhmana who was domestic chaplain to king Brahmadatta of Kâsi, was a friend of king Dîghîti of Kosala. And king Dîghîti of Kosala, O Bhikkhus, went to the place where that Brâhmana, the domestic chaplain to king Brahmadatta of Kâsi, was; having approached him he said to that Brâhmana, the domestic chaplain to king Brahmadatta of Kâsi: "Your lady-friend, my beloved, is pregnant, and the longing of pregnant women has come upon her; and she desires (&c., as above)."

'(The Brâhmana replied): "Well, O king, let us see the queen also."

'Then, O Bhikkhus, the queen-consort of king Dîghîti of Kosala went to the place where that Brâhmana, the domestic chaplain to king Brahmadatta of Kâsi, was. And, O Bhikkhus, that Brâhma*n*a, the domestic chaplain to king Brahmadatta of Kâsi, saw the queen-consort of king Dîghîti of Kosala coming from afar. On seeing her he rose from his seat, adjusted his upper robe so as to cover one shoulder, raised his joined hands to the queen-consort of king Dîghîti of Kosala, and three times uttered this exclamation: "Verily a Kosala king dwells in thy womb! Verily a Kosala king dwells in thy womb!" (And further he said): "Do not despond, O queen, you will obtain the sight at sunrise of an army with its four hosts set in array, clad in armour, standing on auspicious ground, and you will obtain the drinking of the water in which the swords are washed."

6. 'And, O Bhikkhus, that Brâhma*n*a, the domestic chaplain to king Brahmadatta of Kâsi, went to the place where king Brahmadatta of Kâsi was. Having approached him, he said to king Brahmadatta of Kâsi: "Lord, the signs that appear are such, that to-morrow at sunrise an army with four hosts, set in array, clad in armour, must station itself on auspicious ground, and the swords must be washed."

'Then, O Bhikkhus, king Brahmadatta of Kâsi gave order to his attendants: "Do, my friends, what the Brâhma*n*a, my domestic chaplain, tells you."

'Thus, O Bhikkhus, the queen-consort of king Dîghîti of Kosala obtained the sight at sunrise, &c., and the drinking of the water in which the swords were washed.

'And, O Bhikkhus, the queen-consort of king Dîghîti of Kosala, when the child in her womb had reached maturity, gave birth to a boy. They called him Dîghâvu ("Longeval"). And ere long, O Bhikkhus, young Dîghâvu came to the years of discretion.

7. 'And king Dîghîti of Kosala, O Bhikkhus, thought: "This king Brahmadatta of Kâsi has done much harm to us. By him we have been robbed of our troops and vehicles, our realm, our treasuries and storehouses. Should he find us out here, he will have us all three killed. What if I were to cause young Dîghâvu to dwell outside the town."

'Then king Dîghîti of Kosala, O Bhikkhus, caused young Dîghâvu to dwell outside the town. And young Dîghâvu, O Bhikkhus, dwelling outside the town, ere long learnt all arts.

8. 'At that time, O Bhikkhus, the barber of king Dîghîti of Kosala dwelt at the court of king Brahmadatta of Kâsi. Now, O Bhikkhus, this barber of king Dîghîti of Kosala saw king Dîghîti of Kosala dwelling, together with his consort, at Benares, at a certain place near the town, in a potter's dwelling, in disguise, in the guise of a wandering ascetic. When he had seen him, he went to the place where king Brahmadatta of Kâsi was, and having approached him, he said to king Brahmadatta of Kâsi: "King Dîghîti of Kosala, Your Majesty, dwells, together with his consort, at Benares, at a certain place near the town, in a potter's dwelling, in disguise, in the guise of a wandering ascetic."

9. 'Then, O Bhikkhus, king Brahmadatta of Kâsi gave order to his attendants: "Well, my friends, bring king Dîghîti of Kosala and his consort before me."

'And those people, O Bhikkhus, accepted this order of king Brahmadatta of Kâsi (by saying),

"Yes, Your Majesty," and brought king Dîghîti of Kosala and his consort before him.

'Then, O Bhikkhus, king Brahmadatta of Kâsi gave order to his attendants: "Well, my friends, bind king Dîghîti of Kosala and his consort firmly with strong ropes, tie their arms to their backs, have them close shaven, lead them around with loud beatings of drums from road to road and from cross-way to cross-way, then lead them out of the town by the southern gate, hew them in four pieces to the south of the town, and throw the pieces away to the four quarters."

'And those people, O Bhikkhus, accepted this order of king Brahmadatta of Kâsi (by saying), "Yes, Your Majesty," bound king Dîghîti of Kosala and his consort firmly with strong ropes, tied their arms to their backs, had them close shaven, and led them around with loud beatings of drums from road to road and from cross-way to cross-way.

10. 'Now, O Bhikkhus, young Dîghâvu thought: "For a long time I have not seen my father and mother. What if I were to go and see my father and mother." And young Dîghâvu, O Bhikkhus, entered Benares, and saw his father and mother, bound firmly with strong ropes, their arms tied to their backs, close shaven, and being led around with loud beating of drums from road to road and from cross-way to cross-way. When he saw that, he went up to his father and mother.

'And king Dîghîti of Kosala, O Bhikkhus, saw young Dîghâvu coming from afar; seeing young Dîghâvu he said to him: "Do not look long, my dear Dîghâvu, and do not look short[1]. For not by

[1] This enigmatic phrase will be found explained below, § 19.

hatred, my dear Dîghâvu, is hatred appeased; by not-hatred, my dear Dîghâvu, hatred is appeased."

11. 'When he had spoken thus, O Bhikkhus, the people said to king Dîghîti of Kosala: "This king Dîghîti of Kosala is mad and raves. What has this Dîghâvu to do with him? Who is he to whom he says: 'Do not look long, &c.?'" (Dîghîti replied): "I am not mad, my friends, nor do I rave. He who is clever will understand it."

'And for the second time, &c. And for the third time, O Bhikkhus, king Dîghîti of Kosala said to young Dîghâvu, &c. And for the third time said the people (&c., down to:) "He who is clever will understand it."

'Then those people, O Bhikkhus, having led king Dîghîti of Kosala and his consort around from road to road and from cross-way to cross-way, led them out of the town by the southern gate, hewed them in four pieces to the south of the town, threw the pieces away to the four quarters, stationed there a troop of soldiers, and went away.

12. 'Then young Dîghâvu, O Bhikkhus, went to Benares, got strong drink there, and made those soldiers drink it. When they were drunk and had fallen down, he gathered the pieces (of the two bodies), made a funeral pile, put his father's and his mother's bodies on that pile, set it on fire, and raising his clasped hands he three times circumambulated the funeral pile.

'Now at that time, O Bhikkhus, king Brahmadatta of Kâsi had gone up on to the terrace of his splendid palace. And king Brahmadatta of Kâsi, O Bhikkhus, saw young Dîghâvu, who, raising his clasped hands, three times circumambulated the funeral pile. When he saw that, he thought: "Doubtless this man is a relation or kinsman of king Dîghîti of Kosala. Alas for my misfortune, that nobody will tell me (what this means)!"

13. 'And young Dîghâvu, O Bhikkhus, went to the forest. There he cried and wept to his heart's content. Then he wiped his tears, entered the town of Benares, went to the elephant stables near the royal palace, and said to the elephant trainer: "I wish to learn your art, master."

'"Well, my good young man, learn it."

'And young Dîghâvu, O Bhikkhus, arose in the night, at dawn's time, and sung in the elephant stables in a beautiful voice, and played upon the lute. And king Brahmadatta of Kâsi, O Bhikkhus, having risen in the night, at dawn, heard that singing in a beautiful voice and that playing upon the lute in the elephant stables. On hearing that he asked his attendants: "Who is it, my friends, who has risen in the night, at dawn's time, and has sung in the elephant stables in so beautiful a voice, and has played upon the lute?"

14. '(The attendants replied): "A young pupil, Your Majesty, of such and such an elephant trainer, has risen in the night, at dawn, and has sung in the elephant stables in so beautiful a voice, and has played upon the lute."

'(The king said): "Well, my friends, bring that young man to me."

'Those people accepted, O Bhikkhus, that order of king Brahmadatta of Kâsi (by saying), "Yes, Your Majesty," and brought young Dîghâvu to him.

'"Is it you, my good young man, who has risen in the night, &c.?"

'"Yes, Your Majesty."

'"Well, my good young man, sing and play upon the lute (also before me)."

'Young Dîghâvu, O Bhikkhus, accepted this order of king Brahmadatta of Kâsi (by saying), "Yes, Your Majesty," and in order to win (the king's) favour he sung in a beautiful voice and played upon the lute.

'And king Brahmadatta of Kâsi, O Bhikkhus, said to young Dîghâvu: "Be my attendant, my good young man."

'Young Dîghâvu, O Bhikkhus, accepted this order of king Brahmadatta of Kâsi (by saying), "Yes, Your Majesty." And young Dîghâvu, O Bhikkhus, became (a servant) of king Brahmadatta of Kâsi, rising before him, lying down after him, willingly obeying all his commands, agreeable in his conduct, pleasing in his words. And ere long, O Bhikkhus, king Brahmadatta of Kâsi gave to young Dîghâvu an intimate position of trust.

15. 'And king Brahmadatta of Kâsi, O Bhikkhus, said to young Dîghâvu: "Well, my young friend, put the horses to the chariot; we will go a-hunting." And young Dîghâvu, O Bhikkhus, accepted this order of king Brahmadatta of Kâsi (by saying), "Yes, Your Majesty," put the horses to the chariot, and said to king Brahmadatta of Kâsi: "The horses have been put to your chariot, Your Majesty; you may do now as you think fit."

'And king Brahmadatta of Kâsi, O Bhikkhus, ascended the chariot, and young Dîghâvu drove the chariot: and he drove the chariot in such a way that the hosts (of the royal retinue) went one way, and the chariot went another way.

'And after a long drive, O Bhikkhus, king Brahmadatta of Kâsi said to young Dîghâvu: "Well, my young friend, stop now the chariot. I am tired; I would lie down."

'Young Dîghâvu, O Bhikkhus, accepted this order of king Brahmadatta of Kâsi (by saying), "Yes, Your Majesty," stopped the chariot, and sat down on the ground cross-legged. And king Brahmadatta of Kâsi, O Bhikkhus, lay down, laying his head in the lap of young Dîghâvu; and as he was tired, he fell asleep in a moment.

16. 'And young Dîghâvu thought, O Bhikkhus: "This king Brahmadatta of Kâsi has done much harm to us. By him we have been robbed of our troops and vehicles, our realm, our treasuries and storehouses. And he has killed my father and mother. Now the time has come to me to satisfy my hatred,"—(thinking thus) he unsheathed his sword. Then, O Bhikkhus, young Dîghâvu thought: "My father said to me in the hour of his death: 'Do not look long, my dear Dîghâvu, and do not look short. For not by hatred, my dear Dîghâvu, is hatred appeased; by not-hatred, my dear Dîghâvu, hatred is appeased.' It would not become me to transgress my father's word,"—(thinking thus) he put up his sword.

'And for the second time . . . . and for the third time young Dîghâvu thought, O Bhikkhus: "This king Brahmadatta of Kâsi has done much harm to us" (&c., down to:)—(thinking thus) he put up his sword.

'At that moment, O Bhikkhus, king Brahmadatta of Kâsi, frightened, terrified, full of anguish, and alarmed, suddenly arose.

'And young Dîghâvu, O Bhikkhus, said to king

Brahmadatta of Kâsi: "Why do you arise so suddenly, O king, frightened, terrified, full of anguish, and alarmed?"

'(The king replied): "I dreamt, my young friend, that young Dîghâvu, the son of king Dîghîti of Kosala, came upon me with his sword; therefore have I arisen so suddenly, frightened, terrified, full of anguish, and alarmed."

17. 'Then, O Bhikkhus, young Dîghâvu, stroking with his left hand the head of king Brahmadatta of Kâsi, and with his right hand unsheathing his sword, said to king Brahmadatta of Kâsi: "I am that young Dîghâvu, O king, the son of king Dîghîti of Kosala. You have done much harm to us. By you we have been robbed of our troops and vehicles, our realm, our treasuries and storehouses. And you have killed my father and mother. Now the time has come to me to satisfy my hatred."

'Then, O Bhikkhus, king Brahmadatta of Kâsi fell down before young Dîghâvu, inclining his head to his feet, and said to young Dîghâvu: "Grant me my life, my dear Dîghâvu! Grant me my life, my dear Dîghâvu!"

'"How can I grant you your life, O king? It is you, O king, who should grant me my life!"

'"Well, my dear Dîghâvu, then grant me my life, and I will grant you your life."

'Thus, O Bhikkhus, king Brahmadatta of Kâsi and young Dîghâvu granted each other their lives and took each other's hands and swore an oath not to do any harm to each other.

'And king Brahmadatta of Kâsi, O Bhikkhus, said to young Dîghâvu: "Well, my dear Dîghâvu, put now the horses to the chariot; we will go."

'And young Dîghâvu, O Bhikkhus, accepted this order of king Brahmadatta of Kâsi (by saying), "Yes, Your Majesty," put the horses to the chariot, and said to king Brahmadatta of Kâsi: "The horses have been put to your chariot, Your Majesty; you may do now as you think fit."

'And king Brahmadatta of Kâsi, O Bhikkhus, ascended the chariot, and young Dîghâvu drove the chariot; and he drove the chariot in such a way that they soon reached again the hosts (of the royal retinue).

18. 'And king Brahmadatta of Kâsi, O Bhikkhus, having entered Benares, convoked his ministers and counsellors and said to them: "If you should see, my good Sirs, young Dîghâvu, the son of king Dîghîti of Kosala, what would you do to him?"

'Some (of the ministers) replied: "We would cut off his hands, Your Majesty;" (others said): "We would cut off his feet"—"We would cut off his hands and feet"—"We would cut off his ears"—"We would cut off his nose"—"We would cut off his ears and his nose"—"We would cut off his head."

'"This is young Dîghâvu, Sirs, the son of king Dîghîti of Kosala. It is not permitted to do anything to him; he has granted me my life, and I have granted him his life."

19. 'And king Brahmadatta of Kâsi, O Bhikkhus, said to young Dîghâvu: "Why did your father say to you in the hour of his death: 'Do not look long, &c.'—what did your father mean by that?"

'"What my father said, O king, in the hour of his death: 'Not long'—(means): 'Let not your hatred last long;' this did my father mean when he said in the hour of his death: 'Not long.' And what my father said, O king, in the hour of his death: 'Not short'—(means): 'Do not be hasty to fall out with your friends;' this did my father mean when he said in the hour of his death: 'Not short.' And what my father said, O king, in the hour of his death: 'For not by hatred, my dear Dîghâvu, is hatred appeased; by not-hatred, my dear Dîghâvu, is hatred appeased'—(means this): 'You have killed my father and mother, O king. If I should deprive you therefore of life, O king, then your partisans, O king, would deprive me of life; my partisans again would deprive those of life. Thus by hatred that hatred would not be appeased. But now, O king, you have granted me my life, and I, O king, have granted you your life; thus by not-hatred hatred has been appeased.' This did my father mean when he said in the hour of his death: 'For not by hatred, &c.'"

20. 'Then king Brahmadatta of Kâsi, O Bhikkhus, thought: "O wonderful! O marvellous! How clever is this young Dîghâvu, that he understands in its full extent the meaning of what his father spoke so concisely,"—and he gave him back his father's troops and vehicles, his realm, his treasuries and storehouses, and he gave him his daughter.

'Now, O Bhikkhus, if such is the forbearance and mildness of kings who wield the sceptre and bear the sword, so much more, O Bhikkhus, must you so let your light shine before the world that you, having embraced the religious life according to so well-taught a doctrine and a discipline, are seen to be forbearing and mild.'

And for the third time[1] the Blessed One thus

[1] See § 2.

addressed those Bhikkhus: 'Enough, O Bhikkhus, no altercations, no contentions, no disunion, no quarrels!'

And for the third time that Bhikkhu who adhered to the party who were wrong, said to the Blessed One: 'Lord, may the Blessed One, the king of Truth, be patient! Lord, may the Blessed One quietly enjoy the bliss he has obtained already in this life! The responsibility for these altercations and contentions, for this disunion and quarrel will rest with us alone.' And the Blessed One thought: 'Truly these fools are infatuate; it is no easy task to administer instruction to them,'—and he rose from his seat and went away.

End of the first Bhâ*n*avâra, which contains the story of Dîghâvu.

3.

And in the forenoon the Blessed One, having put on his under-robes, took up his alms-bowl and his *k*îvara, and entered the town of Kosambî for alms. Having collected alms in Kosambî, after his meal, when he had returned from his alms-pilgrimage, he put his resting-place in order, took up his alms-bowl and his *k*îvara, and standing in the midst of the assembly he pronounced the following stanzas:

'Loud is the noise that ordinary men make. Nobody thinks himself a fool, when divisions arise in the Sa*m*gha, nor do they ever value another person higher (than themselves).

'Bewildered[1] are (even) the clever words of him who is versed in the resources of eloquence. As wide as they like they open their mouth. By whom they are lead they do not see.

'"He[2] has reviled me, he has beaten me, he has oppressed me, he has robbed me,"—in those who nurse such thoughts, hatred will never be appeased.

'"He has reviled me, he has beaten me, he has oppressed me, he has robbed me,"—in those who do not nurse such thoughts, hatred is appeased.

'For not by hatred is hatred ever appeased; by not-hatred it is appeased; this is an eternal law.

'The others[3] do not know that we must keep ourselves under restraint here; but those who know it, their quarrels are appeased.

'They whose bones are broken (by their foes), who destroy lives, who rob cows, horses, and treasures, who plunder realms,—even these may find conciliation. How should you not find it?

'If[4] a man find a wise friend, a companion who

[1] Parimu*tth*â. Buddhaghosa: 'Parimu*tth*â 'ti mu*tth*assatino.' Mu*tth*assati cannot be connected with mû*lh*a, as Childers supposes, but it is evidently mushitasm*ri*ti (Kathâsarits. 56, 289; compare satisammosa, Mil. Pañha, p. 266). Thus it appears that parimu*tth*a must be derived also from the root mush.

[2] These verses are inserted in the Dhammapada, vv. 3–6.

[3] That is to say, those who do not follow the Buddha's teaching. On this meaning of pare compare parappavâdâ at Mahâ-parinibbâna Sutta V, 62. Professor Max Müller, who in the first edition of his translation of the Dhammapada (Buddhaghosa's Parables, p. lvi) has 'Some do not know that we must all come to an end here,' in the revised edition (Sacred Books of the East, vol. x) renders the phrase, 'The world does not know that we must all come to an end here.'

[4] The following three verses have also been inserted in the Dhammapada, vv. 328–330. The two first recur in the Khaggavisâna-sutta of the Sutta Nipâta, vv. 11, 12.

lives righteously, a constant one, he may walk with him, overcoming all dangers, happy and mindful[1].

'If he find no wise friend, no companion who lives righteously, no constant one, let him walk alone, like a king who leaves his conquered realm behind[2], like an elephant in the elephant forest[3].

'It is better to walk alone; with a fool there is no companionship. Let a man walk alone; let him do no evil, free from cares, like an elephant in the elephant forest[3].'

4.

1. And the Blessed One, having pronounced these stanzas standing in the midst of the assembly, went forth to Bâlakalo*n*akâra-gâma (or, to Bâlaka, the salt-maker's village).

At that time the venerable Bhagu dwelt at Bâlakalo*n*akâra-gâma. And the venerable Bhagu saw the Blessed One coming from afar; seeing him he prepared a seat, brought water for the washing of his feet, a foot-stool, and a towel, went forth to meet him, and took his bowl and his robe. The Blessed One sat down on the seat he had prepared; and

[1] On the juxtaposition of happiness with mindfulness, see the constantly repeated phrase occurring, for instance, in the Tevi*gg*a Sutta I, 49 (at the end). It would perhaps be better to read satîmâ in the text, as Fausböll has done, metri causâ.

[2] That is, who abdicates, and devotes himself in the forest to a hermit's life. This is given as the crucial instance of a happy life in the *G*âtaka Story, No. 10.

[3] Professor Fausböll reads in both verses mâtangara*ññ*o instead of mâtaṅgara*ññ*e.

when he was seated, the Blessed One washed his feet. And also the venerable Bhagu, having respectfully saluted the Blessed One, sat down near him. When he was sitting near him, the Blessed One said to the venerable Bhagu: 'Is it all well with you, O Bhikkhu? Do you find your living? Do you get food without too much trouble?'

'It is all well with me, Lord; I find my living, Lord; I get food, Lord, without too much trouble.'

And the Blessed One, having taught, incited, animated, and gladdened the venerable Bhagu by religious discourse, rose from his seat and went forth to the Eastern Bambû Park (Pâkina-vamsa-dâya).

2. At that time the venerable Anuruddha and the venerable Nandiya and the venerable Kimbila dwelt at Pâkina-vamsa-dâya. And the park-keeper saw the Blessed One coming from afar; seeing him he said to the Blessed One: 'Do not enter this park, O Samana; here dwell three noble youths accustomed to comfort and ease; you must not annoy them.' And the venerable Anuruddha heard what the park-keeper was saying to the Blessed One; hearing that he said to the park-keeper: 'Do not keep off the Blessed One, my good park-keeper; our teacher, the Blessed One, has arrived.' And the venerable Anuruddha went to the place where the venerable Nandiya and the venerable Kimbila were; having approached them, he said to the venerable Nandiya and to the venerable Kimbila: 'Come here, my venerable friends! Come here, my venerable friends! Our teacher, the Blessed One, has arrived.'

3. And the venerable Anuruddha, the venerable Nandiya, and the venerable Kimbila went forth to meet the Blessed One; one took the bowl and the

robe of the Blessed One, the other one prepared a seat, the third one brought water for the washing of his feet, a foot-stool, and a towel. Then the Blessed One sat down on the seat they had prepared; and when he was seated, the Blessed One washed his feet. And also those venerable persons, having respectfully saluted the Blessed One, sat down near him. When the venerable Anuruddha was sitting near him, the Blessed One said to him: 'Is it all well with you, O Anuruddhas[1]? Do you find your living? Do you get food without too much trouble?'

'It is all well with us, Lord; we find our living, Lord; we get food, Lord, without too much trouble.'

'And do you live, O Anuruddhas, in unity and concord, without quarrels, like milk and water (mixed together)[2], and looking at each other with friendly eyes?'

'Certainly, Lord, do we live in unity and concord (&c., down to:) and looking at each other with friendly eyes.'

'And in what way, O Anuruddhas, do you live in unity and concord, &c.?'

4. 'I think, Lord: "It is all gain to me indeed, it is high bliss for me indeed, that I live in the companionship of brethren like these." Thus, Lord, do I exercise towards these venerable brethren friendliness in my actions, both openly and in secret; I

---

[1] We have here the plural Anuruddhâ, meaning Anuruddha and his friends. So in *K*ullavagga I, 13, 6 Sâriputtâ means Sâriputta and Moggallâna.

[2] Khîrodakibhûtâ can scarcely contain an allusion to the Milk Ocean (see Childers, s.v. khîrodaka). Milk and water is frequently chosen by the Indian poets as a type of the most perfect union.

exercise (towards them) friendliness in my words, and friendliness in my thoughts, both openly and in secret. And I think thus, Lord: "What if I were to give up my own will and to live only according to the will of these venerable brethren." Thus, Lord, I give up my own will and live only according to the will of these venerable brethren. Our bodies, Lord, are different, but our minds, I think, have become one[1].'

And also the venerable Nandiya . . . . and also the venerable Kimbila . . . . said to the Blessed One: 'I think also, Lord: "It is all gain to me" (&c., down to:) have become one.

'In this way, Lord, do we live in unity and concord, without quarrels, like milk and water (mixed together), and looking at each other with friendly eyes.'

5. 'And do you live, O Anuruddhas, in earnestness, zeal, and resolvedness?'

'Certainly, Lord, do we live in earnestness, zeal, and resolvedness.'

'And in what way, O Anuruddhas, do you live in earnestness, zeal, and resolvedness?'

'He[2] who first of us comes back, Lord, from the village, from his alms-pilgrimage, prepares seats, gets water for washing feet, a foot-stool, and a towel, cleans the slop-basin, and gets it ready, and puts there (water to) drink and food. He who comes back last from the village, from his alms-pilgrimage, eats, if there is any food left (from the dinner of the others) and if he desires to do so; and if he does

[1] Compare the last poem in the Sutta Nipâta, and especially v. 1143.

[2] Compare IV, 1.

not desire (to eat), he throws it away at a place free from grass, or pours it away into water in which no living things are; takes away the seat, puts away the water for washing the feet, the foot-stool, and the towel, cleans the slop-basin and puts it away, puts the water and the food away, and sweeps the dining-room. He who sees a water-pot, or a bowl for food, or an easing-chair, empty and void, puts it (into its proper place), and if he is not able to do so single-handed, he calls some one else, and thus we put it (into its place) with our united effort, but we do not utter a word, Lord, on that account. And every five days, Lord, we spend a whole night, sitting together, in religious discourse. In this way, Lord, do we live in earnestness, zeal, and resolvedness.'

6. And the Blessed One, having taught, incited, animated, and gladdened the venerable Anuruddha and the venerable Nandiya and the venerable Kimbila by religious discourse, rose from his seat, and went forth to Pârileyyaka. Wandering from place to place he came to Pârileyyaka. There the Blessed One dwelt at Pârileyyaka, in the Rakkhita grove, at the foot of the Bhaddasâla tree. Then in the mind of the Blessed One, who was alone, and had retired into solitude, the following thought arose: 'Formerly I did not live at ease, being troubled by those litigious, contentious, quarrelsome, disputatious Bhikkhus of Kosambî, the constant raisers of questions before the Sa*m*gha. But now, being alone and without a companion, I live pleasantly and at ease, remote from those litigious, contentious, quarrelsome, disputatious Bhikkhus of Kosambî, the constant raisers of questions before the Sa*m*gha.' And there

dwelt also a noble elephant, who was surrounded by a crowd of elephants, she-elephants, elephant-calves, and young elephants; the grass blades he ate had their tips broken; the branches he broke down (the other elephants) ate; the water he drank was turbid; and when he waded into the river and plunged down, the she-elephants came and rubbed up their bodies against him. Now that noble elephant thought: 'I am surrounded by a crowd of elephants (&c., down to:) and rub up their bodies against me. What if I were to live alone, far away from those crowds.'

7. And that noble elephant left the herd behind, and went to Pârileyyaka, to the Rakkhita grove, to the foot of the Bhaddasâla tree, to the place where the Blessed One was. Having approached him, he administered with his trunk to the Blessed One (water to) drink and food, and removed the grass from that place. And that noble elephant thought: 'Formerly I did not live at ease, surrounded by that crowd of elephants (&c., down to:) and rubbed up their bodies against me. But now, being alone and without a companion, I live pleasantly and at ease, remote from those elephants, she-elephants, elephant-calves, and young elephants.'

Then the Blessed One, both regarding his own retirement, and understanding by the power of his mind the thoughts which had arisen in the mind of that noble elephant, on this occasion pronounced this solemn utterance:

'Thus the noble one and the noble, the elephant tusked with tusks like cart poles[1] (and the noble

---

[1] Îsâdanta; see Böhtlingk-Roth, sub voce ishâ.

One among men)—the mind of the one and the mind of the other harmonise in this, that they take delight in dwelling alone in the forest.'

5.

1. And the Blessed One, having dwelt at Pârileyyaka as long as he thought fit, went forth to Sâvatthi. Wandering from place to place he came to Sâvatthi. There the Blessed One dwelt at Sâvatthi, in the *G*etavana, the garden of Anâthapi*nd*ika. And the lay-devotees of Kosambî thought: 'These venerable Bhikkhus of Kosambî have brought much misfortune to us; worried[1] by them the Blessed One is gone. Well, let us neither salute the venerable Bhikkhus of Kosambî, nor rise from our seats before them, nor raise our hands before them, nor perform the proper duties towards them, nor honour and esteem and revere and support them, nor give them food when they come on their walks for alms; thus, when they are not honoured, esteemed, revered, supported, and hospitably received by us, they will go away, or return to the world, or propitiate the Blessed One.'

2. Thus the lay-devotees of Kosambî did not salute any more the Bhikkhus of Kosambî, nor did they rise from their seats before them (&c., down to:) nor gave them food when they came on their walks for alms.

Then the Bhikkhus of Kosambî, when they were no more honoured (&c., down to:) and hospitably

[1] Ubbâ*lh*a; see *G*âtaka I, 300, and Mahâvagga III, 9, 1.

received by the lay-devotees of Kosambî, said to each other: 'Well, friends, let us go to Sâvatthi and let us settle there that question before the Blessed One.' And the Bhikkhus of Kosambî put their resting-places in order, took up their alms-bowls and their robes, and went forth to Sâvatthi.

3. And the venerable Sâriputta heard: 'Those litigious, contentious, quarrelsome, disputatious Bhikkhus of Kosambî, the constant raisers of questions before the Sa*m*gha, are coming to Sâvatthi.' And the venerable Sâriputta went to the place where the Blessed One was; having approached him and respectfully saluted the Blessed One, he sat down near him. Sitting near him the venerable Sâriputta said to the Blessed One: 'Lord, those litigious, contentious (&c., down to:) are coming to Sâvatthi. How am I to behave, Lord, towards those Bhikkhus?'

'Well, Sâriputta, you must side with those who are right according to the Dhamma.'

'But how shall I discern, Lord, what is right and what is wrong?'

4. 'There are eighteen things, Sâriputta, by which you may conclude that a Bhikkhu is wrong according to the Dhamma. In case, Sâriputta, a Bhikkhu declares what is not Dhamma to be Dhamma, or declares what is Dhamma not to be Dhamma, or declares what is not Vinaya to be Vinaya, or declares what is Vinaya not to be Vinaya, or declares what has not been taught and spoken by the Tathâgata to have been taught and spoken by the Tathâgata, or declares something taught and spoken by the Tathâgata not to have been taught and spoken by the Tathâgata, or declares what has not been

practised by the Tathâgata to have been practised by the Tathâgata, or declares something practised by the Tathâgata not to have been practised by the Tathâgata, or declares what has not been ordained by the Tathâgata to have been ordained by the Tathâgata, or declares something ordained by the Tathâgata not to have been ordained by the Tathâgata, or declares what is no offence to be an offence, or declares an offence to be no offence, or declares a slight offence to be a grievous offence, or declares a grievous offence to be a slight offence, or declares (a rule regarding) an offence to which there is an exception to be without an exception, or declares (a rule regarding) an offence to which there is no exception to admit of exceptions[1], or declares a grave offence[2] to be a not grave offence, or declares an offence that is not grave to be a grave offence, —these are the eighteen things, Sâriputta, by which you may conclude that a Bhikkhu is wrong according to the Dhamma.

5. 'And there are eighteen things, Sâriputta, by which you may conclude that a Bhikkhu is right according to the Dhamma. In case, Sâriputta, a Bhikkhu declares what is not Dhamma to be not

[1] Our translation of sâvasesa and anavasesa is entirely conjectural. By the exceptions alluded to here we believe that such clauses must be understood as, for instance, in the sixth Nissaggiya Rule the words: 'Except at the right season;—here the right season means when the Bhikkhu has been robbed of his robe, or when his robe has been destroyed. This is the right season in this connection.'

[2] The term 'Du*tth*ullâ âpatti' is used also in the ninth Pâ*k*ittiya Rule, and the Old Commentary there states that by 'grave offences' those belonging to the Pârâ*g*ika and Sa*m*ghâdisesa classes are understood.

Dhamma, or declares what is Dhamma to be Dhamma (&c., down to :), or declares a grave offence to be a grave offence, or declares an offence that is not grave to be not grave,—these are the eighteen things, Sâriputta, by which you may conclude that a Bhikkhu is right according to the Dhamma.'

6. And the venerable Mahâmoggallâna heard (&c., as in §§ 3–5)—and the venerable Mahâkassapa heard, &c.—and the venerable Mahâkakkâna heard, &c.—and the venerable Mahâkotthita[1] heard, &c.—and the venerable Mahâkappina heard, &c.—and the venerable Mahâkunda heard, &c.—and the venerable Anuruddha heard, &c.—and the venerable Revata heard, &c.—and the venerable Upâli heard, &c.—and the venerable Ânanda heard, &c.—and the venerable Râhula heard (&c., as above).

7. And Mahâpagâpati Gotamî heard: 'Those litigious, contentious, quarrelsome, disputatious Bhikkhus of Kosambî, the constant raisers of questions before the Samgha, are coming to Sâvatthi.' And Mahâpagâpati Gotamî went to the place where the Blessed One was; having approached him and respectfully saluted the Blessed One, she stationed herself near him. Standing near him Mahâpagâpati Gotamî said to the Blessed One: 'Lord, those litigious, contentious (&c., down to :) are coming to Sâvatthi. How am I to behave, Lord, towards those Bhikkhus?'

'Well, Gotamî, hear the Dhamma on both sides. When you have heard the Dhamma on both sides,

---

[1] The name of this Thera is spelt in the MSS. Mahâkotthita and Mahâkotthika. In the Northern Buddhist works he is called Mahâkaushthilya. In the Lalita Vistara (p. 1, ed. Calc.) Kaundilya is a misprint.

then accept the opinion and the belief and the doctrine and the cause of those Bhikkhus who are right according to the Dhamma; and whatever the Bhikkhunîsa*m*gha has to apply for to the Bhikkhusa*m*gha[1], for all that you must apply to the party of those who are right.'

8. And Anâtha-pi*nd*ika the householder heard (&c., as in § 3, down to:). 'How am I to behave, Lord, towards those Bhikkhus?'

'Well, householder, bestow gifts on both sides; having bestowed gifts on both sides, hear the Dhamma on both sides. When you have heard the Dhamma on both sides, then accept the opinion and the belief and the doctrine and the cause of those Bhikkhus who are right according to the Dhamma.'

9. And Visâkhâ Migâramâtâ heard, &c.[2]

10. And the Bhikkhus of Kosambî in due course came to Sâvatthi. And the venerable Sâriputta went to the place where the Blessed One was; having approached him and respectfully saluted the Blessed One, he sat down near him. Sitting near him the venerable Sâriputta said to the Blessed One: 'Lord, those litigious, contentious, quarrelsome, disputatious Bhikkhus of Kosambî, the constant raisers of questions before the Sa*m*gha, have arrived at Sâvatthi. How are we, Lord, to arrange the dwelling-places of those Bhikkhus?'

'Well, Sâriputta, assign separate dwelling-places to them.'

---

[1] See *K*ullavagga X, 1, 4, and the 59th Pâ*k*ittiya Rule in the Bhikkhuni-pâtimokkha.

[2] As in § 8. Instead of 'Well, householder,' read 'Well, Visâkhâ.'

'And if there be no separate dwelling-places, what are we to do then, Lord?'

'Then, Sâriputta, you must separate (some dwelling-places from the rest) and then assign them (to those Bhikkhus). But in no wise, Sâriputta, do I say that the dwelling-place of a senior Bhikkhu must be taken from him. He who does that, commits a dukka*t*a offence.'

'And how are we to act, Lord, regarding (the distribution of) material gifts[1]?'

'Material gifts, Sâriputta, must be distributed among all in equal parts.'

11. And that Bhikkhu against whom expulsion had been pronounced, pondering over both Dhamma and Vinaya, came to the following conclusion: 'This is an offence; this is not no offence. I am an offender; I am not offenceless. I am expelled; I am not unexpelled. The sentence by which I have been expelled is lawful, unobjectionable, and valid.' Then that expelled Bhikkhu went to the expelled Bhikkhu's partisans; having approached them, he said to the partisans of the expelled Bhikkhu: 'This is an offence, friends; this is not no offence, &c. Come now, my venerable brethren, and restore me.'

12. Then the partisans of that expelled Bhikkhu took with them the expelled Bhikkhu, and went to the place where the Blessed One was; having approached him and respectfully saluted the Blessed One, they sat down near him. Sitting near him those Bhikkhus said to the Blessed One: 'Lord, this Bhikkhu, against whom expulsion has been pronounced, says, "This is an offence, friends (&c.,

[1] Such as food, robes, &c.

down to :) and restore me." What are we to do here, Lord?'

'This is an offence, O Bhikkhus; this is not no offence. This Bhikkhu is an offender; this Bhikkhu is not offenceless. This Bhikkhu is expelled; he is not unexpelled; the sentence by which he has been expelled is lawful, unobjectionable, and valid. But since this Bhikkhu, O Bhikkhus, having committed an offence, and having been sentenced to expulsion, sees (his offence), restore now that Bhikkhu, O Bhikkhus.'

13. And the partisans of that expelled Bhikkhu, having restored that expelled Bhikkhu, went to the Bhikkhus who had sentenced him to expulsion; having approached them, they said to the Bhikkhus who had pronounced that sentence: 'As regards that matter, friends, which gave origin to altercations among the Sa*m*gha, to contentions, discord, quarrels, divisions among the Sa*m*gha, to disunion among the Sa*m*gha, to separations among the Sa*m*gha, to schisms among the Sa*m*gha,—that Bhikkhu (who was concerned in that matter), having committed an offence, and having been sentenced to expulsion, has seen (his offence) and has been restored. Come, friends, let us declare now the re-establishment of concord among the Sa*m*gha in order to bring that matter to an end.'

Then the Bhikkhus who had pronounced that sentence of expulsion, went to the place where the Blessed One was; having approached him and respectfully saluted the Blessed One, they sat down near him; sitting near him those Bhikkhus said to the Blessed One: 'Lord, those partisans of the expelled Bhikkhu have said to us: "As regards that matter (&c., down to:) in order to bring that matter to an end." What are we to do here, Lord?'

14. 'Since this Bhikkhu, O Bhikkhus, having committed an offence, and having been sentenced to expulsion, has seen (his offence) and has been restored, let the Sa*m*gha, O Bhikkhus, declare the re-establishment of concord in order to bring that matter to an end. And this declaration is to be performed in this way: Let all brethren assemble together, both the sick and the healthy; no one is allowed to send his declaration of *kh*anda[1] (and to stay away). When you have assembled, let a learned, competent Bhikkhu proclaim the following ñatti before the Sa*m*gha: "Let the Sa*m*gha, reverend Sirs, hear me. As regards that matter which gave origin to altercations among the Sa*m*gha, to contentions, discord, quarrels, divisions among the Sa*m*gha, to disunion among the Sa*m*gha, to separations among the Sa*m*gha, to schisms among the Sa*m*gha,—that Bhikkhu (concerned in that matter), having committed an offence, and having been sentenced to expulsion, has seen (his offence) and has been restored. If the Sa*m*gha is ready, let the Sa*m*gha declare the re-establishment of concord in order to bring that matter to an end. This is the ñatti. Let the Sa*m*gha, reverend Sirs, hear me (&c.[2], down to:) the re-establishment of concord, in order to bring that matter to an end, has been declared by the Sa*m*gha; the division that existed among the Sa*m*gha has been settled; the disunion that existed

[1] See II, 23.

[2] Here follows the repetition of the ñatti and the other solemn formulas belonging to a ñattidutiya kamma in the usual way.

among the Saṃgha has been settled. The Saṃgha is in favour (of this declaration); therefore you are silent; thus I understand." Then let the Saṃgha hold Uposatha and proclaim the Pâtimokkha.'

6.

1. And the venerable Upâli[1] went to the place where the Blessed One was. Having approached him and respectfully saluted the Blessed One, he sat down near him. Sitting near him the venerable Upâli said to the Blessed One: 'Lord, if the Saṃgha, regarding a matter which has given origin to altercations (&c., down to:) to schisms among the Saṃgha, declares the re-establishment of concord, without having inquired into that matter and without having got to the bottom of it, is this declaration, Lord, lawful?'

'If the Saṃgha, Upâli, regarding a matter (&c., down to:) declares the re-establishment of concord, without having inquired into that matter and without having got to the bottom of it,—this declaration, Upâli, is unlawful.'

'But if the Saṃgha, Lord, regarding a matter (&c., down to:) declares the re-establishment of concord, after having inquired into that matter and after having got to the bottom of it,—is this declaration, Lord, lawful?'

'If the Saṃgha, Upâli, (&c., down to:) declares the re-establishment of concord, after having inquired

[1] See the note at IX, 6, 1.

into that matter and after having got to the bottom of it,—this declaration, Upâli, is lawful.'

2. 'How many kinds are there, Lord, of the re-establishment of concord among a Sâ*m*gha?'

'There are the following two kinds, Upâli, of re-establishment of concord among a Sa*m*gha: Concord may be re-established, Upâli, in the letter, but not in the spirit, and concord may be re-established both in the spirit and in the letter.

'And in what case, Upâli, is concord re-established in the letter, but not in the spirit? If the Sa*m*gha, Upâli, (&c., as above) declares the re-establishment of concord, without having inquired into that matter and without having got to the bottom of it,—in this case, Upâli, concord is said to have been re-established in the letter, but not in the spirit.

'And in what case, Upâli, is concord re-established both in the spirit and in the letter? If the Sa*m*gha, Upâli, (&c., as above) declares the re-establishment of concord, after having inquired into that matter and after having got to the bottom of it,—in this case, Upâli, concord is said to have been re-established both in the spirit and in the letter. These, Upâli, are the two kinds of re-establishment of concord among a Sa*m*gha.'

3. And the venerable Upâli rose from his seat, adjusted his upper robe so as to cover one shoulder, bent his clasped hands towards the Blessed One, and addressed the Blessed One in the following stanzas:

'In the affairs of the Sa*m*gha and in its consultations, in the business that arises and in trials, what sort of man is then most wanted? what Bhikkhu is then most worthy of the leadership?'

'Above all he who is blameless in his moral conduct, who watches over his behaviour, whose senses are well controlled, whom his rivals do not reprove according to the law,—for there is nothing for which they could censure him,—

'Such a man, who abides in blameless conduct, is well versed (in the doctrine), and mighty are his words. He is not perplexed, nor does he tremble, when he enters an assembly[1]. He does not disparage his cause by vain talk.

'So also when he is asked questions in the assemblies, he does not hesitate, and is not troubled. By his timely words, that solve the questions, the clever man gladdens the assembly of the wise.

'Full of reverence for elder Bhikkhus, well versed in what his teacher has taught him, able to find out (the right), a master of speech, and skilled in making his rivals fail,—

'By whom his rivals are annihilated, by whom many people receive instruction,—he does not forsake the cause he has taken up, (nor does he become tired) of answering questions and putting questions without hurting others;—

'If he is charged with a mission, he takes it upon himself properly, and in the business of the Sa*m*gha (he does) what they tell him[2];—when a number of Bhikkhus despatches him (somewhere), he obeys

[1] The same idea is put into the Buddha's mouth in the Mahâparinibbâna Sutta I, 23, 24.

[2] We propose to read âhu na*m* yathâ. This seems more satisfactory than the reading and the explanation found in Buddhaghosa's A*tth*akathâ: 'yathâ nâma âhuna*m* âhutipi*nd*a*m* samugga*n*hanti (sic) eva*m* api so somanassagâten' eva *k*etasâ sa*m*ghassa ki*kk*esu samuggaho.'

their command, but he does not think therefrom, "It is I who do this;"—

'In what cases a Bhikkhu commits an offence, what an offence is, and how it is atoned for, both these expositions are well known to him[1]; he is versed in the rules about offence and atonement;—

'By what deeds a Bhikkhu brings expulsion upon himself, in what cases one has been expelled, and the rehabilitation of a person who has undergone that penance,—all this he also knows, well versed in the Vibhaṅgas;—

'Full of reverence for elder Bhikkhus, for the young, for the Theras, for the middle-aged, bringing welfare to many people, a clever one:—such a Bhikkhu is the one who is then worthy of the leadership.'

End of the tenth Khandhaka, which contains the story of the Bhikkhus of Kosambî.

End of the Mahâvagga.

---

[1] For 'Exposition' the text has vibhaṅga, about the technical meaning of which see our Introduction, pp. xv seq. 'Both' refers to the Bhikkhuvibhaṅga and Bhikkhunîvibhaṅga. In the text, ubhayassa must be corrected into ubhay' assa, i. e. ubhaye assa.

KULLAVAGGA.

*K*ULLAVAGGA.

FIRST KHANDHAKA.

THE MINOR DISCIPLINARY PROCEEDINGS.

I. THE TAGGANIYA KAMMA (ACT OF REBUKE).

1.

1. At that time the Blessed One was staying at *G*etavana, in the grove of Anâtha-pi*nd*ika.

Now at that time the Bhikkhus who were followers of Pa*nd*uka and of Lohitaka[1],—who themselves were makers of strife, quarrelsome[2], makers of disputes[3], given to idle talk, and raisers of legal questions in the Sa*m*gha[4],—used to go up to such other Bhikkhus as were the same, and say, 'Do not allow such a one, venerable Sirs, to turn you back. Discuss loud and long. You are indeed cleverer, more wise, more well informed, more able at that (than

[1] These were two out of the six notorious *Kh*abbaggiya Bhikkhus, who are so frequently mentioned elsewhere. Buddhaghosa says, tesa*m* nissitakâ pi Pa*nd*ukalohitakâ tv' eva pa*ññ*âyanti.

[2] In addition to the passages referred to in the two following notes, compare the closing words of the Pâtimokkha, and the 2nd, 3rd, 12th, 13th, 17th, 54th, 74th, and 75th Pâ*k*ittiyas.

[3] Such persons were formerly dealt with according to the 10th, 11th, and 12th Sa*m*ghâdisesas.

[4] Such persons were formerly dealt with according to the 8th and 9th Sa*m*ghâdisesas and the 76th Pâ*k*ittiya. Compare also below, IV, 14, and the 63rd and 79th Pâ*k*ittiyas.

your adversaries are) and do not you be afraid of them. We too will be on your side.' Thereby both disputes arose which had not arisen before; and disputes which had arisen grew hotter.

2. Those Bhikkhus who were modest were annoyed, murmured, and became indignant, saying, 'How can the Bhikkhus who are followers of Pa*nd*uka and of Lohitaka act thus.' And those Bhikkhus told the matter to the Blessed One.

Then the Blessed One on that occasion, and in that connection, convened an assembly of the Order of Bhikkhus, and inquired of the Bhikkhus: 'Is it true, as they say, Bhikkhus, that those Bhikkhus who are followers of Pa*nd*uka and Lohitaka,—who themselves (&c., as in § 1, down to the end)?'

'It is true, Lord!'

The Blessed Buddha rebuked them, saying, 'This is improper, O Bhikkhus, for those foolish persons, not according to rule, unsuitable, unworthy of a Sama*n*a, unbecoming, and ought not to be done. How can these foolish persons, O Bhikkhus, who themselves (&c., as in § 1, down to the end). This will not conduce, O Bhikkhus, either to the conversion of the unconverted, or to the increase of the converted; but rather to those who have not been converted being not converted, and to the turning back of those who have been converted.'

3. And when the Blessed One had rebuked those Bhikkhus in various ways,—speaking of the evils of being hard to satisfy in the matter of support or nourishment, of wishing for much, of discontent, of love of society, and of sloth; and speaking in praise of being easy to satisfy in the matter of support and nourishment, of wishing for little, of the

contented man who has eradicated (evils from his mind), has quelled his passions[1], and is full of faith, of reverence, and of the exercise of zeal,—when he had thus held a religious discourse to the Bhikkhus as to what was fit and suitable in that respect, he addressed the Bhikkhus, and said: 'Let the Sa*m*gha, therefore, O Bhikkhus, carry out the Ta*gg*aniya-kamma (Act of Rebuke) against those Bhikkhus.

4. 'Now thus, O Bhikkhus, should it be carried out. In the first place the Bhikkhus who are followers of Pa*nd*uka and Lohitaka ought to be warned; when they have been warned, they ought to be reminded (of the Rule in the Pâtimokkha against which they have offended); when they have been reminded, they ought to be charged with the (particular) offence; when they have been charged with the offence, some discreet and able Bhikkhu ought to lay the matter before the Sa*m*gha, saying,

'"Let the venerable Sa*m*gha hear me. These Bhikkhus who are followers of Pa*nd*uka and Lohitaka, who themselves (&c., as in § 1, down to the end). If the time is fit for the Sa*m*gha (to do so) let the Sa*m*gha carry out the Ta*gg*aniya-kamma against the Bhikkhus who are followers of Pa*nd*uka and Lohitaka.

'"Such is the motion (*ñ*atti).

'"Let the venerable Sa*m*gha hear me. The Bhikkhus who are followers of Pa*nd*uka and Lohitaka,

---

[1] We have here the substance of that 'religious discourse' (dhammi*m* katha*m*) which the Buddha is so frequently stated to have held before he laid down the rule for the guidance of the Bhikkhus in the particular matter which had been brought before him. It recurs in the Mahâvagga (I, 25, 6), and is constantly to be supplied both there and below.

who themselves (&c., as in § 1, down to the end). The Sa*m*gha hereby carries out the Ta*gg*aniya-kamma against them. Whosoever of the venerable ones approves of the carrying out of the Ta*gg*aniya-kamma against the Bhikkhus who are followers of Pa*nd*uka and Lohitaka, let him remain silent. Whosoever approves not thereof, let him speak.

'"A second time I say the same thing. Let the venerable Sa*m*gha (&c., as before[1]). A third time I say the same thing. Let the venerable Sa*m*gha (&c., as before[1]).

'"The Ta*gg*aniya-kamma against the Bhikkhus who are followers of Pa*nd*uka and Lohitaka has been carried by the Sa*m*gha. The Sa*m*gha approves (the motion). Therefore is it silent. Thus do I understand."'

2[2].

1. 'There are three things, O Bhikkhus, by which, when a Ta*gg*aniya-kamma is characterised, it is against the Dhamma, and against the Vinaya, and difficult to be settled; (that is to say), when it has not been carried out in a full assembly of properly qualified persons, according to law and justice, and in the presence of the litigant parties[3]—when it has been carried out without the accused person having been heard—when it has been carried out without the accused person having confessed himself guilty. A Ta*gg*aniya-kamma, O Bhikkhus, charac-

[1] The motion just proposed is repeated down to the end.

[2] Repeated below, chapters 10, 14, and 19.

[3] All these details are involved in the meaning of the technical term asammukhatâ, which is fully explained in *K*ullavagga IV, 14, 16, and following.

terised by these three things is against the Dhamma, and against the Vinaya, and difficult to be settled.

'There are other three things, O Bhikkhus, by which, when a Tagganiya-kamma has been characterised, it is against the Dhamma, and against the Vinaya, and difficult to be settled; (that is to say), when it has been carried out though no fault has been committed—when it has been carried out for a Pârâgika or a Samghâdisesa offence[1]—when it has been carried out though the fault has been confessed. A Tagganiya-kamma, O Bhikkhus, characterised (&c., as before, down to) settled.

'There are other three things, O Bhikkhus, by which, when a Tagganiya-kamma has been characterised, it is against the Dhamma, and against the Vinaya, and difficult to be settled; (that is to say), when it has been carried out without the accused person having been warned—when it has been carried out without the accused person having been called upon to remember (whether he has or has not committed the offence)—when it has been carried out without the accused person having been convicted. A Tagganiya-kamma, O Bhikkhus, characterised (&c., as before, down to) settled.

'There are other three things, O Bhikkhus, by which, when a Tagganiya-kamma has been characterised, it is against the Dhamma, and against the Vinaya, and difficult to be settled; (that is to say), when it has not been carried out in a properly constituted meeting properly conducted[2]—when it has

[1] Buddhaghosa says, Adesanâgâminiyâ ti Pârâgikâpattiyâ vâ Samghâdisesâpattiyâ vâ.

[2] As in the first paragraph of this section more fully described. The word here used is the same.

been carried out without justice[1]—when it has been carried out without the presence and approval of all the Bhikkhus belonging to the particular circuit[2]. A Tagganiya-kamma, O Bhikkhus, characterised by these three things is (&c., as before, down to) settled.

'There are other three things, O Bhikkhus, by which, when a Tagganiya-kamma has been characterised, it is against the Dhamma, and against the Vinaya, and difficult to be settled; (that is to say), when it has been carried out without the accused person having been heard—when it has been carried out without justice—when it has been carried out without the presence and approval of all the Bhikkhus belonging to the circuit. A Tagganiya-kamma, O Bhikkhus, characterised by these three things is (&c., as before, down to) settled.

'There are other three things (&c., as before, down to) that is to say, when it has been carried out without the accused person having been convicted—when it has been carried out without justice—when it has been carried out without the presence and approval of all the Bhikkhus belonging to the circuit.'

[And in a similar way each of the three things in paragraphs 2 and 3 of this section are united with the two things just repeated in each of paragraphs 4, 5, and 6, to make six further cases in which a Tagganiya-kamma is declared to be against the Dhamma, and against the Vinaya, and difficult to be revoked.]

Here end the twelve cases of a proceeding (Kamma) which is against the law.

---

[1] Adhammena; perhaps 'contrary to the Rules.'

[2] Vaggena for vi + aggena, the opposite of samaggena. See our note on the 21st Pâkittiya, and Mahâvagga IX, 3, 5.

3.

1. 'There are three things, O Bhikkhus, by which, when a Tagganiya-kamma is characterised, it is a proceeding in accordance with the Dhamma, a proceeding in accordance with the Vinaya, and is easy to be settled; (that is to say), when it has been carried out in a full assembly of qualified persons, according to law, and in the presence of the litigant parties—when it has been carried out after the accused person has been heard—when it has been carried out after the accused person has confessed himself guilty. A Tagganiya-kamma, O Bhikkhus, characterised by these three things is in accordance with the Dhamma, and in accordance with the Vinaya, and is easy to be settled.'

[And in a similar way the opposite of each of the twelve propositions in the last section is here laid down.]

Here end the twelve cases of a proceeding (Kamma) which is according to law.

4.

1. 'There are three things, O Bhikkhus, which, when they characterise a Bhikkhu, the Samgha, if it likes, should carry out the Tagganiya-kamma against him; (that is to say), when he is a maker of strife, quarrelsome, a maker of disputes, given to idle talk, and a raiser of legal questions in the Samgha[1]—when he is dull, stupid, full of faults, and devoid of merit—when he is living in lay society, in unlawful

[1] This refers to the Introductory Story, I, 1, 1.

association with the world. There are three things, O Bhikkhus, which, when the Samgha suspects (&c., as before, down to) against him.

'There are other three things, O Bhikkhus, (&c., as before, down to) against him; (that is to say), when he has failed in morality as regards moral things—when he has failed in conduct as regards transgression—when he has failed in opinion as regards the principal matters of opinion[1]. There are three things, O Bhikkhus, (&c., as before, down to) against him.

'There are other three things, O Bhikkhus, (&c., as before, down to) against him; (that is to say), when he speaks in dispraise of the Buddha—when he speaks in dispraise of the Dhamma—when he speaks in dispraise of the Samgha. These are three things, O Bhikkhus, (&c., as before, down to) against him.

2. 'There are three kinds of Bhikkhus, O Bhikkhus, against whom, if the Samgha likes, it should carry out the Tagganiya-kamma; (that is to say), one who is a maker of strife (&c., as in § 1, down to) a raiser of legal questions in the Samgha—one who is dull, stupid, full of faults, and devoid of merit—and one who is living in lay society, in unlawful association with the world. These are three kinds of Bhikkhus, O Bhikkhus, (&c., as before, down to) the Tagganiya-kamma.

'There are other three kinds of Bhikkhus, O Bhikkhus, against whom, if the Samgha likes, it should carry out the Tagganiya-kamma; (that is to say), one who has failed in morality in regard to moral matters—one who has failed in conduct

[1] Compare Mahâvagga I, 36, 8, and our note there.

as regards transgression—one who has failed in opinion as regards the principal matters of opinion. These are three kinds of Bhikkhus, O Bhikkhus (&c., as before, down to) the Tagganiya-kamma.

'There are other three kinds of Bhikkhus, O Bhikkhus, against whom, if the Samgha likes, it should carry out the Tagganiya-kamma; (that is to say), one who speaks in dispraise of the Buddha—one who speaks in dispraise of the Dhamma—one who speaks in dispraise of the Samgha. These are three kinds of Bhikkhus, O Bhikkhus (&c., as before, down to) the Tagganiya-kamma.'

Here end the six permissive cases of Tagganiya-kamma.

5[1].

1. 'A Bhikkhu against whom the Tagganiya-kamma has been carried out ought to conduct himself aright. And herein this is the right conduct[2]: he ought not to confer the upasampadâ—he ought not to give a nissaya[3]—he ought not to provide

[1] This chapter is repeated below for the Nissaya-, Pabbâganiya-, and Patisâraniya-kammas (chapters 10, 15, and 21). The corresponding rule for the first two Ukkhepaniya-kammas is different, and much more stringent (chapter 27, repeated in chapter 31); but that for the third (chapter 33) is again the same as the rule laid down in this chapter. In the second Khandhaka (1, 2) the list of restrictions is again longer.

[2] Sammâvattanâ. See Mahâvagga I, 26, 1; 27, 1; 33, 1; 34, 1.

[3] Buddhaghosa says, âgantukânam nissayo na dâtabbo. The relation of a junior Bhikkhu either to his upagghâya or to his âkariya is alike called nissaya (Mahâvagga I, 36, 1); but the term is more especially applied to the latter (Mahâvagga I, 32, 2, whereas in the corresponding formula for the upagghâya, Mahâ-

himself with a sâma*n*era[1]—he ought not to accept the office of giving exhortation to the nuns[2]—and if he has accepted the office, he ought not to exhort the nuns[2]—he ought not to commit the offence for which the Ta*gg*aniya-kamma has been carried out by the Sa*m*gha against him—nor any offence of a similar kind—nor any worse offence—he ought not to find fault with the proceeding (that has been carried out against him)—nor with (the Bhikkhus) who have carried it out—he ought not to raise objection against a regular[3] Bhikkhu's taking part in the Uposatha ceremony[4]—or in the Pavâra*n*â ceremony[5]—he ought not to issue commands (to a junior inhibiting him from going beyond the bounds[6], or summoning him to come before the elders)—he ought not to set on foot a censure against any other Bhikkhu[7]—he ought not to ask another Bhikkhu to give him leave (to rebuke that Bhikkhu[8])—he ought not to warn (another Bhikkhu[9] whom he supposes to be offending)—he ought

vagga I, 25, 7, the word nissaya does not occur). In other words, nissaya means all that is included in the phrase 'nissâya te vatthabba*m*' (*K*ullavagga I, 9, 2).

[1] Compare Mahâvagga I, 36, 37.

[2] See below, *K*ullavagga X, 9, 4, and also the 21st Pâ*k*ittiya.

[3] Compare Minayeff, Pâtimokkha, p. 63.

[4] Compare Pâtimokkha*m* *th*apetu*m* at *K*ullavagga IX, 2.

[5] Compare Mahâvagga IV, 16, 2.

[6] As, for example, under the rule at Mahâvagga I, 27, 2. Buddhaghosa says, Na sava*k*aniya*m* kâtabban ti aham âyasmanta*m* asmi*m* vatthusmi*m* va*k*aniya*m* karomi imamhâ âvâsâ param pi mâ pakkâmi yâva na ta*m* adhikara*n*a*m* vûpasanta*m* hotîti. He also gives a longer note, partly to the same effect, on the corresponding passage in II, 1, 2, which will be found in our note there, and from which we have taken the second clause in the parentheses.

[7] See the note on this word in the next chapter.

[8] Compare Mahâvagga II, 16, 1. [9] Compare *K*ullavagga IX, 5.

not to call upon another Bhikkhu to remember (whether he has or has not committed an offence)—and he ought not to associate with the Bhikkhus.'

Here end the eighteen duties which follow on a Tagganiya-kamma.

6[1].

1. So the Samgha carried out the Tagganiya-kamma against the Bhikkhus who were followers of Panduka and Lohitaka. And when they had been subjected by the Samgha to the Tagganiya-kamma and were conducting themselves aright in accordance thereto, they became subdued[2], and they sought for release[3]; and going up to the Bhikkhus they spake as follows: 'We, Sirs, have been subjected by the Samgha to the Tagganiya-kamma (&c., down to) release. What now should we do?'

They told this thing to the Blessed One.

'Then, O Bhikkhus, let the Samgha revoke the Tagganiya-kamma carried out against the followers of Panduka and Lohitaka.

2. 'There are five things, O Bhikkhus, by which,

[1] Compare below, chapters 11, 16, 23, 28, 34.

[2] Lomam pâtenti. See the commentary as given by H. Oldenberg at p. 309 of his edition of the text. That our translation is correct is evident from the use of panna-lomo (at Kullavagga VII, 1, 6), that being simply the opposite of hattha-lomo, which signifies 'having the hair of the body erect in consequence of the excitement produced by fear, joy, or amazement;' and hence simply 'troubled, excited.' The opposite of this is 'pacified, subdued.'

[3] Netthâram vattanti. See the commentary in the edition of the text loco citato.

when a Bhikkhu is characterised, a Tagganiya-kamma ought not to be revoked for him; (that is to say), when he confers the upasampadâ—when he gives a nissaya—when he provides himself with a sâmanera—when he accepts the office of giving exhortation to the nuns—and when, having accepted that office, he exhorts the nuns. These are the five things, O Bhikkhus (&c., as before, down to) revoked for him.

'There are other five things, O Bhikkhus, by which, when a Bhikkhu is characterised, a Tagganiya-kamma ought not to be revoked for him; (that is to say), when he commits the offence for which the Tagganiya-kamma has been carried out by the Samgha against him—or any other offence of a similar kind—or any worse offence—when he finds fault with the proceeding that has been carried out against him—or with the Bhikkhus who have carried it out. These are five things, O Bhikkhus (&c., as before, down to) revoked for him.

'There are eight things, O Bhikkhus, by which, when a Bhikkhu is characterised, a Tagganiya-kamma ought not to be revoked for him; (that is to say), when he raises objections against a regular[1] Bhikkhu's taking part in the Uposatha ceremony—or in the Pavâranâ ceremony—when he inhibits a junior from going beyond the bounds—when he sets on foot a censure against any other Bhikkhu—when he asks another Bhikkhu to give

[1] Pakatattassa, that is a Bhikkhu who has not made himself liable to any disciplinary proceeding, has committed no irregularity. It is one of the expressions unknown to the Pâtimokkha, but occurs in the much later Introduction to that work (Dickson, p. 11). See below, III, 1, 1.

him leave to rebuke that Bhikkhu—when he warns another Bhikkhu whom he supposes to be offending—when he reminds another Bhikkhu of a rule against which he supposes that Bhikkhu to be offending—when he associates with the Bhikkhus. These are the eight things, O Bhikkhus (&c., as before, down to) revoked for him.'

Here end the eighteen cases in which there ought to be no revocation (of the Ta*gg*aniya-kamma).

7.

[This chapter is exactly the converse of the last.]

Here end the eighteen cases in which there ought to be a revocation (of the Ta*gg*aniya-kamma).

8[1]

1. 'Now, thus, O Bhikkhus, should the revocation be carried out. Those Bhikkhus who are followers of Pa*nd*uka and Lohitaka should go before the Sa*m*gha, with their upper robe arranged over one shoulder, and should bow down at the feet of the elder Bhikkhus, and squatting down, and raising their hands with the palms joined together, should speak as follows: "We, Sirs, have been subjected by the Sa*m*gha to the Ta*gg*aniya-kamma, and are conducting ourselves aright in accordance thereto; and we have become subdued, and we seek for release, and beg for a revocation of the Ta*gg*aniya-

[1] Compare below, chapters 12 and 17.

kamma." And a second time they should beg [in the same words]. And a third time they should beg [in the same words]. Then a discreet and able Bhikkhu should lay the matter before the Sa*m*gha:

2. '"Let the venerable Sa*m*gha hear me. These Bhikkhus who are followers of Pa*nd*uka and Lohitaka have been subjected (&c., as before), and they are conducting themselves (&c., as before), and they beg (&c., as before).

'"This is the motion (ñatti).

'"Let the venerable Sa*m*gha hear me. These Bhikkhus (&c., as before, down to) and they beg for a revocation of the Ta*gg*aniya-kamma. The Sa*m*gha revokes the Ta*gg*aniya-kamma for the Bhikkhus who are followers of Pa*nd*uka and Lohitaka. Whosoever of the venerable ones approves of the revocation of the Ta*gg*aniya-kamma for the Bhikkhus who are followers of Pa*nd*uka and Lohitaka, let him hold his peace. Whosoever approves not thereof, let him speak.

'"And a second time I say the same thing. Let the venerable Sa*m*gha (&c., as before, down to) let him speak.

'"And a third time I say the same thing. Let the venerable Sa*m*gha (&c., as before, down to) let him speak.

'"The revocation of the Ta*gg*aniya-kamma for the Bhikkhus who are followers of Pa*nd*uka and Lohitaka has been carried by the Sa*m*gha. The Sa*m*gha approves; therefore is it silent. Thus do I understand."'

Here ends the first (Kamma), the Ta*gg*aniya-kamma.

II. The Nissaya-kamma (Act of Subordination).

9.

1. Now at that time the venerable Seyyasaka was stupid, and indiscreet, and full of faults, and devoid of merit, and was living in lay society in unlawful association with the world[1]. So much so that the Bhikkhus were worn out[2] with placing him on probation[3], and with throwing him back to the beginning (of his probationary term)[4], and with subjecting him to the mânatta discipline[5], and with rehabilitating him[6]. The moderate Bhikkhus were annoyed, and murmured, and became indignant

---

[1] There is no rule in the Pâtimokkha in which any of these things are declared to be an offence. The 31st and 85th Pâkittiyas only refer to a Bhikkhu's staying an unreasonable time in a public rest-house, and to his frequenting a village beyond the ordinary occasions. Stupidity, and keeping low company, are not mentioned. Why then should Seyyasaka have been placed upon probation? We think the answer will appear from our note 1 on II, 1, 1.

[2] Pakatâ, 'done up,' explained by vâvatâ. See Oldenberg's quotation from Buddhaghosa at p. 310 of his edition of the text.

[3] Compare Mahâvagga I, 38, 1; Mahâ-parinibbâna Sutta V, 64, 65; and Kullavagga III, 3. On the distinction between these kinds of probation, see also our note below on II, 1, 1.

[4] See below, II, 2, 1. Compare also Subhûti's explanation in Childers, and the passages quoted in the index to Oldenberg's edition of the text, p. 348, sub voce, especially Kullavagga III, 7.

[5] See below, Kullavagga III, 1; III, 4.

[6] See below, Kullavagga III, 2; III, 5.

(saying), 'How can the venerable Seyyasaka be so stupid (&c., as before), that the Bhikkhus are worn out (&c., as before)?'

Then those Bhikkhus told that matter to the Blessed One.

And the Blessed One on that occasion, and in that connection, convened a meeting of the Bhikkhu-sa*m*gha, and asked the Bhikkhus, 'Is it true, O Bhikkhus, as they say, that the venerable Seyyasaka is stupid (&c., as before, down to) with rehabilitating him?'

'It is true, Lord!'

The Blessed Buddha rebuked him (saying), 'This is improper' (&c., as usual, compare I, 2, 3, down to), and addressed the Bhikkhus, and said, 'Let the Sa*m*gha therefore, O Bhikkhus, carry out the Nissaya-kamma (Act of Subordination) against the venerable Seyyasaka: "Thou must remain under the superintendence of others[1]."

2. 'Now thus, O Bhikkhus, should it be carried out. In the first place the Bhikkhu Seyyasaka ought to be warned; when he has been warned, he ought to be reminded[2]; when he has been reminded, he ought to be charged with the offence[2]; when he has been charged with the offence, some discreet and able Bhikkhu ought to lay the matter before the Sa*m*gha (saying),

'"Let the venerable Sa*m*gha hear me (&c., as usual; see above. chapters 1. 4 and 8. 2)."'

---

[1] These are the distinctive and technical words of the Nissaya-kamma, just as the corresponding clause in chap. 13, § 7 contains the technical words of the Pabbâ*g*aniya-kamma.

[2] As explained above, chap. 1. 4.

10.

[Chapters 2–5 are here repeated at length, Nissaya-kamma being substituted throughout for Ta*gg*aniya-kamma.]

11[1].

1. So the Sa*m*gha carried out the Nissaya-kamma against the Bhikkhu Seyyasaka (saying), 'Thou must remain under the superintendence of others.'

And he, when subjected by the Sa*m*gha to the Nissaya-kamma, by resorting to and cultivating the acquaintance of good companions[2], associating with them, getting them to declare to him (the Dhamma), and asking them questions, became wise in the traditions; a man to whom the Nikâyas had been handed down; a reciter of the Dhamma, of the Vinaya, and of the Mâtikas; clever, discreet, wise, modest, full of remorse, and docile; he conducted himself aright, he became subdued, he sought for release, and going up to the Bhikkhus, he spake as follows:

'I, Sirs, after having been subjected by the Sa*m*gha to the Nissaya-kamma, am conducting myself aright, and have become subdued, and I seek for release. What now should I do?'

They told this thing to the Blessed One.

'Then, O Bhikkhus, let the Sa*m*gha revoke the Nissaya-kamma for the Bhikkhu Seyyasaka.

[1] Compare above, chapter 6.

[2] Compare Dhammapada, ver. 357.

2. 'There are five things, O Bhikkhus (&c., as in chap. 6. 2, down to the end of chap. 7, reading throughout Nissaya-kamma for Ta*gg*aniya-kamma).'

12.

[This chapter sets out the mode of revocation by a kamma-vâ*k*â precisely as above in chapter 8.]

Here ends the second (Kamma), the Nissaya-kamma.

III. The Pabbâganiya-kamma (Act of Banishment).

13[1].

1. Now at that time the Bhikkhus who were followers of Assagi and Punabbasu were dwelling on the Kitâ Hill, wicked Bhikkhus, and shameless. Such as these were the evil practices they followed: they used to plant cuttings of flowers, and have them planted; they used to water flowers, and have them watered; they used to gather them, and have them gathered; they used to make them up into nosegays, and have them so made up; they used to make them up, and to have them made up, into wreaths, of the kind with the stalks together, and of the kind with the stalks separate[2], of the kind called mañgarikâ[3], of the kind called vidhutikâ[4], of the kind called vatamsaka[5], of the kind

[1] The whole of this chapter recurs in the Sutta Vibhaṅga on the 13th Samghâdisesa. The proceeding here laid down is really only a later method of acting under the circumstances similar to those for which that rule had previously been the authorised dealing.

[2] The Samanta Pâsâdikâ says, Ekatovantikan ti pupphânam vante ekato katvâ kata-mâlam. Ubhatovantikan ti ubhohi passehi puppha-vante katvâ kata-mâlam.

[3] Perhaps 'like an anklet.' The Sam. Pâs. says, Mañgarî viya katâ puppha-vikati mañgarikâ ti.

[4] Perhaps 'like a fan.' The Sam. Pâs. says, Vidhutikâ ti sûkiyâ vâ salâkâya vâ sinduvâra-pupphâdîni viggihitvâ katâ (mâlâ).

[5] Perhaps 'like a crest.' The Sam. Pâs. says, vatamsako ti

called âve*l*a[1], of the kind called ura*kkh*ada[2];—and they then used to take or send wreaths of each of these various kinds to the wives and daughters and young women and sisters-in-law and female slaves in respectable families;—and they used to eat out of one dish, to drink out of one vessel, to sit on one seat, to lie on one bed, one mat, one coverlet, with the wives and daughters and young women and sisters-in-law and female slaves in respectable families;—and they used to eat food at the wrong time, and to drink strong drink, and to make use of garlands, and scents, and unguents;—and they used to dance, and sing, and play music, and wanton, and all these together in every combination.

2. And they used to amuse themselves at games[3] with eight pieces and ten pieces, and with tossing up, hopping over diagrams formed on the ground, and removing substances from a heap without shaking the remainder; and with games at dice, and trap-ball; and with sketching rude figures, tossing balls, blowing trumpets, having matches at ploughing with mimic ploughs, tumbling, forming mimic wind-mills, guessing at measures, having

avata*m*sako. Compare the close of Rh. D.'s note on vegha for avegha, 'Buddhist Suttas,' p. 37.

[1] Perhaps 'like an earring.' The Sam. Pâs. says, a*k*elo (sic) ti ka*nn*ikâ. Compare Sanskrit âpî*d*a, and *G*âtaka, vol. i, pp. 12, 95, 269.

[2] The Sam. Pâs. says, Ura*kkh*ado ti hâra-sadisa*m* ure-*th*apanaka-puppha dâma*m*. 'Like mail-armour.'

[3] All these games are forbidden seriatim in paragraph 4 of the Ma*ggh*ima Sîla, and the whole list of offences recurs in the Sutta-vibhaṅga, Sa*m*ghâdisesa XIII, 1, 2. See Rh. D., 'Buddhist Suttas from the Pâli,' p. 193. We adhere to the translations there given and based on the Sumaṅgala Vilâsinî.

chariot races, and archery matches, shooting marbles with the fingers, guessing other people's thoughts, and mimicking other people's acts;—and they used to practise elephant riding, and horse riding, and carriage driving, and archery, and swordsmanship;—and they used to run to and fro in front of elephants, and in front of horses, and in front of carriages;—and they used to exhibit signs of anger[1], and to wring their hands[2], and to wrestle[3], and to box with their fists;—and spreading their robes out as a stage they used to invite dancing girls, saying, 'Here you may dance, sister!' and greet her with applause[4]. Thus manifold were the evil lives which they practised.

3. Now at that time a certain Bhikkhu who had spent the rainy season in the country of Kâsi, and was on his way to visit the Blessed One, arrived at the Ki*t*â Hill. And that Bhikkhu in the early morning put on his under garment, and went, duly bowled and robed, to the Ki*t*â Hill for alms. And he was perfect in dignity, with his eyes cast down, and pleasing in appearance, whether in going in or

---

[1] Usse*l*h*enti. We are quite uncertain how to render this word. One might be tempted to think that a denominative verb from usso*l*h*i may have acquired a technical sense appropriate to this passage. But we do not favour any such conjectural alteration of the clear reading of the MSS., at all events at present.

[2] Appo*l*h*enti. See Buddhaghosa's note quoted by Rh. D. in his note on the Book of the Great Decease, II, 19.

[3] Nibbu*ggh*anti, which Buddhaghosa explains by malla-yuddha*m* karonti. Compare ubbu*ggh*ati at *K*ullavagga VIII, 10, and Sutta-vibhaṅga, Pârâ*g*ika I, 10, 26.

[4] The Sam. Pâs. says, Nalâ*t*ika*m* pi denti sâdhu sâdhu bhaginîti attano nalâ*t*e aṅguli*m* *th*apetvâ tassâ nalâ*t*e *th*apenti.

in coming out, in looking or in watching, in bending in his arm or in stretching it forth[1].

Then the people on beholding that Bhikkhu, said, 'Who is this fellow like a fool of fools, or like an idiot of idiots, or like a simpleton of simpletons[2]? Who would give an alms when this fellow comes near! Now our own masters, the followers of Assagi and Punabbasu, are gentle, friendly, pleasant in speech, radiant with smiles, by no means fools, but open in countenance, and the first to speak. To such now it is fit to give an alms!'

And a certain lay-disciple saw that Bhikkhu as he was going along the Kitâ Hill for alms. And on seeing him, he went up to the place where he was; and on coming there he said to that Bhikkhu:

'Has your reverence received an alms?'

'No, my friend, I have received no alms!'

'Come, your reverence! Let us go to my house!'

4. So the lay-disciple took the Bhikkhu to his house, and gave him to eat, and asked him:

'Whither then is your reverence going?'

'I am on my way to Sâvatthi, my friend, to visit the Blessed One.'

'Then let your reverence bow down at the feet of the Blessed One in my name, and say, "The residence on the Kitâ Hill, Lord, has been spoiled. The Bhikkhus who are followers of Assagi and Punabbasu are dwelling on the Kitâ Hill, wicked Bhikkhus, and shameless. Such as these are the

[1] Compare Mahâ-parinibbâna Sutta II, 15.

[2] The Sam. Pâs. says, Samkutita-mukhatâya bhâkutika-bhâkutikâ viya.

evil practices they follow (&c., as in §§ 1, 2, down to the end). And people, Lord, who were formerly believers and full of faith, are now become non-believers and void of faith; the opportunities of alms that were formerly open to the Sa*m*gha are now destroyed; worthy Bhikkhus forsake, and wicked Bhikkhus dwell in the place. Let, Lord, the Blessed One be pleased to send (other) Bhikkhus to the Ki*t*â Hill in order that the residence there may be re-established."'

5. 'Very well, my friend,' said the Bhikkhu, in assent, to that lay-disciple. And rising from his seat, he set out for Sâvatthi, and went straight on to Anâtha-pi*nd*ika's grove, to the *G*etavana in Sâvatthi, to the place where the Blessed One was staying. And on arriving there he saluted the Blessed One, and took his seat on one side.

Now it is the custom for the Blessed Buddhas to exchange words of greeting with in-coming Bhikkhus. And the Blessed One said to that Bhikkhu, 'Do things go well with you, O Bhikkhu? Have you enough for your support? Have you accomplished your journey without too much fatigue? And whence, O Bhikkhu, have you come?'

'Things go well with me, Lord. I have enough for my support. And I have accomplished my journey without too much fatigue. I have spent the rainy season, Lord, in the land of Kâsi; and on my way to Sâvatthi to visit the Blessed One I arrived at the Ki*t*â Hill. And after having dressed early in the morning, I went, Lord, duly bowled and robed, on to the Ki*t*â Hill for alms. And a certain lay-disciple saw me (&c., as above, down to the end of § 4, with the alterations necessary to the narrative form of speech). Thence, Lord, am I come.'

6. Then the Blessed One on that occasion, and in that connection, convened a meeting of the Bhikkhu-Sa*m*gha, and asked the Bhikkhus:

'Is it true, O Bhikkhus, as they say, that those Bhikkhus who are followers of Assa*g*i and Punabbasu, and are dwelling on the Ki*t*â Hill, are wicked Bhikkhus, and shameless; and that such are the evil practices they follow (&c., as in § 4, down to the end)?'

'It is true, Lord.'

The Blessed Buddha rebuked them, saying, 'How can they, O Bhikkhus, foolish persons that they are, follow such practices as these (&c., as in §§ 1, 2, down to the end)? This will not conduce, O Bhikkhus, to the conversion of the unconverted (&c., as usual. Compare chap. 1, § 2, down to the end).'

And when the Blessed Buddha had rebuked them, and had delivered a religious discourse, he addressed the venerable Sâriputta and Moggallâna, and said, 'Go now, Sâriputta and Moggallâna[1], to the Ki*t*â Hill. And on arriving there carry out the Pabbâ*g*aniya-kamma (Act of Banishment[2]) against those Bhikkhus who are followers of Assa*g*i and Punabbasu, to the effect that they may become your Saddhi-vihârikas[3].'

---

[1] On this meaning of Sâriputtâ, see the note on Mahâvagga X, 4, 3.

[2] That is, out of the particular place where they have caused the scandal, not of the Order. When they in anger left the Order, their conduct in doing so is blamed. See chap. 16, § 1.

[3] See Mahâvagga I, 25, 6, and following, and *K*ullavagga VIII, 11, 12, and compare above, 9. 1.

'How, Lord, can we carry out the Pabbâganiya-kamma against those Bhikkhus who are followers of Assagi and Punabbasu; for they are passionate men and violent?'

'Then do you go, Sâriputta and Moggallâna, together with a number of Bhikkhus.'

'So be it, Lord!' said Sâriputta and Moggallâna, in assent, to the Blessed One.

7[1]. 'Now thus, O Bhikkhus, should it be carried out. In the first place the Bhikkhus who are followers of Assagi and Punabbasu ought to be warned: when they have been warned, they ought to be reminded (of the Rule in the Pâtimokkha against which they have offended); when they have been reminded they ought to be charged with the offence; when they have been charged some discreet and able Bhikkhu ought to lay the matter before the Samgha, saying,

'"Let the venerable Samgha hear me. These Bhikkhus who are followers of Assagi and Punabbasu are wicked Bhikkhus and shameless. Their evil practices are both seen and heard, and also that respectable families have been led astray by them is seen, too, and heard[2]. If the time is fit for the Samgha to do so, let the Samgha carry out the Pabbâganiya-kamma against those Bhikkhus who are followers of Assagi and Punabbasu, to the effect that the Bhikkhus who are followers

[1] On this section compare chap. 1, § 4, chap. 9, § 2.

[2] Buddhaghosa points out that whereas the Tagganiya-kamma is directed against quarrelsomeness, and the nissaya-kamma against foolishness, it is scandal to the community against which the Pabbâganiya-kamma is directed.

of Assa*g*i and Punabbasu are not to dwell on the Ki*t*â Hill[1].

'"This is the motion (*ñ*atti).

'"Let the venerable Sa*m*gha hear me. These Bhikkhus who are followers of Assa*g*i and Punabbasu are wicked Bhikkhus and shameless. Their evil practices (&c., as before, down to) is seen, too, and heard. The Sa*m*gha hereby carries out the Pabbâ*g*aniya-kamma against them, to the effect that the Bhikkhus who are followers of Assa*g*i and Punabbasu are not to dwell on the Ki*t*â Hill[1]. Whosoever of the venerable ones approves of the carrying out of the Pabbâ*g*aniya-kamma against the followers (&c., as before) to the effect (&c., as before[1]) let him remain silent. Whosoever approves not thereof, let him speak.

'"A second time I say the same thing. Let the venerable Sa*m*gha (&c., as before). A third time I say the same thing. Let the venerable Sa*m*gha (&c., as before).

'"The Pabbâ*g*aniya-kamma has been carried out by the Sa*m*gha against those Bhikkhus who are followers of Assa*g*i and Punabbasu to the effect that those Bhikkhus who are followers of Assa*g*i and Punabbasu are not to dwell on the Ki*t*â Hill[1]. The Sa*m*gha approves of it. Therefore is it silent. Thus do I understand."'

14.

1. [Here follow the twelve cases in which a Pabbâ*g*aniya-kamma is declared to be against

[1] The corresponding clause to the words 'to the effect,' &c., is wanting in chap. 1, § 4, but occurs in chap. 9, § 2.

the law, and according to law respectively, in the precise wording of chapters 2 and 3, reading Pabbâ*g*aniya for Ta*gg*aniya. Then follow the six cases of permissive suspension in the precise wording of chapter 4, but in addition to the cases there given for the Ta*gg*aniya-kamma, §§ 1 and 2 of this chapter are respectively added at the end of §§ 1 and 2 of that chapter.]

1. 'There are three things, O Bhikkhus, which when they characterise a Bhikkhu, the Sa*m*gha, if it likes, should carry out the Pabbâ*g*aniya-kamma against him; (that is to say), when he is characterised by frivolity[1] of action—when he is characterised by frivolity of speech—when he is characterised by frivolity both of action and of speech. These are the three things, O Bhikkhus (&c., as before, down to) against him.

'There are other three things, O Bhikkhus, which when they characterise a Bhikkhu, the Sa*m*gha, if it likes, should carry out the Pabbâ*g*aniya-kamma against him; (that is to say), when he is characterised by absence of right-doing in action—when he is characterised by absence of right-doing in speech—when he is characterised by absence of right-doing both in action and in speech. These are the other three things, O Bhikkhus (&c., as before, down to) against him.

'There are other three things (&c., as in each of the last paragraphs; the three things here being injury[2] done by him to others in action, in speech, and both in action and in speech, owing to his own

[1] The Sam. Pâs. says, Kâyiko davo nâma kâya-ki*l*â vu*kk*ati.

[2] The Sam. Pâs. says, Kâyika*m* upaghâtita*m* nâma kâya-dvâre pa*ññ*atti-sikkhâpadassa asikkhana-bhâvena upahanana*m* vu*kk*ati.

want of training in the precepts and practices of the order).

'There are other three things (&c., as in each of the last paragraphs, the three things here being evilness of life in action, in speech, and both in action and in speech).

2. 'There are three kinds of Bhikkhus, O Bhikkhus, against whom, when the Sa*m*gha likes (to do so), it should carry out the Pabbâ*g*aniya-kamma; (that is to say), one who is frivolous in action—one who is frivolous in speech—one who is frivolous both in action and in speech. These are the three kinds of Bhikkhus (&c., as above, down to) the Pabbâ*g*aniya-kamma.

'There are other three kinds of Bhikkhus (&c., as in the last paragraph, substituting first, absence of right-doing—secondly, injury to others—and thirdly, evilness of life respectively in action, in speech, and both in action and in speech).'

15.

[This chapter is identical with chapter 5, reading Pabbâ*g*aniya for Ta*gg*aniya.]

16[1].

1. So the Bhikkhu-Sa*m*gha, with Sâriputta and Moggallâna at their head, proceeded to the Ki*t*â Hill, and there carried out the Pabbâ*g*aniya-kamma against those Bhikkhus who were followers

[1] Corresponding to chapters 6 and 11 above.

of Assa*g*i and Punabbasu, to the intent that those Bhikkhus should no longer dwell on the Ki*t*â Hill. And they, when subjected by the Sa*m*gha to the Pabbâ*g*aniya-kamma, did not conduct themselves aright, they did not become subdued, they did not seek for release, they did not ask the Bhikkhus for forgiveness, they reviled them, they found fault with them[1], saying that they were offending by acting in partiality, in ill-feeling, in folly, and in fear[2]; and they not only departed from the place, but also left the Order[3].

Those Bhikkhus who were moderate were offended, murmured, and became indignant, saying, 'How can those Bhikkhus who are followers of Assa*g*i and Punabbasu, after having been subjected by the Sa*m*gha to the Pabbâ*g*aniya-kamma, refuse to conduct themselves aright (&c., as before, down to) leave the Order?' And those Bhikkhus told the matter to the Blessed One.

Then the Blessed One on that occasion, and in that connection, convened a meeting of the Bhikkhu-sa*m*gha, and asked the Bhikkhus:

'Is it true, O Bhikkhus, as they say, that those Bhikkhus who are followers of Assa*g*i and Punabbasu, after having been subjected by the Sa*m*gha to the Pabbâ*g*aniya-kamma, refuse (&c., as before, down to) leave the Order?'

'It is true, Lord!'

---

[1] Compare Sa*m*ghâdisesa 13.

[2] These are the four so-called Agatis, usually occurring as the faults of a judge (Rh. D., 'Buddhist Birth Stories,' p. xxii, and Dasaratha *G*âtaka, p. 1), but compare Sigâlovâda Sutta, ed. Grimbolt, p. 299.

[3] Compare *G*âtaka I, 117, and Mahâvagga I, 39, 5.

'How can those Bhikkhus who (&c., as before, down to) leave the Order? This will not conduce, O Bhikkhus, either to the conversion of the unconverted, or to the increase of the converted; but rather to the unconverted being not converted, and to the turning back of those which have been converted.' And when the Blessed One had rebuked those Bhikkhus in various ways, and had delivered a religious discourse, he addressed the Bhikkhus, and said:

'Then, O Bhikkhus, let not the Sa*m*gha revoke the Pabbâ*g*aniya-kamma. There are five things, O Bhikkhus (&c., as before, from chapter 6, § 2, down to the end of chapter 7, reading Pabbâ*g*aniya for Ta*gg*aniya).'

Here end the eighteen cases in which there ought to be a revocation (of the Pabbâ*g*aniya-kamma).

17[1].

1. 'Now thus, O Bhikkhus, should the revocation be carried out. The Bhikkhu, who has been subjected to the Pabbâ*g*aniya-kamma, should go before the Sa*m*gha (&c., as before in chapter 8, §§ 1, 2, down to the end).'

Here ends the third (Kamma), the Pabbâ*g*aniya-kamma.

---

[1] Compare chapters 8 and 12.

IV.

THE PATISÂRANIYA-KAMMA (ACT OF RECONCILIATION).

18[1].

1. Now at that time the venerable Sudhamma was residing at Makkhikâsanda in dependence upon Kitta the householder, superintending[2] the new buildings he erected[3], and being constantly supplied by him with food. And whenever Kitta the householder wished to give an invitation to the Samgha, or to four or five Bhikkhus[4], or to a single one, he used not to invite them without making special mention of the venerable Sudhamma.

Now at that time a number of the Thera Bhikkhus, including the venerable Sâriputta, and the venerable Mahâ Moggallâna, and the venerable Mahâ Kakkâna, and the venerable Mahâ Kotthita, and the venerable Mahâ Kappina, and the venerable Mahâ Kunda, and

[1] The whole of this story of Kitta and Sudhamma recurs in the Dhammapada commentary, pp. 262–264. There is no Rule in the Pâtimokkha by which giving offence to a layman, the cause of the proceeding described in the following chapters, is considered worthy of censure.

[2] Navakammiko, not 'newly appointed to an office,' as Dr. Rudolf Hoernle translates in the Indian Antiquary, XI, 29, in dealing with one of the Bharhut Inscriptions. See Gâtaka I, 92, and below, V, 13, 3, VI, 5, 2, VI, 17, 1, X, 24. This duty of superintending a new building was even filled by Bhikkhunîs; see the Bhikkhunî-vibhanga, Pârâgika I, where the details of the duty are incidentally mentioned.

[3] Compare below, Kullavagga VI, 5, 2, and Gâtaka I, 92, 22.

[4] This clause, both here and below, is omitted in the Sinhalese MS.

the venerable Anuruddha, and the venerable Revata, and the venerable Upâli, and the venerable Ânanda, and the venerable Râhula, as they were journeying through the country of Kâsi, arrived at Ma*kkh*ikâsa*nd*a. And *K*itta the householder heard the news that the Thera Bhikkhus had arrived at Ma*kkh*ikâsa*nd*a.

Then *K*itta the householder went up to the place where the Thera Bhikkhus were, and on arriving there, he saluted the Thera Bhikkhus, and took his seat on one side. And when he was so seated the venerable Sâriputta taught *K*itta the householder, and incited him, and roused him, and gladdened him with religious discourse. And *K*itta the householder, having been thus taught, and incited, and roused, and gladdened with religious discourse, said to the Thera Bhikkhus, 'May the venerable Theras consent to take their to-morrow's meal, as incoming Bhikkhus, at my house.' And the Thera Bhikkhus signified, by silence, their consent.

2. Then perceiving that the Thera Bhikkhus had given their consent, *K*itta the householder rose from his seat, and bowed down before the Thera Bhikkhus, and keeping them on his right hand as he passed them, went on to the place where the venerable Sudhamma was. And on arriving there, he saluted the venerable Sudhamma, and stood by on one side. And so standing, *K*itta the householder said to the venerable Sudhamma: 'May the venerable Sudhamma consent to take his to-morrow's meal at my house with the Theras.'

But the venerable Sudhamma, thinking, 'Formerly indeed this *K*itta the householder, whenever he wished to give an invitation to the Sa*m*gha, or to four or five Bhikkhus, or to a single one, used not to invite them without making special mention of me; but now he has invited the Thera Bhikkhus without regarding me. This *K*itta the householder is now incensed against me, unfavourable to me, takes pleasure in me no longer.' And so thinking he refused, saying, 'It is enough, O householder.'

And a second time *K*itta the householder said to the venerable Sudhamma (&c., as before, with the same result). And a third time (&c., as before, with the same result).

Then *K*itta the householder, thinking, 'What can the venerable Sudhamma do against me, whether he consents, or whether he does not consent,' saluted the venerable Sudhamma, and keeping him on his right hand as he passed him, departed thence.

3. And at the end of the night *K*itta the householder made ready sweet food, both hard and soft, for the Thera Bhikkhus. And the venerable Sudhamma, thinking, 'I may as well go and see what *K*itta the householder has made ready for the Thera Bhikkhus,' robed himself early in the morning, and went, duly bowled and robed, to the place where *K*itta the householder dwelt; and, on arriving there, he took his seat on a mat spread out for him.

Then *K*itta the householder went up to the place where the venerable Sudhamma was; and after he had come there, he saluted the venerable Sudhamma, and took his seat on one side. And when he was so seated the venerable Sudhamma addressed *K*itta the householder, and said: 'Though this great store of sweet food, both hard and soft, has been made ready by you, O householder, there is one thing yet wanting, that is to say, tila seed cake.'

'Though then, Sir, there is so much treasure in the ward of the Buddhas, yet there is but one thing of which the venerable Sudhamma makes mention, and that is tila seed cake. Long ago, Sir, certain merchants of Dakkhi*n*âpatha went, for the sake of their traffic, to the country of the East, and thence they brought back a hen. Now, Sir, that hen made acquaintance with a crow, and gave birth to a chicken. And, Sir, whenever that chicken tried to utter the cry of a cock it gave vent to a "caw," and whenever it tried to utter the cry of a crow, it gave vent to a "cock-a-doodle-do[1]." Just even so, Sir, though there is much treasure in the ward of the Buddhas, whenever the venerable Sudhamma speaks, the sound is "tila seed cake."'

4. 'You are abusing me, householder. You are finding fault with me, householder. This place, householder, is yours. I must go away from it,' said the venerable Sudhamma.

'I do not intend, Sir, to abuse the venerable Sudhamma, nor to find fault with him. Let, Sir, the venerable Sudhamma still dwell at Ma*kkh*ikâsa*nd*a. Pleasant is this grove of plum trees, and I shall take good care to provide the venerable Sudhamma with those things a recluse requires—to wit, with robes and food and lodging and medicine when he is sick.'

And a second time the venerable Sudhamma said: 'You are abusing me (&c., as before, with the same reply). And a third time the venerable Sudhamma said: 'You are abusing me (&c., as before, down to) I must go away from it.'

[1] Compare *G*âtaka I, 432; II, 307.

'Whither then, Sir, will the venerable Sudhamma go?'

'I shall go to Sâvatthi, O householder, to visit the Blessed One.'

'Then, Sir, let the Blessed One know all, both what you yourself have said, and what I have said. And I should not, Sir, be surprised if the venerable Sudhamma were to return again even to Ma*kkh*ikâsa*nd*a.'

5. So the venerable Sudhamma gathered together his sleeping mat, and set out, with his bowl and his robe, for Sâvatthi. And he journeyed straight on to Sâvatthi, to the *G*etavana, Anâthapi*nd*ika's Grove, to the place where the Blessed One was; and on arriving there he bowed down before the Blessed One, and took his seat on one side. And when he was thus seated the venerable Sudhamma informed the Blessed One of all, both that he himself had said, and that *K*itta the householder had said.

The Blessed Buddha rebuked him, saying, 'This was improper, O foolish one, not according to rule, unsuitable, unworthy of a Sama*n*a, and ought not to have been done. How is it that you, O foolish one, could put down[1] and could lower by your censure[2] *K*itta the householder, he being a man of faith, a believing disciple, and a donor, a provider, and a supporter of the Sa*m*gha?' This will not conduce, O foolish one, either to the conversion of the unconverted, or to the increase of the converted; but rather to the unconverted not being converted, and to the turning back of those who have been

---

[1] Compare Dhammapada, p. 263, and *G*âtaka I, 191.

[2] Compare *G*âtaka I, 191, 356, 359, and Sutta Nipâta, verse 905.

converted.' And after he had rebuked him, and had delivered a religious discourse, he addressed the Bhikkhus, and said: 'Let therefore the Sa*m*gha, O Bhikkhus, carry out the Pa*t*isâra*n*iya-kamma (Act of Reconciliation)[1] against the Bhikkhu Sudhamma, saying, "You are to ask and obtain pardon of *K*itta the householder."'

6. 'Now thus, O Bhikkhus, should it be carried out. In the first place the Bhikkhu Sudhamma ought to be warned: when he has been warned, he ought to be reminded (of the Rule in the Pâtimokkha against which he has offended); when he has been reminded, he ought to be charged with the offence; when he has been charged with the offence, some discreet and able Bhikkhu ought to lay the matter before the Sa*m*gha, saying,

'"Let the venerable Sa*m*gha hear me. This Bhikkhu Sudhamma has put down, and has lowered by censure *K*itta the householder, a man of faith, a believing disciple, a donor, provider and supporter of the Sa*m*gha. If the time is fit for the Sa*m*gha to do so, let the Sa*m*gha carry out the Pa*t*isâra*n*iya-kamma against the Bhikkhu Sudhamma.

'"This is the motion (*ñ*atti).

[1] Childers proposes doubtingly to derive the word Pa*t*isâra*n*iya from the root smar; but that that is impossible is probably sufficiently evident from the meaning of the word, which is quite clear from the context of this, and from the following chapters. Now at p. 530 of the Lalita Vistara the common Pâli phrase sammodanîya*m* katha*m* sârâ*n*îya*m* vîtisâretvâ is represented by the Sanskrit sammodani*h* sa*m*ra*ñg*anî*h* kathâ*h* k*ri*tvâ. It is by no means impossible that this parallel may offer the true solution of the etymology of the Pâli words in question; (compare Sârâga as equal to sa*m*râga, sâratta to sa*m*rakta, &c. &c.) Pa*t*isâra*n*iya would then be equal to pratisa*m*ra*ñg*anîya. See Senart, Mahâvagga, p. 599.

'"Let the venerable Sa*m*gha hear me. This Bhikkhu (&c., as before, down to) supporter of the Sa*m*gha. The Sa*m*gha hereby carries out the Pa*t*isâra*n*iya-kamma against the Bhikkhu Sudhamma with the words, 'You are to ask and obtain pardon of *K*itta the householder.' Whosoever of the venerable ones approves of the carrying out of the Pa*t*isâra*n*iya-kamma against Sudhamma the Bhikkhu, let him remain silent. Whosoever approves not thereof, let him speak.

'"A second time I say the same thing. Let the venerable Sa*m*gha (&c., as before). A third time I say the same thing. Let the venerable Sa*m*gha (&c., as before).

'"The Pa*t*isâra*n*iya-kamma has been carried out against the Bhikkhu Sudhamma with the words, 'You are to ask and obtain pardon of *K*itta the householder.' The Sa*m*gha approves the motion. Therefore is it silent. Thus do I understand."'

19.

[Here the twelve cases of a proceeding against, and the twelve cases of a proceeding according to law are repeated of the Pa*t*isâra*n*iya-kamma in the words of chapters 2 and 3 of the Ta*gg*aniya-kamma.]

20[1].

1. 'There are five things, O Bhikkhus, which when they characterise a Bhikkhu, the Sa*m*gha, if it likes, should carry out the Pa*t*isâra*n*iya-kamma against him; (that is to say), when he goes about to bring

[1] See above, chapter 4.

loss on the laity—when he goes about to do harm to the laity—when he goes about to deprive the laity of their dwellings—when he reviles and finds fault with the laity—when he brings about division between the laity. These are the five things, O Bhikkhus, which (&c., as above, down to) against him.

'There are other five things, O Bhikkhus, which when they characterise a Bhikkhu, the Sa*m*gha, if it likes, should carry out the Pa*t*isâra*n*iya-kamma against him; (that is to say), when he speaks to the laity in dispraise of the Buddha—when he speaks to the laity in dispraise of the Dhamma—when he speaks to the laity in dispraise of the Sa*m*gha—when he puts laymen down, and lowers them by censure—when he does not fulfil a promise made in accordance with the Rules to the laity. These are the other five things, O Bhikkhus, which (&c., as before, down to) against him.

'There are five kinds of Bhikkhus, O Bhikkhus, against whom the Sa*m*gha, if it likes, should carry out the Pa*t*isâra*n*iya-kamma; (that is to say), one who goes about to bring loss on the laity (&c., as in the last paragraph, down to the end).'

Here end the four times five cases of suspicion.

21.

[Chapter 5, as to the right conduct of a Bhikkhu subjected to the Ta*gg*aniya-kamma, is repeated, reading Pa*t*isâra*n*iya for Ta*gg*aniya.]

Here end the eighteen duties which follow on a Pa*t*isâra*n*iya-kamma.

22.

1. So the Sa*m*gha carried out the Pa*t*isâra*n*iya-kamma against Sudhamma the Bhikkhu, saying, 'You are to ask and obtain pardon of *K*itta the householder. And after he had been subjected by the Sa*m*gha to the Pa*t*isâra*n*iya-kamma, though he went to Ma*kkh*ikâsa*nd*a, he was unable, being greatly troubled in his mind, to ask and obtain pardon of *K*itta the householder, but returned again even to Sâvatthi.

Then the Bhikkhus asked him, 'Has *K*itta the householder been induced by you to give you his pardon?'

'Indeed, though I went to Ma*kkh*ikâsa*nd*a, I was unable, being greatly troubled in my mind, to ask and obtain pardon of *K*itta the householder.'

They told this thing to the Blessed One.

2. 'Let, then, the Sa*m*gha, O Bhikkhus, appoint a companion messenger to Sudhamma the Bhikkhu, to ask and obtain pardon of *K*itta the householder.

'Now thus, O Bhikkhu, should the companion messenger be appointed. In the first place the Bhikkhu (who is to be sent) is to be asked (whether he is willing to go). After he has been asked, let some discreet and able Bhikkhu lay the matter before the Sa*m*gha, as follows:

'"Let the venerable Sa*m*gha hear me. If the time seems meet to the venerable Sa*m*gha, let the Sa*m*gha appoint such and such a Bhikkhu as a companion messenger to Sudhamma the Bhikkhu, to ask and obtain pardon of *K*itta the householder.

'"This is the motion (*ñ*atti).

'"Let the venerable Sa*m*gha hear me. The Sa*m*gha hereby appoints such and such a Bhikkhu as a companion messenger to Sudhamma the Bhikkhu, to ask and obtain pardon of *K*itta the householder. Whosoever of the venerable ones approves of such and such a Bhikkhu being appointed as a companion messenger to Sudhamma the Bhikkhu, let him remain silent. Whosoever approves not thereof, let him speak.

'"Such and such a Bhikkhu has been appointed by the Sa*m*gha (&c., as before). The Sa*m*gha approves thereof. Therefore is it silent. Thus do I understand."

3. 'Then, O Bhikkhus, let Sudhamma the Bhikkhu go, together with the Bhikkhu who is the companion messenger, to Ma*kkh*ikâsa*nd*a, and ask pardon of *K*itta the householder, saying, "Pardon me, O householder; I desire to gain once more thy good pleasure." If, when he thus speaks, he pardons him, it is well. If he pardon him not, the Bhikkhu who is the companion messenger should say, "Pardon him, O householder; he desires to gain once more thy good pleasure." If, when he thus speaks, he pardon him, it is well. If he pardon him not, the Bhikkhu who is the companion messenger should say, "Pardon him, O householder; I desire to gain thy good pleasure." If, when he thus speaks, he pardon him, it is well. If he pardon him not, the Bhikkhu who is the companion messenger should say, "Grant pardon, O householder, to this Bhikkhu, in the name of the Sa*m*gha (I ask it)." If (&c., as before, down to). If he pardon him not, the Bhikkhu who is the companion messenger—without going out of sight, and without going out of hearing,

of *K*itta the householder—should make Sudhamma the Bhikkhu arrange his robe on one shoulder, and squat down on his heels, and stretch forth his two hands with the palms together, and so confess his fault.'

23.

1. So the venerable Sudhamma went, with another Bhikkhu as companion messenger, to Ma*kkh*ikâsa*nd*a, and obtained pardon of *K*itta the householder. And he conducted himself aright, and he became subdued, and he sought for release (&c., as above, in chapters 6, 7, down to the end).

Here end the eighteen cases in which there ought to be a revocation of the Pa*t*isâra*n*iya-kamma.

24.

[In this chapter the Kammavâ*k*â of the revocation of the Pa*t*isâra*n*iya-kamma is given in words precisely similar to those of chapters 8 and 12.]

Here ends the fourth (Kamma), the Pa*t*isâra*n*iya-kamma.

V. THE UKKHEPANIYA-KAMMAS (ACTS OF SUSPENSION) for not acknowledging, and for not atoning for, an offence[1].

25.

1. Now at that time the Blessed Buddha was dwelling at Kosambî, in the Ghosita Ârâma. And at that time the venerable *Kh*anna[2], when he had committed a fault, was not willing to acknowledge the fault. Those Bhikkhus who were moderate were annoyed, murmured, and became indignant, saying, 'How can the venerable *Kh*anna act so?' And those Bhikkhus told the matter to the Blessed One.

Then the Blessed One on that occasion, and in that connection, after he had convened a meeting of the Bhikkhu-sa*m*gha, asked the Bhikkhus:

'Is it true, O Bhikkhus, as they say, that *Kh*anna

[1] There is no mention in the Pâtimokkha of any such proceeding. At the close of each of the four Pâ*t*idesaniya Rules there is a form of confession to be observed. It would seem from the following chapters, which are nowhere expressly confined to these four cases, that a similar confession was expected after the commission of an offence against any of the Pâtimokkha Rules. In the closing words of the Sa*m*ghâdisesa Rules, an older proceeding is mentioned, under which an offending Bhikkhu who has not confessed any breach of either of those thirteen Rules is to remain on probation for as many days as he has allowed to go by without confessing.

[2] On *Kh*anna's character, see also below, IV, 14, 1, XI, 1, 12–14, and Mahâ-parinibbâna Sutta VI, 4.

when he has committed a fault, is not willing to acknowledge the fault?'

'It is true, Lord!'

The Blessed Buddha rebuked him, saying, 'How, O Bhikkhus, can that foolish one act so? This will not conduce either to the conversion of the unconverted, or to the increase of the converted; but rather to those who have not been converted being not converted, and to the turning back of those who have been converted.'

And when the Blessed One had so rebuked him, and had delivered a religious discourse, he addressed the Bhikkhus and said: 'Let therefore the Sa*m*gha, O Bhikkhus, carry out against *Kh*anna the Bhikkhu the âpattiyâ adassane Ukkhepaniya-kamma (the Act of Suspension which follows on not acknowledging a fault) to the intent that he shall not eat or dwell together with the Sa*m*gha[1].

'Now thus, O Bhikkhus, should it be carried out.' [Here follow the formal words of the Kammavâ*k*â as in chapter 1. 4, with the necessary alterations owing to the difference of the fault and of the Kamma following on it. And at the end of the Kammavâ*k*â (after the words 'Thus I understand') the following sentence is added.]

'And send a proclamation, O Bhikkhus, from residence to residence[2]; saying, "*Kh*anna the Bhikkhu has been subjected by the Sa*m*gha to the Ukkhepaniya-kamma for not acknowledging a fault."'

---

[1] Compare Mahâvagga I, 79 generally, and § 2 of that chapter on the last clause (asambhoga*m* sa*m*ghena).

[2] On this phrase the Samanta Pâsâdikâ says, Âvâsa-parampara*ñ* *k*a bhikkhave sa*m*sathâ ti sabbâvâsesu âro*k*etha.

26.

[Here follow the twelve cases in which a Kamma is against the law, and the twelve in which it is according to law; and also the six permissive cases in which it may be carried out, if the Sa*m*gha likes, precisely as in chapters 2, 3, and 4.]

27[1].

1. 'A Bhikkhu against whom the Ukkhepaniya-kamma that follows on not acknowledging a fault has been carried out ought to conduct himself aright. And herein this is the right conduct: he ought not to confer the upasampadâ—he ought not to give a nissaya[2]—he ought not to provide himself with a sâma*n*era[2]—he ought not to accept the office of giving exhortation to the nuns[2]—if he have accepted that office, he ought not to exhort the nuns[2]—he ought not to commit the offence for which the Ukkhepaniya-kamma that follows on not acknowledging a fault has been carried out against him—nor any offence of a similar kind—nor any worse offence—he ought not to find fault with the proceeding (that has been carried out against him)—nor with (the Bhikkhus) who have carried it out—[3]he ought not to accept from a regular Bhikkhu reverence, or

[1] As this chapter, containing the sammâ-vattanâ or right conduct, differs from the corresponding chapters of the preceding Kammas (chapters 5, 10, 15, and 21), it is here set out in full.

[2] See the passages quoted above (chapter 5).

[3] The passage between these two figures recurs at II, 1, 1.

service, or salutation, or respect, nor allow him to provide a seat, or a sleeping-place, or water for the feet, or a foot-stool[4], or a foot-towel[5] for him, nor to carry his bowl or his robe, nor to shampoo him[3]—he ought not to harass a regular Bhikkhu with a complaint that he has failed in morality, or in conduct, or in doctrine, or in the mode of obtaining a livelihood—he ought not to cause division between a Bhikkhu and the Bhikkhus—he ought not to wear the outward signs of being a layman, or of being a follower of some other doctrine[6]—he ought not to follow the professors of other doctrines—he ought to follow the Bhikkhus—he ought to train himself in the training of the Bhikkhus—he ought not to dwell under one and the same roof with a regular Bhikkhu, whether in a place formally declared to be a residence, or to be not a residence, or in a place which is neither the one nor the other,—on seeing a regular Bhikkhu he ought to rise from his seat—he ought not to touch[7] a regular Bhikkhu, either inside or outside (of the residence)—he ought not to raise objections against a regular Bhikkhu's taking part in the Uposatha ceremony[8]—or in the Pavâra*n*â

[4] At II, 1, 1. Buddhaghosa explains this word as confined to a stool on which to place feet that have been washed (dhota-pâda-*th*apanaka*m*).

[5] Buddhaghosa says on the same expression in II, 1, 1, pâdakathaliyan (sic) ti adhota-pâda-*th*apanaka*m* pâda-gha*m*sana*m* vâ.

[6] The Samanta Pâsâdikâ says, Na titthiya-dha*g*o ti kusa*k*îrâdi*m* na dhâretabba*m*. Compare the use of arahad-dha*g*a*m* at *G*âtaka I, 65.

[7] The Samanta Pâsâdikâ says, Na âsâdetabbo ti na pâsâdetabbo (compare the use of âsâdesi, *G*âtaka I, 481). Anto vâ bahi vâ ti vihârassa anto vâ bahi vâ.

[8] On this and the following sentences compare the passages quoted above, chapter 5.

ceremony—he ought not to issue command (to a junior, inhibiting him from going beyond the bounds, or summoning him to appear before the elders)—he ought not to set on foot a censure against any other Bhikkhu—he ought not to ask another Bhikkhu to give him leave (to rebuke that Bhikkhu)—he ought not to warn (another Bhikkhu whom he supposes to be offending)—he ought not to remind (another Bhikkhu of a law against which he supposes that Bhikkhu to be offending)—and he ought not to associate with the Bhikkhus.'

Here end the forty-three duties which follow on an Ukkhepaniya-kamma for not acknowledging a fault.

28.

1. So the Sa*m*gha carried out against *Kh*anna the Bhikkhu the Ukkhepaniya-kamma for not acknowledging a fault to the effect that he should not eat or dwell together with the Sa*m*gha. And after he had been subjected by the Sa*m*gha to the Ukkhepaniya-kamma for not acknowledging his fault he went from that residence to another residence. And the Bhikkhus there did no reverence to him, rose not from their seats to welcome him, rendered him not service, offered him not salutation, paid not respect to him, offered him not hospitality, nor esteemed him, nor honoured him, nor supported him. And when he received from the Bhikkhus neither hospitality, nor welcome, nor esteem, nor honour, nor

support, he went from that residence to another residence. And the Bhikkhus there did no reverence to him, rose not from their seats to welcome him, rendered him not service (&c., as before, down to:) he went from that residence to another residence. And when he received no hospitality he returned back again even to Kosambî. Then he conducted himself aright, and he became subdued, and he sought for release, and going up to the Bhikkhus he spake as follows: 'I, Sirs, having been subjected by the Sa*m*gha to the Ukkhepaniya-kamma am conducting myself aright in accordance thereto, and I am become subdued, and I seek for release. What now should I do?'

They told this thing to the Blessed One.

'Then, O Bhikkhus, let the Sa*m*gha revoke the Ukkhepaniya-kamma for not acknowledging his fault carried out against *Kh*anna the Bhikkhu.

2. 'There are five things, O Bhikkhus, [&c., the rest of this section bearing the same relation to the last, which chapter 6, § 2, does to chapter 5.]'

Here end the forty-three cases [in which an Ukkhepaniya-kamma for not acknowledging a fault is not to be revoked].

29.

'There are five things, O Bhikkhus, [&c., as in chapter 7. This chapter being the exact opposite of chapter 28.]

Here end the forty-three cases [in which an Ukkhepaniya-kamma for not acknowledging a fault ought to be revoked].

30.

'And thus, O Bhikkhus, should the revocation be carried out [&c., as before, in chapters 8, 12, &c.]'

Here ends the fifth Kamma, namely, the Ukkhepaniya-kamma for not acknowledging a fault.

31.

Now at that time the Blessed Buddha was dwelling at Kosambî, in the Ghosita Ârâma. And at that time the venerable *Kh*anna, when he had committed a fault, was not willing to atone for that fault [&c., the proceeding in this case being the same, and laid down in the same words as the proceeding in the last case, chapters 25–30].

Here ends the sixth Kamma; namely, the Ukkhepaniya-kamma on not atoning for a fault[1].

[1] It will be seen from the above chapters, and especially from chapter 27, that the Ukkhepaniya-kamma is an Act, not of expulsion, but only of suspension. The ten cases in which a member of the Order could be expelled are those given above in Mahâvagga I, 60; and the technical word for 'expel' is nâseti.

VI. The Ukkhepaniya-kamma for not renouncing a sinful doctrine.

32.

1. Now at that time the Blessed Buddha was staying at Sâvatthi, in the *G*etavana, the grove of Anâthapi*nd*ika. And at that time a certain Bhikkhu by name Ari*tth*a, who had formerly been a vulture tormentor[1], had fallen into a sinful belief of this kind; (that is to say), 'In this wise do I understand the Dhamma preached by the Blessed One, that to him who practises those things which have been declared by the Blessed One to be impediments[2],

[1] In his commentary on the Pâ*k*ittiya, quoted by Oldenberg in his note on this passage, Buddhaghosa explains this expression to mean 'born in a family of vulture slayers.' This does not help us much, vulture slaying as a regular occupation being somewhat incomprehensible, and not referred to elsewhere. Whatever its meaning, the occupation referred to is perhaps the origin of, or should at least be compared with, the statement of Ktesias (circa B.C. 400) in his 'Indika' (ed. C. Müller, Fragment xiii), that the Indians used not dogs but vultures, which they trained for that purpose, in hunting hares and foxes. Lassen in his 'Indische Alterthumskunde,' II, 638, 639, thinks this statement not incredible, very fairly comparing the use of falcons in Europe in the Middle Ages. It is not impossible that the correct rendering here should be 'vulture-catcher,' or 'vulture-trainer;' but we prefer to be literal.

[2] The only one of such things (Dhammâ) known to us elsewhere in the Vinaya Pi*t*aka itself is deliberate falsehood. This is stated in Mahâvagga II, 3, 3 to be an impediment, which is explained by the Old Commentator, at Mahâvagga II, 3, 7, to mean an impediment to the attainment of the *Gh*ânas, and other things of similar nature.

there will arise no impediment sufficient (to prevent his acquiring spiritual gifts)[1].'

Now many Bhikkhus heard that Ari*tth*a, who had formerly (&c., as before, down to:) to be impediments. And those Bhikkhus went up to the place where Ari*tth*a the Bhikkhu, who had formerly been a vulture tormentor, was; and on arriving there they asked Ari*tth*a the Bhikkhu, who had formerly been a vulture tormentor, 'Is it true, friend Ari*tth*a, as they say, that you have fallen into a sinful belief (&c., as above, down to) spiritual gifts?'

'Certainly[2]! I do so understand the Dhamma preached by the Blessed One (&c., as before).'

2. 'Say not so, friend Ari*tth*a. Bear not false-witness against the Blessed One. For neither is it seemly to bring a false accusation against the Blessed One, nor could the Blessed One have spoken so. By many a figure, friend Ari*tth*a, have the things which are impediments been declared to be impediments by the Blessed One, and also to be sufficient to prevent him who cultivates them (from attaining to spiritual gifts)[3]. Lusts have been declared by the Blessed One to be of short taste[4], full of pain, and full of despair, things wherein the danger is great. Lusts have been declared by the Blessed One to be like the bones of a skeleton, full of pain, and full of despair, things wherein the danger is

[1] This is word for word the same speech as that which is condemned in the 68th and 70th Pâ*k*ittiyas.

[2] Byâ is only known to us as an intensive particle occurring in passages like the present one.

[3] So far this section is word for word the same as the 68th and the 70th Pâ*k*ittiyas.

[4] Quoted at Dhammapada, ver. 186.

great. Lusts have been declared by the Blessed One to be like lumps of raw meat, full (&c., as before, down to:) is great. Lusts have been declared by the Blessed One to be like torches made of a wisp of hay . . . . , like a pit full of live coals[1] . . . . , like the visions of a dream . . . . , like a beggar's portion . . . . , like the fruits of trees . . . . , like the sword and the slaughter-house . . . . , like darts and clubs . . . . , like snakes and creeping things, full of pain, and full of despair, things wherein the danger is great.'

Yet notwithstanding that Bhikkhu Ari*tth*a, who had formerly been a vulture tormentor, when thus being addressed by the Bhikkhus, remained steadfastly adhering, in the very same way, and with violence, to that sinful doctrine, declaring, 'Verily I do so understand the Dhamma preached by the Blessed One (&c., as before, in § 1).'

3. Then since those Bhikkhus were unable to move Ari*tth*a the Bhikkhu, who had formerly been a vulture tormentor, from that sinful doctrine, they went up to the place where the Blessed One was; and when they had come there, they told this thing to the Blessed One.

And the Blessed One on that occasion, and in that connection, convened a meeting of the Bhikkhu-sa*m*gha, and asked Ari*tth*a the Bhikkhu, who had formerly been a vulture tormentor, 'Is it true, as they say, Ari*tth*a, that you have fallen into a sinful doctrine of such a kind (&c., as before, in § 1)?'

'Certainly, Lord! I do so understand (&c., as before, in § 1).'

[1] Compare *G*âtaka I, 231, 232.

'How can you, O foolish one, so understand the Dhamma preached by me? Have I not, by many a figure, O foolish one, declared the things which are impediments to be impediments, and sufficient to prevent him who cultivates them (from attaining to spiritual gifts)? Have not lusts been by me declared to be of short taste (&c., as above, down to:) like snakes and creeping things, full of danger, full of despair, things wherein the danger is great? Yet now you, O foolish one, by your having grasped that doctrine wrongly[1], are not only bearing false-witness against us, but you are also rooting yourself up, and are giving rise to much demerit, the which will be to you for a long time for an evil and a woe. This will not conduce, O foolish one, either to the conversion of the unconverted, or to the increase of the converted; but rather to those who are unconverted not being converted, and to the turning back of those who have been converted[2].'

When he had thus rebuked him, and had delivered a religious discourse, he addressed the Bhikkhus, and said: 'Let therefore the Sa*m*gha, O Bhikkhus, carry out against Ari*tth*a the Bhikkhu, who was formerly a vulture tormentor, the Ukkhepaniya-kamma for not renouncing a sinful doctrine, to the intent that he shall not eat or dwell together with the Sa*m*gha.'

4. 'Now thus, O Bhikkhus, should it be carried out. In the first place the Bhikkhu Ari*tth*a ought

[1] Compare Mahâ-parinibbâna Sutta IV, 8–11.

[2] Up to this point the whole chapter recurs as the Introductory Story in the Sutta-vibhaṅga on the 68th Pâ*k*ittiya.

to be warned [&c., as in chapter 25, down to the end of the Kammavâkâ, including the supplementary sentence as to the proclamation].'

33.

[Here follow the twelve cases in which the Kamma is against the law, the twelve cases in which it is according to law, the six permissive cases in which it can be carried out if the Samgha likes, and the eighteen divisions of the right conduct for the convicted Bhikkhu to pursue, precisely as in chapters 2, 3, 4, and 5, reading 'Ukkhepaniya-kamma for not renouncing a sinful doctrine,' instead of 'Tagganiya-kamma.']

34.

1. So the Samgha carried out against Arittha the Bhikkhu, who had formerly been a vulture tormentor, the Ukkhepaniya-kamma for not renouncing a sinful doctrine, to the intent that he should not eat nor dwell with the Samgha. And when he had been thus subjected by the Samgha to the Ukkhepaniya-kamma for not renouncing a sinful doctrine, he left the Order.

Those Bhikkhus who were moderate were annoyed, murmured, and became indignant, saying, 'How can Arittha the Bhikkhu, having been subjected by the Samgha to the Ukkhepaniya-kamma for not renouncing a sinful doctrine, leave the Order?' And those Bhikkhus told the matter to the Blessed One.

Then the Blessed One on that occasion, and in that connection, convened a meeting of the Bhikkhu-sa*m*gha, and asked the Bhikkhus, 'Is it true, O Bhikkhus, as they say, that Ari*tth*a the Bhikkhu, having been subjected (&c., as before, down to) left the Order?'

'It is true, Lord.'

The Blessed Buddha rebuked him, saying, 'How can Ari*tth*a the Bhikkhu (&c., as before, down to) leave the Order? This will not conduce either to the conversion of the unconverted, nor to the increase of the converted; but rather to those who have not been converted not being converted, and to the turning back of those who have been converted.'

And when he had rebuked him, and delivered a religious discourse, the Blessed One addressed the Bhikkhus, and said: 'Let then the Sa*m*gha, O Bhikkhus, revoke the Ukkhepaniya-kamma for not renouncing a sinful doctrine, which has been carried out against Ari*tth*a the Bhikkhu.

'There are five things, O Bhikkhus, [&c., as before, in chapters 6 and 7, down to the end.]'

Here end the eighteen cases in which a revocation of the Ukkhepaniya-kamma on not renouncing a sinful doctrine should be carried out.

35.

'Now thus, O Bhikkhus, should it be carried out,' &c. [Here follows the Kammavâkâ for the revocation of a Kamma precisely as in chapter 8, with the necessary alterations.]

Here ends the seventh (Kamma), the Ukkhepaniya-kamma on not renouncing a sinful doctrine.

Here ends the First Khandhaka, the Khandhaka on the Kammas.

SECOND KHANDHAKA.

PROBATION AND PENANCE.

1.

1. Now at that time the Blessed Buddha was staying at Sâvatthi, in the *G*etavana, Anâthapi*nd*ika's Grove. And at that time Bhikkhus who had been placed on probation[1] used to accept reverence and service and salutation and respect from regular Bhikkhus; and to allow them to provide a seat, or a sleeping-place, or water for the feet, or a foot-stool, or a foot-towel for them; and to carry their bowl or their robe, and to shampoo them[2].

---

[1] There are four principal kinds of probation; the first of which was required when the follower of another of the reforming sects was received into the Buddhist Order, and is described in Mahâvagga I, 38. The other three, which follow on the commission of a Sa*m*ghâdisesa offence, are more particularly described below in the third Khandhaka. The Pâli names of these four are respectively apa*t*i*kkh*anna-parivâsa, pa*t*i*kkh*anna-parivâsa, suddhanta-parivâsa, and samodhâna-parivâsa.

No conclusion should be drawn against this statement from the passage above at I, 9, 1; though Se*yy*asaka's conduct, as there described, would not have rendered him liable to any one of these four principal probationary proceedings. For he is said to have been guilty of many offences (âpatti-bahulo). The accompanying enumeration must be taken, not as a description of those offences, but as additional to them. And the probation imposed upon him must have been for concealing one or more of the many offences not particularly specified.

[2] All these expressions recur above, I, 27, 1.

Those Bhikkhus who were moderate were annoyed, murmured, and became indignant, saying, 'How can Bhikkhus who have been placed on probation accept reverence (&c., as above, down to) shampoo them?'

And those Bhikkhus told this thing to the Blessed One.

Then the Blessed One on that occasion, and in that connection, convened a meeting of the Bhikkhu-sa*m*gha, and asked the Bhikkhus: 'Is it true, O Bhikkhus, as they say, that Bhikkhus who have been placed on probation accept reverence (&c., as before, down to) shampoo them?'

'It is true, Lord.'

The Blessed Buddha rebuked them, saying, 'How can those Bhikkhus (&c., as before, down to) shampoo them? This will not conduce, O Bhikkhus (&c., as usual, down to)[1] turning back of those who have been converted.'

And when he had rebuked them, and had delivered a religious discourse, he addressed the Bhikkhus, saying, 'A Bhikkhu who has been placed on probation ought not to accept reverence (&c., as before, down to) shampoo them. Whosoever does so, shall be guilty of a dukka*t*a offence. I prescribe, O Bhikkhus, to those Bhikkhus who have been placed on probation to do [all the courtesies, duties, and services mentioned above[2]] for one another, according to their seniority. I prescribe, O Bhikkhus, five things (as permissible) to Bhikkhus who have been placed on probation,

[1] See I, 1, 2, down to the end.

[2] That is, in the lists recurring in the previous paragraphs, and given in full at I, 27, 1.

according to their seniority; (that is to say), the Uposatha ceremony, the Pavâra*n*â ceremony, the share in robes for the rainy season, in things dedicated to the Sa*m*gha[1], and in food.

2. 'Therefore, O Bhikkhus, do I make known to you a rule of conduct for Bhikkhus who have been placed on probation, according to which they ought to conduct themselves aright. And herein this is the right conduct. He ought not to confer the Upasampadâ (&c., as above, in I, 1, 5, down to the end)[2].

'A Bhikkhu who has been placed on probation ought not, O Bhikkhus, to walk in front of, or to sit down in front of, a regular Bhikkhu. Whichever belonging to that company of Bhikkhus shall be the worst seat[3], or the worst sleeping-place, or the worst room[4], that shall be given to that Bhikkhu, and there-

[1] Ono*g*anam, which the Samanta Pâsâdikâ explains by 'visag*g*ana*m*.' Compare the use of ono*g*esi at Dipava*m*sa XIII, 29. The etymology of the word is unknown to us.

[2] The Samanta Pâsâdikâ has here the following note on sava*k*aniya*m*, which should be compared with the shorter note on the same word given above, I, 1, 5: Na sava*k*aniya*m* kâtabban ti palibodhatthâya pakkosanatthâya vâ sava*k*aniya*m* na kâtabba*m*. Palibodhatthâya hi karonto, aha*m* âyasmanta*m* imasmi*m* vatthusmi*m* sava*k*aniya*m* karomi, imamhâ âvâsâ ekapada*m* pi mâ pakkami yâva na ta*m* adhikara*n*a*m* vûpasanta*m* hotîti; evam karoti. Pakkosanatthâya karonto, aha*m* te sava*k*aniya*m* karomi, ehi mayâ saddhi*m* vinaya-dharâna*m* sammukhibhâva*m* ga*kkh*âmâ ti: eva*m* karoti.

[3] Buddhaghosa says here, Âsanapariyanto bhattaggâdîsu sa*m*gha-navak-âsana*m* vu*kk*ati, svassa dâtabbo. Pariyanta is used here in the same sense as in the 22nd Nissaggiya.

[4] Vihâra. In later times this word is no doubt always, or almost always, used to designate the whole of a building in which several or many Bhikkhus resided. In the older literature it always,

with shall he content himself. A Bhikkhu who has been placed under probation ought not, O Bhikkhus, to visit the families who support a regular Bhikkhu (by officiating, in order to do so, as the companion who precedes or follows that regular Bhikkhu)—he ought not to devote himself to a forest life—he ought not to devote himself to living on alms personally received[1]—he ought not to cause an alms to be brought out to him with the object of escaping an extension of his probationary term[2], thinking, "Let them not recognise me" (as one who has been placed under probation)[3].

'A Bhikkhu who has been placed on probation ought, O Bhikkhus, to announce the fact of his having been so placed when he arrives at a residence as an incoming Bhikkhu—he ought to announce the fact to an incoming Bhikkhu—he ought to announce the fact at an Uposatha meeting—he ought to announce the fact at a Pavâranâ meeting—and, if he be sick, he ought to announce the fact at such meetings by means of a messenger[4].

or almost always, denotes the dwelling-place, the private apartment, of a single Bhikkhu.

[1] That is, to refrain from salâka-bhatta, &c.

[2] The Samanta Pâsâdikâ says, Tappakkayâ 'ti nihatabhatto hutvâ vihâren' eva nisîditvâ bhuñganto vattiyo ganayissâmi gakkhato me bhikkhû disvâ anârokentassa rattikkhedo (cap. 2) siyâ 'ti iminâ kâranena pindapâto na niharâpetabbo.

[3] Mâ mam gânimsû 'ti mâ mam ekabhikkhu pi gânâtû 'ti ka iminâ agghâsayena vihâre sâmanerehi pakâpetvâ bhuñgitum labbhati. Gâmam pindâya pavisitabbam eva. Gilânassa pana navakammam âkariyupagghâyakikkâdipasu (sic) tassa vâ vihâre yeva akkhitum vattati. Sake pi gâme anekasatâ bhikkhû vikaranti na sakkâ hoti ârokentum gâmakâvâsam gantvâ sabhâgatthâne vasitum vattati.

[4] This paragraph, it will be seen, is omitted in three out of the four following cases, which are otherwise similar in every respect,

3. 'A Bhikkhu who has been placed on probation ought not, O Bhikkhus, to go away from a residence in which Bhikkhus are living to a residence in which no Bhikkhus are living, unless with a regular Bhikkhu, or in time of danger. A Bhikkhu who has been placed on probation ought not, O Bhikkhus, to go away from a residence in which Bhikkhus are living to a place which is not a residence[1] and where no Bhikkhus are living, unless with a regular Bhikkhu, or in time of danger. A Bhikkhu (&c., as before) ought not to go away from a residence in which Bhikkhus are living, either to a residence or to a place which is not a residence, and where Bhikkhus are not living, unless (&c., as before)[2]. . . . from a place which is not a residence, but where Bhikkhus are living, to a place which is a residence, but where Bhikkhus are not living . . . . from a place which is not a residence, but where Bhikkhus are living, to a place which is not a residence and where Bhikkhus are not living . . . . from a place which is no residence, but where Bhikkhus are living, either to a place which is not a residence or to a residence where no Bhikkhus are living . . . . from a place which is either a residence or not a residence, to a place which is a residence, but where no Bhikkhus are living . . . . from a place which is either a residence or no residence, but where Bhikkhus are living, to a place

as regards the right conduct which is laid down for them, to the present case of the Bhikkhus who have been placed on probation.

[1] The Samanta Pâsâdikâ says, (Abhikkhuko âvâso) na hi tattha vuttharattiyo ga*n*anupikâ honti. pakatattena pana saddhi*m* va*tt*ati. Anâvâso nâma *k*etiyaghara*m* bodhighara*m* samma*ñ*gani-a*tt*ako dârua*tt*ako pâniyamâ*l*o va*kk*aku*t*i dvârako*tth*ako 'ti evamâdi.

[2] In the text read âvâso vâ anâvâso vâ.

which is not a residence and where no Bhikkhus are living . . . . from a place which is either a residence or not a residence, but where Bhikkhus are living, to a place which is either a residence or not a residence, but where no Bhikkhus are living, unless with a regular Bhikkhu or in time of danger.

'A Bhikkhu who has been placed on probation ought not, O Bhikkhus, to go away from a residence where Bhikkhus are living to a residence where Bhikkhus are living, but where there may be Bhikkhus of different communities from his own (unless, &c., as before). [The same changes as in the last series are here rung upon this inhibition, down to] . . . . from a place which is either a residence or not a residence, but where Bhikkhus are living, to a place which is either a residence or not a residence, and where Bhikkhus are living, but where there may be Bhikkhus of different communities from his own (unless, &c., as before).

'A Bhikkhu who has been placed on probation ought to go, O Bhikkhus, from a residence where Bhikkhus are living to a residence where Bhikkhus are living, and where there are Bhikkhus of the same community (with himself), if he knows, "This very day I can go there." [Here follow the same permutations and combinations as in the last two series.]

4. 'A Bhikkhu who has been placed on probation ought not, O Bhikkhus, to dwell with a regular Bhikkhu in a residence under one and the same roof—nor in a place which is not a residence under one and the same roof—nor in a place which is either a residence or not a residence under one and the same roof. On seeing a regular Bhikkhu he

ought to rise from his seat[1]; and he ought to offer his seat to a regular Bhikkhu. He ought not to sit down on one and the same seat with a regular Bhikkhu; when a regular Bhikkhu is seated on a low seat he ought not to sit down on a high seat[2]; when a regular Bhikkhu is seated on the ground he ought not to sit down on a seat[3]; he ought not to walk up and down on the same *k*aṅkama[4] with a regular Bhikkhu; when a regular Bhikkhu is walking up and down on a low *k*aṅkama he ought not to walk up and down on a higher *k*aṅkama; when a regular Bhikkhu is walking up and down on the ground he ought not to walk up and down on a (properly prepared) *k*aṅkama.

'A Bhikkhu who has been placed on probation ought not, O Bhikkhus, to dwell (&c., all the other acts mentioned in the last paragraph being here repeated down to the end) with a Bhikkhu senior to himself who has been placed on probation.... with a Bhikkhu who has been thrown back to the commencement of his term of probation .... with a Bhikkhu who has rendered himself liable to the Mânatta discipline[5] .... with a Bhikkhu undergoing the Mânatta discipline .... with a Bhikkhu who is in a position to receive rehabilitation[5].

'If a meeting of four Bhikkhus, of whom one is

[1] This recurs in Khandhaka I, chapter 27.

[2] Compare the 69th Sekhiya.

[3] Compare the 68th Sekhiya.

[4] A narrow space of open ground, levelled and cleared of jungle, for the purpose of being used to walk up and down upon when meditating. See our note on Mahâvagga V, 1, 14.

[5] On these disciplines and on rehabilitation, see the following Khandhaka.

a probationer, should place a Bhikkhu on probation, or throw him back to the beginning of his probationary course, or subject him to the Mânatta discipline—or if a meeting of twenty Bhikkhus, of whom one is a probationer, should rehabilitate a Bhikkhu, that, O Bhikkhus, is an invalid act, and need not be obeyed[1].'

Here end the ninety-four duties encumbent on a probationer.

2.

1. Now the venerable Upâli went up to the place where the Blessed One was; and on arriving there, he saluted the Blessed One, and took his seat on one side. And when he was so seated the venerable Upâli said to the Blessed One: 'Now in what case, Lord, can there be an interruption of the probationary period of a Bhikkhu who has been placed on probation[2]?'

'There are three ways of interruption of the probationary period, O Upâli, of a Bhikkhu who has been placed on probation; (that is to say), by

[1] Compare Mahavâgga IX, 4, 1.

[2] Literally, 'breaking of the nights.' The time of probation was reckoned, not by days, but by nights; and in either of the three cases which follow the reckoning was interrupted, and had to begin afresh.

dwelling together[1], by dwelling alone[2], and by not announcing[3].

'These are the three ways of interruption to the probationary period, O Upâli, of a Bhikkhu who has been placed under probation.'

3[4].

1. Now at that time, since there was a great company of the Bhikkhus gathered together at Sâvatthi, those Bhikkhus who had been placed on probation did not know how to carry out their probation correctly.

They told this thing to the Blessed One.

'I prescribe to you, O Bhikkhus, to carry out your probation correctly. Now thus, O Bhikkhus, ought you to postpone[5] the probation. The Bhikkhu who has been placed on probation is to go up to a single Bhikkhu, and arranging his robe on one shoulder, and squatting down on his heels, and stretching forth his hands with the palms together, he is to say: "I postpone my probation." Then the probation is postponed. Or he is to say: "I postpone

[1] Buddhaghosa explains this to mean when the probationer has done any of the things forbidden in II, 1, 4.

[2] That is, when the probationer has done any of the things forbidden in II, 1, 3.

[3] That is, when the probationer has omitted to make any of the announcements prescribed at the end of II, 1, 2.

[4] This chapter is repeated below, chap. 8, in reference to Bhikkhus undergoing the Mânatta discipline.

[5] That is, if it should be impossible during the time immediately succeeding the imposition of probation to fulfil all the thereto necessary duties, then a Bhikkhu might postpone the fulfilment to some more convenient season.

the duties (i. e. of a probationer)." Then also the probation is postponed.'

2. Now at that time the Bhikkhus who were at Sâvatthi went away hither and thither, and the Bhikkhus who had been placed on probation were not able to carry out their probation correctly[1].

They told this thing to the Blessed One.

'I prescribe to you, O Bhikkhus, to take upon yourselves again the probation (which had been postponed). Now thus, O Bhikkhus, ought you to take it upon yourselves again. The Bhikkhu who has been placed under probation is to go up to a single Bhikkhu, and arranging his robe on one shoulder, and squatting down on his heels, and stretching forth his hands with the palms together, he is to say: "I take my probation again upon myself." Then the probation is resumed. Or he is to say: "I take the duties (i. e. of a probationer) upon myself again." Then also is the probation resumed.'

Here end the duties encumbent on a probationer.

4.

1. Now at that time Bhikkhus, who had rendered themselves liable to be thrown back to the commencement (of their probationary course)[2], used to

---

[1] The Samanta Pâsâdikâ here says, Eva*m* vatta*m* samâdiyitvâ parivutta-parivâsassa mânatta*m* ga*n*hato puna vatta-samâdâna-ki*kk*a*m* n' atthi samâdinna-vatto yeva hi esa. Tasmâssa *kh*âratta*m* mânatta*m* dâtabba*m*, *k*i*nn*a-mânatto abbhetabbo, eva*m* anâpattiko hutvâ suddhante pati*tth*ito tisso sikkhâ pûretvâ dukkhass' anta*m* karissatîti.

[2] This is fully explained in the next Khandhaka.

accept reverence [&c., as before in chapter 1, reading throughout 'Bhikkhus liable to be thrown back to the beginning of their probationary course' for 'Bhikkhus who had been placed on probation[1];' and omitting in chapter 2 the announcements referred to there in our note].

5.

[In this chapter the same rules are laid down, word for word, as in the last, reading throughout for 'Bhikkhus liable to be thrown back to the beginning of their probationary course,' 'Bhikkhus liable to be subjected to the Mânatta discipline[2].']

6.

[In this chapter the same rules for the Mânatta, or Penance, are laid down word for word as those in chapter 1, §§ 1, 2, 3, and 4, for the probation, reading throughout 'Bhikkhus who are going through the Mânatta discipline' for 'Bhikkhus who have been placed under probation.' There are, however, one or two minor points of difference, which are as follows:

1. At the end of the announcements (chapter 1,

[1] In the text alter the words 'Instead of sa*m*ghena parivâso dinno hoti read sa*m*ghena mûlâya pa*t*ikassanâraho kato hoti' into 'Instead of parivâsikâ bhikkhû read mûlâya pa*t*ikassanârahâ bhikkhû.'

[2] This is fully explained in the next Khandhaka.

§ 2) there is inserted the injunction, 'He ought to announce the fact every day.'

2. In the passages about going from one residence to another (chapter 1, § 3) read 'unless with the Saṁgha' instead of 'unless with a regular Bhikkhu.'][1]

7.

1. Now the venerable Upâli went up to the place where the Blessed One was; and on arriving there, he saluted the Blessed One, and took his seat on one side. And when he was so seated the venerable Upâli said to the Blessed One: 'Now in what case, Lord, can there be an interruption of the Mânatta discipline[2] of a Bhikkhu who is undergoing that discipline?'

'There are four ways of interruption of the Mânatta discipline, O Upâli, of a Bhikkhu who is undergoing that discipline; (that is to say), by dwelling together[3], by dwelling alone[3], by not announcing[3], and by living with less than four other Bhikkhus[4]. These are the four ways (&c., as before, down to) undergoing that discipline.'

---

[1] It will be seen, therefore, that there is very little, one might almost say no practical, difference between the Parivâsa, which we have rendered 'probation,' and the Mânatta, which we have usually left untranslated, and sometimes rendered 'penance.' Neither the one nor the other are at present enforced anywhere among the Buddhists.

[2] See chapter 2, note 1.

[3] See the notes above on chapter 2.

[4] The Samanta Pâsâdikâ says, ûne gaṇe ti kattâro vâ atirekâ vâ.

8.

[In this chapter the means of postponing and resuming the Mânatta penance are laid down, word for word, as in chapter 3, reading 'Bhikkhus who are undergoing the Mânatta discipline' for 'Bhikkhus who have been placed on probation.']

9.

[This chapter is word for word the same as chapter 1, reading 'Bhikkhus who have rendered themselves capable of receiving rehabilitation' for 'Bhikkhus who have been placed on probation.']

Here ends the Second Khandhaka, called the Khandhaka on Probationers, &c.

THIRD KHANDHAKA.

PROBATION AND PENANCE (CONTINUED).

1.

1. Now at that time the Blessed Buddha was staying at Sâvatthi, in the *G*etavana, Anâthapi*n-d*ika's Grove. And at that time the venerable Udâyi committed an offence, to wit, the first Sa*m*ghâdisesa offence, and did not conceal it. He told the Bhikkhus, saying, 'I have committed an offence—the first Sa*m*ghâdisesa offence—and do not conceal it. What now shall I do?'

They told this thing to the Blessed One.

'Then, O Bhikkhus, let the Sa*m*gha lay the Mânatta penalty on Udâyi the Bhikkhu for the space of six days on account of that offence—the first Sa*m*ghâdisesa—which he has not concealed.

2. 'Now thus, O Bhikkhus, ought it to be laid upon him. Udâyi the Bhikkhu ought to go up, O Bhikkhus, before the Sa*m*gha; and, arranging his robe on one shoulder, he ought to bow down at the feet of the elder Bhikkhus, and squatting down on his heels, and stretching forth his hands with the palms together, he ought to say as follows:

'"I, venerable Sirs, have committed an offence—the first Sa*m*ghâdisesa—which I have not concealed. I ask the Sa*m*gha (to impose upon me) the Mânatta penalty for six days on account of this offence—the first Sa*m*ghâdisesa offence—which I have not concealed."'

[This speech is repeated three times.]

3. 'Some discreet and able Bhikkhu should then lay the matter before the Sa*m*gha, as follows:

'"Let the venerable Sa*m*gha hear me. Udâyi the Bhikkhu has committed an offence—the first Sa*m*ghâdisesa offence—which he has not concealed. And he asks the Sa*m*gha for the Mânatta penalty for six days on account of that offence—the first Sa*m*ghâdisesa offence—which he has not concealed.

'"If the time seem meet to the Sa*m*gha, let the Sa*m*gha impose a Mânatta of six days' duration on Udâyi the Bhikkhu for that one offence—the first Sa*m*ghâdisesa offence—which he has not concealed.

'"This is the motion (*ñ*atti).

'"The Sa*m*gha hereby imposes a Mânatta of six days on Udâyi the Bhikkhu for that one offence—the first Sa*m*ghâdisesa offence—which he has not concealed.

'"Whosoever of the venerable ones approves of the imposition of a Mânatta (&c., as in the last paragraph, down to) not concealed, let him remain silent. Whosoever approves not, let him speak.

'"A second time I say the same thing (&c., as before in the last two paragraphs). A third time I say the same thing (&c., as before).

'"The Sa*m*gha has imposed a Mânatta of six days' duration (&c., as before, in the words of the motion, down to) not concealed. The Sa*m*gha approves thereof. Therefore is it silent. Thus do I understand."'

2.

1. When he had done the Mânatta he told the Bhikkhus, saying, 'Friends, I committed an offence—the first Sa*m*ghâdisesa offence—which I had not concealed. And I asked the Sa*m*gha for a Mânatta of six days' duration for that offence—the first Sa*m*ghâdisesa offence—which I had not concealed. The Sa*m*gha imposed upon me a Mânatta (&c., as before, down to) not concealed. Now I have accomplished that Mânatta. What now shall I do?'

They told this thing to the Blessed One.

'Then, O Bhikkhus, let the Sa*m*gha rehabilitate Udâyi the Bhikkhu.

2. 'Now thus, O Bhikkhus, ought he to be rehabilitated.

'Udâyi the Bhikkhu ought to go up (&c., as in chapter 1, § 2, down to) he ought to say as follows:

'"I committed, venerable Sirs, an offence—the first Sa*m*ghâdisesa offence—which I did not conceal. I asked the Sa*m*gha (to impose upon me) a Mânatta of six days' duration for that offence—the first Sa*m*ghâdisesa offence—which I had not concealed. The Sa*m*gha imposed upon me a Mânatta of . . . . for . . . . not concealed. I, having accomplished that Mânatta, ask the Sa*m*gha for rehabilitation."'

[This speech is repeated three times.]

3. 'Then some discreet and able Bhikkhu [&c., as before in chapter 1, § 2, the rest of the kammavâ*k*â bearing the same relation to the petition as it does there].'

3.

1. Now at that time the venerable Udâyi had committed an offence—the first Saṁghâdisesa—which he had for one day concealed.

He told the Bhikkhus (&c., as before).

They told this thing to the Blessed One.

'Then, O Bhikkhus, let the Saṁgha impose a probation of one day on Udâyi the Bhikkhu for an offence (&c., as in the first paragraph of this section down to) concealed.

2. 'Now thus, O Bhikkhus, ought it to be imposed—.'

[Here follows the kammavâkâ precisely as in chapter 1, §§ 2 and 3, with the necessary changes in the wording, a. of the offence, b. of the penalty.]

4.

1. When he had passed through the probation he told the Bhikkhus, saying, 'I committed, friends, an offence—the first Saṁghâdisesa—which for one day I concealed. I asked the Saṁgha to impose upon me a probation of one day for the offence . . . . concealed. The Saṁgha imposed . . . . concealed. I have passed through that probation. What now should I do?'

They told this thing to the Blessed One.

'Let then the Saṁgha impose upon Udâyi the Bhikkhu a Mânatta of six days' duration.'

2, 3. [Here follows the kammavâkâ as in chapter 1, §§ 2, 3, to the end.]

5.

1. When he had accomplished the Mânatta he told the Bhikkhus, saying, 'I committed (&c., as 4. 1, down to) for one day concealed. I asked, &c. . . . The Sa*m*gha imposed a probation, &c. . . . When I passed through that probation the Sa*m*gha imposed a Mânatta of &c. . . . for &c. . . . I have accomplished that Mânatta. What now shall I do?'

They told that matter to the Blessed One.

'Let then the Sa*m*gha, O Bhikkhus, rehabilitate Udâyi the Bhikkhu.'

2, 3. [Here follows the kammavâ*k*â as in chapter 2, §§ 2, 3, to the end.]

6.

[This chapter is the same as chapter 3, reading 'for two—three—four—five days concealed,' and 'probation of two—three—four—five days.']

7.

1. Whilst he was undergoing that probation, he committed an offence—the first, &c.—which he did not conceal.

He told the Bhikkhus, saying, 'I committed, &c. . . . I asked the Sa*m*gha, &c. . . . The Sa*m*gha imposed upon me a probation of two—three—four—five days. Whilst I was undergoing that probation, I committed, &c. . . .'

They told that matter to the Blessed One.

'Let then the Saṃgha, O Bhikkhus, throw back Udâyi the Bhikkhu to the commencement (of his probationary course).'

2, 3. [Here follows the kammavâkâ as in chapter 1, with the necessary alterations.]

8.

1. When he had undergone that probation, and was liable to the Mânatta, he committed an offence—the first Saṃghâdisesa—which he did not conceal.

He told the Bhikkhus, saying, &c. . . .

They told this matter to the Blessed One.

'Let then the Saṃgha, O Bhikkhus, throw back Udâyi the Bhikkhu to the commencement (of his probationary course).'

2, 3. [Here follows the kammavâkâ in the same form as is given in chapter 1.]

9.

1. When he had undergone that probation he told, &c. . . .

They told, &c. . . .

'Let then the Saṃgha, O Bhikkhus, impose upon Udâyi the Bhikkhu a Mânatta of six days' probation for these offences.'

2, 3. [The kammavâkâ as before.]

10.

1. While he was undergoing that Mânatta he

committed an offence—the first Sa*m*ghâdisesa—which he did not conceal.

He told the Bhikkhus, saying, 'I committed, &c. . . . I asked the Sa*m*gha. . . . The Sa*m*gha imposed [&c., going through all that had happened, down to the end of the first paragraph in this chapter].

They told, &c.

'Let then the Sa*m*gha, O Bhikkhus, impose upon Udâyi the Bhikkhu a Mânatta of six days' duration, throwing him back to the commencement (of his Mânatta).

[The kammavâ*k*â as before.]

11.

1. When he had accomplished that Mânatta, and while he was worthy to be rehabilitated, he committed an offence—the first Sa*m*ghâdisesa offence—which he did not conceal.

He told the Bhikkhus [all that had happened from chapter 6 onwards down to this last offence].

They told, &c.

'Let then the Sa*m*gha, O Bhikkhus, impose upon Udâyi the Bhikkhu a Mânatta of six days' duration, for that he when he had (&c., as in first paragraph down to) not conceal, throwing him back to the commencement (of his Mânatta).

'Now thus, O Bhikkhus, [here follows the kammavâ*k*â as before.]

12.

1. When he had accomplished that Mânatta he told the Bhikkhus [all that had happened].

They told, &c.

'Let then the Sa*m*gha, O Bhikkhus, rehabilitate Udâyi the Bhikkhu.

'Now thus [here follows the kammavâ*k*â as before].

13.

1. Now at that time the venerable Udâyi committed an offence—the first Sa*m*ghâdisesa—and for half a month he concealed it.

[The rest of this chapter is precisely the same as chapter 3, reading 'for half a month' instead of 'for one day.']

14.

1. Whilst he was undergoing that probation he committed an offence—the first Sa*m*ghâdisesa—which for five days he concealed.

He told, &c. . . . 'I committed, &c. . . I asked, &c. . . . The Sa*m*gha imposed a probation of half a month, &c. . . . Whilst I was undergoing, &c. . . . What now shall I do?'

They told, &c.

'Let then the Sa*m*gha, O Bhikkhus, for that whilst (&c., as in the first paragraph) throw Udâyi the Bhikkhu back to the beginning of his probationary term, and impose upon him an inclusive probation (to include his new offence together) with the former offence[1].

'Now thus, O Bhikkhus, [here follow two kammavâ*k*âs, one for the throwing back, and one for the additional probation, each of them as in chapter 1.]'

15.

1. When he had undergone that probation, and while he was liable to the Mânatta, he committed an offence—the first Sa*m*ghâdisesa—which for five days he concealed.

He told, &c. . . . [all that happened, from chapter 13 downwards].

They told, &c.

'Let then the Sa*m*gha, O Bhikkhus, for that he when he had (&c., as in the first paragraph) throw Udâyi the Bhikkhu back to the commencement of

---

[1] Samodhâna-parivâsa. It is clear from the next chapter that this probation did not affect the Mânatta to which he was liable for that first offence. The Mânatta always lasted six days, and was preceded by a probation equal in length to the time during which the offence had been concealed. If now, during that probation, another offence was committed and concealed, the penalties for this new offence and for the old one were not accumulative but concurrent. The offender lost the advantage of the probation he had already undergone, he was thrown back to the commencement of his term of probation, and had to begin again. But the new term of probation—equal in length to whichever was the longest of the two periods during which he had concealed the two offences—satisfied both the concealments, and the Mânatta which still, as it would have done before, followed at the end of the probation, satisfied both the offences. See our note below on chapter 20.

his probationary term, and impose upon him an inclusive probation (for this and) for the former offence.

'Now thus, O Bhikkhus, [here follow two kammavâkâs, as in the last chapter.]'

16.

1. When he had undergone that probation he told the Bhikkhus, &c. [all that had happened since chapter 13].

They told, &c.

'Let then the Samgha, O Bhikkhus, impose upon Udâyi the Bhikkhu a Mânatta of six days' duration for these offences[1].

'Now thus, O Bhikkhus, [here follows one kammavâkâ in the form given in chapter 1.]'

17.

1. While he was undergoing that Mânatta he committed an offence—the first Samghâdisesa—which he for four days concealed.

He told, &c. . . . [all that had happened, from chapter 13 downwards].

They told this matter to the Blessed One.

'Let then the Samgha, O Bhikkhus, for that while (&c., as in the first paragraph) throw Udâyi the Bhikkhu back to the commencement (of the probationary term he had already undergone), and impose

[1] As in chapter 9.

upon him an inclusive probation (for this and) for the first offence, and also a Mânatta of six days' duration.

'Now thus, O Bhikkhus, [here follow three kammavâkâs, one for the throwing back, one for the inclusive probation, and one for the new Mânatta, each of them on the same form as that given in chapter 1.]'

18.

1. When he had accomplished that Mânatta, and while he was worthy to be rehabilitated, he committed an offence—the first Samghâdisesa—which for five days he concealed.

He told, &c. [all that happened, from chapter 13 downwards].

They told this matter to the Blessed One.

'Let then the Samgha, O Bhikkhus, for that when he had (&c., as in the first paragraph) throw Udâyi the Bhikkhu back to the commencement (of the probationary term he had already undergone) and impose upon him an inclusive probation for this and for the first offence, and a Mânatta of six days' duration.

'Now thus, &c. . . . [Here follow three kammavâkâs as in chapter 17.]'

19.

1. When he had accomplished the Mânatta he told the Bhikkhus [all that happened, from chapter 13 downwards].

They told this matter to the Blessed One.

'Let then the Sa*m*gha rehabilitate Udâyi the Bhikkhu.

'Now thus, O Bhikkhus, [here follows the kammavâ*k*â as in chapter 5.]'

Here end the proceedings on the breach of the first Sa*m*ghâdisesa.

20.

1. Now at that time a certain Bhikkhu had committed numerous Sa*m*ghâdisesa offences, one of which he had concealed for one day, one for two days, one for three days, [and so on down to] and one for ten days.

He told the Bhikkhus, saying, 'I have committed, (&c., as before, down to) and one for ten days. What now shall I do?'

They told this thing to the Blessed One.

'Let then the Sa*m*gha, O Bhikkhus, impose upon that Bhikkhu an inclusive probation according to one of those offences which has been concealed for ten days[1].'

'Now thus, O Bhikkhus, ought it to be imposed.'

---

[1] From this and what follows it is clear that however many are the offences, and however various the periods of concealment, the probation is only to last for the same period as the longest of the concealments has lasted. Thus the Samanta Pâsâdikâ says here: agghasamodhâno nâma sambahulâsu âpattîsu yâ ekâ vâ dve vâ tisso vâ sambahulâ vâ âpattiyo sabba*k*irapa*t*i*kkh*annâyo tâsa*m* agghena samodhâya tâsa*m* rattipari*kkh*edavasena avasesâna*m* ûnatarapa*t*i*kkh*annâna*m* âpattîna*m* parivâso diyyati. Yassa pana sata*m* âpattiyo dasâhapa*t*i*kkh*annâ, apara*m* pi sata*m* âpattiyo dasâhapa*t*i*kkh*annâ ti, eva*m* dasakkhattu*m* katvâ âpattisahassa*m* divasasatapa*t*i*kkh*anna*m* hoti, tena ki*m* kâtabban ti? Sabba*m* samodhâpetvâ dasa divase parivasitabba*m*, eva*m* eken' eva dasâhena divasasata*m* pi parivasitam eva hoti. Vutta*m* pi *k*' eta*m*:

dasasata*m* rattisata*m* âpattiyo *kh*âdayitvâna
dasarattiyo vasitvâna mu*kk*eyya pârivâsiko.

[Here follows the kammavâkâ in the form given at chapter 1, §§ 2, 3, to the end.]

21.

1. Now at that time a certain Bhikkhu had committed numerous Samghâdisesa offences, one of which he had concealed for one day, two for two days, three for three days, [and so on down to] and ten for ten days.

He told, &c.

They told, &c.

'Let then the Samgha, O Bhikkhus, impose upon that Bhikkhu an inclusive probation equal in duration to the longest time during which he has concealed any one or more of those offences[1].'

[Then follows the kammavâkâ as before.]

22.

1. Now at that time a certain Bhikkhu had committed two Samghâdisesa offences which he had concealed for two months. And it occurred to him, 'Lo! I have committed two Samghâdisesa offences which I have concealed for two months. Let me now ask the Samgha for a probation of two months for one offence concealed for two months.' And he asked the Samgha for a probation of two months for

[1] Literally, 'according to the value of whichever offences among those offences have been the longest concealed.'

one offence concealed for two months. And the Sa*m*gha imposed upon him a probation (&c., as before, down to) for two months. Whilst he was undergoing that probation, shame overcame him in that he thought, 'I have committed, &c. . . . And it occurred to me, &c. . . . And I asked, &c. . . . And the Sa*m*gha imposed . . . . And whilst I was undergoing . . . . (&c., as before, down to) for two months.'

'Let me now ask the Sa*m*gha for a probation of two months for the other offence concealed for two months.'

2. He told the Bhikkhus [all that had happened]. They told this thing to the Blessed One.

3. 'Let then the Sa*m*gha, O Bhikkhus, impose upon that Bhikkhu a probation of two months for that other offence concealed for two months.'

[Here follows the kammavâ*k*â as before.]

'Then that Bhikkhu, O Bhikkhus, should undergo probation for two months from that date[1].'

23.

1. 'Now in case, O Bhikkhus, a Bhikkhu have committed two Sa*m*ghâdisesa offences [&c., as before, in the first paragraph of the last chapter down to the end]. And he asks the Sa*m*gha for a probation of two months for that other offence concealed for two months. And the Sa*m*gha imposes upon him a probation of two months for that other offence

---

[1] Tadupâdâya; see chapters 23. 1 and 2, 24. 3.

concealed for two months[1]. That Bhikkhu, O Bhikkhus, ought to continue on probation for two months from that date.

2. 'Now in case, O Bhikkhus, a Bhikkhu have committed two Sa*m*ghâdisesa offences, which he has concealed for two months. And he is aware of one offence, but of the other offence he is not aware. And he asks the Sa*m*gha for a two months' probation for that offence of which he is aware, concealed for two months. And the Sa*m*gha gives him a probation of two months for an offence concealed for two months. And whilst he is undergoing that probation he becomes aware of the other offence. Then it occurs to him,

'"Lo! I have committed two Sa*m*ghâdisesa offences (&c., as in the last paragraph, down to) I became aware of the other offence. Let me now ask the Sa*m*gha for a probation of two months for that other offence concealed for two months."

'And he asks the Sa*m*gha for a probation of two months for that other offence concealed for two months. And the Sa*m*gha imposes upon him a probation of &c. . . . for &c. . . . That Bhikkhu, O Bhikkhus, ought to continue on probation for two months from that date.

3. 'Now in case, O Bhikkhus, a Bhikkhu commit two Sa*m*ghâdisesa offences, which he conceals for two months; and one offence he recollects, but the other offence he does not recollect. And he asks the Sa*m*gha (&c., as in the last section, down to the end, reading "recollect" for "be aware of").

[1] This is merely repeated to lay a basis for the following variations. See below, chapter 25.

4. 'Now in case, O Bhikkhus, a Bhikkhu commit two Sa*m*ghâdisesa offences, which he conceals for two months; and of one offence he is not doubtful[1], but of the other offence he is doubtful. And he asks the Sa*m*gha (&c., as in the last section, reading "is doubtful" for "does not recollect").

5. 'Now in case, O Bhikkhus, a Bhikkhu commit two Sa*m*ghâdisesa offences, which he conceals for two months; and one offence he conceals wittingly, but the other offence he conceals unwittingly. And he asks the Sa*m*gha for a probation of two months for those two offences concealed for two months. And the Sa*m*gha imposes upon him a probation of two months for those two offences concealed for two months. And whilst he is undergoing that probation there arrives a Bhikkhu who is versed in the traditions, acquainted with the tradition, a custodian of the Dhamma, of the Vinaya, and of the Mâtikâs[2], clever, discreet, wise, modest, sensitive, willing to learn. And he speaks thus:

'"What has this Bhikkhu, O friends, been guilty of, and why is he on probation?"

'And they reply: "This Bhikkhu, O friend, has committed two Sa*m*ghâdisesa offences, which he concealed for two months; and one offence he concealed wittingly, and one offence he concealed unwittingly. He asked the Sa*m*gha for a probation of two months for those two offences concealed for two months. And the Sa*m*gha imposed upon him a probation of two months for those two offences con-

---

[1] In chapter 34, § 1, di*tth*î, instead of nibbematiko, is put in opposition to vematiko.

[2] See our note above, on Mahâvagga II, 21, 2, and compare VII, 1, 7; VIII, 32, 1; X, 1, 2; *K*ullavagga I, 11, 1.

cealed for two months. Therein, O friend, is this Bhikkhu guilty, and therefore is he on probation."

'And he rejoins: "The offence which he wittingly concealed, O friends, for that the imposition of a probation is valid, and by reason of its validity it takes effect[1]. But the offence which he unwittingly concealed, O friends, for that the imposition of a probation is invalid, and by reason of its invalidity it does not take effect. For this offence, O friends, the Bhikkhu is liable to a Mânatta."

6. 'In case, O Bhikkhus, a Bhikkhu commit two Sa*m*ghâdisesa offences, which he conceals for two months. And one offence he conceals recollecting it, but the other offence he conceals without recollecting it.'

[Here follow the same remarks as in the last section, down to the end, reading 'recollecting it' for 'wittingly.']

24.

1. Now at that time a certain Bhikkhu committed two Sa*m*ghâdisesa offences which he concealed for two months. And it occurred to him, 'Lo! I have committed, &c. . . . for two months. Let me now ask the Sa*m*gha for a probation of one month for &c. . . .' He asked the Sa*m*gha for a probation of one month for &c. . . . The Sa*m*gha imposed upon him a probation of one month for &c. . . . Whilst he was undergoing that probation, shame (for the way

---

[1] This expression recurs below, chaps. 25, 27, &c. Compare the use of rûhati at Mahâvagga VI, 14, 5.

in which he had acted) overcame him. 'Let me now ask the Sa*m*gha for a (further) probation of one month for the two Sa*m*ghâdisesa offences concealed for two months.'

2. He told the Bhikkhus [all that had happened, in the words of § 1, and asked them], 'What now shall I do?'

They told this thing to the Blessed One.

3. 'Let then the Sa*m*gha, O Bhikkhus, impose upon that Bhikkhu a probation for a further month for those two Sa*m*ghâdisesa offences concealed for two months.'

[Here follows the kammavâ*k*â in the form given in chapter 1, §§ 2, 3.]

'Thus that Bhikkhu, O Bhikkhus, should undergo probation for two months from that date[1].'

25.

1. 'In case, O Bhikkhus, a Bhikkhu commit two Sa*m*ghâdisesa offences which he conceals for two months. And it occurs to him (&c., as in last chapter). . . . And he asks . . . . And the Sa*m*gha imposes . . . . And whilst he is undergoing that probation, shame (&c.) overcomes him, &c. . . . And he asks the Sa*m*gha for a probation of a further month for those two Sa*m*ghâdisesa offences concealed for two months. And the Sa*m*gha imposes upon him a further probation, &c. . . . Then, O Bhikkhus, that Bhikkhu should from that date undergo that further

[1] See above, chap. 22. 3.

probation of one month for those two Sa*m*ghâdisesa offences concealed for two months[1].

2, 3. 'Now in case, O Bhikkhus, a Bhikkhu have committed two Sa*m*ghâdisesa offences, which he conceals for two months. And of one month he is aware, but of the other month he is not aware . . . . one month he recollects, but the other month he does not recollect . . . . one month he wittingly conceals, but the other month he unwittingly conceals.'

[This chapter is word for word the same as chapter 23, reading 'month' for 'offence.']

26.

1. Now at that time a certain Bhikkhu had committed numerous Sa*m*ghâdisesa offences; but he was not aware of the degree of the offences[2], and was not aware of the duration of the times[2]; or he did not recollect the degree of the offences, and did not recollect the duration of the times; or he was uncertain as to the degree of the offences, and was uncertain as to the duration of the times.

He told the Bhikkhus, saying, 'I have committed, &c. . . . but I am not aware, &c. . . . I do not recollect, &c. . . . I am uncertain, &c. . . . What now shall I do?'

They told this thing to the Blessed One.

'Then let the Sa*m*gha, O Bhikkhus, impose upon that Bhikkhu a probation of complete purifi-

[1] This repetition of the last chapter is again only to afford a basis for the succeeding variations, as above, in chap. 23.

[2] That these are plurals, and not singulars, is clear from § 3, below.

cation (that is to say, a probation for as many days as have elapsed since the date of his upasampadâ)[1].

2. 'Now thus, O Bhikkhus, should it be imposed.' . . .

[Here follows the kammavâ*k*â in the same form as is given in chapter 1.]

3. 'In the following cases, O Bhikkhus, is the probation of complete purification to be imposed; and in the following cases is the (ordinary) probation to be imposed. Now in what cases is the probation of complete purification to be imposed? When he is not aware of the degree of the offences, nor of the duration of the times; when he does not recollect the degree of the offences, nor the duration of the times; and when he is not certain as to the degree of the offences, nor as to the duration of the times—then is the probation of complete purification to be imposed.

'When he is aware of the degree of the offences, but not of the duration of the times; when he does recollect the degree of the offences, but not the duration of the times; when he is certain as to the degree of the offences, but not as to the duration of the times—then is the probation of complete purification to be imposed.

'When he is aware . . . . recollects . . . . is certain . . . . of the degree of some, but not of others of the offences, and is not aware of . . . . does not recollect . . . . is not certain of the duration of the times[2]—then &c.

'When he is not aware . . . . does not recollect . . . .

[1] Suddhanta-parivâso. The Samanta Pâsâdikâ says, Ta*m* gahetvâ gahita-divasato yâva upasampadâ-divaso tâva rattiyo ga*n*etvâ parivasitabba*m*.

[2] This and the following sentences are given in the text in full, as in the last paragraph.

is not certain . . . . of the degree of the offences, and is aware . . . . recollects . . . . is certain . . . . of the times of some, but not of the times of the others—then, &c.

'When he is aware . . . . recollects . . . . is certain of the degree of the offences, and is aware . . . . recollects . . . . is certain of the times of some, but not of the times of others—then, &c.

'When he is aware . . . . recollects . . . . is certain of the degrees of some of the offences, but not of others; and is aware . . . . recollects . . . . is certain of the times of some, but not of the times of others—then, &c.

'In these cases, O Bhikkhus, is the probation of complete purification to be imposed.

4. 'And in what cases, O Bhikkhus, is the (ordinary) probation to be imposed? When he is aware . . . . recollects . . . . is certain of the degree of the offences, but is not aware . . . . does not recollect . . . . is not certain of the duration of the times—then is the (ordinary) probation to be imposed.

'When he is not aware . . . . does not recollect . . . . is not certain of the degree of the offences, but is aware . . . . recollects . . . . is certain of the duration of the times—then &c. . . .

'When he is aware . . . . recollects . . . . is certain of the degree of some of the offences, but not of others; and is aware . . . . recollects . . . . is certain of the duration of the times—then &c. . . .

'In these cases, O Bhikkhus, is the (ordinary) probation to be imposed[1].'

Here ends the probation.

---

[1] That is to say, shortly; if the guilty Bhikkhu can determine the time during which the offence has been concealed (on which the length of the probation depends), then he is to undergo the

27.

1. Now at that time a certain Bhikkhu, whilst he was under probation, threw off the robes. Afterwards he came back again, and asked the Bhikkhus for upasampadâ. They told this thing to the Blessed One.

'In case, O Bhikkhus, a Bhikkhu throws off the robes whilst he is under probation, there can follow no probation to him, O Bhikkhus, so long as he is out of the Order. If he afterwards receive the upasampadâ, the original probation (previously imposed upon him, still remains obligatory) upon him. A probation once imposed, is imposed for good; a probation once undergone, is undergone for good; if any (portion of the time) remain over, the probation must be again undergone (from the beginning).

'In case, O Bhikkhus, a Bhikkhu, whilst he is undergoing probation, becomes a Sâma*n*era. There can happen no probation to him, O Bhikkhus, so long as he is a Sâma*n*era. If he afterwards receives the upasampadâ (&c., as in the last paragraph, down to the end).

'In case, O Bhikkhus, a Bhikkhu, whilst he is undergoing probation, goes out of his mind . . . . becomes weak in his mind . . . . diseased in his sensations . . . . is suspended for not acknowledging an

corresponding probation. If not, he is to undergo the so-called 'probation of complete purification,' which, as it is computed from the date of his ordination, is quite certain to be as long as the time of the longest concealment of any offence.

offence .... for not atoning for an offence .... for not recanting a sinful doctrine[1]—there can happen no probation to him, O Bhikkhus, so long as he is out of his mind .... weak in his mind .... suspended, &c. If he afterwards becomes not out of his mind .... becomes not weak in his mind ..... is restored from the suspension, the original probation is still obligatory upon him. A probation once imposed (&c., as in the first paragraph, down to the end).

2. 'In case, O Bhikkhus, a Bhikkhu, whilst he is liable to be thrown back to the commencement of his probation, throws off the robes (&c., as in all the paragraphs of section 1, reading "liable to be thrown back," for "undergoing probation").'

3. [The same for a Bhikkhu who throws off the robes, or becomes any of the seven things specified, whilst he is liable to be subjected to the Mânatta discipline;

4. Or is undergoing the Mânatta discipline;

5. Or is fit to be rehabilitated.]

Here end the forty[2] cases (of interruption to a major disciplinary proceeding from a change of state in the person undergoing that discipline).

28.

1. 'In case, O Bhikkhus, whilst a Bhikkhu is undergoing probation, he commit numerous Saṁghâ-

---

[1] The text has a separate paragraph for each of these cases.

[2] That is, on any of the above eight events occurring in any of the above five cases.

disesa offences, definite[1], but not concealed, that Bhikkhu is to be thrown back to the commencement of his probation.

2. 'In case, O Bhikkhus, whilst a Bhikkhu is undergoing probation, he commit numerous Sa*m*ghâdisesa offences, definite, and concealed, that Bhikkhu is to be thrown back to the commencement of his probation, and an inclusive probation is to be imposed upon him according to the duration of time since the first of the offences which he has thus concealed.

'In case, O Bhikkhus, whilst a Bhikkhu is undergoing probation, he commit numerous Sa*m*ghâdisesa offences, grievous, and some of them concealed, some of them not concealed, that Bhikkhu must (as in the last paragraph to the end).

'In case, O Bhikkhus, whilst a Bhikkhu is undergoing probation, he commit numerous Sa*m*ghâdisesa offences, not definite, and not concealed .... not definite, and concealed[2] .... not grievous, and some of them concealed, others not concealed .... some definite, and some not definite and not concealed .... some definite, and some not definite and (all) concealed .... some definite, and some not definite, some concealed, some not concealed—then that Bhikkhu is to be thrown back, and an inclusive probation is to be imposed upon him, according to the duration of

[1] Parimâ*n*â, the meaning of which is open to much doubt. The Samanta Pâsâdikâ merely says, Antarâ sambâhulâ âpattiyo âpa*gg*ati parimâ*n*â pa*t*i*kkh*annâyo ti âdisu âpatti-pari*kkh*edavase parimâ*n*âyo *k*' eva appa*t*i*kkh*annâyo *k*â 'ti attho. The only conclusion to be drawn from this is that the word is acc. fem. plur., and not an adverb. Compare chap. 33, below.

[2] The text has a full paragraph for each of these cases.

the time since the first of the offences which he had concealed.'

[The same if the offences are committed whilst he is liable to the Mânatta discipline, or undergoing the Mânatta discipline, or pending his rehabilitation.]

Here end the thirty-six cases (of fresh offences being committed whilst under probation)[1].

29.

1. 'In case, O Bhikkhus, a Bhikkhu who has committed numerous Sa*m*ghâdisesa offences, but has not concealed them, throw off the robes, and he, having afterwards again received the upasampadâ, does not conceal them. A Mânatta, O Bhikkhus, is to be imposed upon that Bhikkhu.

'In case, O Bhikkhus, a Bhikkhu (&c., as before, down to) throw off the robes, and he, having afterwards again received the upasampadâ, does conceal them,—on that Bhikkhu, O Bhikkhus, a probation is to be imposed according to the duration of the time during which he has concealed any offence in the batch of offences thus afterwards concealed[2]; and after that a Mânatta is to be imposed.

[1] This chapter is repeated below, chap. 33, for the cases in which a new ordination has followed after the offences have been committed.

[2] The Samanta Pâsâdikâ says, Pa*kkh*imasmi*m* âpattikkhandhe ti eko 'va so âpattikkhandho, pa*k*i*kkh*âditattâ pana pa*kkh*imasmi*m* âpattikkhandhe ti vutta*m*. Purimasmin ti etthâpi es' eva nayo.

'In case, O Bhikkhus, a Bhikkhu who has committed numerous Sa*m*ghâdisesa offences, and has concealed them, throw off the robes, and he, after having again received the upasampadâ, does not conceal them,—on that Bhikkhu, O Bhikkhus, a probation is to be imposed according to the duration of the time during which he has concealed any offence in the batch of offences thus previously concealed[1]; and after that a Mânatta is to be imposed upon him.

'In case, O Bhikkhus, a Bhikkhu who has committed numerous Sa*m*ghâdisesa offences, and has concealed them, throw off the robes, and, after again receiving the upasampadâ, he does conceal them, —on that Bhikkhu, O Bhikkhus, a probation is to be imposed corresponding to the duration of the time during which he has concealed any offence either in the first or in the batch of offences thus afterwards concealed; and after that a Mânatta is to be imposed upon him.

[2]2. '[In case, O Bhikkhus, a Bhikkhu have com-

---

[1] See the close of the last note.

[2] This section should correspond to chap. 31, section 2, but as noted by H. O. in his edition of the text, p. 312, there is very great confusion in the MSS. We ought to have four cases of which the distinctions are as under. Those offences

1	concealed before	are afterwards	not concealed	+ −
	not concealed before	„	not „	− −
2	concealed before	„	not „	+ −
	not concealed before	„	concealed	− +
3	concealed before	„	concealed	+ +
	not concealed before	„	not concealed	− −
4	concealed before	„	concealed	+ +
	not concealed before	„	concealed	− +

All these four cases are required to make up the one hundred

mitted numerous Sa*m*ghâdisesa offences, and some of his offences have been concealed, and some not concealed; and he, having thrown off the robes, and again received the upasampadâ, does not afterwards conceal those offences which he had previously concealed, and does not afterwards conceal those offences which previously he had not concealed,—on that Bhikkhu [the penalty is to be the same as in section 1, paragraph 4].]

'In case, O Bhikkhus, a Bhikkhu [&c., as in last paragraph, down to] does not afterwards conceal those offences which he had previously concealed, and does conceal those offences which previously he had not concealed,—on that Bhikkhu [the penalty is to be the same as in section 1, paragraph 4].

'In case, O Bhikkhus, a Bhikkhu (&c., as in last paragraph, down to) does afterwards conceal those offences which he had previously concealed, and does not afterwards conceal those offences which previously he had not concealed,—on that Bhikkhu [the penalty is to be the same as in section 1, paragraph 4].

'In case, O Bhikkhus, a Bhikkhu (&c., as in last paragraph, down to) does afterwards conceal those offences which he had previously concealed, and does afterwards conceal those offences which previously he had not concealed,—on that Bhikkhu [the penalty is to be the same as in section 1, paragraph 4].

3. 'In case, O Bhikkhus, a Bhikkhu have committed numerous Sa*m*ghâdisesa offences, and of some

cases mentioned in the title at the close of chap. 30; but the first is altogether omitted in the text, and the others are not properly discriminated. We have supplied the first in brackets, and corrected the others accordingly.

of them he is aware, but of some of them he is not aware; and he conceals those offences of which he is aware, but does not conceal those offences of which he is not aware; after having thrown off the robes, and again received the upasampadâ, those offences of which he had previously been aware, and which he did then conceal, of them, afterwards, he is still aware, and he does not conceal them; and those offences of which previously he had not been aware and did not then conceal, of them, afterwards, he becomes aware, and does not conceal them,—on that Bhikkhu [the penalty is the same as in section 1, paragraph 3].

'In case, O Bhikkhus, a Bhikkhu (&c., as in the last paragraph, down to) and again received the upasampadâ, those offences of which he had previously been aware, and which he did then conceal, of them, afterwards, he is still aware, and he does not conceal them; and those offences of which previously he had not been aware, and did not then conceal, of them, afterwards, he becomes aware, and does conceal them,—on that Bhikkhu [the penalty is the same as in section 1, paragraph 4].

'In case, O Bhikkhus, a Bhikkhu (&c., as in the last paragraph, down to) which he did then conceal, of them, afterwards, he is still aware, and does conceal them; and of those offences of which previously he had not been aware, and did not then conceal, of them, afterwards, he becomes aware, and does not conceal them,—on that Bhikkhu [the penalty is the same as in section 1, paragraph 4].

'In case, O Bhikkhus, a Bhikkhu (&c., as in the last paragraph, down to) which he did then conceal, of them, afterwards, he is still aware, and does conceal them; and of those offences of which previously he had not been aware, and did not then conceal, of them, afterwards, he becomes aware, and does conceal them,—on that Bhikkhu [the penalty is the same as in section 1, paragraph 4].'

4. [This section is the same as the last, reading 'he recollects' for 'he is aware,' and 'he does not recollect' for 'he is not aware.']

5. [This section is again the same as section 3, reading 'he is certain' for 'he is aware,' and 'he is not certain' for 'he is not aware.']

30.

1. [The whole of the last chapter is repeated in the case of a Bhikkhu who, having committed offences, becomes a Sâma*n*era, goes out of his mind, or becomes weak in his mind[1], and the text then goes on] 'He becomes diseased in his sensations. His offences are some of them concealed, some not concealed. Of some offences he is aware, of some he is not aware. Some offences he recollects, some he does not recollect. Of some offences he is certain, of some he is not certain. Those offences of which he was not certain, those he conceals; those offences of which he was certain, those he does not conceal. Then he becomes diseased in his sensations. When he has recovered power over his sensations, those offences of which he previously had been certain and had concealed, of those he is afterwards still certain, but does not conceal them; and those offences of which he previously had been

[1] See above, chap. 27, and Mahâvagga II, 22, 3; IX, 4, 7.

uncertain and had not concealed, of those he became certain but did not conceal them. Those offences of which he previously had been certain and had concealed, of those he was afterwards still certain and did not conceal; while those offences of which he previously had been uncertain, and had not concealed, of those offences he afterwards became certain and did conceal them. Those offences of which previously he had been certain, and had concealed, of those offences he was afterwards still certain and did conceal them; while those offences of which he previously had been uncertain and had not concealed, of those offences he afterwards became certain, and did not conceal them. Those offences of which he previously had been certain, and had concealed them, of those offences he was afterwards still certain and did conceal them; whilst those offences of which he previously had been uncertain and did not conceal them, of those offences he afterwards became certain and did conceal them,—on that Bhikkhu, O Bhikkhus, [the same penalty is to be imposed as in chapter 29, section 1, paragraph 4.]'

Here end the hundred cases[1] in which a Mânatta (is to be imposed after a change of state in the guilty Bhikkhu).

---

[1] The hundred cases are made up thus: Chap. 29, §§ 1, 2, 3, 4, 5 contain each of them four cases (after our correction of 29. 2); so that chap. 29 gives altogether twenty cases. Then in chap. 30, each of these twenty cases is repeated in the four other cases there given; so that chap. 30 gives altogether eighty cases. Of these eighty cases, as usual, at the end of a repetition, the last (four cases) are set out in full.

31.

1. 'In case, O Bhikkhus, a Bhikkhu who is undergoing probation is guilty meanwhile of a number of Sa*m*ghâdisesa offences, and without concealing them then throws off the robes, and he, when he has again received the upasampadâ, does not conceal those offences—that Bhikkhu ought to be thrown back to the commencement (of his term of probation).

'And in case, O Bhikkhus, a Bhikkhu (&c., as before, down to) and he, when he has again received the upasampadâ, does conceal those offences—that Bhikkhu ought to be thrown back to the commencement (of his term of probation), and an inclusive probation ought to be imposed upon him (corresponding to the time which has elapsed since) the first offence among those offences which he has concealed.

'And in case, O Bhikkhus, a Bhikkhu who is undergoing probation is guilty meanwhile of a number of Sa*m*ghâdisesa offences, and, concealing them, throws off the robes; and he, when he has again received the upasampadâ, does not conceal those offences—that Bhikkhu ought to be thrown back to the commencement of his term of probation, and an inclusive probation ought to be imposed upon him (corresponding to the period which has elapsed since) the first offence among those offences which he has concealed.'

[The same judgment if he has concealed the offences before he throws off the robes, and also after he has again received the upasampadâ.][1]

[1] This section corresponds to chap. 29, section 1.

2. 'And in case, O Bhikkhus, a Bhikkhu who is undergoing probation is guilty meanwhile of a number of Sa*m*ghâdisesa offences, and some of them he has concealed and some of them he has not concealed; and after he has thrown off the robes and again received the upasampadâ, he does not afterwards conceal those offences which previously he had concealed, and he does not afterwards conceal those offences which previously he had not concealed—[the judgment is the same as in the last paragraph of § 1].'

[In the same case down to] he does not afterwards conceal those offences which previously he had concealed, and he does afterwards conceal those offences which previously he had not concealed [the judgment is the same].

[In the same case, down to] he does afterwards conceal those offences which previously he had concealed, and he does not afterwards conceal those offences which previously he had not concealed [the judgment is the same].

[In the same case, down to] he does afterwards conceal those offences which previously he had concealed, and he does afterwards conceal those offences which previously he had not concealed [the judgment is the same][1].

3. 'And in case, O Bhikkhus, a Bhikkhu who is undergoing probation is guilty meanwhile of a number of Sa*m*ghâdisesa offences, and he is aware of some of those offences, and not aware of others; and he conceals those offences of which he is aware, but does not conceal those offences of which he is

[1] This section corresponds to chap. 29, section 2.

not aware. After having thrown off the robes and again received the upasampadâ, those offences of which he had previously [&c., as in chapter 29, section 3, down to] on that Bhikkhu [the penalty is the same as in the last section, chapter 31, § 2].'

[The rest of this chapter corresponds exactly to chapter 29, §§ 4, 5, and chapter 30; the penalty being always the same.]

32.

1. 'And in case, O Bhikkhus, a Bhikkhu who has rendered himself liable to the Mânatta discipline, or is undergoing the Mânatta discipline, or is fit to be rehabilitated, is guilty meanwhile of a number of Samghâdisesa offences which he does not conceal; and he then throws off the robes, and again receives the upasampadâ,—then with regard to the Bhikkhu so liable to the Mânatta discipline, or undergoing the Mânatta discipline, or fit to be rehabilitated, the same rules are to apply as in the case of a Bhikkhu so acting while undergoing probation[1].

'And in case, O Bhikkhus, a Bhikkhu who is fit to be rehabilitated[2] is guilty meanwhile of a number of Samghâdisesa offences which he does not conceal; and he then becomes a Sâmanera, goes out of his mind, becomes weak in his mind, or becomes diseased in his sensations; his offences are some of them

[1] As laid down in chap. 31.

[2] This includes, of course, the two other cases of a Bhikkhu who has rendered himself liable to, or is undergoing the Mânatta discipline.

concealed, some of them not concealed . . . . [and so on, as in chapter 30, down to the end, excepting that the penalty is here the same as it is in the previous chapters 31 and 32].'

33.

1. 'And in case, O Bhikkhus, a Bhikkhu is guilty of a number of Sa*m*ghâdisesa offences, definite, and not concealed—not definite, and not concealed—of one designation, and not concealed—of various designations, and not concealed—similar, and not concealed—dissimilar, and not concealed—connected[1], and not concealed—disconnected, and not concealed—and then throws off the robes[2].' . . .

---

[1] On the opposition of vavatthita and sambhinna, compare Minayeff Pâtimokkha, p. 29, where these two expressions are used of language.

[2] The chapter is translated as it stands. To supply the implications involved, the words 'a Bhikkhu' at the beginning should be understood as 'a Bhikkhu undergoing probation, or liable to the Mânatta discipline, or undergoing the Mânatta discipline, or fit to be rehabilitated.' And the conclusion should be supplied as in chap. 28, except that the penalty in each case is not an additional probation, but a probation corresponding in length to the period which has elapsed since the first of those offences which the re-ordained Bhikkhu has concealed (either before or after the second ordination). The details are only worked out, in chap. 28, of the first of the several pairs here enumerated, and are intended to be supplied here for each of the other pairs in a similar way. All the pairs recur in chaps. 35, 36.

34.

1. 'Two Bhikkhus have been guilty of a Sa*m*ghâdisesa offence, and as touching that Sa*m*ghâdisesa offence they are of opinion that it is a Sa*m*ghâdisesa offence[1]. One of them conceals, the other does not conceal it. He who has concealed it should be compelled to confess himself guilty of a dukka*t*a offence, and a probation corresponding to the period during which he has concealed it having been imposed upon him, a Mânatta should be imposed upon them both.

'Two Bhikkhus have been guilty of a Sa*m*ghâdisesa offence, and as touching that Sa*m*ghâdisesa offence they are in doubt. One of them conceals, the other does not conceal it. [The penalty is the same.][2]

'Two Bhikkhus have been guilty of a Sa*m*ghâdisesa offence, and as touching that Sa*m*ghâdisesa offence they are of opinion that it is a mixed offence[3]. One of them conceals, the other does not conceal it. [The penalty is the same.][2]

'Two Bhikkhus have been guilty of a mixed offence, and as touching that mixed offence they are of opinion that it is a Sa*m*ghâdisesa offence. One of

---

[1] Compare chap. 23, § 4.

[2] The concluding words of the last paragraph are here repeated.

[3] The Samanta Pâsâdikâ says, Missakan ti thulla*kk*ayâdîhi missita*m*; that is an act which involves not only a Sa*m*ghâdisesa, but also some one or other of the lesser offences. Compare the use of missaka at *G*âtaka II, 420, 433, and at Mahâ-parinibbâna Sutta, ed. Childers, p. 22.

them conceals, the other does not conceal it. [The penalty is the same.][1]

'Two Bhikkhus have been guilty of a mixed offence, and as touching that mixed offence they are of opinion that it is a mixed offence. One of them conceals, the other does not conceal it. [The penalty is the same.]

'Two Bhikkhus have been guilty of a minor offence[2]; and as regarding that minor offence they are of opinion that it is a Sa*m*ghâdisesa offence. One of them conceals, the other does not conceal it. He who has concealed it should be compelled to confess himself guilty of a dukka*t*a offence, and both of them should be dealt with according to law.

'Two Bhikkhus have been guilty of a minor offence, and as touching that minor offence they are of opinion that it is a minor offence. One of them conceals, the other does not conceal it. He who has concealed it should be compelled to confess himself guilty of a dukka*t*a offence, and both of them should be dealt with according to law.

2. 'Two Bhikkhus have been guilty of a Sa*m*ghâdisesa offence, and as touching that Sa*m*ghâdisesa offence they are of opinion that it is a Sa*m*ghâdisesa. One of them thinks: "I will tell (the Sa*m*gha of it)." The other thinks: "I will not tell (the Sa*m*gha of it);" and during the first watch of the night he conceals it, and during the second watch of the night he conceals

[1] The concluding words of the last paragraph are here repeated.

[2] That is, any offence less than a Sa*m*ghâdisesa. The Samanta Pâsâdikâ says, Suddhakan ti Sa*m*ghâdisesa*m* vinâ lahukâpattikkhandham eva.

it, and during the third watch of the night he conceals it. After the sun has arisen the offence is a concealed one. He who has concealed it [&c.; the penalty is the same as in section 1, paragraph 1].

'Two Bhikkhus have been guilty of a Samghâdisesa offence, and as touching that Samghâdisesa offence they are of opinion that it is a Samghâdisesa offence. They set out, intending to tell (the Samgha of it). On the way there springs up in one of them a desire to conceal it; and during the first watch of the night he conceals it, and during the second watch of the night he conceals it, and during the third watch of the night he conceals it. After the sun has arisen the offence is a concealed one. He who has concealed it [&c.; the penalty is the same as before].

'Two Bhikkhus have been guilty of a Samghâdisesa offence, and as touching that Samghâdisesa offence they are of opinion that it is a Samghâdisesa offence. They go out of their mind; and afterwards when they have recovered their senses one of them conceals, the other does not conceal it. He who has concealed it [&c.; the penalty is the same as before][1].

'Two Bhikkhus have been guilty of a Samghâdisesa offence. When the Pâtimokkha is being recited they say thus: "Now do we come to perceive it; for this rule they say has been handed down in the Suttas, is contained in the Suttas, and comes into recitation every half month." As touching that Samghâdisesa offence, they (thus) come to be of

[1] It is probably to be understood that a like rule is to apply in the other similar cases mentioned in the last paragraph of chap. 32.

opinion that it is a Sa*m*ghâdisesa offence. One of them conceals, the other does not conceal it. He who has concealed it [&c.; the penalty is the same as before].'

35.

1. 'And in case, O Bhikkhus, a Bhikkhu is guilty of a number of Sa*m*ghâdisesa offences—definite, and not definite—of one designation, and of various designations—similar to each other, and dissimilar—connected with each other, and disconnected[1]. He asks the Sa*m*gha for an inclusive probation on account of those offences[2]. The Sa*m*gha imposes upon him an inclusive probation on account of those offences. He undergoing that probation is guilty meanwhile of a number of Sa*m*ghâdisesa offences, definite ones, which he does not conceal. He asks the Sa*m*gha to throw him back on account of those intervening offences to the commencement (of his term of probation). The Sa*m*gha [does so] by a lawful proceeding that cannot be quashed[3], and fit

[1] See chap. 33 for this list.

[2] In accordance with the rule laid down in chap. 28, which shows that by 'a Bhikkhu' must be understood 'a Bhikkhu who is under probation;' and the offences he has committed must have been concealed by him.

[3] Akuppa. The technical term kamma*m* kopeti is not to revoke the valid decision of a kamma regularly held, but to show that the kamma by reason of some irregularity was no real kamma, and its whole proceedings therefore void. One may compare akuppâ me *k*eto-vimutti spoken by the Buddha immediately after he had attained Nirvâ*n*a under the Bo Tree (Ariyapariyosâna Sutta in H. O.'s 'Buddha,' p. 429) and the opposite idea in Sutta Nipâta IV, 3, 5.

for the occasion; and it also imposes a Mânatta upon him, but by an unlawful proceeding, and then by an unlawful proceeding rehabilitates him. That Bhikkhu, O Bhikkhus, is not purified from those offences.

'And in case, O Bhikkhus, a Bhikkhu is guilty of a number of Sa*m*ghâdisesa offences—definite, and not definite—of one designation, and of various designations—similar to each other, and dissimilar—connected with each other, and disconnected. And he asks the Sa*m*gha for an inclusive probation on account of those offences. The Sa*m*gha imposes upon him an inclusive probation on account of those offences. He undergoing that probation is guilty meanwhile of a number of Sa*m*ghâdisesa offences, definite ones, which he does conceal. He asks the Sa*m*gha to throw him back on account of those intervening offences to the commencement (of his term of probation). The Sa*m*gha [does so] by a lawful proceeding that cannot be quashed, and fit for the occasion; and it also imposes upon him an inclusive probation by a lawful proceeding, and imposes upon him a Mânatta, but by an unlawful proceeding, and by an unlawful proceeding it rehabilitates him. That Bhikkhu, O Bhikkhus, is not purified from those offences.'

[The same decision is given if, of the intervening offences, all of which are definite, some have been concealed, and some not concealed.]

2. [The same if the intervening offences have been not definite and not concealed, or not definite and concealed, or all not definite but some concealed and some not concealed, or all not concealed but some definite and some not definite, or all concealed

but some definite and some not definite, or some definite and some not definite and some concealed and some not concealed.]

Here end the nine principal cases (which serve as a basis for the variations in the following chapter) in which a Bhikkhu is not purified (by undergoing a term of probation).

36.

1. [The same nine cases of the throwing back is carried by unlawful proceeding, though the Mânatta and the rehabilitation are by a lawful proceeding.]

2. 'And in case, O Bhikkhus, a Bhikkhu is guilty of a number of Sa*m*ghâdisesa offences—definite, and not definite—of one designation, and of various designations—similar to each other, and dissimilar—connected with each other, and disconnected[1]. He asks the Sa*m*gha for an inclusive probation on account of those offences. The Sa*m*gha imposes upon him an additional probation on account of those offences. He undergoing that probation is guilty meanwhile of a number of Sa*m*ghâdisesa offences, definite ones, which he does conceal. He asks the Sa*m*gha to throw him back on account

[1] These offences must be understood to be offences committed while under probation, and concealed. See the note on chap. 35, § 1.

of those intervening offences to the commencement of his term of probation. The Sa*m*gha [does so] by an unlawful proceeding that is liable to be quashed, and unfit for the occasion; and it also imposes an inclusive probation upon him, but by an unlawful proceeding. He thinking, "I am undergoing that probation," is guilty meanwhile of a number of Sa*m*ghâdisesa offences, definite ones, which he does conceal. When he has arrived at this condition he calls to mind the other offences committed while the first offences were being committed, and he calls to mind also the other offences committed while the latter offences were being committed.

'Then it occurs to him, "I have been guilty of a number of Sa*m*ghâdisesa offences (&c., as in the whole of the section from the beginning to the end of the last paragraph, down to) and I called to mind also the other offences committed while the latter offences were being committed. Let me now ask the Sa*m*gha to throw me back on account of those offences committed while the former offences, and while the latter offences, were being committed, to the commencement of my term of probation, by a lawful proceeding that cannot be quashed, and is fit for the occasion; and let me ask for an inclusive probation to be imposed by a lawful proceeding, and for a Mânatta to be imposed by a lawful proceeding, and then for rehabilitation by a lawful proceeding."

'And he asks the Sa*m*gha [accordingly], and the Sa*m*gha [does so]. That Bhikkhu, O Bhikkhus, is purified from those offences.'

[The same if some of the offences in each case have been concealed and some not concealed.]

3, 4. [The Bhikkhu is not purified from such intervening and remembered offences as are specified in the last section, if the Sa*m*gha has proceeded, as in the first section of this chapter, by an unlawful proceeding.]

Here ends the Third Khandhaka, on the Accumulation of Offences.

NOTE ON ABHIHA*TTHUM*.

In the 7th Nissaggiya, in the 34th Pâ*k*ittiya, and in the 36th Pâ*k*ittiya there occurs the phrase abhiha*tth*u*m* pavâreyya, regarding the correct translation of which, as will be seen from the note on the first passage, we were in doubt. The connection is always 'if A should offer B,' &c.; and the only difficulty is the force of the word abhiha*tth*u*m* which precedes the 'should offer,' and in some way qualifies it. In all three passages the Old Commentary preserved in the Sutta-Vibhaṅga explains the two words abhiha*tth*u*m* pavâreyya by 'Take just as much as you want' (yâvataka*m* i*kkh*asi tâvataka*m* ga*n*hâhi), which does not solve the difficulty. On the following words of the third passage, however, the Old Commentary (see H. O., 'Vinaya Pitaka*m*,' vol. iv, p. 84) uses the word abhiharati in its usual sense of 'he brings up to, offers to, hands over to,' as practically equivalent to abhiha*tth*u*m* pavâreti; and Buddhaghosa, in the Samanta Pâsâdikâ on the 7th Nissaggiya, uses abhiharitvâ as directly equivalent to abhiha*tth*u*m*.

Now in a passage quoted from the Thera-gâthâ in H. O.'s 'Buddha, sein Leben, seine Lehre, und seine Gemeinde' (p. 425, note 1), nikkhamitu*m*na occurs as the gerund of nikkhamati instead of nikkhamitvâna. The existence in Prâkrit of corresponding gerunds in -tu, -tu*m* for -tvâ, and in -tû*n*a, -tuâ*n*a for -tvâna, is laid down in Hema*k*andra II, 146 (Pischel, vol. i, p. 62). And Professor Weber has given corresponding forms (âha*tt*u, ka*tt*u, &c.) from the *G*ain dialect in his Bhagavatî I, p. 433.

What we have in the phrase in question is therefore simply a gerund in -tu*m*, and the two words taken together mean, 'if A should lay before and offer to B,' &c. The thing offered in one case is robes, in the other two cases food; and abhiharati is the usual word in Pâli for serving food, laying it before another person. Compare thâli-pâka-satâni abhihari at *G*âtaka I, 186; and the phrase bhattâbhihâro abhihâriyittha constantly repeated in the Mahâ-sudassana Sutta (Rh. D., 'Buddhist Suttas,' in the last paragraph of chap. II, §§ 12, 29, 31, 33, 37).

TRANSLITERATION OF ORIENTAL ALPHABETS ADOPTED FOR OF THE SACRED BOOKS OF THE EAST.

CONSONANTS.	MISSIONARY ALPHABET. I Class.	II Class.	III Class.	Sanskrit.	Zend.	Pehlevi.	Persian.	Arabic.	Hebrew.	Chinese.
Gutturales.										
1 Tenuis	k	...	...	क	𐬐	[illegible]	ك	ك	כּ	k
2 „ aspirata	kh	...	...	ख	𐬑	[illegible]	...	...	כ	kh
3 Media	g	...	...	ग	𐬔	[illegible]	گ	...	גּ	...
4 „ aspirata	gh	...	...	घ	𐬖	[illegible]	...	...	ג	...
5 Gutturo-labialis	q	...	...	...	...	...	ق	ق	ק	...
6 Nasalis	ṅ (ng)	...	...	ङ	𐬢 (ng) 𐬣 (N)	...	...	...	...	...
7 Spiritus asper	h	...	...	ह	𐬵 (𐬷 hv)	[illegible]	ه	ه	ה	h, hs
8 „ lenis	ʼ	...	...	...	...	...	ا	ا	א	...
9 „ asper faucalis	ʻh	...	...	...	...	...	ح	ح	ח	...
10 „ lenis faucalis	ʼh	...	...	...	...	...	ع	ع	ע	...
11 „ asper fricatus	...	*ʻh*	...	...	...	...	خ	خ	ח	...
12 „ lenis fricatus	...	*ʼh*	...	...	...	...	...	...	...	...
Gutturales modificatae (palatales, &c.)										
13 Tenuis	...	*k*	...	च	𐬗	[illegible]	چ	...	...	*k*
14 „ aspirata	...	*kh*	...	छ	...	...	...	...	...	*kh*
15 Media	...	*g*	...	ज	𐬘	[illegible]	ج	ج	...	...
16 „ aspirata	...	*gh*	...	झ	...	...	غ	غ	...	...
17 „ Nasalis	...	*ñ*	...	ञ	...	...	...	...	...	...

CONSONANTS (*continued*).	MISSIONARY ALPHABET. I Class.	II Class.	III Class.	Sanskrit.	Zend.	Pehlevi.	Persian.	Arabic.	Hebrew.	Chinese.
18 Semivocalis	y	...	...	य	[glyph] [glyph] [glyph] } init.	[glyph]	ي	ي	י	y
19 Spiritus asper	...	(ẏ)	...	...	...	...	...	...	...	...
20 „ lenis	...	(ẏ)	...	...	...	...	...	...	...	...
21 „ asper assibilatus	...	*s*	...	श	[glyph]	[glyph]	ش	ش	...	...
22 „ lenis assibilatus	...	*z*	...	...	[glyph]	[glyph]	ژ	...	...	*z*
Dentales.										
23 Tenuis	t	...	...	त	[glyph]	[glyph]	ت	ت	תּ	t
24 „ aspirata	th	...	...	थ	[glyph]	...	...	...	ת	th
25 „ assibilata	...	...	TH	...	...	...	ث	ث	...	...
26 Media	d	...	...	द	[glyph]	[glyph]	د	د	דּ	...
27 „ aspirata	dh	...	...	ध	[glyph]	...	...	...	ד	...
28 „ assibilata	...	...	DH	...	...	...	ذ	ذ	...	...
29 Nasalis	n	...	...	न	[glyph]	[glyph]	ن	ن	נ	n
30 Semivocalis	l	...	...	ल	...	[glyph]	ل	ل	ל	l
31 „ mollis 1	...	*l*	...	ळ	...	...	...	...	...	...
32 „ mollis 2	...	...	L	...	...	...	...	...	...	...
33 Spiritus asper 1	s	...	...	स	[glyph]	[glyph]	س(ث)	س	שׂ	s
34 „ asper 2	...	...	s ([glyph])	...	...	...	...	...	ס	...
35 „ lenis	z	...	...	...	[glyph]	[glyph]	ز (ذ)	ز	ז	z
36 „ asperrimus 1	...	...	z (ʒ)	...	...	...	ص	ص	צ	ʒ, ʒh
37 „ asperrimus 2	...	...	z ([glyph])	...	...	...	ض	...	...	...

Dentales modificatae (linguales, &c.)										
38 Tenuis	. . .	*t*	. . . .	ट	. . . .	. . .	ط	ط	ט	. . .
39 „ aspirata	. . .	*th*	. . . .	ठ	. . . .	. . .	ظ	ظ	. . .	. . .
40 Media	. . .	(*d*)	. . . .	ड	𐬛	[illegible]	. . .	. . .	. . .	. . .
41 „ aspirata	. . .	*dh*	. . . .	ढ	. . . .	. . .	. . .	ض	. . .	. . .
42 Nasalis	. . .	*n*	. . . .	ण	𐬣	. . .	. . .	. . .	. . .	. . .
43 Semivocalis	r	. . .	. . . .	र	𐬭	[illegible]	ر	ر	ר	. . .
44 „ fricata	. . .	*r*	. . . .	. . .	. . . .	. . .	. . .	. . .	. . .	*r*
45 „ diacritica	. . .	. . .	R	. . .	. . . .	. . .	. . .	. . .	. . .	. . .
46 Spiritus asper	sh	. . .	. . . .	ष	𐬴	[illegible]	. . .	. . .	. . .	sh
47 „ lenis	zh	. . .	. . . .	. . .	. . . .	. . .	. . .	. . .	. . .	. . .
Labiales.										
48 Tenuis	p	. . .	. . . .	प	𐬞	[illegible]	پ	. . .	פּ	p
49 „ aspirata	ph	. . .	. . . .	फ	. . . .	. . .	. . .	. . .	פ	ph
50 Media	b	. . .	. . . .	ब	𐬠	[illegible]	ب	ب	בּ	. . .
51 „ aspirata	bh	. . .	. . . .	भ	. . . .	. . .	. . .	. . .	ב	. . .
52 Tenuissima	. . .	*p*	. . . .	. . .	. . . .	. . .	. . .	. . .	. . .	. . .
53 Nasalis	m	. . .	. . . .	म	𐬨	[illegible]	م	م	מ	m
54 Semivocalis	w	. . .	. . . .	. . .	[illegible]	. . .	. . .	. . .	. . .	w
55 „ aspirata	hw	. . .	. . . .	. . .	. . . .	. . .	. . .	. . .	. . .	. . .
56 Spiritus asper	f	. . .	. . . .	. . .	𐬟	[illegible]	ف	ف	. . .	f
57 „ lenis	v	. . .	. . . .	व	»	[illegible]	و	و	ו	. . .
58 Anusvâra	. . .	*m*	. . . .	अं	[illegible] ã	. . .	. . .	. . .	. . .	. . .
59 Visarga	. . .	*h*	. . . .	अः	. . . .	. . .	. . .	. . .	. . .	. . .

VOWELS.	MISSIONARY ALPHABET. I Class.	II Class.	III Class.	Sanskrit.	Zend.	Pehlevi	Persian.	Arabic.	Hebrew.	Chinese.
1 Neutralis	0	. . .	. . . .	. . .	. . . .	. . .	. . .	. . .	ְ	ă
2 Laryngo-palatalis	ĕ	. . .	. . . .	. . .	. . . .	. . .	. . .	. . .	. . .	. . .
3 „ labialis	ŏ	. . .	. . . .	. . .	. . . .	ا fin.	. . .	. . .	. . .	. . .
4 Gutturalis brevis	a	. . .	. . . .	अ	𐬀	𐬀 init.	َ	َ	ַ	a
5 „ longa	â	(*a*)	. . . .	आ	𐬁	𐬁	َا	َا	ָ	â
6 Palatalis brevis	i	. . .	. . . .	इ	𐬌	. . .	ِ	ِ	ִ	i
7 „ longa	î	(*i*)	. . . .	ई	𐬍	[illegible]	ِي	ِي	ִי	î
8 Dentalis brevis	*li*	. . .	. . . .	ऌ	. . . .	. . .	. . .	. . .	. . .	. . .
9 „ longa	*lí*	. . .	. . . .	ॡ	. . . .	. . .	. . .	. . .	. . .	. . .
10 Lingualis brevis	*ri*	. . .	. . . .	ऋ	. . . .	. . .	. . .	. . .	. . .	. . .
11 „ longa	*rí*	. . .	. . . .	ॠ	. . . .	. . .	. . .	. . .	. . .	. . .
12 Labialis brevis	u	. . .	. . . .	उ	𐬎	. . .	ُ	ُ	ֻ	u
13 „ longa	û	(*u*)	. . . .	ऊ	𐬏	ا	ُو	ُو	וּ	û
14 Gutturo-palatalis brevis . . .	e	. . .	. . . .	. . .	𐬈(e) 𐬉(*e*)	. . .	. . .	. . .	ֶ	e
15 „ longa . . .	ê (ai)	(*e*)	. . . .	ए	[illegible], [illegible]	[illegible]	. . .	. . .	ֵ	ê
16 Diphthongus gutturo-palatalis	âi	(*ai*)	. . . .	ऐ	. . . .	. . .	َيْ	َيْ	. . .	âi
17 „ „	ei (ĕi)	. . .	. . . .	. . .	. . . .	. . .	. . .	. . .	. . .	ei, êi
18 „ „	oi (ŏu)	. . .	. . . .	. . .	. . . .	. . .	. . .	. . .	. . .	. . .
19 Gutturo-labialis brevis	o	. . .	. . . .	. . .	𐬊	. . .	. . .	. . .	ָ	o
20 „ longa	ô (au)	(*o*)	. . . .	ओ	𐬋	ا	. . .	. . .	וֹ	. . .
21 Diphthongus gutturo-labialis	âu	(*au*)	. . . .	औ	[illegible] (*au*)	. . .	َوْ	َوْ	. . .	âu
22 „ „	eu (ĕu)	. . .	. . . .	. . .	. . . .	. . .	. . .	. . .	. . .	. . .
23 „ „	ou (ŏu)	. . .	. . . .	. . .	. . . .	. . .	. . .	. . .	. . .	. . .
24 Gutturalis fracta	ä	. . .	. . . .	. . .	. . . .	. . .	. . .	. . .	. . .	. . .
25 Palatalis fracta	ï	. . .	. . . .	. . .	. . . .	. . .	. . .	. . .	. . .	. . .
26 Labialis fracta	ü	. . .	. . . .	. . .	. . . .	. . .	. . .	. . .	. . .	ü